AN ANCIENT FIRE

Book Three of the Discovery Trilogy

F. D. Brant

F. D. Brant

GRESHAM, OREGON

Books Written by F. D. Brant

Science Fiction Adventure

Of Gods Strangers and Messengers

Survival Trilogy

Time of Isolation

Desperate to Survive

A Taste of history Past

The Harsh Lands

Post-Apocalyptic

Unexpected Unplanned and into the Unknown

Discovery Trilogy

The Ones Before

Discovery

An Ancient Fire

Contemporary Christian Fiction

The Woman in the Snow

CHAPTER ONE

Dan crouched on the hilltop overlooking the canyon below. There was movement down there and he needed to know who it was and what their intentions were. His clothing was such that it blended well with the surrounding soils and vegetation. As long as he remained still he was invisible to any who might actually look his way. But he doubted any would do that since the area he was in held no promise of anything that would be of interest. His hair was silver showing his age, but his eyes were still sharp, at least when looking at distances – close work was another thing altogether.

They had been lucky to find this place. An accidental discovery long ago after they – he and his family – had escaped the destruction of their village. His mate all their offspring and their mates had been away from the village that day celebrating the arrival of a new member to their personal clan. At this time the village was attacked and destroyed, leaving them homeless and hiding until such time as the attackers left. The good news was all of his family had survived. The bad, all their supplies, their emergency packs had been destroyed or stolen when the village burned. So their escape had been long, difficult, and full of forging to keep enough with them so that they didn't starve.

They had moved a great distance away from their stomping grounds into these desolate hills and valleys. It was here just above where he now crouched that he; well they as a family had made the discovery. To say that this place was old was an understatement. Whoever had been the one to build this had planned well, and had an eye towards survival. Much of what they found was strange, but the amount of food, seed, and supplies that were stored here showed them that whoever it had been had planned well, and had made sure that whatever had happened that he and his family would survive. Yet, this place lay untouched and undiscovered until they found it. So whatever it was that had befallen the creator of this haven, he never returned. Now it was theirs, and he hoped that it would remain so.

The world they lived was a violent one, with many wandering tribes, clans, raiders, slavers, few villages, and fewer still, larger ones they called towns that because of their size was ignored or at least avoided by the marauding bands. The smallest of the villages were not so lucky, and while the one where they had lived wasn't one of the smallest, it was a very long way from being the largest. Isolation had been their safety, but also, and in the end their downfall. With no other close, there was no support. And how it was discovered is an unknown, but it was, and now it's gone.

He wasn't a big man, in fact was only of average height and weight. Had a narrow hawk like face which held both a full beard and mustache. He needed to wait until he was sure whoever this was had left the area. So there would be no fires for cooking, no smoke produced that could be smelled or seen, and no movement to lead one to investigate as to why. So he waited and watched as the dust from their passing began to settle, except where the winds picked it up again. Whoever this was remained in the washes and soon the last of the dust of their passing disappeared and he felt that now it would be safe to move. Yet, tonight, and possibly for the next couple of days they would have no fires to give them away.

He feared that whoever this is that they might be the ones responsible for the destruction of the village that they had been members of. To be truthful he had no way of knowing considering how far they were from that destroyed village, let alone that time factor. It was tough enough to survive without being attacked by these many roving bandits and murderers. While many, with what was left of the world, tried to rebuild – with no laws on the land – these others destroyed. Since the collapse of civilization over three generations ago chaos, death, murder, rape, and the darker side of man had come forth and risen to the top. With the semblance of civility destroyed with the plummeting of earth by a meteor which in reality had been a very large asteroid everything had changed in that instant. Had it only been one then they may have recovered, but it was not destined to be that way. This asteroid was grabbed by the moon's gravity, striking a glancing blow on the moon shattering the rock into a million pieces, and then plummeting towards earth formed a deadly halo of destruction that reigned terror down upon them, destroying almost all buildings and millions upon millions of people. Leaving, in the end, no more than five percent left alive and scattered across the wounded earth.

With the amount of fire falling from the sky very little was left standing. Fires raged out of control and the earth spewed forth vast volcanoes that had been dormant along the tectonic plates changing the very shape of the continents. More died of exposure and starvation as the atmosphere had heated, and carbon dioxide levels rose because of those fires and volcanoes. Vegetation almost completely disappeared furthering the possibility that this fire from space would completely sterilize the planet and make it lifeless. Yet, now the planet was beginning to show small signs of recovery – very small signs.

Borders were gone; the petty differences that once existed between the nations of this world were gone, as were the nations. Now it was simply a fight for survival and to remain hidden from the ones who destroyed. And because of the constant battle between the ones who only wanted to destroy, and the ones who were trying to survive, protect their families and what they had, the odds were against the species surviving, with extinction just over the horizon. *So much destruction, so much loss of life,* he thought. *Why is it that these who only destroy cannot see beyond their next conquest, the next bit of misery and death they cause?* All he could do was shake his head. It really made no sense. These were more like the swarms of locusts that devoured all and moved on leaving nothing by death and destruction behind them. *What would they do once they had destroyed everything? Probably turn on themselves until there would be no one alive to mourn the passing.*

For the women it was much worse. They became property, a commodity to trade, a way to get a favor. They had no worth at all. At least in the villages that they had been members of, they held to the old traditions of husband and wife and family. But as each of these villages were located and destroyed it became less likely that the old ways would be kept and honored. As he continued to look in the direction that the unknown group had taken he heard someone approaching from behind. Looking around he found his oldest son approaching quietly. He signaled him to stealth and when he came up next to him Dan said, "There's a rather large group that just passed us by down there in the lower areas. They kept to the places that would keep them from being seen, or being located. From the way they moved I do not trust them. Pass it on that there can be little or no movement outside, and that the fires will not be lit. Until I know for sure that they are out of the area we cannot take any chance. With the size of that group we'd stand no chance of surviving if they find us."

"Okay dad. This won't go over well with your grandchildren. They hate being cooped up inside, but we'll do the best we can. The loss of our last place is still too new to ignore." He quietly left leaving Dan still staring out in the direction where they had disappeared. *I really need to thank whoever it was who had built this place.* He saw a bright streak heading across the heavens and knew that another meteor had entered the atmosphere. Thankfully the frequency of these events had dropped tremendously and it now happened no more than a moon cycle apart instead of hundreds if not thousands in the same time. He watched it until it went out of sight and reluctantly left his post and headed back into the hidden shelter.

Keeping low and from long habit he moved quietly and with care taking advantage of what little ground cover there was. After all this is a desert, although there was much desert, it was different in the fact that there were grasses and trees; he believed that the trees that were here were called spruce. But he knew that this was an old name and much of the old was slowly disappearing as were the buildings, the materials scavenged from the ruins, and whatever equipment that still functioned. Again, he thanked whoever the stranger had been that originally built this place. He had thought it out well. There were no entrances into the underground living area that could be observed – quite a feat for the desert. So he crouched and went around a small sand and rock hill, looked around, and entered taking the ladder down into their hidden home.

He had to wait a moment for his eyes to adjust to the dim light and when his eyes adjusted he saw his family looking at him anxiously. He shrugged, "I don't know what it means or whether they are just passing through. I really do hope that they are doing just that – because if they aren't then, even with this place being so well hidden, we'll be located. With as many as we have living here, and the fact that we've explored some of the surrounding area, something we've probably left will be found and that will make them curious, driving them to look for other signs.

"They continued on out of my sight, but they kept to the low areas not far from that small river that heads through this desert. From what I observed there didn't appear to be any family groups looking for a new home somewhere. Most were men; in fact there was a complete lack of women, which really bodes ill for us. It most definitely speaks that they easily could be another large group of raiders like the ones that destroyed our village. In fact it could be the very same one. But none of us knows what those raiders look like since we were fortunate enough to be away at the time of the attack.

"The lack of women suggests that they are a part of that large network of slavers who captures and sells women and children, making them a commodity, property, and subservient. Oh, I saw no children either further confirming my first observations. As you all are aware, they are a force of destruction in this world full of destruction. They've become the predators, and any unsuspecting village, hidden farm, or family is their prey. They only care to torture any male that they capture, the females they rape and then sell, and whatever they can steal they will. They aren't looking to the future but only now and what they can gain and not anything else. So I truly hope that their passing through this area is just that, and once they leave that this will be the last we see of them. I know I'm repeating myself, but this type of scum scares me to death.

"So for the next several days we are stuck inside, except for our forays outside to see if they have backtracked and are searching the area for entertainment and profit – namely ones like us. We will only go out at dusk, night, or just before sunrise. Any other time is too much of a risk." He smiled although it was a sad one. *This place wasn't meant for this many people. It works, but we'll be tripping over each other for a while. And I'm sure our tempers are going to rise, and there's nothing any of us can do about it.* "I have no answers, and I hope that in the end, we won't have to abandon this place and face the dangers out here again." Shaking his head, he shrugged. "I really wish I had better news for all of you.

"As you know, what we've found here in this place is the very thing that those murderers and thieves are looking for. Any of the old technology brings a high price, especially since most of it is disappearing. None of it was built to last, and with no one still alive that can repair it, it is disappearing rapidly. It won't be very long until it's all gone. And what's here would support a force that size for close to a year. And you women would bring a high price in the slave centers. This place is a raider's dream. Stuff to steal and sell, women to rape and trade, and a hidden oasis in the middle of the desert to operate and raid from. We cannot let them find us, it's really that serious. And I, and I'm sure the rest of the males here, don't want to be the center of their form of entertainment as they would enjoy the torture they would do to us. Taking bets to find out how long we would last before we die – then, before dying, knowing that we have failed our women folk. And knowing that their lives would end up being a living hell, with an end similar to our own, only it would be further down the road. So please be careful, and let's try to make the best of a bad situation."

He looked around his family and saw the fear in their eyes, and it was understandable. After all they had survived, only by luck, the other attack. And again it was by luck that they had found this place hidden deep in the desert. Like those suspected raiders, they had moved slowly and with care away from the destroyed village moving east in the Oregon territory until they had reached the desert. The desert scared all of them; after all, it was a barrier they knew very little about. Then they found that small river and had followed it. Yet, not knowing where it might lead, they, at dusk and at dawn, would climb to a high point to study the surrounding land. It had been on one of these dawn-dusk trips they had stumbled upon this place. In fact, because they had felt safe, all the family had climbed to the top. There were plenty of low areas to keep one hidden, and one of the grandchildren had stumbled upon the secondary exit – not the one they presently used. But again, whoever have planned and built this thing had thought about more than one way in and one way out.

Afraid that someone was around that lived in this place they pulled back. He and Seth his oldest son entered, and with a small torch explored the discovery. The first thing they noticed was the smell – one of long abandonment. There was heavy dust on everything, with no tracks or even the small animals that always seemed to find a way into their homes. At the point where they had entered there was a small pile of sand that had blown through the closed entrance. As they explored they found much that would allow them to not only survive, but to live in relative safety. It was divided into a number of different living spaces – a food prep area, bathroom that serviced more than one at a time, sleeping space, and a meeting and relaxing area. While not huge, especially for the number of people that would be using it, it would do.

Later they discovered the secondary units. Some for storage, which had food, seeds for growing their own food, an area that had a transparent skylight to grow the food out of sight, and a water source that continually moved water throughout the hidden facility. Plus, and they had yet to figure this out, there was hot water – honest true and never ending hot water. All he and the rest of his family could figure out was somehow it was tied to the sun for the heating. Yes, someone had invested much thought, time and effort in creating this place, but from the evidence, they never got to use it. He suspected that this had been built before the destruction, before the ancient fires from the skies. And, most likely, the owner had been one of the many who had been killed when all that death that reigned from the skies began.

He did wonder if the one who had constructed this place had a family. And he suspected just from the size that the obvious answer was yes. But from what he and the rest could determine this place had never been used. So like so many others the tragedy extended to this unknown benefactor's whole family. *To faithfully plan for one's family and their protection, and to be able to carry it through like this, only to most likely die, leaving the rest to their unknown fate.* He could think of no worse end – although that end might be theirs also. *Why did it have to go this way?* One would think that everybody would want to survive and work together and solve this crisis that our species faced. But here's where fiction met reality. And reality was harsh with the pecking order taking over. *Oh well, enough of this. It'll change nothing. We've got to do our own surviving and protecting. Otherwise we will become no more, like the one or ones who had originally built this place.* "Okay, let's figure out what we can do and let's be careful. I really want to see a lot more sunrises and sunsets."

There was some sighing and grumbling, but no complaining. While it had been close to a year since the destruction of the village, it was still fresh enough in everyone's minds to be a stark reminder of what could happen if one became careless. As the family members started breaking up and heading back to what they had been doing Dan grabbed Joel, his second son, pulled him aside and said. "Wait until everybody has cleared out and then come topside with me. You're the best in the wild of all of us. Yes, I know I'm pretty good, but the years have worn on me and my eyesight isn't nearly as good as it once was, and I've slowed down tremendously. So much of this type of stuff I've got to pass on."

"Okay dad", Joel replied, "what do you have in mind? If I got the gist of what's happening, the ones who just passed through did just that, pass through."

"Yeah, but I've a feeling about that. From what little I could see it appeared that they were searching for something, and the lack of any apparent family members at all bothers me greatly. I suspect that while they continued north until they were out of sight, I really feel that they'll be back. You know how those canyons, valleys, and deep ravines twist and turn. Later I plan on having most of us out when I'm sure that nobody can see us so we sweep this area and make sure we've left nothing to raise their suspicions."

"You didn't say anything about that, why not?"

"Easy enough, I've no proof, only this feeling that we've not seen the last of them. Although I've been right more often than wrong, still there's no hard proof. And that's where you come in, with my support of course. This is a two person job. We'll take one of the distance glasses we found here. I don't know what they were originally called, but I know that there's still a few around – not many, but we were fortunate to find a couple of pairs here. Again, whoever it was who built and stocked this place had planned very well."

Thinking about his first two sons Seth the oldest had been the one that met him outside when he was watching the settling dust. Seth took more to his wife Marta's side of the family, while Joel his side. Seth was taller and athletically built having blonde hair and a light complexion. Seth had married one of the villagers a few villages back and they presently had two children – girls that resembled their mother who was a dark beauty. When one first looked at her one would suspect from her apparent tan that she was out in the sun all the time. But when one became friends with her and her family it was immediately realized that this darker apparent tan was their natural skin tone. Her name was Tasha and she came to Seth's shoulders – always outgoing and friendly, easily making friends and lighting a room whenever she entered. She had stated that her coloring had come from the Portuguese in her blood line.

Joel was lithe and sinewy, quick on his feet and a little shorter than his older brother, with an inner strength that remained hidden. Quiet, sure of himself, he moved like a ghost through the natural world – something that Dan had always been able to do. Only now with the years piling upon him he realized that he wasn't nearly as good as he once was. The advantage he had was experience. But that didn't make up for the loss of hearing and eyesight – both critical when you scouted. So, slowly over time, Dan had been training and moving the scouting responsibilities to Joel. And he had to admit that the two of them made a pretty good team. Dan felt that the testing for all of them was just about to be upon them and he hoped that when it was over and done that all of them would still be here.

Still survival was not a guaranteed thing. There were enough natural traps out there to take one's life. Add to it the many traps by the bandits, raiders, slavers, and such, so your chances of living went down tremendously. Unfortunately all required the same to live – water, food, shelter. It took time to grow the crops, to raise the herd animals. But the scourge would only take, killing raping, destroying. With so many roving bands doing this, eventually there would be nothing left and then these bands would turn on each other until there would be no one left standing. Unfortunately if this happened they could only blame themselves, since the opportunity to recover had been here. Well, whether they survived as a species or not lay in the future. He just wanted to make sure that they were part of that survival and not fall victim to that bad element that seemed to exist. At times it gave the appearance that there were more of them than the good.

With both of them standing there quietly he waited until there was just the two of them, signaled Joel to follow and they headed topside. It was a few hours until darkness arrived and the warm desert winds struck them as they climbed out of their shelter being temporarily blinded by the bright daytime sunlight. This exit slash entrance sat below the top of the hills and was hidden within a small dry ravine completely invisible unless one happened to walk upon it. By using the ravine one would remain hidden until he or she was far away from this point furthering the chance of discovery to be almost nil. Once away the ravine entered a series of washes that ran in many directions allowing any who traveled this way to remain hidden, only visible to the large birds of prey that worked the thermals gliding effortlessly above, seeing all that was below them.

Taking the right branch they headed for one of the storage containers that was buried deep in the soils and was even more hidden than the entrance to the living spaces. *Yes, whoever it had been who built this place had thought long and hard on safety and security,* Dan thought. Heck, they'd been here for at least three moon cycles before they discovered this hidden treasure. And treasure it truly is – stored food, water, clothing, supplies, repair equipment, weapons of many different kinds, books of knowledge and of recreation, and so much more. It was the weapons they were most interested in now, and the packs that had been put together for such as what they planned. There had been three metal containers buried deep and at least one hundred yards away from the living shelter. Two were exclusively supplies, but the third, the one between, contained equipment for repair, and fabrication. While only eight feet wide, all three were forty feet long.

When they had finally discovered these buried containers it was completely by accident. Taking the ladder down to a concrete floor that the containers sat on they found, as their eyes adjusted to the very dim light only being admitted through the opening that they had climbed through, that all were locked. And not with just a single lock but with multiple locks each requiring a different key. With such security whatever was inside had to be precious. Of course the grandchildren had thought romantically that it had to be treasure of gold and jewels and such, but when the keys were finally located, and they entered each one what they found was more precious than anything the grandchildren had imagined. Eventually they located a skylight, hidden, with a cunning construction, that once closed would be completely hidden, but once opened allowed enough light for all to be able to work in the open area in front of these containers.

They had worried about water, since this was a desert, even though a short way away ran a small river that went whoever knew, because they didn't. But then again their long dead benefactor had thought this out also and had dug a well, and arranged the piping in such a way that there was, again, a buried tank that held, from what they could determine, thousands of gallons of water, and the tank was located above the living shelter so it used gravity to move the water down to where they needed it. He suspected that the waste water was handled with the same efficiency as the rest of this hidden oasis had been constructed. It was obvious, from plans that they had found, that eventually the one who had put all of this together was going to attach all the areas together with constructed tunnels, but this had never been done, with only the beginnings of one they had found that went nowhere.

So with them in front of the containers Dan said, "Look, I want to wait until dusk before we move. Then we will swing wide and take advantage of any all cover and topography that we can. I don't know how far they continued, but there is no reason for such a force to be here. There's absolutely nothing here to support them. I hate to do this, because the supply of ammo is really finite. Even though whoever built this place has set up a reloading bench with powder, lead, primers and brass that supplies all that's here we have no other source. I think that we'll take the rifles as secondary long range weapons and rely on the crossbows. Their range is much shorter, but at least we can make new arrows easier than gunpowder and lead. Primers we can forget about, once they're gone they're gone."

"Sounds good," Joel replied, "But I think we should probably add a couple of combat knives along with our other weapons. We really know nothing about the ones who passed through. We don't have any idea of their wilderness skills, or anything. Still, by them coming out here they can't be newbies. And from your description, with no family groups at all, it doesn't bode well for us, especially if they find this place. I think that if they've stopped then we have more worries. I, like you, can only hope that they continued on completely out of this area, and continue to move on out of the region and leave us alone. But again, like you, I suspect that they are here for a reason. I know it's not for us." Joel paused looking down at the floor in deep thought. He took a deep breath, let it out slowly. "I've seen enough in my short life to know that we are completely on our own. And from the size of this group as you described them, no matter how well we defended this place, in the end we'd be dead, or worse captured and severely abused before being sold into slavery. So I agree whole heartedly, we've got to be more than careful. I suggest that we stay together, and move cautiously and with as much stealth that we can. And if it takes us all night, so be it. There's just a sliver of moon tonight so it's not going to be completely dark. But whether that's to our advantage or theirs I don't know.

"Look why don't we add a couple of pistols to our packs just in case things get dicey and we've got to deal with some of them up close and personal. But, then again, it may not be a good idea and just leave it to the knives. After all firearms are becoming more and more difficult to find and if the ones we are to spy tonight are what you think then hearing a firearm discharge could bring them down upon us with force. These firearms would be something that they'd desperately want. Plus if they found this place, wiped us out, then they would have a base of operations to be able to work from – attacking the surrounding areas and disappearing back into this desert. I know you said that, but it bears repeating Well dad, it's your call, what do you think?"

"I couldn't have said it better myself. In fact let's just leave the firearms alone and go strictly with the crossbows and knives. We don't need to alert them to the fact that we're actually here, and we have firearms." They reopened one of the containers and placed those precious weapons back into the gun safe, left the container, closed and locked it down. *I truly hope I'm wrong,* Dan thought as they stood next to the buried containers. *And I've just misread that small army. But we really have to be cautious, and check out every incursion into this area . . . To be careless at any time leads to one's death.* "Okay Joel, it won't be long before we head out. But first I need to let your mother know what's up, and how long we should be gone. I know she'll still worry, but at least it may not be as bad as it would be if we just leave and inform no one. Be back in a few."

Joel watched as his father climbed the ladder out of the buried containers, and once through the trap door he closed it leaving him on his own. Joel knew that this move was important, but also knowing his mother, she'd worry herself sick while they were away. But what else could they do? Not go and not know, or try to discover what this group was up to, taking the necessary risk, and the slight possibility that they'd be seen. It seemed longer than it should have been, but staying down by the containers in the shadows and coolness was such a sacrifice. The desert had a tendency to get warm. Well, this was desert, but a mild one he'd been told. Heck it even snowed here. To pass some of the time until his father returned he went through both of their packs to be sure that they had everything they needed. As he was finishing his inspection his father returned. Looking up questioningly he waited.

Dan smiled and said, "Telling your mother what we will be doing isn't the easiest, and she always has many arguments as to why we shouldn't. But she really knows that this time I'm right and there is no room for discussion or changing of my mind. We have to know, it's just that simple – that important.

Look it's not too long until the sun sets. So let's head out and away from this area so that we can approach their suspected camp from a different direction. The only good thing about all this sand is that we'll not leave any tracks that can be followed back to here."

It was close to midnight when they finally located the camp. This large group had found a narrow gorge that hid them quite well. If Dan and Joel hadn't been familiar with most of the land around here they'd be easy to miss. Staying far away and watching from the top of a cliff they could see that there were a number of fires burning down in the camp. With careful observation they came to the conclusion that with the rough estimate there had to be somewhere between 75 to 100 people down there – a very large gathering. Again, because of night, they felt safe to use the distance glasses. And what they saw wasn't good. Dan signaled Joel to head for the far end of the cliff they were observing from and to confirm the numbers. He also signaled him to pull back once he'd completed that and both of them would meet back at the predetermined point they'd set up once they had a good idea as to where these people were.

It was probably pushing 2:00 AM when they met back up. Joel, shaking his head whispered, "This doesn't look good at all. I'm all for heading back."

"Agreed. They appear to be in the beginning stages of setting up a semi-permanent camp. There must be something that has drawn them here, and I wish I knew what that is. Any way you look at it, I don't like it, but we are going to have to deal with it. I suspect that soon they're going to be all over these hills making it very uncomfortable for us. Okay then, let's head back and give the family the bad news. I have to admit that at this point I have no answers."

"Me either, dad, me either. Okay, it's going to be just after the sunrise before we get back so let's make time."

* * *

With the camp located, and fortunately not close by, three days had passed and not one of the members of that group had been spotted, which was a good thing. But eventually some would probably work back this way. Although, since they had passed through it might be a while. They might consider it searched. Again, not knowing what the ones in the camp were looking for, left them without vital information. The pressure was building since the whole family was on edge, nervous, and worried. All knew, right down to the grandchildren, what would happen if they were found. The best they could hope for was no discovery, the worst, well, none of them wanted to go there. While the women had been hidden after the destruction of the village, the men had returned to find the carnage that the attack from that band had left behind. It wasn't a pretty sight. Most of the bodies had been mutilated, and the bodies of the women that they did find showed signs of rape, and worse before they were killed. In the end death had been kind. But the time leading up to death hadn't. They had spent that day and few after that burying the dead. There was nothing left alive in that village and not one building or shelter left standing. Even the pets were slaughtered.

So here they were, a much smaller family unit with probably the same type of individuals that had attacked and destroyed the village as next door neighbors, so to speak, and no way to protect themselves from that many. What had brought them here? That was the question that kept going through all of their minds. And this was a real problem. By not knowing it left them helpless as to know what to do. It really made no sense for this small army to be here. There were no major trails or old roads nearby, and with the time that they, as a family, had been here, there had been little to no travel through the area. Also they were days if not weeks away from seeing others, adding to the unknown reason for these to be here.

After that first foray at night to scout them out, Dan and the rest of the family stayed away not wanting to give this army of misfits and probably slavers a hint that they were here. Still by not continuing to keep tabs on them, it made it more difficult to know what to do at all. So during the days they stayed within the confines of the shelter, and only came out briefly in the early evening, just past dusk where, behind some of the sand hills and completely out of sight, the children were allowed out. And children being children had to be admonished time and time again to keep quiet. Sound traveled far in the desert or any open country. Thank goodness for what they had as far as shelter. Otherwise they'd be out in the open subject to discovery and destruction.

Finally after a week of this Dan and Joel headed back out after dark. They had to know what was transpiring with that small army of malcontents, murders, and thieves. The plan was simple, since they knew the last location, and with the partial moon they'd be able to see, and with this ability, to search out the tracks of what this army had been doing, but, at the same time, not approach the campsite at all. With the time that had passed, there would be a good possibility that there would guards set on the ridges now, making any approach very dangerous for not only the two of them but for the family if they were discovered. By staying well away, they would circle the area searching out the outgoing tracks, and maybe discern what their purpose was.

First they headed to the far side opposite of where they had first approached the camp, remaining far away and behind the small hills so as not to silhouette themselves to the sky. This time, as in the last, they stayed together or within a short distance of each other, and began searching out the many tracks heading in both directions. Working their way to the east they found the same sign. Careful now as they'd have to cross the same canyon that this army was camped, again found many tracks leading in and out. Then once safely across and up the other side to their relief the tracks going and coming were less, and as they came back around completing the circle, there were very few. More like the ones who would be coming to the top to guard the camp, than searching. So maybe they had considered what they passed through already known.

Still it was obvious that they were interested in something out here, but what could that be? Of course when Dan and the family had arrived in the area they had found nothing and had originally planned on just passing through using the small river as a direction to travel, stopping only when their haven had been discovered. Yet, as far as they knew there was nothing else out here. They'd been cautious, once their present home had been located, as they searched the surrounding hills and desert; they had found nothing to indicate any others at all. And definitely no towns or villages, old, new, partially or fully destroyed – nothing but this oasis. Not that they had done a complete search. It was on the "to do" list but far from complete. Yet, the amount of tracks that they had observed spoke of a search for something. At this moment all they could hope was that whatever it was wouldn't be located and this danger would move on and leave the area and they untouched. The pressure on them was becoming unbearable. At least for the moment, they knew that this danger was looking in a different direction, but for how long? How long until they changed that direction of searching and came their way? From the amount of tracks that Dan and Joel had observed they were leaving no stone unturned, and if they changed their search to their direction then it would almost be guaranteed that this haven, this place of safety would be discovered.

There had been many arguments, discussions, and family meetings trying to come up with a solution. Even leaving had been suggested. But it had been pointed out that with the amount of, well for a better word, patrols, searches, and such that were being sent out, it would leave them vulnerable to discovery and the very bad results that would come with that discovery. As long as they stayed where they were they would leave no tracks to be followed, and leave no sign that there was anybody around. So it was decided to wait it out. It was the best of the many bad choices they were left with at this time – not that in this time in their history there were many good ones. Keep out of sight, remain so, leave no tracks, become ghosts, and hope that eventually this element would not find what they searched for, and would move on, leaving the area none the wiser that others were here. If only they would be so lucky, yes, if only.

CHAPTER TWO

It had taken a while, but eventually all the hard work had paid off and they'd located that village. It was well hidden, and wouldn't be the easiest to attack. But so far they hadn't been discovered and by staying far away, studying the village through the long view glasses he could search out the area and begin to formulate the plan for attacking and destroying it. He saw that while not large, there would be plenty of women, females from here to use and then the ones that survived to sell into slavery further east in the now thriving slave markets. With the success of this attack, the resulting loot and fun that they would have, followed by the profits made east in those markets they would take some time off and enjoy the rewards from their raiding. But first they had to be successful here. So he continued studying the area from the ridge top looking down into that small hidden valley. This would have to be a complete surprise, nothing short of this would guarantee victory – and it was a farming village too. Which meant, grains, and meat animals, and so much more that they'd use, and what they couldn't, sell – definitely, in his mind, a rich take.

He retreated, heading down the hill before standing once again. He was far enough down now to be hidden from any who lived in that hidden valley. He knew that there were many such places, and while not all of them had such wealth as this, there was a greater chance of finding these communities here than anywhere else that they had searched. He smiled, from what he could determine, and those of the others that were out and watching this place, nobody knew that they were here. They'd been in the area for over a week now and the longer they remained in the area the greater the chances that they would be discovered, alerting the ones below of their presence. Only one more day, and on the morrow it would change. If all went to plan by early afternoon there would be a village no more with only ruins and smoke from the fires rising to the heavens.

Skar, as he was known to the ones who followed him, thought. *Yes this is ours. And with their isolation no one will know that we are here – no one. This lets us work over this place at our own pace. And when everything of value that we can take is with us, only then will we move on, only then.* He looked forward to his time with many of these females, and the screams from the males that they would torture. *Yes, much entertainment ahead.* He laughed softly, there wasn't anybody around that could stop any of this, and only another roving clan might possibly stop him, and his men.

Then that next day when the sun crested the surrounding hills and began to light the valley below they attacked. It had been very successful with the loss of only a couple of his men. The surprise had been complete. One moment it was that peaceful village, the next the screams of the dying and of the ones that they used up, followed by days of torture and rape, beating down the ones that they had kept, killing most of the males, only keeping the male children alive. They would bring a good price in the markets. They stripped the village and then burned it to the ground leaving the bodies to rot in the sun and disappeared leaving a silent world behind them with no obvious life. No animal, no human, not one escaped.

So they began their trek east towards the markets. With what they had the trek would be pleasant for them. After all they had females to keep them comfortable, and the goods, field animals, grains, and such to keep them fed, and what remained when they reached the markets would be sold. Then, for a while, they'd break up enjoy their share, later coming back together with new intel refreshed and ready to plunder again. There was no law to stop them, no one to challenge them, and with as large as this continent was, very little chance of running into another such army as this. The destruction that the ancient fires had brought from the skies to the earth had left very few alive, emptying the lands of the living, scattering the few that survived far and wide. Only during the second generation after the event did people start coming back together and forming small communities. Although with the rocks still falling out of the skies, and the damage to the very earth itself, there was still a very good chance that one would be destroyed – and many were, but now it appeared that the skies were emptied of their deadly rocks, and they fell less and less. Those ancient rocks, ancient fires from the skies were finally diminishing and soon the earth would begin the healing process and start over again.

So by his generation, the third after the incident, one could almost go where he or she pleased and would have a chance of surviving without being destroyed from above. The small communities were becoming more numerous, and armies like his were also becoming more prevalent leaving the ones who were attempting to build a new life vulnerable to the ones who only wanted to use, to take, to kill, to destroy. It was unknown at this point in time which would survive. And he really didn't care. After all death was the final outcome no matter what one did in life. So he felt that grabbing anything and everything was his right. And if others disagreed, well, they could feel his blade just as much as any he had killed.

He remembered watching his mother being raped by such as what he had become. And once they had finished what they were doing they killed her right in front of him and laughed. He had vowed to avenge her, but they laughed, grabbing him as he was tied and then sold him in the same slave markets they were presently going. This had followed with many tough years, but he never forgot, and when the opportunity came, he killed his owner, escaped, and began his search for the ones who had destroyed his world. Of his father he never heard anything, but suspected that he'd been killed outright. In a way he hated him, for no other reason than the man had failed to protect them. Yet he knew that if he thought it out, there probably was no way his father could have protected them, or would have survived. There had been too many, and like he and his at this last village, the surprise had been complete.

He remembered looking back, crying, and desperate. Seeing the small farming village burning with a dark boiling smoke rising high in the sky, bodies naked and bloated lying everywhere, gross in death – no different than the village they'd just left. He remembered learning the hard way to defend himself. Being alone for that time after escaping left him captured once again by another small army, but instead of becoming a victim again and being sold once more into slavery, he joined them, learned their ways becoming as ruthless as they. And after one of the successful raids and his share given he left, hunted down the ones who had destroyed his home and his life and killed them. And with revenge complete he began to form his own.

It was that scar that ran from the top of his head by his left ear to his neck that he took for his name. He became Skar, and whatever his original name, as far as he was concerned, it had died when his family had died. Now he was no more than what the ones who had set him on this pathway were. He destroyed, and cared not for any who tried to build. What they had was his, if he and his army could find them, and as long as he lived it would be that way. He planned to live long, but in this new world of violence, destruction, and death, there were no such guarantees at all. Although he had to admit that he had shortened many lives, so he had no expectations for his own. He was sure that there were many who would love to see his end.

So, once the destruction, murder, rape, looting, and the taking of prisoners for the slave markets was over they headed out leaving a dead silent world behind that time would erase, leaving no sign that there ever had been a village here, a place where people gathered, laughed, cried, made love, had families, grew crops and tried to bring understanding out of the chaos of this present world. It was another nail in the coffin of mankind, and there was no kindness in it at all. What they took they planned on using up, and what survived to be sold for a profit. Taking their time they began the trek to the eastern markets. None of those markets existed in the west as of yet, but who knew, most likely with all the open spaces, myriad canyons, valleys, mountains, and so much more there was a good possibility that some would eventually open out here. Now it would take them three weeks to simply reach one of those markets. At least they had companionship to warm their sleep sacks at night, even if the ones who would join them wanted nothing to do with them. He laughed at this thought.

They had been two weeks into their journey when the attack came. The canyon that they were traversing appeared to be empty with only them being here, suddenly there were shots ringing out from the higher areas. They'd walked into an ambush. And in the ensuing chaos of the battle one thing came through clear and sharp, there was less attacking than the number in his army. But they had the ancient weapons, these that attacked. And from the amount of ammunition that they expended, must have also found a large cache of bullets somewhere. There wasn't a chance in hell that they could overpower such firepower. With their one or two ancient weapons and a very limited ammo supply for the same, followed by the bows, swords, knives, and clubs they were no match. In the first thirty minutes he lost at least a third of his men.

Whoever these attackers were, they were good. Very rarely exposing themselves, they moved like ghosts from one place of cover to another. And where he and his men were located there was very little cover. He felt that they had taken out at least a few, but really had no proof of that. One thing for sure, if they remained here, they'd be cut to ribbons. With hand signals he signed to tighten the defense and once this had been accomplished he followed it by retreating back down the same canyon they had just entered. He was proud watching the discipline of his men as they began an orderly retreat – no panic showing. As they began this retreat the firing from the hidden enemy stopped and a deathly silence lay over the battlefield. Taking advantage of this lull, he had his men move a little faster. At this moment an increase of fire from above towards the area of their retreat caused them to pause. When they attempted to change direction the fire increased there also. It was apparent that whoever had control over this army knew what he or she was doing. So all they could do was hold where they were and see what would transpire.

Skar didn't have long to wait when on one of the closer ridges a group appeared holding the flag of meeting. Looking as close as he dared he made out at least four individuals in this group. But the clothing they were wearing made it difficult to be sure. If they didn't move, then they were almost invisible, so close to the colors of the rocks and soils were those clothes. Taking a deep breath and knowing what was coming he sent up his own flag, the one stating agreement to the meeting, waited until the acknowledgement from the ones above, stood, and hoped that they would abide by this. He personally knew that there was no guarantee that any would. This method had been used as a way to pull others into a trap. Yet, that had already happened, and he felt that if this continued, eventually his army would be devastated and while he felt that they would have returned much the same thing, in the end all there would be is a bunch of dead and no advantage to either side.

He took his second, only known as Bear, with him, putting their weapons away, but close enough for easy access if this turned out to be a ruse. The ones from above started down a hidden trail and stopped half-way expecting Skar to approach them, which he did. After all, what choice did he really have? He noticed that there were three in the forward group and behind these three and just out of hearing range were six more – a definite show of strength and superiority. Not wanting to be on lower ground and instantly putting him in the inferior role he first headed towards and away from this group looking for ground of his own choosing, making them at least adjust their stance to face him. When he reached his chosen point he stopped and waited. This part was always a game. He'd been on both sides of these meetings and knew that what was happening at this moment was very common. It would be a few moments before they would join him there. Looking up at Bear, who was a huge specimen of a man at least six feet six inches tall, and weighing in at least three hundred pounds, none of it fat, he waited. Bear could move with unbelievable speed for one his size, and had unbelievable strength. Highly intelligent he had never wanted to lead, but enjoyed the role of being the second. All weapons that he carried looked to be no more than toys in his hands. Skar whispered, "I have a feeling that this isn't going to be a very comfortable conversation. Whoever these are they are good. Our forward scouts, and our trailers never had a hint and we walked into this very well planned attack. Listen well, just in case I miss something. It could mean the difference of any of us getting out of here alive, or have all of our carcasses rotting in the sun."

As they reached the higher point he looked around and was surprised by what he saw. Had they taken the high road, so to speak, it would have been obvious that this area had been struck by one of those rocks from the sky. The area was close to barren with boulders strung around haphazardly. Vegetation was just beginning to return with small patches of dead grass. Much of the soils were lose making it difficult to climb. So the two of them took it slow and careful climbing higher than the three before dropping down to the small flat area that the others were standing on. Once closer, it became obvious as to why their weapons had seemed so ineffective against the attackers. They were wearing vests of some kind that obviously gave them protection. The weapons that they carried were definitely ancient, but appeared to be in good repair. Strapped around them in bandoleers were massive amounts of ammo.

The apparent leader was a woman. One who was huge. She had to be as tall as bear and wasn't a beauty by any means. Of course this could easily be an illusion. Looking close he saw intelligence in those eyes and on her right hand bore was the mark of a slave – one of the two standard places where those marks were placed. Looking at the rest he saw similar marks. Comprehension came immediately. This small army was escaped slaves, and he knew instantly what would be demanded of them, but knew that if he and the remainder of his army wanted to survive this encounter he would have to give them what they wanted and be thankful that they were allowed to live. He saw the hate in her expression for him and his kind. And in a way he understood it since it was probably someone like him that had sold her into slavery.

The two of the finally came within voice range and stopped, remained silent with arms crossed and waited for this woman to speak. The winds were picking up creating small dust devils, blowing the dark hair of the woman around her face. He suspected that her hair color was black, but with the dust that was in it, lightening the color somewhat, he couldn't be sure. Those winds held heat telling him that most likely they were on the northern end of the Utah territory, maybe even the southern end of the territory of Idaho. He looked around in the distances and saw high plateaus, low growth vegetation, and the heat radiating from the ground. It was a silent world, except for the sounds that the wind created as it whistled around these hillsides.

She looked him over and spat on the ground saying with a venomous tone, "Listen slaver, or whatever or whoever you claim to be, I will hear nothing from you. You are lower than the snake. I will dictate what will happen here, and if you do not agree then we will wipe you out completely. I'm sure this world would be a better place if I went ahead and did just that. Then your carcasses would fertilize these lands and at least some good would come out of you. But alive you are worse than any predator that has ever existed. At least they do what they do for survival. While you do it for the cruelty and the pleasure that you can delve from the misery and death of others. As you can see we are former slaves delivered to the markets in the east by scum like you.

"Also, as you can see we are well armed, and protected so any thought of counter attacking or trying to trail us back to where we camp will be met with death. And I mean death to everybody in you pitiful army. We will follow you out of this area, this place of death to be sure that once this is over that you have left. We move around so don't expect to come back here with a larger army and take us, and what we have, and return us back to the slave markets. Others have thought of this and they are no longer alive. At least we do not torture as you and your kind. Take this as your one and only warning. When you leave, forget about us, because we will not forget about you. We've marked every one of you in our memories and if we even suspect that you are returning you will die. It is just that simple, so simple that even you and your kind can understand.

"Here is what you will do. You have ones that you were going to sell at the slave markets. Now these are mine. You will turn them over to me, and we will confirm that you've complied completely. We've been following you for a while and know how many you have and what you've been doing to them. Ahead is an open area. You will move your entire group – your pitiful army – into that area and on the east side is a flat area that is more open. It is here you will place your prisoners and remain until we signal you that all are there. Once you receive that signal you will retreat back the way you came and disappear from our sight. I do not want to hear a word from your mouth so just nod that you agree.

"Oh if you wonder about our weapons, our protection, understand that we discovered a cache from the ancient times. And while what we have is finite, for our needs it is close to infinite. So the puny weapons of today, and your shields and such are no match for what we have, and what we will continue to have until we are no more. Yes, you can use your imagination and decide to come back and try to locate this but it isn't here, it isn't close, and we do not live in this desolation so you will not be able to find the location. Besides", she laughed an ugly laugh," we dare you to try. We can always use the target practice." She stopped talking and stood waiting with her arm crossed.

The one-way conversation angered him, but he and his were helpless. She'd pointed out the obvious and made it clear that either they obey or they were dead. He could see there would be no room for negotiation at all. So he waited trying to hold what little power in this situation that he could, but it was really a lost cause. They were outclassed, out gunned, and were targeted by a hidden enemy. With nothing showing on his face he nodded once confirming that he understood completely. Both he and Bear backed up and took their leave heading back down the hillside to join the rest. They'd been beaten, and beaten soundly. They would be leaving with their lives, but little else.

As the proceeded back down the hill the winds picked up, strongly filled with heat and dust pelting them with fine granules of sand, which they ignored, with other thoughts on their minds, like survival. Never looking back he felt his back itching expecting the ones above them to change their minds and finish what they'd started. No names had been exchanged but he wasn't surprised by this. After all why should there be? It was obvious that the victors had no need to brag and the losers no want to grovel at their feet. It presently was a very uneasy truce and if they did not do as ordered, well Skar knew what that final outcome would be. Eventually they reached the floor of the small narrow canyon and joined the rest. "We are going to be able to leave with our lives, but that is all. Everything we removed from that farming village will remain and we must leave by the way we came." He could see the protest being formed by many of them. He raised his hand to silence them and continued. "We do not have the fire power to counter what they have. All of those above us have the ancient weapons, plenty of ammo for those weapons and are wearing protective gear. Yes we could fight, but why? We'd lose, plain and simple. Somewhere in the wastes they've discovered a large cache of this old stuff, but again we were warned not to try and follow or to attempt to find that stash. The leader stated that they like us move around a lot. And even if we were to search every inch of this area we'd not find it – if they let us search that is.

"We were also warned that if we attempt to scout them out, follow them in any way that they will kill us – and that would be all of us. And I believe them, because you see, every last one of them are escaped slaves. So they have no reason to love us since we are bringing a fresh supply to the slave markets. The leader of this army is a woman and I can tell you she isn't someone to trifle with. We were not allowed one word was told only to listen and once she finished speaking told us that we were to either nod in agreement or to shake our heads in disagreement – either way once we answered, to leave. And she didn't care which way we decided. So we must head a little further east where there is an open flat area. It is there we are to leave what we captured, turn around and go back to the west.

"Remember, we had flankers out, we had scouts leading us, we had trailers, and at no time did we see the ones who trapped us here. So we are not talking about some amateurs who don't know what they are doing. I would say at this juncture that they are much better at this than we are. I feel we are pretty good, and with the successes we've had I really thought so. Yet, we've run into someone who is better, much better at this than we. So we must lick our wounds and retreat to fight another day, to loot another day, to find females to pleasure us another day. This simply means that if we abide by what we were ordered, there will be another day. If not, then our carcasses will litter the sands right here, right now. I vote for another day and hope in the future not to run into this army again. We've been down this canyon a number of times on our way east and have never had the occasion of meeting this army, which reinforces what we were told that like us they move around a lot. If you need confirmation of what I'm telling you ask Bear. But do it quickly as I suspect they will not tolerate too much of a delay before they act." At this point he walked away to give the surviving members a time to talk with Bear if they so desired.

The woman smiled as she watched what was transpiring down below. "It looks as if he's explaining the facts of life to them and they aren't very happy about it." This brought laughter from the ones who were close enough to hear her comment. "Let's pull back just in case one of them feels lucky. While this armor will protect vital areas there is still other ways we can be killed." With her honor guard she walked between them and back up the trail to the top of the ridgeline that overlooked the defeated ones below. She turned to one who had a sniper rifle and said, "Let's see if we can hurry them along. This stuff gets hot after a while, and I'd love to take it off soon." She looked the one in the eyes and smiled, sweeping her arms in the direction of their enemy, "Any time, if you would?"

Smiling back at her he responded, "With pleasure ma'am." Sighting down the canyon to a large boulder that was just on the other side of the ones in the canyon he fired a single shot. They saw them react and at that moment the woman yelled, "We are becoming impatient, are you ready to die? If so we will be more than willing to fulfill those wishes."

Looking at the scar that the bullet had left and the sound of the shot still echoing down the canyon, Skar shook his head saying, "It will have to now or never. Shall we go where they demand we go, or shall we be stupid and try to fight it out?" He saw that the shot fired had made up their minds and even though there was some grumbling all of the ones who were still alive headed east to an unknown area just ahead where they'd lose what they'd taken.

* * *

After being sure that the ones that they had defeated moved away heading back the way they had come, the woman in charge of this small army of escaped slaves said. "Let's have someone go and welcome those who we've just rescued into our fold. I'm sure they are quite traumatized and are worried that what is going to happen to them will be worse than what they just were dealing with. So let's welcome them with open arms." She paused a moment, deep in thought, while turning around and facing another of her team. "You know that leader of those who have just vacated this place doesn't look to be one who will give up on this. Yes, we beat them on every level in this fight, but we did have the element of surprise, and from what I can see these are the lowest of low. We probably should have wiped them out like we would any other vermin, but didn't. So send a couple of our best scouts out and watch them closely. In fact make it three that way one can come back in and report what this one and his army is doing. I want no surprises."

Turning back to the one she had first been conversing with she said. "We need to bring the ones that were left into our temporary camp. There's enough of everything that they can at least get a decent meal, and clean up a little. Then after our doctor checks them out and he feels that they are able to go with us we'll head back to one of our main camps and see if we can catch up on what's been happening in the other areas." She smiled an ugly wicked smile saying. "We've much work ahead of us. There seems to be more of the vermin out here than any of us thought. I would say, as they did in our past, we've got job security." This brought a laugh from the ones around her.

She shifted gears and asked, "So how bad were our losses this time? We are much smaller in size than the ones we are trying to eliminate or at least bring under control."

Another came forward stating, "Ma'am, one dead from being too careless – probably better off without him anyway. Kept doing stupid things and couldn't find his way out of our camp let alone on the trail. Other than that, we've a few minor injuries that won't delay us at all. I suspect that our delay will be because of the time necessary for those who will be joining us will need to recover sufficiently enough to be able to join us on the trail."

"Okay then, let's go see to our new recruits."

* * *

It had been three days and they continued heading west although Skar suspected that they were being tailed. He had no proof, had seen nobody, but one did not live in the outback, the wilderness without sensing something other than what could be seen. They were presently in the desert trying to decide whether to continue west all the way to the coast or to possibly change directions heading north towards the Washington territory. While contemplating this decision he remembered a mention somewhere by someone, and in both cases – somewhere and someone – he couldn't remember at all. But there was mention that whoever this was, of a destroyed town sitting in the desert close to a small river, and when this one had gone through the area that there had been nothing touched. He had shown him some of the loot that he had grabbed – but, had stated that, at the time, he was simply trying to get away from the desert, and really didn't have a way of taking much with him. Still what little he had with him was convincing.

At the night fire he discussed this with Bear who after listening to the whole thing including the speculation of this town shrugged. "It is a good fairytale, is it not?" Bear replied. "But we've lost everything and it is far to the coast and places for us to raid. I sense unease within our ranks. With the anticipation of what all of us were going to gain when we sold what we had in the markets, and then come away with less than nothing has left a bad taste. No, no, no one is blaming you for this. After all if blame needs to be placed it should be on our own scouts, our out-runners and trailers, they were the ones who allowed us to fall into that trap. What you did was correct. Remember I was at that meeting and the rest of them here weren't. They really do not understand how close we came to death; although I suspect a number know.

"So is it worth it to go off on this tangent and try to find something like this that we have very little knowledge of? A place where even the location is vague, and this desert is huge. Yes, I know, compared to the ones south of here it is small, but even so we can walk through it and never find anything but more sand, rocks, snakes, scorpions and so many other bad things. Yet I think I understand. Something needs to be found and found soon, otherwise we may begin to fight among ourselves, and following this, break up and head to the four winds." Again he shrugged, "I really do not know, I really don't. But, I'll go by any decision you make. Other than this one defeat we've been pretty successful, and have had much pleasure from what we've taken over time."

Skar had no illusions; he knew that he could only hold this army together as long as what they did was successful. On this front he had to admit that overall they had, but many would consider this defeat a reason to replace him with a different leader. And the one thing he understood that in a group like this there were always others who wanted his position and were willing to do whatever necessary to procure it – definitely one of the major problems when dealing with ones like these. One could never trust, or take their word for anything, and definitely one did not turn their backs on them. If one did then a knife in the back could easily be the result. "Okay, I think we'll, at least, look since we're here anyway. It'll only cost us a few days anyway, and since there is a river, well nothing like that big one that runs through that gorge area, there will be water. At least we still have plenty of food. We were allowed to keep that. Although where there's a river there should be game and such depending on that water as much as we need too."

"Okay boss", Bear answered, "just how do you want to go about it? Announce it or what?"

Shaking his head Skar said, "No, don't think so. We'll just work the river for a few days, and if asked only then state what our true purpose for hanging by the river is all about." Looking up he saw the night sky was bright with stars. It was only in his generation that the skies began to clear, and only up until this clearing of the skies began was the night sky described but never seen. It sent a shiver through him because these lights seemed cold and heartless looking down and laughing at the insignificance of this small world. *Why am I here? And just what would my life had been if,* and here he laughed quietly, *yes that big word if.* Shaking his head, it did no good to go that way. He couldn't even remember his family, what his life had been before all had been destroyed and he became a slave, only to escape later, joining the ones that had led to where he was presently.

He remembered crying himself to sleep too many nights at the beginning. The misery and pain, too little food, and too much work for his small body to handle – the uncaring comments, the punishments when it appeared he hadn't done enough to satisfy his owners. At least he'd been fortunate in one way. His owner was not a lover of boys as others were. At times he'd have brief contacts with others such as he, owned by others, and had this described to him in graphic detail. It helped strengthen his resolve to one day escape and bring war to the slavers and try and end this reign of terror on the people who were just trying to survive, to raise their families in what little safety they could find, to be left alone and help the world heal. Yet, here he was part of that destruction, part of the very thing he'd swore that he would destroy. Again, he laughed a bitter laugh. *Yeah, not funny how things worked out in the end.*

When the world was destroyed, and civilization along with it, the resulting collapse allowed the wolves and jackals, the ones who would take, steal, murder, rape, falling on the any that they could take advantage, to become the ones who ruled. At the beginning there was plenty, not because much wasn't destroyed, because it had been. But with the reduction in the population to probably less than five percent remaining, what was still available to that small amount would help the few that survived to remain so. Yet, many thousands died because they didn't know how to survive in this new world. Many thousands of others perished because of the gangs, and small armies that were ravishing anything and everything that they found. Chaos was on and in the world, and the sun's light was hidden with smoke and ash in the skies. There were heavy layers of smoke, from the many fires that ravaged the world – not including the many strikes from above, followed by the acid rains that continued to destroy much of the surviving natural world.

Mankind was on the brink of total collapse and extinction, and the many battles over limited resources did nothing to further the chances of survival. Only by living off the dead carcass of the civilization that once was did any survive. Yet, as time continued to move in the direction of his generation slowly things began to sort themselves out and it appeared that there was a good chance that mankind might survive all of this. But even to this present day there was no guarantee of that at all. He had to admit, whether he really wanted to or not, that he was one of the many pushing mankind towards extinction. Did it bother him? He had been down this road too many times, and still hadn't come up with any kind of answer. Well, he wasn't going to find one tonight, and with the rising sun he and the rest would be out working this river, and with only he and Bear knowing what they were really searching for, continue to keep up the illusion that they had a true destination to the west.

It was probably time to move the camp anyway since nothing had been found except sand, rocks, some type of desert trees, and grasses where the river flowed. There was absolutely nothing to indicate that there had been a town out here. But what did he expect? It had been at least two hundred years since it had been destroyed, and as such, could easily be buried in these sands. Although, the sands didn't give the appearance of moving, like the sands of the great dunes, that they had spied in the distance on one of their forays into the desert in the past. That had been another one of those searches, like this one, where there had been rumors of a hidden village deep in the dunes that had survived and because of the shifting sands, and the oasis that was there to support it, had survived the initial apocalypse, and also the aftermath because of their isolation.

This place was supposed to be filled with wealth that any small army would covet. But his attempt, like others that had tried to find this place, had failed. At least to make up for it they had spied a caravan of horses and mules moving on the hidden trails, attacked and destroyed it taking all for themselves. Yet, that had been years ago and the treasures and loot gained from that venture long gone. So here on this morning they would be moving, and like the scavengers that they truly were, try to locate a destroyed town that at one time had been living and breathing. To strip it of anything precious in their minds, and who knows, maybe find some of those ancient weapons and head back getting revenge on that army of escaped slaves. *What a profit we would make if we could take escaped slaves back to the markets. They always bring a much higher price.*

* * *

"They have to be looking for something. I would have figured after we defeated them that they would continue on to the coast. How do you feel about it?" The scout asked as he turned to the other two scouts, "We're going to need to let our leader know. I'm not comfortable with their stopping here. Still too close to us, and you saw their leader, he's the kind that doesn't admit or take defeat very well. Look, one of you needs to go back and inform her of what we are seeing. We'll withdraw back to the hilltop where we're safe and will designate that a meeting area. So when you return if we aren't there, wait, and we will meet. Just be careful, we cannot be seen at all, or let them know that we've been following them."

The other two looked at each other then back at the one who had talked. The smaller of the two said, "I'll do it. I'm very good at hiding and covering a lot of ground. Should be back in seven or eight days – be careful, if the catch you, well we all know what will be the outcome on that. So I'll leave it that way." He immediately, keeping to the low ground, headed back east in a roundabout direction to remain hidden from the ones they were watching.

CHAPTER THREE

"Dad", Joel stated, "it's getting crowded out here." Shaking his head as both of them crouched behind a small hill looking up towards the ridgeline. "I would never guess that we'd be seeing so many out here. We know what that first group is, but who are these other three that are out and about?"

"Wish I had an answer, but I do agree it seems to be a bit crowded if one considers that we probably have around one hundred people in ten square miles of desert. Yet, like us, these three appear to be keeping track of that army. Fortunately they've been so interested in the army of bad guys that they haven't realized we are here. For now I'd like to keep it that way. I almost walked into them myself but fortunately their attention was drawn elsewhere. The problem we face is; who are the ones watching and what is it that they want? I worry that they may be a rival army and have decided to extend their territory, or maybe the one that came through here a short time in the past and have remained in the area is doing that, I just don't know. But this I do know, it's going to get harder to remain hidden with as many as we are and with this many tramping around the desert, the river, the small canyons and such. We cannot remain hidden inside our hole forever. But we don't have much of a choice for now."

Both were using the distance glasses and were careful to keep them shaded so that the sun didn't reflect off of them giving their location away. They could see the three behind a hill that kept the three out of sight of the small army. It was obvious they were discussing something, but what there was no way to know. By observing Dan and Joel knew that these three were good, very good at moving and remaining hidden. Much better than the two of them, so there was no way they'd chance an approach to be able to overhear what they were discussing. Lying flat on the sandy ground they continued to watch, and then one of the three took off to the east leaving the two. "Now what does that mean?" Joel asked.

"I've got a bad feeling about this, and I hope I'm wrong."

Putting the glasses down he turned towards his father and asked, "What do you suspect?"

"I feel that it's going to get very much more crowded around here shortly, and by not knowing anything but what we have observed, I have no idea how bad it's going to get."

"More crowded?" With a questioning look Joel closed his eyes and thought about what his dad had just stated. Taking a deep breath he realized that if the three had been scouting the others, and one had just left heading east, most likely, the one that had left was heading somewhere to report what they had been watching. "Ouch, and we don't have anywhere to fall back to . . . No place that we can pull back and let this play out and be out of the way. So what do you want to do?"

"Son, I don't think there's much we can do. This country is too open to move freely, but you and I need to begin to search to the south away from both groups and see if we can find a place to fall back to. Our best defense and at this moment, offense, is to remain unseen, and unknown to these two groups. I don't know how we're going to pull this off, but somehow we must if we want to survive." Sliding back slowly to remain hidden from the ones who had the higher point Dan signaled his son to follow. As they slid back they went deeper in a ravine where they crouched moving slowly as the sides of the ravine became deeper allowing them to stand. Dan whispered, "Let's head back to the shelter and be very careful as we do. It would be easy to concentrate on one and miss the other like the three did with us. They may be able to afford to be that way, we can't." He looked both ways and with care they continued their return to the shelter being careful to remain hidden the full distance.

Odds were quickly piling against them and there still was a great chance that before this was over, that they'd be either dead or slaves, and wish they were dead. They went past the hidden entrance to the shelter taking a roundabout path to keep anyone from discovering they were here and to keep the entrance a secret. Eventually with care they approached the entrance and one at a time entered the shaft closing the door behind them. Both worked their way to what had become the family room and saw what would have been considered a normal domestic scene with children playing with their toys on the floor, and family members sitting around in chairs talking, reading, or watching the children. Sunlight streamed in from a small skylight creating areas of light and shadows, with fine dust drifting in and out of the sunlight. *How long will it be this way? And will we survive this latest difficulty?* These questions and so many more kept going through Dan's mind, painfully aware that luck and God had kept them alive so far. But now everything was becoming ever more complicated, and with no real solution or answers coming to him he was at a complete loss as how he being the patriarch of this family, thusly the unofficial leader was going to get them out of this situation. It had been good for so long.

All of them had assumed, and here he had to laugh a bitter laugh, yes, they all had assumed because this was semi-desert that they'd be left alone. All of them had felt that it was providence when they found this place. So they had moved in making this place their home, thinking by its very location that they should be safe for a very long time. *What has brought that first army here in the first place? And who are those others?* His mind kept running in tangents. So with the discovery of this place they had searched, explored, but never far enough as it was now painfully clear. He had failed all of them by not finding another place that they could retreat to if necessary. After all, why would it be necessary? They were in a desert for heaven sake, why should they need another place? Well, he knew that he wasn't going to find any answers right now, and he had nothing good to report to the family as he stood there enjoying the scene.

Inwardly shaking his head he called for attention. "Additional trouble has arrived. I'm afraid that our little corner of the desert is becoming quite crowded. Not only do we have to dodge and avoid that army of suspected slavers, but now we have another that's unknown that has become part of this. Joel and I have spotted what we consider three scouts that are doing the very same thing we are – watching that army. It was only because they were concentrating so hard on remaining out of sight and watching the others that we were not caught. We, Joel and I, were doing the very same thing that these others. In fact they were in the very place where we were heading. Fortunately we saw them before any turned around and faced us. We took notice and quickly, quietly withdrew." He could hear the intake of breath from a couple of the family members and suspected that it probably was the women. Unfortunately, in this time of their history it was women who suffered the most, not that torture was a nice way to die.

"I don't know any more than that, other than the fact that at some point we may have to leave and find another place of safety." Here again he paused, since everything was slowly turning from bad to worst. What could he do? Nothing was the obvious answer, nothing at all. The time to be prepared was in the past and they couldn't return there and start over. "It's obvious that whoever this other group is, they are very interested in that small ruffian army. This makes it so much more difficult for us. And to add to it and you know that I'll never hide anything from any of you, one of the scouts headed out to the east. Probably to make contact with whomever they are a part of. This means that soon, and again I don't know what soon means, soon we may have another army here in this area. And with two it will almost be impossible to remain hidden.

"I want all of you to be prepared to move at a moment's notice if we must. This is becoming serious, very serious, and I, at this moment, do not know what will be the outcome of any of this, or if it will be safer for all of us to just remain here hidden until all of this has blown over, if it does. I really never expected this to happen, but it has, so we'll need to make the best of a worsening situation. At this point, until we know more, none of us, except when we are scouting for information, will leave. We are stuck inside until this plays out or we have information to the contrary that says that either army, if we find a second arriving, is friendly." Taking a deep breath and expelling it slowly he continued. "That's all I have for you – wish it was better news, I really do." Finishing what he had to say Dan turned to leave, deep in thought, thinking about their unknown benefactor once again. But before he could leave his wife interrupted his thoughts, "Yes Marta, what is it?"

"I know that you're beating yourself up over this. Remember I've been with you too long to not know how you think. I suspect that you're blaming yourself for this situation. But you must remember that there are many of us here and all of us are to blame as far as seeing this coming, which we did not. It's obvious to all of us that we should have planned much better. We all felt that like you, once we moved in here we'd remain safe and untouched. We've been shown that we are wrong – all of us. So, like we had to do before we found this place, we will do what we need to live, to survive, to insure our children and grandchildren are here after this, this situation is done one way or the other. It's been very uncomfortable with the grandchildren not being able to go outside except briefly to let off their pent up energy, but they understand as we do. So we will do whatever we must to stay alive, and if that means we live here underground and not coming out for a while, well, so be it.

"Look, you and Joel need to begin training the rest of us so that we can at least help, and if the worst does happen, to be able to have some of us escape. I know that this is a bad time to begin this, but again what choice do we have? There may come a time that we'll have to scatter to the four winds giving at least some of us a chance. I hope beyond hope that it doesn't come to this, but it could. So, while we all know much because it was necessary for our flight from our last village, God Bless their souls, we need to learn more. You know that the two of you, you and Joel are the best at this. I have a feeling that at night the two of you are going out to watch our enemies or possible enemies, but we need someone here who can watch our backs while you're away. So let's begin the learning right here and now. Let's set up some schedule so that even our grandkids can learn."

"Yeah, you know me too well. Yes, I do blame myself for not realizing that what is happening could happen. And we all know why this scouting has fallen to me and Joel, but what you've said is valid. We have no guarantees at all. We let our guard down, became complacent, didn't think this through and allowed this to happen – not that we had any control over this, so yes, it is a very good idea." He turned to Joel and said, "Joel can you start with the grandchildren and show them a few things. I need to check on a couple of things inside this place, and then I'll begin working with the rest." Turning towards Tasha he said, "You can be with your children, and of course if Seth wants to join you that's fine. Between the two of you, you can help Joel get the message across. After all you are the children's parents and know what will work best." Turning back to the rest Dan finished by saying, "I want to be sure that everything is in working order, especially that area where we grow our food. Be back shortly." He took his leave and headed off to make what he considered needed inspections. Not that this was something that they neglected, but when things became really difficult, like now, he'd feel better knowing all was okay.

Just who are these others? And why do they have an interest in this band of ruffians anyway? He had no answers, just questions. The area they were in presently was so isolated he never thought in what remained of life that they'd see another human, yet it was becoming unbelievably crowded. By looking at the numbers that were presently roaming these desolate hills there were probably more out and about than the total number of people that had been in that village. It was fortunate that this hidden place sat close to the top of this small mountain and the country rolled away from here. Again, whoever had built this place spent the necessary time and thought of placement. There were a lot of desert trees about, he believed that they were called desert cedar, but that was only a guess.

Where they had escaped from, far to the southwest, near the forested mountains, across a rolling plain with much signs of ancient volcanic activity, in one of the many hidden canyons had been their village. It had taken them a couple of cycles of the full moon for them to reach this area. And like that band had followed the river into this apparently parched land. Yet this river that they had followed wasn't small. It didn't compare to that large one that ran to the ocean to the west, but with the volume it wouldn't be running dry anytime soon.

It had been fortunate that they found that river. For at that time they were close to starving, running out of water the day before as they had crossed a vast flat area devoid of life, with little to no vegetation growing, no wild grains to harvest to help sustain them, no small animals. It seemed that they were the only life and for them at that moment, they were not sure of their own survival. Then they dropped down into that narrow canyon coming across the river. With no sign that it had been here, you know, things like trees growing along the banks, or the smell of water as one approached, or the increase of wildlife, just nothing. Standing there stunned for a moment, then as one all of them stumbled towards the bank looking in awe at that rapidly flowing water. Carefully they worked their way down the bank to find a place that they could put their heads into that life giving liquid and drink their fill.

Here they stopped for a short time, building fish traps and broiling the fresh fish over coals of a small smokeless fire, eating their fill, and not moving. Looking around Dan knew that this place by the river was not necessarily a safe place to break, but all of them were exhausted. So with some nervousness he allowed all of them to stay for a few hours. Here, at this point of discovering the river, they were completely out in the open. Eventually, even though there had been no sign of anybody other than them here he got the family moving again and they began following this river to the northeast looking for a place to hide and hold out for a few days to give everyone time to recover from their ordeal.

After passing through the narrow canyon to reach this river the area had opened up looking like that it would be a good area to farm. Looking at much of the ground in the area, he saw that much of it was sub-irrigated, meaning that water was close to the surface. And in some areas he saw the water standing on the surface. All he could do was shake his head. Because he knew that in a different time and place that this would be a great place to farm and raise a family, but not now, not at this time. This area was too open, too easy to find, almost impossible to defend, or protect what you built here. So with regret he moved everybody further down this valley looking for a place to hide while they recovered. After what they had just been through it was oh so difficult to continue, but continue on they must. He could see the fatigue and pain in his family, and it hurt deeply. But if they chanced it and remained, they might end up becoming permanent residents here as in dead with their eyes staring sightlessly up at the skies, leaving their bodies to the many scavengers that probably roamed these lands.

This outcome had come close to happening too many times and for whatever the reason they were still here; still alive, even though others who may have been better suited for survival were not. He had no answers as to why it was so, but he did not want to push whatever luck they had. So they continued pass this promising land onward to where the canyon began to close in on them again. Looking up at the hillsides all were bare of vegetation, being only of volcanic rock and loose soil, showing off the area for what it really was – semi desert. With the only sign of anything living being in that valley and close to this fast flowing river.

As Dan thought on this it pushed his mind ever further back. Back to after the attack on the village they'd called home, and the fact they had to close their ears to the screams of terror and pain, and still even now after this time that desperate time flowed and he couldn't stop it.

It had been a desperate run across the open spaces with little cover, very little water, and some food that they added as they crossed that barren area. The days had been hot and the nights cold. He'd have preferred to run in the opposite direction towards the coast where the great forests provided many places to hide, the water plentiful, and thusly the game to provide food for the family. But with little time available to them when the attack on the village happened they had no choice but to retreat to the east. As they temporarily left the area all of them had to close their ears to the screams of the tortured and dying. They knew that if they tried to assist in any way that they would be joining the ones who were either dead or heading quickly that way. Why was it this way? These people were their friends. And all of them were only interested in their families, being able to provide the basics, shelter, a comfortable life, have food at their tables, and to raise their families. And in an instant it was gone forever and they the ones who were left alive would be forever scarred.

The flight was toughest on the grandchildren who were five and seven respectively – much too young to be on such a flight. Much too young to have heard all those terrified screams. And it was obvious that it had left its influence upon them with the nightmares and the clinging to their mother. But they couldn't stop, and they couldn't console them with no time to stop and help them face those fears. Even if the two had been boys he suspected that the results would have been the same. When one is this young it is a place for the fantasies of imagination, not the reality of this desperate world. He and Marta would watch with worry in their souls, discussing late into those troubled nights, ways to help their grandchildren through this. But they knew to survive they had to keep moving, and to be forever vigilant and diligent or through some minor error or omission they too would fall victims to this vermin that attacked and killed without mercy, without care, without compassion.

The direction they had been pushed appeared to be a mistake. As far as they could see, which was quite a distance; there was nothing – no movement, no sign that any animals lived here, no sign of any other humans. No tell-tale smoke rising into the skies in the mornings showing a village or camp, no sound of voices drifting on the winds, no abandoned campsites, just nothing but the dust, winds, sparse vegetation, a high flying predator stating that at least there were small rodents here. But even these small creatures remained hidden. At one point, when they were quite desperate, they had come upon a canyon that split this flat plain they were on. It ran across their chosen path deep with no obvious way across. It was as if the earth had been stretched thin at this place and finally had pulled apart so steep were the sides of this broken area. Broken and jagged with not a hint of how one could climb down one side and then find a way up the other. Having no choice they headed south along its rim. Looking northward from the point of discovery all they saw was a widening of this canyon and the country becoming harsher, if that was truly possible.

Their flagging strength and reserves almost spent it took them a few days to find their way around this, and once around and a bit further they found an abandoned city. It had been destroyed by the ancient fire from the skies. Very little remained, but they were virtually out of everything. At least, by finding this place, they knew that there had to be water somewhere close by. Again, they were careful in their approach and scouted the area around for any life that might still be here. But after a careful, a very careful and cautious search, they came to the conclusion that like this vast plain it was empty of life and had been for a very long time. So they entered the rubble and silence of what once had been a place that like their now dead village had people with their hopes and dreams, with their families, and friends, all gone now, all just a silent dead world, leaving only the spirits to roam the ruins. With the many dust devils dancing on the hot pavement where pavement still existed, it left them feeling even more alone.

From what little he could discern they appeared to be the first in this lost vacant and destroyed city. It might be easily because the distance from the mountains through that hot dry plain, followed by that raw split, which was that very narrow canyon, discouraged any from heading any deeper in this forsaken land. When one looked in any direction, there seemed to be nothing but this plain, the steel blue skies, hot breezes, and very little else – nothing to encourage one to explore past that barrier, past that narrow canyon with the sides seemingly impossible to scale. It was only desperation that had pushed them past that barrier and onward to this place of ancient death. Yet sometime in the past this had been a large community one that serviced the surrounding areas, supplied families, businesses, and who know what. Now all gone, destroyed, and leaving nothing but skeletons lying around. And with so much death there was no one left to give these dead a proper burial. All that remained were the ruins, the dust, the winds, the silence, and the feeling that there were spirits of these unburied dead roaming in the shadows.

He knew that what they were witnessing here had happened everywhere on this world when the ancient fires from the sky struck the lands and oceans. This had been the beginnings of hell on earth. With the great wounds laid upon the earth, the earth reacted with volcanos becoming active once again all along the areas where the plates met. And along with the old new ones became active changing the lands, where they erupted, forever, or as close to forever as it could be. And with the damage caused by the fires from the sky, the earth added its own ancient fire in the form of those volcanos, adding thousands of tons of toxic gases and carbon dioxide to the air – weakening further the life that still clung to earth's surface or lived in the skies. What hadn't been destroyed or touched by the falling skies, were touched by these ancient fires that the earth herself had created. Thusly pushing the earth's living closer to extinction. To becoming close to no different than the majority of planets in this solar system and space – just a dead and sterilized piece of rock with no chance of life ever coming forth in all its glory.

But somehow, and in a short amount of time, very short when one considered the age of this world, things began to settle down, the skies slowly cleared and life crawled out of its many hiding places to begin again. But now the dominant life form seemed to be bent on self-destruction, and if this life form wasn't careful, very soon it would succeed, and they would be no more. And like so many other species that this world had seen, they too would pass into obscurity. Just another extinct experiment that in the end failed, with the earth saying, "There's always time for another before the star that keeps me alive dies."

Here they spent a week searching the ruins, adding to their supplies and replenishing their water skins. With the destruction there was nothing left to identify the name of this dead city so like so many in this wounded world it would return to the earth unknown, and uncared, forever forgotten. For a short time it brought the grandchildren out of their fear and brought some excitement to their eyes that up to now were full of fear, sadness, and tears. It was a place of adventure. Even so, they never strayed far from the family always looking for approval and still clinging to their mother when they heard something they couldn't identify. All Dan could do was shake his head. He wanted so dearly to reach out and take those fears away from them, to hold them close and tell them that everything would be okay, and it would work out to their advantage in the end. But he couldn't, because he knew that he didn't believe it himself.

Looking around in the distances he saw no changes, nothing to suggest that there would be any difference if they continued in the easterly direction they were presently heading. One thing for sure they couldn't retreat, so live or die they were committed to wherever this path led. At least this brief stop had given them a chance to recover at bit. And finally the day came when they had to move on, because this dead place of respite was only that. There would be no way to survive a lifetime with what little remained. So with some regret they left this unknown dead city behind and continued their generally eastern journey. A sorry looking family group looking for shelter from the storms that ravaged this earth, and these storms were not of nature but of man.

The situation at hand brought him out of his thoughts and back to reality. He couldn't afford to be distracted at this point and time. Too much was riding on him and Joel. *Why, why now?* He shook his head and shrugged thinking. *Why not?* There was nothing special about any of them, nothing at all. No reason for any of them to expect any special treatment or to be considered the best of what still lived. It was only by accident and circumstance that had kept them alive so far. He saw that by changing just one small thing in their past, one moment in time, one change in direction, that it would have been they who would not be alive now, and this place of refuge would either still be empty, lying undiscovered, or some other family or individual would be using it. By knowing that whoever the one who had constructed this place had been a victim, easily led one to realize that even the best of plans could still have an unhappy ending, and everything one did still wouldn't change that outcome.

He came out in the bright sunlight seeing the desert cedars throwing short shadows. Remaining low and keeping the surrounding countryside in view he quickly made his way to the entrance to the underground facility for growing of food. This had been built close to a large boulder patch. And with careful work the builder had placed skylights up through the middle of those boulders, and had set the light path to be available from morning to dusk. From the outside these rocks appeared to be no different than the many thousands of similar piles that were the remains of ancient eruptions, very ancient eruptions from long dead volcanos. So there would be no reason for any to climb on top to check out what might be among them. Again he marveled at the ingenuity and thought that had went into this hidden place. He knew from conversations with his father, and grandfather that at the time before the ancient fires from the skies that people used something call currency for exchange and purchasing of goods and services. Not the bartering and trading that was common today. So this would have been something that would have cost much to create, let alone to build and hide.

Taking one more look around, he opened the hidden door and entered into the growing area, first entering the shadows that promised nothing but another storage area. Walking down a narrow short hallway he turned to the right, followed by an immediate left and entered the growing area, temporarily blinded by the bright sunlight streaming into this space. He smelled the moisture, felt the humidity, and smelled the grains that were growing here. He went around these to the opposite side where there were vegetables growing. One of the benefits of such as this was the fact that there were no seasons down here. So one could grow what they needed year round, insuring that there would always be this kind of food. He assumed that whoever this had been that they had planned on protein from animals also, because some of the seeds were of the plants that could be used for animal fodder. But when they arrived and found this place, if originally there had been any domestic beasts, they were long gone and wild if any had survived.

He worried that something might go wrong with all that made this function. And he knew that none in his family including himself could do any more than minor repairs. In a sense this place was a trap. Not the kind where one was led to capture or death, but of another kind. Instead it was a trap of one's needs. The need of the basics, food, shelter, and safety, making one want to stay and not move on. Because here it all was a known, while out in the savage world there was absolutely no guarantees for any of this. This trap had a tendency to make them lower their guard, to become complacent, to accept that they were safe and should, because of that unknown benefactor, remain so. Now he knew, with some regret, that soon they might have to abandon all of this and leave it vacant once more. Taking a deep breath and letting it out slowly Dan walked the narrow areas between the growing tables insuring all was okay.

He heard the outer door swing open, followed by the same closing. He turned towards the entrance and waited not knowing who or how many were coming down here to join him. He had to admit to himself that he was somewhat depressed and at a loss as to what to do at this moment. As wide open as this country appeared to be with so much, in truth, it was no more than vacant lands. Where one would spend days if not cycles of the moon and not see another person, as it had been when they had crossed that plain coming here. Now this small area was becoming much too crowded and dangerous. And with the increase came trouble for them. After all, if these newcomers to this area had been farmers, or even travelers who moved from place to place, only protecting their own, then this would probably come to a peaceful end. But it was not to be.

Seth with Marta entered into the area with Seth saying, "This is becoming too serious. I know that so far we've not been discovered. But you know, as I that with the time we've been here, and with the children out playing and exploring as kids do, plus the rest of us, after all, we're a large group of people, there's just no way that we can cover all the sign saying to the world that we don't exist. It's a very worrisome thing. I know that whoever built this place had considered defense as well. And while we do have some ancient weapons and the ability, at least for a short while to replenish the ammo that they require, it is far from enough for an army of that size. And those others, who are they and why are they watching, keeping tabs on them? I'm afraid, as is Tasha, that we may see another army here shortly." Here he laughed bitterly. Shaking his head he continued, "I don't know why we call them armies, but we do. In reality they are no more than gangs of thugs, and murderers who do as they please because there are none that can enforce rules on such as these. I know that so far we've been safe and they do not know we are here – but for how much longer? Can we afford to stay?"

Marta looked at her husband with a sad smile, as she said. "This is almost as bad as when that last village was attacked. I see the worry in the other women, our daughters and once again those nightmares have returned to your granddaughters. I hear them cry themselves to sleep, and it hurts me deeply that it must be so. I'm not trying to add to your burden, you have done well in keeping all of us safe. Even though, at the beginning, I had questioned your direction of moving us to east, it has worked out well for all of us. I know that we must remain as ghosts, but this is wearing on all of us. I'm beginning to see small arguments, fights and irritation. I guess that comes from too many in a small area and no space to be alone."

She looked down at the floor before returning her gaze to his eyes. He saw a pleading there which tore him apart. She continued saying, "I know that you and Joel are doing everything that you can to keep us safe and to let all of us know what is happening outside of this place. Unfortunately with the circumstances being what they are, the two of you are the only ones getting outside. We've got to come up with something soon; otherwise things are going to get very bad. Somewhere and somehow we've got to get everybody out and away from each other so that this doesn't come to physical fights. I know we all cannot get out at the same time, but even a couple at a time would help relieve the tension and pressure that's building."

Absolutely everything the two of them were saying was true. But what did one do to change what they were facing? *I don't have any real answers,* he thought. "Oh I know exactly what you mean, and I know that with this unknown threat hanging over us that it makes it so much more difficult just to stand by and wait for the proverbial hammer to fall. But at this very moment I have no real answers. Fortunately, as you know, this one gang or army has remained in that canyon and has been searching away from us . . ."

They heard the entrance open and close again and in a few moments Joel made an appearance saying, "I hate be the one bringing more bad news, but the ones we've been watching have packed up their camp and are heading our way. Although from what I can see they are remaining in the valley below. I'm still sensing that they are searching for something. And those scouts we saw, the two that are remaining are shadowing them on the high points. So there's a chance that they could come right by here."

Alarmed Dan asked, "Which way are they moving?"

Trying to keep it somewhat light Joel asked, "Which group? The ones scouting or the ones that are moving in the canyons and valleys bellow us?" He briefly shook his head when he saw his father about to interrupt him. Taking a deep breath he said, "The army is heading west, which means that they'll pass far below us if they stay in the low areas. But you know that from here, actually a little further down, others can watch any movement that happens below. So there's a good chance they'll, those scouts that is, come close to where we are, maybe right over the top of us, I don't know."

Turning back to his wife and oldest son Dan said, "Better get back to the rest and let them know. Unfortunately things appear to be ramping up instead of down. See if we can keep everybody quiet. It shouldn't take too long for the ones below to pass our location, which means, I hope, that these scouts will do the same. Let's move on this, we may not have much time." He turned back to Joel saying, "We'd better do a quick sweep and make sure there's very little that these two can pick up on, then join the rest of the family in that, I guess we can call it a bunker." *Why now? Why when I was just warned that everything is about ready to come apart because we're much too close and nobody has a place to go to get away?* He had no answers as all of them headed back out with Seth and Marta heading for the main living area, and he with Joel preparing to do a sweep. As he watched the two disappear inside he turned to Joel admonishing him to stay away from the west facing areas so that his movement wouldn't leave the army curious as to what was moving up here. They couldn't afford that many coming up here to search. They'd be discovered and from what they knew that would be the end for all of them one way or another.

"Joel, work the southwest side working back to the south and I'll work the northwest side, doing the same. Once you've run your area get back inside and don't wait for me. Let's move on this, I don't know how much time we really have."

"Fortunately, dad, I was working my way back towards that camp trying to both keep out of sight, and watch both the ones scouting that same army and that army. I was being more careful about the scouts since they were closer, so I didn't realize until I really looked down that the army was beginning to move. I waited just long enough to confirm their direction and came back as quickly as I could. Okay, hope to see you back inside soon." With that Joel headed out and began his sweep.

Dan headed to his area which had a drop off that they had to avoid, but at the same time he needed to make sure that there was no debris from their time here that may have fallen over that edge. The soils here were heavily volcanic with many small rocks making footing difficult, and making it even more difficult to move with stealth. He didn't know how soon those two scouts would show up, and knew that it would be from his direction that they would come, if they decided to climb to these heights. So with care he worked his area keeping that ridge line and drop off until last.

* * *

The second scout asked of the leader of the two, "What do you think? They have to be looking for something. With the time that they spent looking to the east and searching all over the lands in that direction, it seemed that there for a while even we would be found."

"I don't know. I really thought that they would continue across that barren plain and head into the mountains on the other side where there'd be more people, communities and such for them to prey on, but there's something out here that interests them, and by not knowing, it's a bothersome thing. And I have a feeling that it doesn't bode well for someone once they find what they are looking for."

"Yeah, it'd be nice if the one we sent back with the report would return so we know what the lady wants to do. I don't have a problem doing this assignment, but what is it all about anyway?"

"Don't know, and I'll never try and second guess her, but she's never led any of us wrong so far. And, if you remember, it was she who led us to and found that weapons cache. So, as far as I'm concerned, she can lead us, and tell us what she wants to accomplish, when she decides to."

Putting his arms out in front of him with his palms out the second said, "Hey don't take this wrong. I wasn't criticizing her at all. If it wasn't for her and what she's been doing some of us would still be slaves. And that attack on this group was brilliant. They didn't have a clue we were there, let alone anywhere in the area. I suspect that she sensed something about this leader and his second. Did you see the size of that one? He's huge! One would suspect that someone that size would be slow, both in mind and movement. But watching him move and looking into his eyes you could see that he's anything but. He'd tear any two of us apart and probably not even raise a sweat."

CHAPTER FOUR

Abe, the scout that was returning to report on the movements of the thieves and murderers pulled into the area where they had set up for meetings, but no one was here. In a way he wasn't surprised. Most likely their leader had remained at that one camp so that the ones that they had taken from that army would, at least, recover somewhat. He had seen them come in and these twenty five or so would need some time to at a minimum rest before moving on. Yet, he knew that the way things worked inside this army, and what else could one call it, he'd have to wait until at least one showed up. He also knew that if he went back to where they'd camped in the past that they wouldn't be there. This woman that led them was uncanny in her ability to locate hidden camps, and even as long as he had been with them he knew very few of them. So he sat down to wait, knowing that it might be a day or two before someone joined him. In a sense it was time he couldn't afford. As it was it had taken him a week to get right here, and he knew personally that much could happen in a week. Too bad they didn't have that instant communication capability that it was rumored that their ancestors had.

* * *

Madam, as she was known to her army, paced with impatience showing in her steps. Also showing was disgust in the way the ones they had rescued had been treated. Many of the women barely had any clothing left to hide their modesty, most having nothing to cover their breasts. The young children being half naked and the rest so close to it that they might as well have been, showing that none escaped the violence. All showed physical and mental abuse. Some so severe that she wondered if they would survive. In a sense it might be better for these few to die ending their misery and try to help the ones who had a chance to recover. It was obvious that all of them had been raped and beaten often, including the children. The ones who did this were less than the animals and in her mind did not deserve to live. And when the condition of these refugees became clear she was glad that she had sent out those scouts to follow. Her anger was rising, and she felt like she wanted to crush the vermin that had brought this kind of horror down on others.

So once the assessments had been made they remained here overnight, and in the morning moved slowly, because of the injuries to the ones they'd rescued, to one of her many hidden areas that was close to this trail. After her escape and subsequent years out here and before forming this army she had searched out the distant places, the unknown areas, where she would be safe. Now all of those many places were her army's refuge and she had what could be considered hundreds of them – although, the exact number was probably much less. Every time they rescued people from the ones like this army, gang, or whatever you wanted to call them, it would take her back to her own past to her own torture and misery, and the misery of the many around her. She wished that life on no one, and it was the only reason now for existing. To be those avenging angels that swoop in like the hawks and eagles, wiping out where they could, any who perpetuated this style of life. There was no reason for it. They, all of them in this wounded world, were trying to survive and rebuild their lives and come back from near extinction. But if these others had their way it wouldn't be long before it wouldn't matter because each death brought them closer to the end.

Approaching her second, she asked, "Did we have enough clothing to allow these women to be able to cover themselves? And how are these children faring?"

Her second, only known as *the second,* replied, "Barely. There were more here than we expected. So we've been sharing where we can." Shaking his head he continued, "I've seen a lot of abuse brought down on others since I've joined your army, not that it wasn't something I've never seen. But, the animals that took these are the worst. I doubt if many of them would be alive to reach the slave markets in the east by their present condition. And if they had, well, they wouldn't have brought the scum much. He looked down and spit in disgust and with anger asked, "Why do such as they have to exist, and what are your plans for them?"

Smiling a wicked smile Madam said, "At the moment there's not much we can do. We have to nurse these few back to health, at least enough so that we can move. And once they are back into our main hidden camp, and safely into the care of the ones, who can help them, we *will* see – yes we *will* see. Which reminds me, since we'll be stuck here for a while, I need a couple to head out to our rendezvous point to meet with one of the returning scouts so that we know what is transpiring with that trash. Can you get right on it? I must pay a visit to those we've rescued to reinforce that they are now safe and we are not in any way close to the ones who had captured them."

"Yes ma'am, will get right on it. And in a way, I hope that this trash, as you have called them, have disobeyed and have remained in the area allowing us another reason to eliminate them."

"Yes, in many ways my feelings also, but in any fight no matter who has the advantage, it can turn in an instant, and we could lose, we could find ourselves heading back into slavery, and this time, I suspect that we'd all be killed and slaughtered as an example to others that this is what happens to escaped slaves. I, for one, would rather remain free, and out here being those avenging angels freeing others who are on their way to becoming what we've already experienced."

"Yes, not to mention that some of us killed our owners to escape. I'm sure that the sellers would love to get their hands on us as well as the major owners. I'm sure our deaths wouldn't be easy, and it would take us a very long time to die, leaving a strong example for the ones who are still slaves."

"So", Madam said, "let's not give them the opportunity. It may not be in my lifetime, yours, or many down the road of time, but if the human species is to survive then somewhere along the line this must end. I'd like to see it end with us, but it's too wide spread. But knowing this isn't going to prevent me from doing what I can to eliminate it wherever I can."

The second spoke vehemently, "I agree with my whole being. But you're right, with so little of us we have to be careful. We have to pick our fights, and even those have to be tempered in such a way that we come out on top. I know we've been lucky so far, and it's because not too many know of us. But if we become a pain to those in the east I'd suspect that they'd begin to try to hunt us down and destroy us. And all those ancient weapons and such that we have will mean nothing with us under siege from an overwhelming force."

She laughed, even though it was a bitter laugh. "Yeah, and at times it frustrates me that it must be so. But I think that if any of this vermin did locate our main hidden facility they'd be in for a big surprise. They have no idea what surprises we'd have waiting for them – no idea at all." Shaking her head she said, "Let's change the subject, and hope that we are safe there. Of course I heard of a large canyon that stretches for miles in the Arizona territory that has many places and side-canyons to hide in. And even though it is in a desert there's supposed to be a river that runs through it. So if worse comes to worst, we can always retreat to the south and head there. And no before you ask, I've never been there, and only have a vague idea where it is located.

"Someday if we continue to increase in size, and there's no reason for that not to happen, then maybe we can have more than one army of ex-slaves, and have them spread out here in the west all the way from the deep southern borders to the ice in the Alaskan territory. It's a great thought, but, again, it's something I'll probably not live to see. Look, we've kind of headed off on a tangent here. I do need to see how the ones we rescued are doing, and reinforce to them that we are not here to harm them, but to free them, and help them heal. So get those ones out so that we can get the information back from our scouts." Again she shook her head, "It would be nice if we had some of those devices that allowed our ancestors to communicate instantly, but none of that exists now, or if it does we don't understand it and can't make it work." She turned and left heading towards where the ones they had recovered were.

The Second watched as she left, a large woman with sweat glistening on her dark skin, darkened because of the sun, and roughened by the winds and blown sands. Her black hair blowing in the wind, leaving one with a picture of a strong-willed leader who would do what was necessary. And being a woman, at the same time, showing compassion where it was needed, something he hadn't seen from the slave owners or the trash they'd defeated just a short time before. He turned and headed off in a different direction. It was time to get the ones out to that rendezvous point.

She didn't know if she was up for this meeting or not. On her way over she had learned that one of the rescued had passed away. It was a child, and that hit her hard. *Why does it always have to be a child? Why do they have to suffer so?* Yet, she understood why the slave markets wanted children. After all, she had been one at the time she had been sold into slavery and the following years to the time of her escape had been as close to hell on earth as any could be. Not that the boys fared any better. There were owners who liked boys as well as girls and because both were property if one did not do as ordered, then the punishment was severe, so severe in fact that in some cases one died from it. Plus, from the owner's point, it was easier to control a child, to make them what the owners wanted. While adult males were mostly considered too much of a problem and were not wanted – although there were times when the slave markets had requested a particular supply of them. Probably to work in some type of a dangerous location, such as mining or in the hot dry places where one did not last long under the intense heat of the sun.

Steeling herself for the encounter she approached the area that had large tarps spread both on the ground, and above to provide shade from the direct sun, and to provide a little cleaner surface to lie on as the sick and injured were being taken care of. She smiled at the refugees even though the smile was a forced one. She looked over the ones here and cringed inside. From their poor condition she wouldn't be surprised if, in the end, that more of them died before they could move them to a better place. She saw the really young children clinging to their mothers, who were attempting to put forth a brave face for the sake of the children, but in the end, was doing a very poor job of it. She saw the shock, the trauma; these had suffered, and would continue to suffer for a very long time. She hoped that time would help heal, but knew that like her, there would be permanent hidden scars – scars that would surface now and then, and be bared to the real world. She hated it when hers would surface, and with difficulty and much discipline she'd force them back to those hidden places deep inside of her.

Approaching one of the mothers who had two young children clinging to her she saw that at least clothing had been provided. But the dirt, and obvious unhealed wounds and a look that held hope, but one still filled with fear awaited her. Crouching down she could see that her size scared the children. *Oh well this is something that I can do nothing about.* Taking a deep breath she again smiled with what she hoped was encouraging. "I'm known as Madam, and no I don't need to know your names or who you are at this time. It is enough to know that for now you are safe. I know that this is something that's nearly impossible to believe, but it's really true. We are not taking you from your captors just to become your new captors.

"You see we are what you were just about to become, not that you didn't know this. We", and here she waved her arms around encompassing the whole camp, "we are or were slaves." At this point she opened her right hand and showed this woman the mark that identified her as a slave. "You would have been receiving your own marks soon. You were only about a week from the slave markets and while what you have endured up until this time seemed like hell, it would have only been the beginning. You would have been separated from your children and most likely, and I can guarantee this, you would never see each other again. Later, when all of you have had a chance to recover, I will tell you my story, but for now understand that we were able to prevent what your future would have been.

Looking at the woman and her two children she said. "I cannot change your past; I can only hope that you can grow beyond what has already happened to you and the rest here." She stood up and looked at all that was here. "I know that some of you women here will end up carrying a child from the rapes and beatings that all of you endured. And because of this it would be easy to hate this child, but I'm asking you not to do this." She knew that because of her deep voice that what she was saying to this woman and the rest of the women here that they'd hear what she was stating. "And the reason I did not need your name, by the way, is that it's not important at this time. You see, if you had made it to the slave market your name would have been taken from you, and a new one given. That is why we go by the names we do. Most of us, including myself do not remember the names we were given at our births, only the ones given to us by our *masters*." When she said that word it was as if it was something totally disagreeable and needed to be spit out.

"I do not need any of you to speak or say anything. We fear that a couple more of you will die from the abuse all of you received. Before we can move, the ones here who can get a little healthier will need to do that. We have a great distance to travel, and with the physical conditions I see here it will be a slow trek. I'm not going to honey-coat any of this; where we go is not close, and it is not easy to get there. We face danger all along the way including the possibility that the ones we took you from will be looking for revenge. If we are attacked then I need all of you to head to the center where we can protect you. At that point my second, who prefers to be known as The Second, will lead you to what is considered a safe place away from the battle. Yes, I know that he is a male, and that is an issue right now, but trust me on this, you are safe with him or any of the other males that are with me. We will be traveling south initially, and that's really all you need to know, other than we have a large hidden village where we take such as you. It is a place of safety and because of the size and location nearly impregnable, and that's if someone happens to find it.

"And as far as any of the males here, just to let you know this, they were children at the time of their initiation into the world of slavery and grew up slaves. So they understand what would have awaited, as I, the children. And believe it or not, it would have been worse for them than it would have been for you. Some of us took the chance and just escaped, while others, including myself, killed our *masters* so there is a heavy price on all of our heads for capture and return to the markets. And if we are ever captured there will only be humiliation followed by slow torture with only our deaths awaiting us. So we have reasons to save all we can, and to be careful that we remain hidden, and protect each other." She stood back up began to walk away, stopped as she thought of something, turned back around saying, "Now get better. The sooner we can move, the sooner we can get all of you to a much safer place, and hopefully a place that you can heal, well, heal as completely as you can. Some things always remain with us as open wounds."

She headed back towards the center of camp shaking her head. These had been the most abused she could remember and she knew that there would be no way to avoid a few pregnancies out of this. Unfortunately it was the way of the world, when male a female came together eventually a new life would begin. And if the relationship was forced it could lead the woman to not only hating the growing child inside of her, but her own body for being a traitor and allowing this to happen. But in the field as they were, they couldn't provide more than rudimentary care and she wanted to get all of them back to their main village as soon as possible. She had a future date with this bandit or slave army and some scores to settle. Yet, one thing confused her, and that was the leader of this rabble, he had the mark of a slave on his palm as did all of them – although they had never revealed their palms to him or his second. Why had he become what he had? It didn't make any sense to her at all. Well, if nothing else by looking over these refugees it was obvious to her that they would be here a few days, but hopefully no more than that. If they remained in one place too long it left them vulnerable to attack and while she felt confident with their abilities no battle had guarantees.

* * *

"It's 'bout time someone showed. I've been here now for at least one full day plus arriving earlier the day before that," the returning scout said. "What's going on? I really expected to meet everybody here not just you."

Yeah, understood, but you see the ones we recovered were in worse shape than we originally thought. Anyway, as you know, when we started to follow that scum we had found them by accident. After all we were just doing a sweep to see if we could add to our growing army of escaped slaves, but instead found them. Once we recovered the prisoners that they had we found them sorely abused. Even after we began caring for them one of them died. I really didn't get a close look but I think before this is over we'll lose a few more. But because of their condition, we're stuck for at least a couple of days before we can move."

"Damn! We don't need that. Look I need to get back to the other two so that we can continue watching. So here's the report to take back, and for sure this group hasn't gone far enough away, so I think we'll be dealing with them again." The scout then passed on all the information that he had up to the time that he left bringing the runner up to date and once finished took a deep breath saying, "I've got to go. I know that we're in the middle of this day but it's not good for any of us to be out here alone so I suggest you head back immediately. Wish there was a way to speed this up. It must have been nice for the ancients when they talked over great distances instantly instead of having to do this this way."

"Okay, sounds good, hope to see you soon. And yes it would be nice, but we don't, so I guess we're stuck." With that he stood watching as the scout headed back out and disappeared from sight. He was tired from his rapid pace he had kept to get here so took a little time sitting around the small smoldering fire that was putting up very little smoke. Looking around at the barren hills that surrounded him he sighed, put out the fire, scattering the ashes to give the appearance that it was an old fire. He knew that if one really inspected the site that they'd know that it had been recently used, but for ones just passing it would at least seem to be a very old camp – a very old stopping place. Finally he headed off in the opposite direction of the one who had reported, immediately disappearing into the surrounding hills, covering his tracks as well as he could. The information he had was important, and he wondered why those thieves and murderers had stopped in the area that they had and appeared to be hunting for something.

* * *

Skar was frustrated, but at least they had found what seemed to be an old well-traveled trail, not presently but in the past, and not in the recent past but in the distant past. It was one of the clues that the person had left for him as to the route to this lost village – well village would be stretching it he had been told. Still to find such a place largely untouched meant possible riches, and if it was as small as he had been told, at least there would be something they could scavenge that would make up for some of the loss they had suffered when they lost their merchandise. This was really desolate land, but for that river that ran through it, there'd be no reason to be here at all. Yes from a distance with those trees it appeared to be a much nicer area than it really was, and he saw that it could bring some unsuspecting soul into the area, but why? It was just a place to pass through, not to live, so why was there such a place as he was trying to find? He had no answers, but who knew why people did what they did? Of course it was said that the ancients could travel vast distances in a single day and if that was the truth, then this place might have been at a point where it would have been logical as a stopping point, but again, it was all guesswork and supposition.

The day was heating up and it promised to be another one where you'd want to find shade and stay out of the sun, as the heat radiated off the ground. He saw heat waves already forming and it was still morning, late morning yes, but still morning. At least with the sounds of the flowing river it gave a sense of coolness even if it was only an illusion. Well, he felt that soon they could find an area where the water flowed a bit slower and they all would go in for a swim. *Probably a good idea, since I'm sure we all stink anyway.* This thought brought a quiet chuckle because most of the time he was sure that they were pretty ripe.

At least here in the bottom of this valley the lands were relatively flat and green far beyond the river that was flowing through this area. Again with all the searching to the east they had found nothing, and the surrounding hills and mountains promised even less. From a distance these areas above gave the appearance of flowing water and cooler temperatures, but if one believed that it might easily lead to their deaths. The trees that promised much were a desert variety that required little water so one would be drawn with expectations only to have those expectations dashed. While at least on the valley floor the water was here and here in abundance. So following the canyon walls they headed slowly in a generally westerly direction doing a careful search as they went. He knew with the amount of time that had passed since the village was destroyed, well, if he remembered right, in that time it would have been considered a town, but that word had fallen out of favor, could easily be almost invisible blending in with the natural world that it would be returning to.

It getting close to dusk when the first inklings of what may have been what he was looking for began to make its presence known. But he would need to wait until the morning as it was becoming too dark to do anything at all. They had traveled what he suspected was around eight or nine miles or about thirteen or fourteen kilometers. Both measurement systems were still being used although he suspected that eventually both would just go away and something else would replace them. He heard the grumbling of his men. It still was a thorn in their sides that they had lost their prizes and what monies would have come out of the sale in those markets in the east. Well, if things went well, not that they had to this point, maybe there'd be enough here, if this was here, to at least recover some of their losses.

He did notice that the further they traveled to the west that the hillsides were covered with less and less of vegetation making it harder for any to hide. So he felt pretty safe, although where they had been attacked and thoroughly defeated had been similar. The difference being that this area was more open than that narrow canyon where they had been caught. Turning towards Bear he said, "I think to be safe, even with this as open as it is, we'll post our nightly guards. And before it gets too much darker I need a couple to run the perimeters and check for obvious, and the not so obvious hiding places. Then send out a group to gather firewood. That wild cow we took down earlier today will provide for at least a couple of days of meat. And I suspect from the looks of this area that's all we're going to need." He looked around in the failing light and thought. *Yeah this looks like what was described . . . will definitely know in the new day's light.*

"Okay boss, will get right on it." Bear turned to give out the assignments with Skar watching him go. He still had that defeat weighing heavily on his mind. *How did they get the upper hand so fast? And why, of all things, with the runners, trailers, and forward scouts out, didn't we see them, or even have a hint that we were watched? And a woman leading them – who'd of thought that?* He kept going over what had happened in his mind, but in the chaos of the fight, and the rapid end he never did find a pattern or figure out the tactics that were used. Well, if it happened again then the outcome would be different. After all there was that very ancient saying that stated: "Fool me once, shame on you. Fool me twice, shame on me." And he wasn't about to let it happen again. He wished that there was a way to go over the grounds where the fight happened so that between his trackers, Bear, and him, they could figure out the pattern of events and begin to develop a counter to what happened. Shaking his head, he thought. *Nothing I can do about it, and there's no way to go back and search it out, or to even worry about it. Just move on, and do better next time.* Here he laughed a bitter laugh. *Right, if there's to be a next time.*

For some reason he felt that indeed there would be a next time. Partly because they hadn't continued on towards the mountains as ordered, and while he had no proof he suspected that they had been shadowed ever since retreating from that area to the east. Sort of a sixth sense that kept warning him that they were being watched – no proof, none at all, yet he had come to trust this uneasiness. It had been correct more times than not. Still with all of them being all over these hills to the east there had been no sign of anybody following, let alone any sign of other people being here. Other than the valley floors, it was a dry desolate world. Not one that would invite any to live here. So, again he wondered, why had people done it? Why had people lived here? Yes the valley floor could have been farmed, but again why? There were much better places to the west close to the base of the mountains.

Although, that one very large mountain still put up smoke and steam. And when one was in the area, you could personally view the many flows and destruction that the volcano had produced. This was also the result of those many thousands of impacts from those ancient fires from the skies. In many of the areas recovery was happening with new growth replacing what had been destroyed when the volcano had become active once again. It had to been hell to have lived during that time – peaceful one day, and then the very skies dropping fire leaving no place to hide, and then to have the very earth add to the fury and destruction. No, he'd take this time with all its savagery, over living at that time when the event had taken place.

Skar took another look around in the failing light, running through his mind the landmarks given by that one so very long ago. Still he knew that this had been a very small community when it had been here and active, so once again he felt they would find something although the amounts wouldn't be great. Yes, that lake was close by them and it was obvious that it had been formed when the fires from the sky had struck here digging a crater, and because of the high water table had, over time, filled in with water forming this lake. It had been this same impact that had destroyed this place and with time the scars that were still visible from it would be gone completely, leaving only the lake as any visible sign that this had happened here. It was fortunate, for them, that this hadn't been a direct hit or there would be nothing to scavenge. Nothing known to man could stop these fires from the skies, and in the areas where they had struck there was total destruction. So any of the towns, villages and whatever they were called at the time, being hit by these fires were totally consumed leaving only rubble and very little of that behind.

Well, tomorrow we'll know if this is really worth the chance. We were told in no uncertain terms to be well out of the area or face that woman's retribution. It shouldn't take us too long to go through this and then continue west, and maybe south. Shaking his head he found that he was restless and needed to walk. So leaving the camp he headed towards that lake and once he reached it was in awe when he actually began to realize how large it was. Although it could be an illusion in this failing light, and with the coming of the dawn and the sun it might be much smaller than it appeared at this moment. Staring out at nothing he began to wonder why things went the way they did. After all it was ironic how one's life turned, and here he was referring to himself, although he knew it could apply to any. So, how much of what he had become was a conscious decision, or was it the fates which seemed to have dictated it? After all, somewhere back towards the beginning he had been someone growing up in a loving family, probably in some small village, again probably not much different than the one they had destroyed awhile back. But this was so far in his past he really remembered nothing about it at all.

He heard someone approaching and turned to see who it was. It was full on dark and only by having the individual lit by the night sky could he determine who was approaching. Bear was easily two of any of the others and so was easily recognizable. "Hey Bear, need something?" He asked in a quiet voice.

"Just checking in to let you know that all that you wanted accomplished has been . . . Saw you heading off in this direction, so once I confirmed that it was so I came to find you to bring you up to date."

"Okay, so Bear just a minor question, or maybe not so minor, why are we here?"

Not sure what Skar was asking he shrugged, "I thought it was to find that old town and to scour the ruins to find something from the past that we'd sell in the markets to the south, where they value the old ways, and the materials of that time."

"Yeah, that's true, but I was thinking more along the line or direction of our lives. I mean that somewhere along that line we changed and headed in this direction, became what we became, and I know that there were some influences in the past that led us here. Who knows there may have been other such things that we do not remember that might have sent us in another direction."

"Sorry boss, but I never think about the past. It is just that and I cannot go back and change a thing. So I only deal with the now, and really don't think much about the future." Here he laughed, "After all, I leave that to you, and you've done a pretty good job of figuring that one out. Oh I know that none of us is infallible, and we are going to have things happen or go wrong from time to time, like that incident that just happened, but so far you've done all of us good. Look, you know how it is in this world and especially with people like we have here – murderers, rapists, thieves, liars, and yes, even cowards, they can and will turn on you in an instant given the chance, but it hasn't happened. Partially because of me, I guess, but also because you've been a good leader.

"So, back to your question, I really have no answers for you. As far as my path I have nothing there that personally I'm proud of, and in this place and time it's really unimportant anyway. I worry about our next meal, where we may be heading or sleeping, and as far as the future goes, I suspect that somewhere along the line I'll end up dying a violent death. After all, I've personally been responsible for sending many to the grave, and for many their deaths were slow. So, can I expect less? Because of this I do not dwell on the past, the future, or truthfully the present. It means very little in the overall scheme of things. I don't know, for all I know I may be helping our species to its end, but in another hundred years, whatever I've done won't matter, as much as I won't matter." Again he shrugged, "And that's just the way I am."

Shaking his head and smiling, Skar replied, "I wish I could be that way. It'd surely simplify things, but that's not the way I'm put together."

Laughing quietly Bear said, "And that's exactly why we've been successful up to now. So you continue being what and who you are, and I'll be who I am and we'll get to where our road leads us and our lives end as all do." At this point Bear turned around had headed back to camp leaving Skar to his thoughts.

* * *

Looking out over the valley where the lake was located he asked himself. *What are these doing here? And with the fires – there are a lot of them. Here I thought I was alone and had found a place to hide and they show up, now what?* Sam E Kaytrova was just about eighteen and had been on his own for at least two of those eighteen years. He had stumbled upon this place at least a year before and had found many places to hide among the ruins, and there was very few of them. Only the ones that had been partially protected from the blast had left any signs that there had been a community here. But with the time that he had he had been able to find much to survive on. After all one didn't require a lot, and for one there was plenty. Yet it was obvious things were about to change, and not for the better. From what he could determine these was raiders, and slavers. He really needed to remain out of sight. But how could he hide the fact that he'd been living here? There was just too much that he'd done to make it more livable so it would be obvious to these that someone had been here. Well, he'd have to pull back and disappear to one of those other places that he'd found and hope that he wasn't followed or trailed.

Heading back to his main living area he began gathering everything that he could carry, and made his first trip up and out of the valley floor heading up into the mountains that surrounded this area. This was going to be a very long night and he'd have to make sure that his trips up the mountain were as quiet as possible. Sound traveled too well at night. At least he knew where he was going and the many ways to get there. His final trip would be to attempt to cover his tracks and the path he'd been using. Because he hadn't seen anyone in the time he'd been here and the isolation of the area he felt that he was safe and nobody would be around to bother him. Here, was proof that he was so very wrong, and now he hoped that he could escape – but where? He knew that where he was heading would only be temporary, again because there would be no way to cover all his tracks, and with amount of people that seemed to be with these raiders it would take little to no time at all to find his tracks out of the area. *Maybe if I head back in the direction that they came, after all, there'd be plenty of tracks from them. That way mine would be no different, just another set of tracks, except mine would be leaving and not arriving. Darn! That won't work either. Guess all I can do is get this stuff moved, put that emergency pack back together and head for the top of these mountains to another of my caches and then head in the direction that they came from. At least that way I might be safe, but what if they backtrack? Now stop that. You remember both mom and dad saying that you can "what if" yourself to death. Just stick to what you've planned and go from there.*

It had taken him over half the night to move what he figured he needed up and out of the area. It was really surprising to him the amount of stuff he had accumulated over the time he'd stayed here. But most of it would have to stay and only the items that would help him survive would be with him. Fortunately one of his greatest finds was a small private weapons cache from those times. So he had a pistol, shotgun, and hunting rifle with plenty of ammo for all three. It was surprising to him that the ammo was so heavy, but it was also very precious as there would be no replacing it once it was lost or used. So these items were the first he had taken up the mountainside. He knew that at the time of the raining of the ancient fires from the skies that many had owned such things, although from what little history he could find in this town there had been a movement to take them away. He wondered why? After all, with all the bad that existed in the world, and especially now that civilization was no more, one needed some type of protection to keep the bad ones away, or at least to make them cautious.

Out of breath he took a break. He knew that he needed to make one more trip and wondered if he would have the time to do it. Dawn wasn't far off, as he reckoned it. And one thing for sure, he didn't want to be anywhere close to that place when dawn arrived. In fact he considered himself much too close now, but once he had all that he needed he would move on to another place he had marked that wasn't close at all and should be far enough away to be safe – at least he hoped so. Because safety was relative, and he knew that he could handle one or two of these baddies, but more than that he'd better be able to run.

* * *

The two scouts looked over the area where the raiders were camping with the one in charge turning to the other saying, "Looks like they may have found what they were looking for. Can't say for sure, but it looks like this is almost as permanent a camp as the other further east. I suspect that they may have found one of the many unknown, hidden destroyed areas from our ancient past. Maybe this is why they've hung around. Well, in the end, it doesn't matter. They were warned and they are still here."

"Yeah, but I find something curious, and it has nothing to do with the ones we're following. I swear that I saw someone leaving that place of interest. But it was almost full on dark so I can't really be sure. But if there is someone down there, they are in very serious trouble. And it could complicate what we are doing. Right now it's easy to watch the raiders and stay out of sight. But, if we have to deal with yet another unknown group, or even one, we might run into each other, and the surprise could reveal us to our enemy."

"I can't be sure that you actually saw anything. You said it yourself, you're not sure. So until we have some proof we'll consider it a possibility, but concentrate on the ones we're here to watch. And on that note our third should be returning any time. We need to watch for him. We're quite a bit west of where we were. I know that we marked our trail so that he'd follow, but he doesn't know where we ended so it would be easy to pass us by and miss us completely."

"So, what do you want to do? I don't think it's smart to drop us down to just one to watch these."

"Neither do I. I guess we'll just have to hope he can figure it out. In the meantime dawn is almost upon us, so we had better be sure we can't be seen, but still can monitor what's happening down in that canyon." Both of the scouts pulled back up the hill and out of the canyon where they had approached in the dark to insure that what they were suspecting was fact. But now to remain so was to be discovered, and they felt confident that the raiders had no idea that they were here. Being careful in the semi-light of the dawn they hid their trail and carefully placed their feet so as not to knock some rock or loose soil free alerting the world to their presence. The direction they were heading had been chosen the night before so that they wouldn't accidently place themselves into a box canyon or a dead end where they would have to retrace and reveal themselves.

Finally back on top where there was a decent, if incomplete, view of the valley floor the leader had to the one that was with him to pull back a little further where they presently had their dry camp and to get some sleep. He'd wake him about midday and do the same. For now they only had two things going on, monitoring the ones below them and to watch for the returning member of their team.

Watching, the leader saw the beginnings of movement in the raider camp and knew that soon that there would be full activity and probably some initial scouting of this area. So it would be critical to stay out of sight and move as little as possible. Since the eye would catch any movement and especially that which would be out of place and it was a lesson that they had learned well.

* * *

Sam was tired and it had taken all night to haul out what he needed and what he wanted to save, but he knew that his tracks and his sign was everywhere. There'd been no time to even start to eliminate proof that he had been living here. This scared him because this was a really large group of raiders. He suspected that once they had found that someone had been here that they would come looking. Just how was he going to be able to hide from that many anyway? As the morning progressed he could see increased movement in the camp and as the breezes changed from down canyon to up canyon, his mouth watered as he smelled the odor of meat cooking over the fires and he had to admit that it smelled delicious and his stomach growled in protest of having missed a couple of meals because of his hasty flight from his home below. One thing for sure, it wouldn't be any more, so it was time, as soon as it was safe, to head out and try to locate something similar somewhere else. But he had accidently discovered this place, and really had no idea what direction to go, or even where to begin a new search.

At least with what he had with him, although how he was to carry everything he now had he didn't know, he probably should last a couple of moon cycles before running into difficulties. Well, that move was for later. Now he would have to wait out the day until the dusk before he could safely move further away from this place. *Darn, double darn, damn! This place has been as close to perfect. Plenty of water, plenty of game so that I have meat when I wanted or needed it, and enough wild grains to at least have a change in food. The isolation is nice also. I haven't seen anybody since I found this place, at least, I don't know, maybe a couple of years ago.* Shaking his head he continued his thoughts. *I guess all good things must end sometime. But this looked like a place that would remain safe. Now all I can hope is that where I am right now will be until I can move again.*

He dug into the pack that he had and pulled out some jerked meat and gnawed on it, thinking that it was a poor substitute to what he smelled. At least he was well hidden, and he knew that soon his guard would be dropping. He had been moving his supplies all night long and he had to admit that he was tired. As the sun arose of the hills that surrounded this valley he felt the morning chill evaporating and a comfortable warmth replacing it. He continued to watch the area below and the camp but found that as the sun warmed him that he was becoming less alert and then without realizing it fell into a deep exhausted sleep.

It was his snoring that awakened him and he jumped knowing that such a sound would carry a very long way. He didn't know how long he'd been out, but it didn't matter, he had failed himself by doing that. He did a quick survey of the area where he was hidden and then slowly searching outward until he finally searched the camp and the place he had been living. It was obvious that he hadn't been sleeping long since the sun hadn't traveled too much further in the sky and the first few in the camp were beginning to reconnoiter the destroyed town below. At least the little sleep he had gotten seemed to have refreshed him somewhat, so maybe he'd stay awake until tonight, make his move to his next safe area, and then get some real sleep. But until then he'd have to be careful, very careful indeed. They might have captured him while he had passed out and it would have been a very easy thing. He shuddered with that thought knowing what his fate probably would have been at that point. He was young, and he definitely wanted to live to be older.

Dan hoped these scouts that were shadowing the raiders that were moving to the west in the lower areas would be concentrating so hard on them that they wouldn't see the clues that existed right here where they were. He could tell that it was close to a lost cause as far as making the area completely clean of any sign that someone's here. They had been here much too long, and even though they had been careful he could see small signs of habitation. Places where the grandchildren had played in the dirt building their imaginary worlds, bits of debris that would only have come from someone living nearby, stuff largely unnoticed until they were in this situation where they could be discovered. He saw that even though they had tried hard to eliminate trails between the buried structures that they lived, he now saw where paths were developing. One thing for sure, if they survived this all of them would have to come outside and figure out how to hide what he was seeing at this very moment, and he suspected it would be the same for Joel. But there was absolutely nothing either of them could do about it now, nothing at all.

He took a careful look over the side and watched the dust rising from the movement of the raiders and once he established their location he pulled back, did a final check, being sure that the ones that were following the raiders hadn't shown yet, headed back to the central unit, arriving just behind Joel who saw him approaching, and together they entered into their sanctuary. Dan looking at Joel said, "They're definitely on the move, although I really have no idea why they're staying around, because there seems to be only wilderness and us. We're not close to anything or anyone and much too far out for a base camp from which they could attack the surrounding areas from. Any ideas at all?"

"No dad, none. We can hope that they're heading out of the area but I suspect that we've not seen the last of them or these others. I don't know what it means, but I think we're very far from the end of the crisis." Shaking his head he shrugged, "I have no proof of anything, just a feeling that we're a long way away from this being over and done, and that it's going to become very dangerous. I'm only surmising here, but why would they camp here? Yes, I know there's water down there, and anywhere you can find water in the desert it's a place to remember. But both of us know with all they had out searching the area there's much more to it than that. And why do we have them being shadowed by these scouts? To me we are probably facing another group, maybe a rival army of raiders. And if this is so, what are their plans? And if I'm right here, then we may have another army in the area shortly making it more likely with all the skirmishes that would be going on, all the scouting between the rival armies that there'd be nowhere to hide.

"We may need to move and move soon. But, again, all of this is just guesswork so it could be just dust in the wind." He tipped his head to the side and shrugged again. "I just don't know, but the feelings I'm getting scares the hell right out of me. The ones that are here are a known only because we know what they are from the way they act. If we have another army arrive we'll know nothing, and worse their movements will so complicate things for the ones outside of this – you know us."

Silent for a moment, Dan replied, "I could deny all of this, but unfortunately I've had the same feelings. I know that I said it earlier but we screwed up, and very badly. Once we found this place and began our lives anew, we forgot about the very thing that we're facing right now. We've dropped our guard, we don't have a secondary cache, we don't have plans in place to leave this place, or have a place to head to if we did.

I'm sort of the unofficial leader of our family being the oldest member, and I dropped the ball, period.

"Now what we do about what we're facing I have no answers, and I guess we're in a waiting game now, and from what your mother passed on to me it's not going to be an easy thing. Too many people in too small an area and with the known threat, tensions are rising, small arguments over nothing are breaking out, tempers are short, and she's worried that soon it would move beyond that into actual violence. That's what we were talking about when you came down there and warned us that the raiders were on the move." Sighing and shaking his head Dan continued, "I guess if we survive this as a family, although I suspect I said that when we survived the destruction of our village . . . Anyway, in many ways this time it's far worse, so if we do survive this as a family we should come out of it so much stronger, or at least I hope so. But at the same time this could tear us apart and scatter us to the four winds. Our strength is family, and at the same time it is our weakness. Okay, let's get down the rest of the way and bring the family up to date. This isn't going to be good news any way we present it, and again since I'm the one whose more or less in charge I'll break the bad news."

Both of them continued down the ladder through the hatch that divided the entrance from the living area and joined the rest of the family. When they entered the tension in the air was so thick that it could almost be felt, tasted, and smelled. It was obvious that all of them knew the seriousness of what they now faced and with expectant eyes they waited for him to bring them up to date as to what was transpiring outside.

* * *

It had been seven days since they had discovered the raiders on the move and everybody was beat. Very few had gotten any decent sleep and when Dan looked at his granddaughters it tore him up inside. Their eyes were wide and sunken and he saw the fear in their faces. They had become lethargic and seemed to jump at any imagined shadow or noise. Yet, the last couple of days had been quiet. Still he didn't let this quiet fool him and he could tell that the others here knew, as he did that their once secure world was beginning to crash around them. So like the prairie dogs that they had heard about they were hunkering down in their burrows to avoid the predators that lay above waiting in ambush. Quietly he turned to Marta, his wife, and said, "Wish, so much that this would end one way or the other so that we can just let the pressure off this boiling kettle. This place has closed in on everybody and all are now walking as if the floors were covered in broken glass. Look, I plan on making a large sweep tonight and will be gone at least a couple of days. Seth has his hands full with his girls so please lean on Joel and the other children. We really need to know what's going on and if we finally can come up for some fresh air.

"One thing for sure, once this is over we are going to have to re-evaluate everything and be a little more proactive plus providing other places to fall back on. We've been very lucky so far that we've not been discovered. And no, before you ask, this is better done by one person, and I've lived a good life with you, while all of our children still have much of their lives ahead of them. So if the worst happens to me I'll know that the rest of you are safe and that our children still have a chance at their own lives. By being alone I'll know that any strange noise or sound will possibly be an enemy and not friendly. It's so much easier to hide as a single individual, and also know that I can only depend on myself and not expect or plan on covering for another. And no I'm not telling any of the others. You can tell them once I'm gone. Oh just one last thing, if I'm late coming back do not under any circumstances come looking for me. First off you'll compromise this place, and truthfully while you'll have a rough idea of where I went you will really only be guessing." He reached out and hugged her knowing that what he had told her really scared her.

She, looked up into his eyes, even though she was almost his height, then looked down shaking her head not saying anything. The forced smile said all that needed to be said. For some reason she felt that once he left, and again she knew that she wouldn't be able to change his mind, and besides she knew that he was right, she wouldn't see him for a very long time. The feeling was so strong that it had taken any words that she may have wanted to say and rob her of them. So she laid her head on his shoulders and hugged him desperately. She really hoped that she was wrong in her premonition, but others that were this strong have proven out in the past. She felt her emotions building and she knew that if she tried to talk at all she'd be crying instead. How long had the two of them been together? It was a very good question to ask, because the years had just flown and here they had grown children that seemed only yesterday that she had held them in her arms for the first time. Yes she saw the silver and gray in his hair and beard and she was sure that it was a surprise to him when his hair had begun its change. Finally she whispered, "Just be careful." And even these words were almost enough to bring on the tears.

Smiling, although he knew that she couldn't see it, since she had her head on his shoulder, he said, "I always am. After all, I've got you to come back to and all that are our family who will be waiting. How could I not want this with all of my being?" He gently pushed her back, kissed her lightly, saying nothing just relishing the moments that the two of them could be holding each other just like this. Eventually they separated reluctantly and headed in different directions to get those chores done that never seemed to end.

* * *

There'd be no moon tonight, so carefully he left the shelter of their hidden home and worked his way north up the mountainside to get away from their shelter and where, even in the darkness, he'd see a greater distance. If he was going to leave any sign of his passing he wanted it to be away from here. He, carefully taking his time, covered and erased any tracks or sign of his passing close by. He had all night so he had to be careful and he could take the time to do this right. As far as he knew, at this moment, they were the only ones in the area, but with all the activity he wasn't sure so from the beginning he moved as if he and the area were under surveillance. After all it just might be.

* * *

Madam paced back and forth in the darkness. She was restless and worried. They had stayed here much too long, and the one she had sent away to make contact with her scouts hadn't returned yet. Not knowing was driving her crazy, and the fact that it was taking longer than she liked for the injured to recover enough to be moved added to her agitation. Anyway she looked at it, tomorrow, or as words and phrases changed over time, she was beginning to hear "on the morrow", as often as tomorrow – anyway they would have to move and get these people into their permanent village so that they would be safe. There was a good chance that they would run into the returning runner since they'd be generally heading into the same direction anyway. So with the decision made she headed outside of her tent and headed through their camp. Giving an encouraging word here, reinforcing an idea there, and just generally being available to her people. She found that it was very important to be available, to listen, to absorb the feelings, and sense the ambiance of all who were surrounding her.

Time is an interesting thing, she thought, *it moves at the same speed always, well that's the idea anyway.* She had read in a book somewhere, and yes she was glad that she could read, more and more were unable as *time*, and here she laughed as that word was there again – anyway somewhere in the past she had read that there had been a scientist or something like that who have proved that time wasn't constant. It was all according to where you were, and how fast you were moving, well she couldn't prove or disprove it, but from her view time flowed in a constant way. *Yet, as I walk this camp time seems to drag – especially since I need us to be out of here, be out of this area. Yet, when we are in battle, or are in a fight or need to get somewhere by a specific time, time does seem to fly.* Yet, as far as she determined, time was indifferent, not caring what was happening because of it. Time was just here, and they moved through it like they did these wild lands. But unlike these wild lands they couldn't leave a mark on time, although time left its mark on them.

Her second approached and interrupted her thoughts asking, "Are the plans to move out in the morning? I know when we separated that you were leaning that way even though some of the ones we rescued are still weak."

Nodding she said, "Yes. I know that we might be putting them in further jeopardy but we just cannot remain here. So yes we will move out and head for our home base where these can get better care. After the morning meal I want a full contingent of scouts out to search the surrounding area to be sure that we are truly alone and the raiders that we defeated don't do the same to us that we did to them – follow. After all, with the recovery of these women and children we are more vulnerable to ambush and attack since we cannot move fast or with the regular stealth that we usually do." Here she smiled, although in the dark she was sure that he couldn't see it. "Besides, they are not the only baddies out here, and we can become overly concerned about them only to miss another band of raiders. So, as we usually do, when we successfully pull off one of these operations, we'll double our forward and rear scouting and increase our outriders, assign two or three to remain with the ones we rescued and add a couple of days to our return."

"Yes ma'am, standard practice. I'll get everything heading in that direction. And, ma'am, I suspect you want us on the trail just before midmorning."

"Yes, exactly, and even though I don't need to remind you or any of the others that is with us, be aware of attack while we are distracted just before we hit the trail."

In a quiet voice the second said, "No ma'am you don't. It's a tactic we've used successfully ourselves, and it would be embarrassing to have the same done successfully to us." At that he took his leave and passed the word to the rest of the camp.

"Okay, where was I?" She asked herself quietly. She headed to just outside of the camp found a large rock and sat down breathing in the cool night air listening to the sounds of the night. *Such a peaceful place* . . . She laughed at that idle thought. After all, the night in the natural world is anything but. Prey and predator were fighting for their very lives – the prey, to not be eaten by the predator, and the predator needing the protein that the prey would provide. Thusly the world has been this way from the beginnings of *time* – ah there's that word again – to what unknown future still lay before them.

With this world in the chaos that it presently seemed to be in, what did one do to guarantee their survival? She had no answers as there were more ways to die than there was to remain living. Heck, if she wanted to truly admit it, there were enough predators in the natural world that would look upon any of them as food, and then there were those accidents, unexpected changes in the weather, so many ways to die that nature would provide on her own. Then one looked at the race she was part of. They appeared to be worse than anything that nature could throw their way, and while there was no revenge, hate, or malice, when the natural world took your life, there surely was when the species of man did. And sometimes when dealing with her species death probably was preferable to what they could do to one physically and mentally. *Are we really worth saving? Or should we just die out and allow some other species to become the top dog?* One thing for sure, she wasn't going to help it come about. There were too many good people out in this wounded world that deserved to live, to have their families carry on into the unknown future.

With those thoughts she took a deep breath and let it out slowly, stood up, and did a final inspection of the perimeter of the camp. There was only one last thing she wanted to do before she retired and face the coming day and that was to head outside of camp, and see how visible it was. It was a habit she had developed years in the past, and it had saved them a number of times since then. But on the way out she would give the refugees one more visit, both to encourage them and to let them know from her personally that on the morrow they'd be moving out, which brought her back full circle wondering if this rescue would be permanent or temporary, leaving these to become slaves to that scum in the end.

When she left the tent the next morning with dawn's gray just coloring the full black of night she found one of the guards waiting for her. Smiling she asked, "You have something for me?"

Remaining quiet, the guard just nodded his head and waited which is what he considered proper when addressing the leader.

Exasperated because as far as she was concerned in the day-to-day stuff everybody had their things that they had to do and all were equal, and it was difficult for her to have to accept this "respect" for her position. She understood it, but to keep what they did moving well she needed an easy flow of communications to go through all, not any pomp and circumstance. She knew that all of them had been slaves – that all of them had been subservient, that all of them had been abused, and for all of them it had been something they faced most of their lives. So to make such a change in a short period of time was almost too much to expect, but expect it she did. After all, if they were to survive, to continue their vendetta against the slavers, the slave markets, and the owners that would have to change. With some frustration showing in her voice she said, "Out with it man."

"Ah, sorry ma'am. The ah scout returned very late last night and has just now been awakened now that we know you're out. He'll report to you immediately. The rest of the camp is in the process of breakdown, and after all is packed our meals will be eaten and we should be heading out on time."

"Thank you. I assume that the scout reported what he found out to the one in charge last night, am I right?"

"It wasn't on my shift ma'am, so I truly don't know, but suspect it is so."

Nodding she said again, "Thank you, you can return to your duties as we all have much to accomplish in a very short time." The guard bowed showing respect and withdrew. She knew that whatever hadn't been needed for overnight had already been packed and they were down to what was necessary. She hoped that the information that the scout had for her was good news and those raiders had completely left the area as she demanded. It would be a little while before he arrived and she needed to make that morning nature call before it demanded more of her attention.

When she returned to the camp she saw that the tents were coming down and the camp breakdown was in full swing. Other than the pots and pans necessary for making the morning meal all was being placed in the packs, and the pack animals were being loaded. There was a chill in the morning air that made one look for the heat from one of the cooking fires and she headed to the closest one putting her hands towards the flames feeling the warmth as it penetrated her cold flesh. While she was doing this the scout approached just as one of the people making the meal handed her some coffee. She knew that this stuff would continue to get harder to find as the finite supplies ran out over time. Eventually they'd have to find something to replace it, but she really had no idea what could do that. Turning to the scout with her cold hands around the warm mug she asked, "So do you have good news, or something else?" Both of them heard the crackling of the fires which was a comforting sound.

"Wish it was good news ma'am, but it appears that they haven't completely vacated the area." He then went into the full explanation, and what the others who were following the raiders thought might be transpiring. The total information took about ten minutes to relay, and after that the scout left heading back to what he needed to do.

She stood there in silence staring into the fire not seeing it at all, unconsciously sipping her coffee. *Damn, why can't things be simple? Those raiders, and specifically the leaders were told flat out that they were to continue all the way out and not hang around or there'd be hell to pay, and yet . . . No time for that now. We've got to get these refugees to a place of safety. And once that's accomplished we'll deal with them.* Looking up from the fire she realized that one of her group was attempting to get her attention. "Sorry, I know that you heard what the scout relayed, and it means we'll have to face them again, maybe this time we'll just wipe them out or at least break up this army and scatter them." She saw that the woman was trying to hand her a plate of food which she took and thanked her. *Why does it seem to always go this way?* She had no answers and no time to dwell on the questions anyway. It was a few days travel to get these to safety and that took precedence over everything else at this moment.

In her mind she drifted back to that time when she had been a slave. There had been times when she was alone and didn't have to spread her legs for some male at the request of her master, or do some other horrible act to entertain them. She had learned to read during this time and had discovered Westerns and loved to read about their fictional escapades throughout a time in their history that really wasn't much different than the time she was living in. Along the way she discovered a writer whose locations were real, and she found that in the beginnings of many of his books were maps of the areas that he had written about. Slowly she learned how to read these maps, small though they were, and found to her surprise that she was just east and south of many of the stories. It was at this time that she began to plan her escape.

Through the underground that existed between the many slaves there were slight hints that many had escaped their masters. Although the punishment if one was captured and returned was too gruesome to discuss. The masters and owners swore that none escaped, but if that had been the truth, then there would be no need of the type of punishment that they were warned about by their owners. She began to hear stories, over the years, of many that had been successful in their escape and that they were still free and out in the desolations where they were safe from retribution. And because of this she began to hope that she would become one of them. Life as a slave sucked, and it was worse for a female who had to submit anytime for anyone at the whim of one's owner. She also knew that as she aged, since she had seen it happen too many times to keep count, that she would be passed on to the houses where her services would be sold and she would be earning money as a prostitute for her owner.

While she and any other woman's lives were hell within the households of their masters, it was far worse when they were moved into the houses where sex was rented. In those places one received all kinds and all sorts of wants and desires. From the simple need, to being tied up and tortured for the pleasure of the one who had rented the time. She had known a few of the women placed in these houses who had not survived these encounters and she swore she would not be one of them. And she had a slight taste of how this could play out when she had been passed out to the guards to use as they pleased. They were rough, and couldn't care less for her feelings or the pain they placed upon her body. She had to endure, hope that the time was quick, and that they would tire of her, and eventually send her back. And once back it would take weeks for the marks, bruises, and the soreness of her female parts to heal and she'd almost feel normal once again, if such was possible.

It was after one such session that she had discovered, in one of those books, a place in the Wyoming territory that might be a great place to escape. So secretly she began to gather what little information and maps existed of the area. She had found that in a couple of his Western books that he had mentioned an area that had been used by the outlaws of those days. Not fictional ones, but real ones. And it was because of its remoteness, narrow passes, and the many ways in which one could escape if discovered that it became a favorite hideout for a number of years. She began to listen to the traders as they came into the area specifically their discussions about where they had been and what others had passed on and found no mention at any time of this area. So she began to hoard small items, hiding them wherever she felt they might remain hidden. The day might come where she'd have her chance and she'd have to be ready.

* * *

Hearing the clinking of the plates she returned to the present and realized that she had eaten her food without even realizing it. She stood up headed over to the bucket that was there for rinsing the plates, rinsed the plate and handed it to the woman who was responsible for packing the final items up. She headed back to the fire briefly, feeling the warmth from this particular fire for the last time, before they were back on the trail, took a deep breath and looked around. She saw that the site was completely broken down and packed, with the ones responsible for extinguishing the fires now going around doing just that. She headed over to where the refugees were and gave them an encouraging smile. She had to admit that even with all the encouragement and such that they still looked to be fearful. Well, there was nothing she could do about that.

She turned around and signaled to her second to move. Finding a rock that was easy to climb, he got on top, pulled out a small horn, and gave the signal to head out. While the main group remained for a few moments the forward scouts headed out, with the trailers dropping back and then the flankers headed out and once all of these were out of sight the rest began their movement. They had quite a distance to travel and the sooner it was over, the sooner they'd return to eliminate this other problem. Of course, the raiders may have already left the area by then, and if so, then there would be no problem.

The weather seemed to be cooperating and this would be helpful. Once winter arrived, in its full fury, the hidden village would be buried under feet of snow. Still it was home, and it was safe, well, as safe as any place could be in these times. She longed for a better situation for all of what she considered the good people. The ones attempting to eke out a living from the lands, raise their families, and want for no more than that. In her mind instead it was a time of vermin the ones who preyed on others not caring at all to the pain, death, and suffering they caused. Only caring for that moment's pleasure, or entertainment, or to figure out what they could steal. *If only there'd be a way to bring this scum under control, or to completely eliminate them.*

Of course, from her personal experience, the slavers, the slave markets, and the ones who purchased, sold, and owned slaves were the worst. The slave markets supported the continued deprivations on the ones who were trying to keep their families safe. She felt that if they were eliminated, then much of what supported this bad element would disappear, and thusly the raiders would become less organized, and easier to destroy. In her mind it would be the beginnings of a new direction.

She knew very little of what the world was like before the ancient fires fell from the skies. Only that it was the combination of this rock striking their moon breaking up and then showering the earth in fire, death, and destruction. Then, and she didn't understand how, the moon would continue to kick the fire to the earth continuing the destruction. Whatever was before was gone and this is what had replaced it, and she hated it. And presently it was one of the reasons that she personally carried thoughts that said she did not want to bring a child into this. So with the establishment of her hidden village, and the slow growth over the years, to where the population probably numbered close to a thousand, and with the fertile land, although the growing season was short, it was a success she could feel proud of. It was the beginning of what she hoped was true change to the existing status quo.

They had to cover the distances crossing the Idaho territory, Montana territory, and eventually into the Wyoming territory. Until they reached Wyoming where there were many rolling hills and grasslands and as they traveled they'd be working in and out of heavily forested areas. Many places ripe for ambush like the one she had pulled on those raiders, so they would travel with care. She really wished, at this moment that she had the full army with her instead of this patrol as they swept the areas. If she had, then she would have wiped out the raiders. But she wasn't sure with what she had that she would have been successful. Yet, the outcome had been positive. Now once back and all had a chance to recover, and the new ones had been placed, at least initially in the large houses where everybody shared space, she could plan for the return and subsequent destruction of the raiders. She really looked forward to that and to look into the dead eyes of leader and his second, knowing that they had removed another blight, and in the end, the world would be better for it.

* * *

With the dawn Dan was far away from their present hidden home and heading west staying on the high points and trying to remain hidden as well as he could. He needed to find somewhere where he'd be able to catch a few hours' sleep – a hole or something. He didn't need someone finding him while he was most vulnerable. Looking around with his eyes burning and feeling heavy he found a place where the cedars had died, with a few new one replacing the old, leaving the dead trees and their many fallen branches. Finding a hole he crawled into the center and was completely hidden to even a close inspection, if someone happened to pass by, and was almost instantly asleep. His plan was simple – travel at dusk to dawn and try to stay out of sight during the daylight hours. Before finding his hole he had figured that most likely he had covered about four miles in the darkness. He had no plans on moving fast or be careless. There was too much at stake.

He wished that they were living in a different time and place and not have to face these dangers, the death and destruction that were constant companions. But he knew that every period of time had its own problems to face. He thought the place they were presently living was proof of that. If the time when this place had been constructed was peaceful and there was no sign of trouble on the horizon, then this place wouldn't have been built, wouldn't exist. Yet, exist it did, and while he had no way of knowing why or what was happening that had caused the original owner to have it constructed, it had to have been something major. Bartering was the way of things now, but they still found coins and such from where currency was used instead. And by guessing he figured that it had been very expensive to build.

He didn't know what wakened him but he was wide awake and laid still for a few moments as he gathered his wits about him. He found that he had been very deep down and whatever it was that had awakened him had reached down to his subconscious telling him something wasn't right. Taking a deep slow breath he let it out blinking his eyes looking up at the dead juniper branches that were above him. Right now remaining still was the key. To leave this hiding place would require moving through some of that dead material giving himself away with the noise it would create. He strained to hear anything and then slowly since it had to be in the distance somewhat he heard voices. Voices so faint that he couldn't make out the words being spoken, or even the gender of the speakers. Whatever they were speaking about was beyond him and the winds kept sweeping the sounds away. Slowly the voices drifted off and seemed to be moving in the same direction that he was heading. *So things are getting crowded and more complicated. Who'd have thought that in a place like this that is so isolated that it would become this way?*

He continued to listen but whoever it had been either had quit speaking or were now away from the area. From the shadows he could tell that he'd only been asleep for a few hours and needed more if he was to be alert and fresh. So carefully he found a semi comfortable position and drifted back to sleep. Dusk would be here soon enough.

* * *

The scouts met on top of one of the many foothills that were in the area. This had been the point where they had marked the trail for the one returning from Madam and their patrol. One would return here periodically to wait until he showed up. Now united once again the three of them discussed plans on how they would watch the raiders, or slavers if one wanted to be more accurate. The leader spoke saying, "We've got to be even more careful than we've been. I'm sure that we've not been seen by any, but from what I can judge they suspect that they've been followed. That leader, what's his name, right Skar, isn't stupid. And I guess that makes sense. One doesn't stay in that position if one is stupid.

"And I thought that I saw someone leaving that destroyed town. Can't be sure because whoever it is, is very good at concealing him or herself. For obvious reasons, whoever it is, is watching that army, and not for anybody else that might be around. From the ease of his movements I'd say he has a good grasp of the lands around here. Although again, this all could be my imagination as I never really saw anybody – just a shadow now and then and something out of place. But I think it's better that we consider it as such so that we can be a little more aware. And if there is someone who has been living down there, we just might have to consider that there are others." He saw the doubt in their eyes with that last statement, he smiled and shrugged. "Look I just said it's a possibility. Think about it really. If you were one wanting to stay away from ones like we are scouting what better place than this? Who'd think to search for someone here in this desolation? It surprised me the first time through this area to find that river. Come on, a river here in this dry land?

"Enough on this, we need to get back to where we can watch those raiders. Who knows what they are up to anyway? And we really need to watch for others more diligently. We haven't been doing that and it would be easy for another group or army to have snuck up on us with us none the wiser until it's too late. We've been concentrating so hard on them that it would have been easy to do. In fact, and I hate to admit it because it's true, I think an untrained child could have done it, and embarrassed the heck out of us." The three of them got up from behind the boulders where they had met and headed out to the west not knowing that they were within a few hundred feet of one of those unknown people who had claimed this area as their home.

* * *

When he awakened the second time it was dusk and time to be moving. He crawled out of his hole, emptied his bladder, grabbed his pack and headed out to the west behind the three scouts neither aware of the others. It was shortly after he began his trek in that direction that he came upon the tracks of the three and that brought back the memories of being awakened earlier to the sound of voices somewhere in the distance. At least this confirmed that it wasn't his imagination and that there had been someone out there. Now the question became; is it the raiders, or is it the ones that appeared to be watching them? *Now what? Do I change my direction and avoid the ones who've made these tracks? Or do I chance it and follow behind them. It's been at least half a day since I think I heard them talking so they have a decent lead on me.* It was another one of those dilemmas that one faces too many times in one's lifetime. Decisions from these situations could literally change one's direction in life.

Staring out in the direction that he needed to go he knew that there'd be a little of the moon tonight – first quarter, he thought. So while it wouldn't be as bright as a full moon at least it wouldn't be so dark that it would be dangerous to travel. In the end he decided that he would stay with his original plan and add additional caution for this other unknown group. He started out making good time as the dusk deepened. Then as full darkness fell, he slowed his progress way down, and carefully advanced to the west. While the moon would be rising it wouldn't be until later. So the first part of the night would be quite dark, and with the lay of the land it would be easy to make a misstep and fall. And some of the places where he had to travel there were cliffs a plenty, and if he fell into one of these he would only see death. If not instant, a possible slow one because of the injuries he would sustain, and with no one knowing his location, there'd be no rescue.

The moon was well into the night sky when he caught the slight glow of a campfire hidden far back from the overlook where one could watch the canyons below. Curious, he knew that it was important to find out who was at that fire so he headed further up and above the location of where he thought the campfire might be. But as he pulled out from his location it disappeared from sight. Before approaching the area he hiked up and down the mountain for a small distance and it was only in that one place that the fire was visible. Wherever this was it had been chosen for just that reason – invisibility. Taking a deep quiet breath he slowly approached from the only direction where the fire was visible. He figured that once he truly had it located that he would change his direction, try to get above the camp and see who might be there. Plus he hoped that he could overhear anything that might be spoken around the fire so that he might be able to know who he was dealing with. After all, they might be part of that large army of raiders that kept them on the edge for much too long. He didn't want to reveal to them that there were others here and increase the intensity of their search.

Eventually he got as close as he dared, and moved as quietly as he could to a higher point that was a distance away, then slowly worked his way back down to what he hoped would be the camp location only to find that he had gone too far to the west. So he backtracked and worked his way back east. What he worried more about was the fact that most likely there would be someone on watch and he hadn't been able to locate that individual or individuals who would be doing that. He still had no idea how many was by that fire. Eventually he heard the crackling and popping of the fire and knew that he was close – now what? He could hear it but couldn't see it, nor could he determine how many.

CHAPTER SIX

Skar stood by the lake staring out at nothing. The first day here hadn't produced much. But it was obvious to him and to any of the others that someone was living here. From what evidence that they had gathered it appeared to have been only one individual. But whoever this person they had been here quite a while. Add to it that this occupation was recent and it left him in a quandary as to just strip this old site of anything of value, or try and find this individual and see if he or she, they hadn't determined that, had been stockpiling finds somewhere else. Darkness had fallen and on the morrow they'd begin the real deep search looking for tech stuff that would do well in the eastern markets. It still galled him that they had lost their prizes which would have brought much wealth into their hands once they had reached the slave markets. Shaking his head he thought, *Got to get that out of my mind. There's nothing I can do to change what happened. We've done the same to others, so why shouldn't it happen to us?* His self-loathing for that one failure was broken when Bear came up and joined him.

"Okay Skar, we've come to the conclusion that the individual who's living here is male. In the small caches that we've found there are not the types of things that a female would collect, at least none that we know. My feeling is that we should forget about him, because I guarantee this, he knows this area better than we do, and would probably be able to avoid us no matter how we try to catch him. Besides I suspect it will only be a matter of time, if we do not move on, *as we were so ordered*, that we might face that escaped slave army again."

"Yeah, you're probably right . . . hmmm, a thought just entered into my mind, but I'll need to think about it for a while, and probably will disregard it anyway."

With a questioning look Bear asked, "What's going through your mind now boss?"

Smiling a wicked smile he said, "Now what do you think the owners would pay if we brought in all those escaped slaves? Plenty, I'm thinking, and if that's so then we could probably just quit doing this and go find our own hole and disappear."

Shaking his head Bear replied, "Don't think that's the best idea you've ever come up with. They beat us soundly and could have wiped us out if the whim had crossed their minds."

"True, but we didn't know that they were around or that they had that kind of fire power. Oh well, it's just a thought anyway. Probably nothing will come of it, and you're right, we were outclassed in every way possible. And who'd have thought that a female would be leading them? Not me, I only see one use for them – well two if I want to be honest, and that's for a man's pleasure, and producing babies. Other than that they are worthless and cause nothing but problems and dissention among the males, when others won't share.

"But, I have to admit that she's a force in herself." Shaking his head and smiling, he continued, "And huge. She's probably the largest female I've ever seen and from what little I saw she wasn't fat. She towered over her second and the others that were there. I'd say it's easy to figure out how she escaped."

Intrigued by Skar's line of reasoning Bear asked, "Really? How so?"

"Oh I can't prove it, but I suspect that until she grew into what she is now that she probably was no different from the other female slaves. You know, docile, obeying, giving her master pleasure, and the others she would be required to service. But at some point she became who she is, and because of her size I suspect her master, whoever he was, decided that she needed to be moved to one of the houses. Now both you and I know what happens in those houses, and no female ever comes out of them alive. Somehow she probably got word of that future and decided that there's no way that's going to happen to her. So once the opportunity presented itself she escaped. I suspect that she probably overpowered any of the guards, even if there were more than one.

"There are still two measuring systems being used from the ancient times. I know this because at the time I was a slave I was required to learn history. I don't know why, it meant nothing to me, but here I learned the old weights and tables as they were called. In one she would be well over six feet tall, and the other around two meters. You Bear range in the six foot range and under two meters, so she is even taller than you, but not by much. And no, don't you think about it, about taking her on. Even with your strength, in the end, I don't think you'd win."

Here Bear laughed. "Don't worry about it boss. I have no aspirations towards that one. I don't know why, but I'm drawn towards those small females, and the ones her size have no draw at all. Although I have to admit that it would be fun to try and tame her." He shrugged, "But you're probably right. Wonder if she killed her master when she escaped? After all it is a possibility."

"Hmmm, something I didn't think about, but there is a great possibility that is the way of it. Maybe when we get back to those eastern markets we'll ask around, find out if there's anything known." He shrugged once again, "Or maybe not. Hmm, might not be worth the time or trouble to be truthful. I suspect that if it is the way it happened that it has been kept a secret. After all, the slave owners don't want it known that one of their own was killed by their own slaves – might give others ideas."

"True, and like I said boss, we should just leave it alone. Even if they weren't competent with their tactics, the firepower that they possess would be enough to overcome any shortcomings that they might have. But I have to admit that operation was precise and efficient. Together they make an unstoppable force. Again like I said when we first started talking on this – leave her and her army alone unless you want to die young. And because of who they were, there will be no mercy. The other facts in all of this lies with the fact she doesn't need to recruit to fill her losses. With all the escaped slaves out there, for them to have a chance to strike back would be first on their minds. And you have to admit that is exactly what they are doing."

Smiling once again Skar replied, "I told you it was just a thought. But who knows, there just might be some opportunity in the future that will present itself to us. Still what you've said is accurate and as such, it is something that should be left alone." He shrugged one last time, "Okay, back to what you originally said, you're probably right. If it is only a single male then it's not worth the effort to find him. Had it been a female then we probably could have improved morale around here by using her up. One wouldn't be worth saving for the markets." Taking a deep breath he said, Okay then, on the morrow let's strip whatever we can find and get out of here before she and her army shows up to finish what they started. And I really do wonder why."

"Why boss? Why what?"

"Simple really. They knew what we are, and yet they let us live."

"True, but we still had our captives, and they might have injured or killed them in the fight."

"True, but once they had them they still could have done it."

"Yes, but they gave their word that they wouldn't"

Nodding Skar said, "True, and that my friend may be their weakness, they actually keep their word. After all, when one is working from the point of strength, the ones who have lost have nothing to negotiate with, and you know that if it had been us in the position of power we would have promised anything, but in the end our promises would have meant nothing."

Bear had to admit that what Skar had just stated was quite true. After all if you won there was no reason to bargain. Make the losers believe that they would get something and then show them the reality of the world. "I'll let the rest know and we'll see how fast we can do this. I wonder if there might be other such places as this. I know we have been pressured to leave for the coast, but if there is one like this out in the middle of this semi-desert, there has to be more. And, most likely, like this one they would be close to this small river."

"Hmmm – didn't think about that. And it appears that this sort of runs westerly, maybe that's exactly what we'll do." Turning away from Bear now in deep thought he walked off towards the edge of that small lake leaving Bear standing there. Bear shrugged, turned around and headed back to camp.

* * *

In a way Madam pushed all of them, even the ones they had rescued. She had a feeling that the raiders that they had taken these few from would need another lesson, and she felt that her army was the ones who would be the givers of that lesson. So each day they rose early and pushed on until dark. Her heart went out to those they had rescued because it was obvious that the abuse that they had received made it difficult for them to keep up this punishing pace. She and the rest continued to encourage them and support them wherever it was necessary, and soon they were in familiar lands which brought a smile to her face.

The last contact with the scouts had put the raiders in the desert by that small river. It was obvious they were looking for something, so maybe they'd be around long enough for her full force to return. *One can only hope. No time to think about that now, must keep my mind on the present – still a chance to be ambushed, even though we know these lands like our own bodies.* She signaled the alert and with hand signals had more scouts and runners out, and with a second set of signals had their main force spread out so that they wouldn't be easy targets. After all, if they had been able to keep the raiders in the dark there would be others that would do the same to them.

Soon the pass they were looking for came into view and she knew that by night they would be inside their hidden village completely unknown to the world outside, and as far as she was concerned, it would remain that way. Turning around she signaled break and assemble. This would be the final meal, a cold trail affair, before eating their first meal back at their personal homes. She wished that they could just remain there and forget the violence of the outside world, but knew that if it was left to its own devices that eventually it would spill over into their world, and there was no way to her dying breath that she'd allow that to happen.

* * *

They'd come through the pass with the final dying rays of the setting sun, changing the full lingering clouds to brilliant oranges and reds before turning gray and fading slowly from sight. They saw the village in the distance with many of the residents out and watching their approach. Yes tonight there'd be a celebration for their safe return, and for the rescue of the ones that had been bound for the slave markets. And to sleep in one's own bed, even if it was only to be a day or two, would be a nice change. Every once in a while she'd take a lover, and she had one waiting for her. With her past it wasn't something that was easy to do, but found that the companionship was something that she looked forward to. But enough of these personal thoughts it was time to get them organized and the ones rescued into their temporary shelters, then on to the celebration, followed by the speeches and then the cleanup and everybody retiring, feeling good that others had been rescued and then added to their growing village. On the morrow would come the logistics of integrating these that they had rescued into the village and for them to begin their new lives.

Right now a smile came to her face as they entered the village. A bon fire had been built in the center of the village and most had turned out to see theirs return. After all many that went with her had families, and always when they headed out beyond this hole-in-the-wall there was a chance that one wouldn't return. So it was always uplifting to see the joy that these reunions brought. She saw the tears of joy from the women who had mates that were a part of her army as they flew into each other's arms. This part was always fulfilling to her. Yet, she did not have a mate, and felt because of her position that she would not take one. A lover now and then would have to suffice. With those memories always with her, from things that happened twenty one years ago, she just couldn't do it. She still would awaken from the nightmare of that time. But now wasn't the time to think of this, but to enjoy the moment, get the new settled, get a good night's sleep, and prepare the army for a force march to see if indeed those raiders had done as they had been ordered. If not, with the firepower available to her and her army, the raiders, all of them, would cease to exist.

And she had to admit that a bath, a hot bath would be something to look forward to, but for now she smelled the spitted cooking meat and it made her mouth water in anticipation. Yes this celebration would go deep into the night with all sharing in their freedom, and the bounties that the fields, and animals provided. Before she could find a place to sit and relax one of the servers pushed a plate of food in her hands and guided her to the head of the tables that had been placed in the square for this occasion. Smiling and protesting did nothing and she found herself pushed gently down into the chair. She looked at the plate of food and it was piled high with the best cuts of the roasted meat, and plenty of the grains and vegetables that she loved. And there in a large mug was some of the local wine that they made right here. Giving in, she thanked the one and raised her mug in celebration of their safe return, which was answered with a cheer from the rest of the village and patrol.

* * *

The three scouts that were shadowing the raiders stood around their own fire that was small and hidden so as to not give them away to the ones that they trailed. Looking at the meager trail rations that they had been living on for what seemed too long the leader said, "I don't know about this, I suspect that our patrol is probably back and enjoying a homecoming with lots of freshly cooked foods with their friends and families. Here we stand with nothing around us enjoying the great cuisine that has to rival what they are now enjoying." This brought a chuckle out of the other two. All of them missed their friends and families, and yes the celebrations when they returned from their patrols – especially if one of the patrols had been successful in rescuing others on the way to the slave markets, or saving someone's life because of the too numerous bad ones out in the world right now. When the odds were such that one wouldn't be caught or punished for what one did, then why not do your worst?

The one that had the night duty sighed saying, "Guess I'd better head out and watch", he paused and smiled, "and oh mighty cook, it was a great meal." This brought laugher from all of them. He backed from the light of the fire and disappeared into the darkness and was gone as if he had never been. He, once away from the fire, moved with stealth and in a roundabout way worked away from their camp before circling back to the point where they would watch everything that was happening with the raiders. The locations allowed clear views of the valley where the raiders were camping, and the ruins that they were stripping. The ones guarding on the outskirts of the camp were visible and with care he made a rough headcount and determined how many guards they had out. Even though this bunch had remained in the area of these ruins it would not surprise him if they put out small patrols to be sure that they were alone, and that there wouldn't be a repeat of what had happened to them on their way east.

He suspected that their own army would be heading back soon and would push through and be here in a few days. He knew from what they had observed that there had been no serious stripping of the ruins as of yet. They appeared to have been checking the area out as if there had been someone living here. He remembered that one of the other two had mentioned that they had thought they had seen someone leaving, but wasn't sure. In a sense what they saw from the raiders confirmed that there must have been. He hoped that whoever it was, that this one wasn't female. Seeing what these did to the ones they rescued he wished no such fate on his worst enemy. And if the one was female then he was sure that there would be patrols out to find her so that they'd have their "entertainment" to help pass the time.

Of course, there was a second reason that he hoped that the one was male, and it was this; by being male they wouldn't bother, and any patrol that they would have out would only be for their own protection. If they were looking for someone then it would become so much more difficult to remain hidden themselves, and so much easier to accidently run into each other, and this was the last thing he or the others wanted. So far they had been successful in remaining hidden, but knew by the observations of the leader that the leader suspected that they were being shadowed by someone. So far, as he knew, their scouting team had left nothing to confirm his suspicions, and he wanted it to remain that way. *Come on Madam and the rest of you. I'd like to see this end soon. There's no way that we can continue to remain hidden. Eventually one of us will reveal ourselves and then it will be over. And who is and where is the one or ones who were living in those ruins?*

Whoever it was seemed to be very good at remaining out of sight, but how long can this one continue to do it? Of course, he realized, that this individual or group, or however many there were, would know the area intimately, and thusly know the best places to hide, the way to move from one place to another and remain out of sight. And so far they had done just that. From the short time that he'd been in the area he knew that as convoluted as the land seemed to be, there had to be hundreds, if not thousands of places to hide. Although, he had to admit, it always came back to water. No one can live very long without it. And yes they had ways of transporting the precious fluid, but it was always finite. So this probably eliminated many of the hiding places that would only be used temporarily. So when one began to think along those lines it made it a little easier and narrowed the areas where one could disappear.

This was the desert for heaven sake so the sources were few. Although not like any desert he'd ever seen. The soil was rocky and hard, and there were trees – trees, man – who'd have thought? It gave the illusion that there was much water, and such here, but that was all it was – an illusion. In the deserts that he'd been in there were areas of sand dunes, there the particles were fine and the winds continued to pick them up and piling them in those hills with each morning all tracks from the previous day being wiped out. The dunes were traps in themselves. No water, and with the shifting sands no landmarks, and ones' tracks disappeared almost as quickly as they were made. Yes much of the desert was rocky and vegetation seemed to grow far apart and every one of those plants had thorns, needles and such, all wicked defenses against any who might think that the plant could be of some benefit. But even in these rocky areas there was sand, course yes, but it still was sand.

Here none of the familiar existed, yet it was a desert. It didn't make sense to him. So like the rest they called the trees "desert trees". They looked so much like the ones in the alpine forests and he knew that those required lots of water. So relying on past experience would do one no good here because experience said that these trees should only grow where there was water, but it was a lie. Still, down by that small river one would find the normal stuff. Trees that required lots of water, grasses, and plenty of wild beasts that needed that forage and water to survive. Once away, and only a short distance it returned to this unforgiving land. Why would anyone want to live here? Yet those ruins below said that people at one time did.

One thing for sure, since joining madam's army of escaped slaves, he and the rest had seen a lot of territory, and had viewed sights that if someone had described it to any of them they wouldn't have believed it. Those stone arches, and red stone spires that seemed to be on the verge of collapse, areas where boiling water spewed forth high in the sky in columns with a sound of roaring waterfalls, desert that was perfectly flat as far as they could see, and here a desert of hard soils and trees. Of course everybody knew about the volcanos, and those ancient fires from the skies, but to hike an area where the molten rock had flowed or to see the crater that had formed when one of those ancient fires actually hit made one feel very vulnerable and very small. Who could fight or overcome any such as that?

He did another quick survey of the camp and everything appeared to be normal, not much happening, which was just as he, and the others who were with him, liked it. With the time that they had been following the raiders there had been a number of close calls where they were almost discovered, but so far their luck had held. Yet, how long could it continue this way? Sure they were only three and it was easy for so few to remain hidden, out of sight, but when they were running those search teams out it had become a dance with death trying to move from one point to another trying avoid detection and at the same time trying to figure out what they were doing. There'd been no time to cover their tracks and fortunately it became unnecessary because of the number of teams the raiders had sent out. Eventually things settled down, the teams were pulled back in and the raiders had moved to where they were presently. Looking over the camp once again it still appeared to be quiet – *may it stay that way.*

* * *

Bear decided that once it became full dark that he would go out and search the hillsides above them. While he knew that the squatter that had been living in these ruins was male, there could easily have been another. And Skar still believed that they were being shadowed. So by taking this personal recon he figured that he would, if nothing else look back on their camp and see if he could find any weaknesses in their setup. Important stuff, after all, like the boss, he felt that they were pushing their luck by remaining in the area and that eventually they'd face that army that defeated them. In his mind, even though he didn't expect to find the one who had left, he would have a great opportunity to critically view their camp. *No moon tonight, not good . . . Makes it even easier for someone to remain out of sight, and it makes moving around that more difficult.* How did one remain quiet when you couldn't see where to place your feet? Well, he'd just have to move a bit more careful, and take his time. After all, he had all night if he wanted it that way.

Eventually he made the ridgeline that was behind that lake. Unknown to him he was now on the opposite side to the scouts that were trailing them. He found that once he reached the ridgeline that it was somewhat brighter and easier to see and maneuver around. Looking across to the other side he thought he saw what might be the glow to a campfire, but it was so faint that it might simply be a star in the sky touching the rim. Shaking his head, there seemed to be no life here at all. He wondered why the ones who had lived here in the past had. It made no sense to him. Yes the river flowed by this location, but there was nothing else. No reason at all to live here. Well, it was unimportant, and this was where his curiosity ended. After all, it's all in the past, and much of that past is very dead as is this town, so it was nothing to concern himself with. Now the only value lie in what they could salvage from what remained here, move on, and hope that what they found would at least allow them some time to relax, visit the houses where one could have a female or two, eat good food, and drink much alcohol. It had been that anticipation with the captives that they had that all of them were looking forward to, but now they were scavenging with little hope of coming up with enough to cover their loss of the ones they were planning to sell in the slave markets to the east.

He cursed their luck, but then just shrugged. After all, it could have as easily been them doing the attacking and taking the captives instead of the way it happened. He hiked the ridge looking down on their many fires, and truthfully wasn't able see where their guards were posted which meant that they were doing their job. He knew where each one was approximately, but even with this knowledge he couldn't mark their location. With the silence that surrounded him up here, he found nothing to indicate that anybody had ever been up here, and with no proof that what he had seen across the canyon and up on the opposite ridge was anything, he headed back down, hiked around the other side of the lake, located the guard that was on this side of the camp, made himself known, and headed for his own portable shelter, as they were becoming known, there was much to do on the morrow.

For the ones that were on the other side of the canyon it was a good thing. Two of the three groups had small fires burning, but they had thought out their locations to hide them as much as possible and unknown to them they had been successful. After all, light is easily seen at night. Bear didn't have the sixth sense that Skar seemed to have, and he, after his trip to the top felt that it had to be Skar's imagination. With all the movement that they'd been doing in the last cycle, with the patrols, and search teams that they had out, they had found no sign of anybody – living or dead. It was a hot silent unforgiving world that they were presently traveling through. And to why there had been a town here was beyond him. Especially since the area to the west was much more inviting than this desolation. Yes there was the river, but it was only a small oasis in a dead world as far as he was concerned. Still he felt the tension in the air, one that spoke of something coming, something unknown. It had been the reason for leaving camp and climbing that hill to see what might be found, but all had been quiet, all had been normal, there was just nothing . . . So why the feeling?

* * *

The scouts had rotated twice since darkness fell, and each reported to the replacement that all was quiet. Without the moon to light the area it was very dark and the only movement that could be discerned was any who moved through the flickering light of the many fires down in that camp. As the night had progressed there was less and less until complete silence lay upon the land. The only ones awake down there were the ones guarding and they remained both silent and out of the light. The scouts appreciated the discipline that they were showing, but wished it not to be so. They were sure that as the night deepened that the cool air would settle into that canyon and their camp making it chilly. The desert was that way – hot during the day and cold at night. So those fires would be very inviting. Yet not one of the guards had come close to any of the fires, or the revealing light. There was one central campfire that seemed to be maintained while the others slowly burned down to coals, showing a dull red glow that became fainter as the night passed until they burned out and could not be seen any longer.

When the last change of the scouts arrived just before dawn the one that had been watching shivered saying, "It's finally gotten chilly here. I surely would like to get warm before I get back to my sack. Any hot drink left?"

"Yes, but it's not fresh by any means. In fact I suspect that if you aren't careful that it will jump up and bite you."

Laughing quietly, the one who would be heading in stated, "I don't care . . . I'm ready for a fight of that kind – get me warm anyway. Nothing happening, just the one fire being maintained, and I've never seen anybody put wood on it, but somebody has to be, so they are quiet about it. Now that makes me worry. I know that it's dark and it's not easy to see any moving around, but to put wood on that fire requires someone to come into the light, and usually when wood is added it's just tossed into the fire and sparks rise, followed by a flare once the new fuel is added. None of that has happened."

"Hmmm, did you think that they may have stacked it in such a way that it would self-feed?"

"Yes, I actually did, but it would require someone coming by periodically to be sure that it didn't need any more, and while I've watched the whole surrounding area, as we need to, I've kind of kept that fire as a focal point, and nothing, and I mean nothing." He shrugged before continuing, "Not that I wouldn't have missed something. After all it is dark, and for whatever reason it has been a very dark night. Anyway, what I'm trying to say here is this; it shows me that they are better than they appeared to be when we attacked them successfully. It might be that we were very lucky and they are much more disciplined than we first thought. I know that with the one who is second down there, no one in their right mind would cross him. So I suspect that he is the power behind the leader. And from observing the leader he isn't stupid either. This is something that I think that we need to remember and tell Madam and when I get back to our small fire I'll pass this on to Abe also. It needs to be known. We cannot take these lightly just because we beat them once."

Thinking about what the one just about off his shift stated he replied, "Good information, and you're right, critical to be truthful. It would be so easy to think that we will have an easy time the next time we face these raiders in battle, and to underestimate them. But if we really want to be honest to have been as successful as they seem to be there would have to be someone very strong and cunning at the top, and a second that would enforce the laws. And it appears that both exist here." He saw the other yawn, and smiled. "Okay, head back in. Dawn isn't far off and any sleep you can get will help. I suspect that the raiders will get very busy today searching those ruins in earnest."

He watched as the relieved scout disappeared into the darkness, turned back around and looked down on that sleeping camp, one that seemed to be so innocent and normal. But here was a falsehood, the ones down there were more deadly than a viper, or a wild cat, and had no morals or codes of conduct, or truth to them. If you became their victim you could expect nothing but the worst that man could do. He looked back over the sleeping camp thinking that it would be mid-morning when Abe came to relieve him, so there was much time ahead of him.

* * *

Dan was in a quandary. Once he had located this small camp he cast about far from its location trying to determine if there were any others around or if this one person was all there was. In the darkness it was difficult to be quiet, and he needed to be. He didn't want to alert whoever this was until he was sure of exactly what he faced. So he took his time, hunted far and wide and found no evidence of any others. *So who is this single one? Where is he living, and why is he where he is?* What he was seeing made no sense. So back to watching whoever this was became his goal. He needed to know more, but still had to remain hidden. So far that hadn't been difficult because of the night. Well, he'd have to make a decision before dawn on what his course of action would be. Once it became light then it would become obvious to whoever this was that someone had been around his camp. So what to do – what to do?

* * *

Marta awoke. It had been another terrible night without Dan being next to her. She missed him terribly, but knew that what he was out doing was necessary. Their quiet world had been unraveling for a while since that raider army had shown up. And even though they had moved to the west there was no guarantee that they would remain there. And who are those others that seemed to be shadowing that army? It had been luck and only that which kept them from being discovered. If those others hadn't been concentrating so hard on watching, then Dan and Joel would have been discovered. She took a deep and quiet breath blinking the sleep from her burning eyes. Her body ached and from the way she felt she knew that sleep would not be coming. Slowly she pushed the covers back, climbed out of bed placing the slippers on that had belonged to the woman who would have come here after the initial fires from the skies struck, but apparently never had the chance. She headed for the necessary space – they'd been calling that since they had found a small sign attached to the door with those words on it. It must have been some joke between the owners because she knew that they were still using the same words today that they did back then. It was known as a bathroom.

She took care of the morning nature call and decided that a shower might help her shake off the cobwebs in her head, but that seemed to require effort, and right now she just didn't have it. So she sat down on the lid of the toilet, leaning forward with her ears ringing, taking deep, slow breaths. Finally she sighed, pushed herself up and started the water in the shower. When the water warmed, which was almost instant, she slipped out of her nightclothes and into the hot cleansing flowing water from the shower. She remained in there for who knew how long, but looking at her skin she saw that it was wrinkled from being in the water far too long. Again sighing she shut the water off, grabbed a towel and dried off. Once complete, she, with the towel wrapped around her headed back to the bedroom and got dressed. From the lack of sounds she knew that she was the only one up.

Once dressed, she headed for the kitchen and it had a small sign like the bathroom that simply said "food prep area". Again she suspected that it was some inside joke between the long dead family members, something to add a little humor to what would have been a bad situation. Turning on the light, such a marvel in her mind, she began preparing a meal for herself, and would probably add food later for the rest of her growing family. As she began to work around the area she began humming a tune not really paying attention to it at all. With her back to the doorway she heard a small shuffle of feet, turned and saw her granddaughter standing there in her pajamas rubbing her eyes. Well, breakfast would have to wait. Smiling Marta asked, "So Jana, my little one, what are you doing up so early?"

Jana replied, saying, "I just couldn't sleep. Caron was having a nightmare and was kicking me in her sleep. I heard something in here and came to see and found you grandma."

Smiling at her grandchild Marta said, "Well I couldn't sleep either. Without your grandfather around it's harder for me to do just that. So come over and let me hold you for a while then both of us can be comforted, what do you say to that?" She saw a huge smile as Jana ran to her and jumped in her arms. Marta carried the small burden over to a rocker just outside the kitchen and rocked her. It was here the rest of the family found them later that morning still arm in arm with Jana in Marta's lap and both asleep.

* * *

Finally coming to the conclusion that the one around this small now smoldering fire was alone he now had to come to a decision. Should he contact this one, or should he just head off and continue monitoring the raiders? Inwardly he shrugged. *This area that we've been living has become more crowded than I ever expected. Unfortunately I have the feeling that it's going to get much worse before it gets better. Yes these raiders have moved, but I've the feeling they won't be here that long. And who is this, and where are those others we spotted earlier?* Questions, questions, questions, and he had absolutely no answers. Why did it seem that was the way of things, of life? He laughed quietly as he found that he had just added more that had no answers. So what to do, should he go ahead or not? Finally he decided to make contact.

Looking into that small camp he saw that the one person had his head forward and on his chest and probably was dozing – not a comfortable position at all. He quietly approached the camp and softly hailed the camp. With a jerk the male snapped awake looking around to see where the sound had come from, and with a look that said that he wasn't sure if it was a dream or reality he took a deep breath. Dan watched as this one was searching desperately with his eyes trying to see anything beyond his camp. Again softly Dan asked, "May I come into your camp?"

The one in the camp snapped his head around in the direction of the voice grabbing a knife which he held loosely in his hand he asked, "Who may I ask is requesting this and how'd you find my camp?"

Being able to finally see his face Dan realized that the one had to be in his teens and from the observation of the raiders there were nobody that young with them making this one living out here as they were. "Look, I'm not a part of the ones camping below. If I had been do you think that I would have hailed your camp?"

Sam realized that what this stranger had asked was true. If it had been the raiders he would have been a prisoner right at this moment. Trussed up and heading for a very painful death. "Okay, you're right. Come on in, but be slow about it. I'm very good with this knife if I need be." The person stepped out of the darkness and once in the light displayed open hands showing no weapons. Sam's first impression was that whoever this was wasn't young, but at the same time had a fluidity of movement that spoke of one who had been long in the wilderness. He realized that with that silver hair and beard he would have been easily recognizable, and from his observations there was nobody in that camp below that looked like him at all. At least he knew to count this one out as being a part of the raiders.

Dan read much going across his face including fear, conflicting thoughts about who he – Dan might be, and how was he discovered. Standing in the dim flickering light of the dying campfire he said, "I'm Dan, and you are?"

"Oh, sorry, I . . . I haven't seen anybody around in so long, well at least until they showed up. Until then I just considered myself the only one out here. Oh yeah, my name is Sam."

"Well, Sam, if it's any consequence to you, we thought, until they showed up, that we were alone."

"We? Are there more of you out in the darkness?"

Laughing Dan thought. *I know I'm taking a chance on this, but it's quite obvious he's alone.* "No, no more out in the darkness beyond the fire. But I have others that I'm responsible for who are not close." He didn't want to reveal more than that, and by stating it like he did there was no way anyone would guess where his family might be. "Is there any more with you? I scouted your camp and the surrounding area and only found your tracks, although it took some searching in the dark to do that."

Sam wondered what he should reveal. After all he was alone, and being that way meant that he only had to depend on himself, but at the same time it meant that he had no one to cover his back. But it did appear that this one was honest, but it was easy to be fooled. Finally he shrugged, it was obvious that this Dan had scouted his camp and the area around it and yes he could lie but the facts would show that he was doing just that. "No, I'm alone, lost my family nigh on a couple of years ago. Since then I've been on my own, and until they arrived, living in those ruins doing quite well, thank you. But when they showed up I had to leave in a hurry."

"Yeah, know what you mean. They are the reason I'm here, and there is another small group around here also."

"Another group?" He asked alarmed. *Why haven't I seen them?*

Smiling, although it was a sad smile Dan continued, "Yes, so it seems that we are getting quite crowded for this desert. There are, I believe, only three and they've been shadowing the raiders. I almost tripped over them a while back. But they were concentrating so hard on the raiders that they didn't see me, and I'm sure they are quite unaware of my existence. But it does lead one to wondering why they would be doing this. You haven't seen them?"

"No, but I've been trying to stay ahead of those down in that camp. I had to leave so quickly that I was afraid that they would follow me. Fortunately I have small caches throughout these hills, but I left much of what I scavenged down there in those ruins."

"I hope you're not planning on going back down there and try to recover your finds."

"Yeah I thought about it, but I'm really not that stupid. There's just too many of them, and it would be too easy to get caught, and I know what they do to males, and I have no desire to become their entertainment."

"Me either, but why the fire? Even with the great job of concealing it as you did, a fire can be seen a very long way off, and if nothing else the smoke can drift down into the canyon leading to someone to investigate."

"Yeah, I know, but I needed something to cheer me up, and it was cold. I figured that if I kept it small and hidden like this I'd be okay. Besides with all the fires they have going in their camp I doubt that they'd smell mine."

Smiling and shaking his head Dan said, "Never assume, that's when one can guarantee trouble." Dan joined Sam at the fire and until the sun broke the top of the hills they talked of many things, trying not to give away too much, but at the same time appreciating the companionship. After all in this present world trust was something that had to be earned.

The celebration of their safe return had been nice, and while most of the patrol with their rescued women and children were tired, all stayed up to enjoy the festivities and the friendship that was extended to them. This was so different from the real world outside of this hidden oasis, in a world filled with death and destruction. With the morning light they would be heading out once again, but this time it would be with her full force to bring war down upon those raiders – these *slavers*. When they left, again there would be worry, and anxiety with the ones who remained behind. The worry with her taking most of her force was the protection that would be lacking. So far this place had never been located by any of their enemies, but one could not always count on such to continue. Yet, there had been no time to locate a second hidden location for them to fall back to if the unthinkable happened.

With the gray of dawn she was up and feeling like hell. It had been another bad night and that nightmare had returned once again. Would she ever escape it, and move beyond? Madam didn't know. Heck the incident that the nightmare was based upon had happened twenty one years in her past when she was nine. Exhaling loudly trying to make herself feel more alive she finally stood up, but lost her balance and fell back on the bed. She began giggling. *What's wrong with you madam? Can I even stand up and get out of bed?* Shaking her head, at least she saw some humor in this ridiculous situation. Again breathing out loudly she tried again and headed off to take care of the reason for waking this early. Her bladder was aching and wasn't going to allow her to sleep until she emptied it. So she headed off to the privy.

She wondered about her children. Yes they were hers, but she never had gotten to see them. All four had been taken from her at the time of their births. It was only through the rumor mill that she even learned the sex of them. And with the loss of each one taken from her she cried for what seemed weeks. But she was only a slave and had no say at all. She learned that three of her children had been girls, but, thankfully in her mind, had not survived. They didn't need to be brought up to face what she was facing every day. The other child had been male, but that was all she ever learned. She had her first child at thirteen, second when she was about to turn fifteen, third at seventeen, and her last when she was eighteen. With the last she swore that she would escape this imprisonment, this slavery, and help bring an end to this. So while she could not escape the continual abuse she received as a slave, and the requirement that she warm too many beds, eventually because of her size the demands had at least lessened somewhat. Some of the ones that she had to spread her legs for were becoming fearful of her and were afraid that she would kill them in their sleep.

When this began to happen she knew that it would only be a matter of time and she would be shipped off to the houses where no one returned alive. It was the final stop for any of the slaves, and to be assigned there was a death sentence. So with the birth of her last child she began the serious planning of escaping, and wreaking some personal revenge on her owner. As she could, she began to hoard small items that she felt would help her in her escape attempt and slowly it was coming together. But somehow the owner got wind of her hiding this stuff, had the slave quarters searched, and located all of her hard won supplies. She was severely beaten, and for a time her punishment included servicing all of the guards, and cleaning all of the chamber pots. Her food was cut back, and she wasn't allowed to bathe. And to make the point quite clear to her she was told that another incident like this would immediately put her into those houses.

She endured the pain and humiliation, and some of the weird needs of the guards. And she put on a front of repentance, but deep inside she seethed with anger, and this anger further strengthened her resolve. At least, so far in her young life, she hadn't caught anything from these men that she had to service. Yet, how long could she count on that? She felt that one of the other slaves had probably given her away. But there wasn't any proof, and knowing the situation, it wouldn't have surprised her. So once her time was over she was even more careful, and it took a while to gather what she felt that she needed. This time none of her hoarded items were kept within the slave quarters. She had found a place outside close to the fields that worked quite well. And she had to travel past this area every day, and it turned out to be a convenient place to rest – no one became suspicious.

With her twenty-first year she felt she had enough hidden away and it was time. She sensed that soon she would be moved to that final destination so she really didn't have anything to lose with this attempt. During those years since she had been caught she had been studying much of the routines of the house staff, the guards, and the comings and goings of the ones that would visit. Then on a very dark moonless night, long after all were asleep she made her move. Slipping out of the slaves quarters, heading around the building where she had hidden a knife at least a year before, she moved with a stealth the belied her size. Periodically she would check to make sure it was still there and still hidden, and it always had been. She knew that she would need something more substantial, but this would do for her first part of the her plan, which was to take out the guard grab his long knife and ancient weapon, a pistol, and whatever rounds he had. She knew that she would catch him in mid-shift, and if all went well she would be well gone by the time his body was discovered.

She felt her heart pounding in her chest and it seemed so loud, how could any miss it? But she knew that it was strictly herself that could feel and hear it. So she waited in the deeper shadows impatient for this to be over, knowing that every second that she hid made it a greater possibility that she would be found. Eventually she heard the crunching of the sandals that the guard wore, on the gravel like surface and she tried to make herself even smaller, and tried to pull deeper into those shadows. She found that her breath had to be controlled since she felt herself on the verge of panic. *What if this fails – then what?* Doubts continued to enter her mind and she almost screamed out, but with iron discipline and control developed over her life as a slave she got herself under control. Then she saw the guard and he passed by her unaware. When she saw which one had this shift tonight she actually smiled. This particular guard had been rough with her, and had been physically violent so she wouldn't feel sorry once he was gone. Any of the female slaves who had to service him had come back with injuries all the way up to broken bones.

She rose out of her hiding place and quietly approached the guard who seemed to be unaware until the very last moment when something must have alerted him and he began to turn. But it was too late and she buried the knife deep into him while at the same time had placed her other hand over his mouth so he couldn't let out a warning. She could see recognition in those dying eyes as he saw who had done this to him, and then he was dead. She carried the body back to the shadows and quickly searched the body taking everything of value and adding it to her personal pack. She then carefully picked up the body and deposited it out further so that it would appear that the attack had come from somewhere else. The pistol was for last resort, because firing it would rouse the whole compound and she knew if that happened she would be caught and her life would be over.

It would have been easy to leave at this point in time, but she had another appointment with destiny. She wasn't going to let her owner live. He had brought too much misery on too many in her mind, and while she knew that there would be others to replace him, this one would be gone. So now armed with both her small knife and the long knife of the guard she worked her way along the planned route that would keep her in the shadows. It was still in the middle of the late night shift and because of human nature most were less alert at this time of night. She still had two guards to take out that roamed around the outside of the master's home. Then once inside there would be others. She hoped that whoever the master was bedding that night wouldn't scream or give her away. So with the same ease that she had dispatched the one guard that was working the slave compound she took out the two separately from the shadows, and not a sound left the dead men's lips. She added their weapons and whatever else to her growing pack, but not knowing what awaited her out in the wilds she took what she thought she needed. There would be a final raiding of the dry goods in the pantry of this main house before she left so that she would have what she hoped was enough food to get her far away.

She knew that the front entrance door squeaked when it was opened, so she went through an open window instead. It took her eyes a moment to adjust to the deeper gloom that existed inside the house. To her surprise the guard that was inside, the downstairs one was snoring, asleep on one of the plush chairs. She quietly approached the sleeping guard from the rear, grabbed his mouth a slit his throat. She continued to hold the struggling guard until he quit moving. She was glad for her size and strength at this moment. Since, in his death throes, it had taken all of her strength to keep him there, and avoid making noise. That left only one more that she knew of, but his location was unknown. Although she suspected that he was somewhere upstairs. This was a rather large house with many rooms, and the owner was fond of entertaining.

Quietly she worked her way upstairs being careful to step over the one step that made noise if you put your weight on it. Once on top she made her way along the railing listening and then in she heard what sounded like heavy breathing and a little grunting and realized that the guard was being serviced by one of the slaves. She knew that she really only had a short time to take care of this last guard and followed the sounds to an end room that was far away from the master room. She could see candle light through a partially cracked door and pushing the door open to see more she saw the guard getting off of one of the female slaves who was crying softly. Well, she'd be the revenge for her tonight. Again with stealth that seemed impossible she came quietly into the room and with the guard standing there still naked and watching the slave he had just taken, she took a large step forward and buried the long knife deep into his back. She saw and felt the surprise in his body as it reacted and then he was dead. She also saw the fear in this young female slave. She put her finger to her lips signaling that this one should remain quiet.

She stood there in a quandary for a moment, not sure what to do. One thing for sure she didn't want to harm this young woman. Quickly coming to a decision she went over to her to find out, in the short time that she had, if she would be worth taking with her. She didn't want any witnesses left behind as to who was responsible. When she really saw the age of this female she knew she couldn't leave her here. She couldn't be much more than ten or eleven – *Much too young to have to face this.* So quickly and without passion she told this one to dress, to take everything of value from this one who had just raped her, to head downstairs to the pantry and grab food that they could use on the road – things like bread, and dried meats, and flours. Then to wait there and she would be down and meet her there. And to be sure that she was dressed for the road for what lay ahead of them would not be easy.

She quickly left hoping that this one would do what she had asked. There was only one more chore she needed to perform before she left and this would only take a few moments. She went down the hallway to the familiar room, one she had been in too many times, slipped in, and sure enough there was another female warming his bed. Both were asleep, so she quietly approached the bed and stabbed the owner through the covers. She saw his eyes fly open in the gloom, and in those eyes she saw the realization of death. He tried feebly to grab her, but there was no strength in those hands or arms. Whoever the one that he had bedded was a heavy sleeper and hadn't even moved. For this she was thankful. She went to the other side of the bed and looked down upon the victim of this night and knew her. She was somewhat pretty, and as a slave that had been a curse. So she had been abused more than others. But somehow throughout the years of abuse she had held it together. She didn't know at the time, when she had entered here whether she was going to kill both the owner and the female slave that warmed his bed, but now decided that since she had already saved one she would try and save this one also.

She had one more chore and this was something she had thought about doing as a warning to others who participated in the slave trade. She threw back the covers exposing both as naked which woke up the other in the bed who blinked a few times trying to figure out why she was suddenly cold. Madam quickly put her hand over her mouth so that she wouldn't scream and whispered to her who it was. The one in the bed nodded an acknowledgement and Madam uncovered her mouth. Madam whispered, "I haven't a lot of time, but if you want a chance to escape this it is now."

The decision came quickly and the one said, "I'm with you, what do you want me to do?"

"Get yourself dressed in something that will work for the road and head downstairs to the kitchen and the pantry. There is a young girl there gathering stuff for the road, and you can help. Just do it quickly. I have one more thing I need to do here and then I'll meet the two of you there and we will be on our way. Do not waste time on any frills and such. Take what will sustain us, the three of us." She watched as the one got up and quickly grabbed what she had and headed out the door. Madam knew that in the rooms next to this one were other things that this one could change into that would be more appropriate for the road. And once she was out of the room Madam cut off his private parts and stuck them in the dead man's mouth as a warning to any of the others that this would be their fate if they continued in their ways. In her mind it was only right that even though dead that he choked on the very things that had terrorized so many women. It was an empty jester, but it made her feel better. He was dead, and by doing this meant nothing to the body at all.

Heading out of the room and closing the door she headed quickly downstairs. So far everything had moved well and rather quickly. Although, she had to admit that she hadn't planned on taking anybody with her, and now she had already added two others. Shrugging, she knew there was very little she could do about it. She joined the other two women, even though it was stretching the point with the youngest.

Still she had to submit like the rest so she qualified. She saw that the two of them had been busy and had filled a couple of cloth sacks with goods. Smiling with what she hoped was an encouraging smile she signaled them to go to the back door that led from the kitchen to the outside where the trash and scraps were removed. Quickly she went through the scrap bucket grabbing meat scraps and stuck them in another smaller sack. She then exited the kitchen and joined the other two.

Time was of the essence and she could see, in the darkness that these two were not dressed well for what lay ahead of them and with some impatience whispered, "Look, we have to escape, and do it now. Both of you go back inside and see if you can find some man's clothes to change into. What you are wearing will not work, period. Now go, and don't take long, we haven't the time." Both of the women disappeared back into the master's house and were gone for what seemed much too long. She began to worry that it was just about to unravel when both showed up now looking more like boys with long hair than the females that they were. She nodded approvingly and signaled that they follow her. She had planned this out as completely as she could. But it was only good until they were free of the compound. Once past and into the world at large it would be a guessing game. None of them, once they had been purchased by this owner, had ever been allowed outside of the compound. So what was waiting them was an unknown.

Madam knew that they had only a short time before the change of the guards and everything became undone. She led them across the fields trying to keep them in the shadows as much as possible. With the fields having low vegetation it was difficult to remain hidden. She could only hope that the darkness and their stealth would suffice. She knew that one of the exits from this place was guarded by dogs, and only patrolled and checked if the dogs raised an alarm. So over time she became friendly with the animals, by feeding them scraps of meat, and carefully petting them when no one would observe. She hoped that this befriending of the dogs would now work. But with the others along and not she alone, she wasn't sure. As they approached the exit she signaled the two women to wait and she quietly approached the two dogs whispering sweet nothings that she had used when she made friends of the dogs. She heard them whine in response and in the darkness she could see their tails wagging. She felt a large pressure life off her chest. She came up to them petted them and fed them the scraps, for which they sat and with a happy woof scarfed down the scraps.

Carefully she released the dogs, she wanted them with her after all, she then went back to where the others were waiting, and the three, plus the two guard dogs exited the compound into what she hoped would be freedom. The only time she wanted to see this place again would be when she could return and free the others. With the owner confirmed as dead she really had no idea what would happen, but knew that there were always others ready to take this one's place. Why was it so, she really didn't know, but at this moment they had far to travel and somewhere during this initial run they needed to hide their tracks as well as they could. In the dark it was impossible, so they attempted to put as much distance away from this place as possible. She knew that until the sun rose in the morning that she wouldn't be sure of her direction. She guessed that to reach the area where she wanted to go would require traveling both north and west. This place was located somewhere at the edge of the Great Plains and her destination was in the mountains.

She led them away from the settlement and deep into the wilderness, a place that supposedly was full of danger. But she knew that now there was more risk staying close to the settlements then what the wild lands would send their way. They were now escaped slaves, criminals to the ones in this settlement. The lowest of the low, and the punishment, if caught would be a very slow painful death. Better for one to take their chances and remain in the wilds then be found and returned. So that first night she pushed them hard, but could tell that the others were beginning to lag – Especially the youngest, which had to be hurting from what had happened to her when Madam had walked in on them. She had seen the blood and knew that the girl had to have been torn a little from the rough treatment. At least she wouldn't have to worry about that again, unless they were captured. And it was this that she reminded both of them that they faced if they did not keep moving.

Somehow they covered many miles that first night – how many she didn't know. But if there had been pursuit, it had gone in a different direction. Madam knew that within a couple of hours that the deed would have been discovered and soon the pursuit would have followed. She was sure that it wouldn't begin until dawn, and she hoped because of her direction into the wilderness that this would be the last direction expected. So by dawn they found a small creek that had many what she thought were cottonwood trees, much fallen branches and downed trees, no tracks of anything but animals coming to drink, so it was here she called a halt. She could see the relief in her companions' eyes. She led them back away from the stream and into that tangle of fallen and broken trees and told both of them to sleep. She would wake one of them later to take her place. They would spend the day here, and with the night move again.

She watched as both disappeared into that tangle and she sat on one of the fallen logs waiting for the rising sun so she could get her bearings. Once that was accomplished she would set landmarks that she hoped she'd be able to follow in the night, and they would begin their trek to what she prayed would be their sanctuary. So far her – their luck had held out and there was no sign of pursuit. The two large dogs sat next to her looking out over the lands. She saw curiosity in their eyes. At that moment she realized that if she remained as she was she would be visible to any one passing by. So she shifted her position, sat on the ground and leaned back on the fallen tree trunk – my, was she ever tired. She stared out into the semi-light of dawn to what appeared to be a serene scene. There was a soft chilly morning breeze caressing her, one that would send a chill up her spine now and then, leading to goose bumps rising on her arms. At those moments she would try to shrug them away which would send more chills down her back.

As the skies lightened from the rising of the sun she slowly was able to discern a little more of her surroundings and found that once again luck had been on their side. Where they were presently, resting and hiding, was only one of many such places. From what little she was able to determine there appeared to have been a flood or something like one in the past that had piled debris and knocked over many of the trees that ran along the stream's banks. It was a tangle of dead wood, brush, and young trees replacing the ones that had been destroyed. She realized that she could hear the creek flowing and it too was such a nice relaxing sound. Taking a deep breath, a breath that might be considered one of freedom she realized, she glanced around trying to take in the whole area. Having lived her life almost totally within the slave quarters and the compound of the slave owner she didn't know how to really see.

In many ways what all of them were facing was overwhelming. Three women alone in the wilderness with no experience, little supplies, and she had no idea if what the two had grabbed would help or hinder. She had to admit that she wasn't even sure what to take. After all, none of them had ever been away from a kitchen or food availability. Yes, the food, most of the time, had been poor, but at least it was something to put into an empty belly. Now once their stolen supplies were gone they would have to fend for themselves – could they really do it? She honestly didn't know. Plus there were others out here that would as soon do to them what they had faced back in that compound. Could she, could they really make it? Or would they die out here? Both were very good questions, but as far as she was concerned, to die out here free was far better than the fate that awaited all of them back there.

She sat there staring out at nothing as the area lightened and finally the sun became visible, but she found that it was more comfortable to just sit here and let her mind drift. They wouldn't be leaving until this night so they would be here in this hiding place all through the daylight hours. It was the growling of the dogs that had remained by her side that brought her awake. With some guilt she realized that she had fallen asleep and had failed in what she was trying to do. It made her mad that she had given in so easily. Blinking her eyes a little to clear them she placed her hands on the two dogs to quiet them, which they did immediately. *Thank god,* she thought. *Okay what has gotten the two of you excited?* She only thought this since she felt that any voices or whispering probably could be heard.

Carefully she looked around and remained still afraid that any movement would give her away. She remembered in those fictional books that dealt with a past time when this country was probably as open and without people as it was now, that the eye was such that it would detect movement and naturally go to where that movement had been seen. At least where she was located she wouldn't be visible unless she made a move. The dead grasses were somewhat tall here and where she sat they came almost to her eyes. She was looking more through them than over them. So as long as she sat still they should be okay. Slowly looking around she finally found what had attracted the dogs' attention. There was a herd of some type of wild animal out there. They had horns, and were both grazing and heading to that creek for water. There must have been hundreds of them. She could see that even though they were eating, they, at the same time were alert for any danger that might exist. She sat in awe of what she was witnessing and then realized that the sun was high in the sky and she had been out for hours. She heard a rush of water and realized that one of the other women had to be awake and had just taken care of nature. Again out here that would be a new experience since there were no privies, or pit toilets to take care of one's needs.

She turned around and saw the one that had been bedded by the slave owner peek her head over the downed tree and place her hands under her head. She was staring out at the same grazing animals as Madam. She said in almost a whisper, "The dogs awakened me, and it took me a little while to realize where I am. Then my bladder said, take care of me, which meant no more sleep for a little while." She took a deep slow breath, "Aren't those animals magnificent?"

Madam looked up and smiled, she had to agree. It also meant that they were the only ones here other than the animals. It also meant that they had to be downwind, or if not, and she wasn't sure, these were not afraid of ones like the three of them. Although she suspected that there were wild dogs, and other such that would be enemies of the wild animals. Her tummy rumbled and she realized that it had been the evening meal yesterday that was the last time that any of them had eaten. Slowly getting up she climbed over the log and joined the other two. The young female was still out, and there were a few blood stains on her pants showing Madam that the escape to this point had not been easy on this one. They were still too close to the town that they had escaped from, and she wouldn't feel safe until they had put at least seven days behind them. Looking up from the sleeping, well she could call her child since she was probably ten years younger than her twenty one years, she said, "Let her sleep. It will help heal those wounds, only the physical ones of course. I'm hoping that with her youth that she can get over the many rapes she's had to face since becoming a slave. I know personally, as I'm sure that you do, that it something that all of us faced too many times to count."

The other smiled, but it was a sad smile that said it all. All of them had come from families somewhere in their past, and with the slavers those families had been destroyed, and they had been sold into slavery. "Yes, I was twelve when it happened and I'm eighteen now. It really has been hell on earth. So how long have you had to endure this?"

Madam smiled back and like the other it was a sad smile. "I was nine when I was captured, and I'm twenty one now. I knew that if I didn't escape soon, there'd be no chance at all. I knew that soon because of my size, I'm over six feet tall, that I would be sent to those houses where no one survives. So I felt that there was nothing to lose. I really had only planned on me, but plans change." Shaking her head and looking down, she had to admit that right at this moment she felt a companionship with the others that were with her. They all had something in common and it could very well strengthen what had started here. "Look, we haven't said our names, and my birth name was taken from me anyway, so I go by another. But for now I don't want any of us giving each other our names. That's for protection, well I think it is. If one of us ends up being captured and returned then other than physical descriptions we cannot identify each other. Does that sound fair?"

"More than fair. The one who owned us has always been rough on any of us that had to go to his bed, and it had been that way when you came in and rescued me, so to speak. I wasn't sorry to see that pig die. He'd terrorized every female that he owned and laughed about it. I know that you stayed behind after you sent me down to help the one that is sleeping there. What were you looking for, if I may inquire?"

She laughed a wicked laugh. "Oh I wasn't looking for anything other to be sure he was dead, and I know it was an empty jester on my part since he was dead, but I just couldn't help myself. I cut off his private parts and stuffed them into his dead mouth. I thought it was only fitting."

This brought laughter from the other. "Now that's something I'd like to have seen. He deserved that and worse."

Both heard the sound of someone waking up and stretching followed by a small voice saying, "I had the most wonderful dream. The dream spoke of me escaping from them, oh how I wish it were so. None of them are kind, and I hate it." There was a brief pause followed by a sound of disbelief, "It wasn't a dream, was it?"

The other two turned towards her with Madam saying, "No little one, it wasn't a dream. For now we are away from there and safe. If you need to take care of nature just head deeper in and find a branch to sit on, we have none of the modern conveniences here. It is something all of us will have to learn to deal with. For a man it is an easy thing, but this will be learning all over again. After all, how do you keep your pants and feet from getting wet? I surely don't have a clue, but we'll learn."

The one she had heard taking a leak earlier said, "Yup, surely is. I just took mine off, and tried to keep my feet up . . . Wasn't totally successful." She shrugged, "Try something else, a different way next time."

Now with concern Madam asked, because she knew what had happened just before she had killed that guard, "Are you going to be okay? I noticed the blood stains, and this flight couldn't have been easy."

The youngest gave her a brave smile. "Oh I hurt, and the pain was with me the whole time, but had I still been there all I could look forward to was more of the same. Believe me", she said with emotion, "I'll take the pain I have now knowing that I'll heal and will not have to submit to those pigs again!"

Madam could tell that she needed to go, smiled and said, "Just go take care of your need, we'll be here until dusk, and we will move again. I don't want any of us out and about during the daylight hours for now. At least, until we have a good distance between us and where we escaped." She watched as the youngest of the three as she worked her way deeper into the tangle and disappeared from sight. She turned around and watched the herd that was grazing its way slowly to the water's edge. It was warming quickly and there was no sign of the coolness of the early dawn. It was time to check out what they had for food, and to determine how they would continue their travel. With her falling asleep like she did, and the sun now directly overhead it was impossible to determine a direction at all. But if she had to guess she figured that they had traveled east, not the direction she wanted to go at all, but better than finding out that they had traveled south.

South would have been a very bad thing. Her destination, well their destination was northwest, and right now only she knew that. She knew that the other two was now her responsibility and that hadn't been in the works or her plans either. *Well I guess I just have to be flexible and adjust. Heck, I really didn't know if I could pull this escape off anyway. So why not have it go like it did anyway? So now what? I know that by myself I probably could have remained out of sight, and pushed harder, but now with these two it is a complete unknown.* Inwardly she shrugged; it was funny how things went. *Maybe having some companionship will be a nice thing . . . maybe.*

The problem she faced other than the obvious, was the fact that these two companions were complete unknowns. Until the encounter in the master's house she had never met either of them and as such couldn't determine what they could or couldn't handle. In the coming days, weeks, and probably months how would they do, how would they survive? Could they handle the hardships that Madam knew was ahead of them? Heck, if she wanted to admit it, and she really didn't know at this time, whether she'd handle what was ahead of them? Too late now, they were committed whatever the outcome.

* * *

Nancse was scared, and that had been that way ever since she had been captured and sold into slavery. She had just turned eleven and found that being a slave as one of the most horrible things that could happen to someone – especially if that someone was female. She knew about sex, and had watched animals breed on their small farm. She knew that it was the way of life, the way of the new generation. So she imagined how it would be when she found her own mate. But that didn't appear to be her future now.

She had been captured, and she learned what rape was and she had cried for many days, but that didn't change anything or her situation. So that night when the guard had grabbed her and forced her upstairs and proceeded to rape her again there was nothing she could do about it. And in her misery she was crying softly, dejected, seeing her life as a living hell having to satisfy whoever her owner pushed her way, and then when no longer wanted sold to the houses where death was a guarantee.

As it had been with others, this one had not been gentle or thoughtful. She was something to use, and when done, sent back to be used again – whenever. She knew that once again that she was bleeding and that he had damaged her, but there would be no mercy from this one or any of the others. So she lay there naked, crying softly not knowing what to do or how to get out of this very bad situation. Her spirits were just about as low as they could go, since she knew that there were too many others that had been in her situation, who had wished to escape, but died here either on the owner's lands or in those houses. She was just another in the long list of slaves who lived and then would die here.

Then as he stood up, naked himself, looking down at her she wasn't sure at that moment if he was going to attack her again, but instead she thought she saw the door opening and this scared her even more, because she believed that another guard might be coming in to get his share of her. In the shadows she couldn't see who it might be, and the guard was just staring at her completely unaware, or, she assumed, knew who was entering. This brought fresh tears since she felt that more of the same was just about to take place. Instead something flashed in the darkness and the guard grunted and then slumped to the floor. To her surprise what she saw was a woman, a very tall woman standing over the body making sure that he didn't move and was dead. It was then she was told to get dressed and head downstairs to the pantry and put together food, they would be leaving this place forever.

At this point the woman left and she got up gingerly and felt a warmth that told her that she was still bleeding. So with care she placed a compress that she made from a cloth that was there and pressed it tightly, dressed, and slowly because of the pain, headed downstairs. Could it be that her chance to escape was upon her? Just when she was a her lowest, with thoughts and desires saying she had to leave, but knowing that like most she would die here? Once in the kitchen she grabbed some sacking and began to put together items that she thought they could use once away. And while doing this a second woman arrived smelling of sex as she probably did, and the two of them continued to do as this other woman had told them.

This other woman eventually showed up and eyed they critically then sent them away to change into something else, something that they could steal from this household, something that would hold up better in the unknown travels that lay ahead of them, and now she was here. She hoped that it wasn't a dream and she would wake up and find that she was still in the slave quarters. If so, it would be so devastating that she didn't know what she would do. "But it isn't a dream", she whispered, "this is real and we are leaving." She could almost feel her heart skip a beat from the joy she felt. Still they could be recaptured, and those brands on their right hands would identify them as escaped slaves and there would be no mercy given.

* * *

Laura had been chosen to be the bedded companion of the owner for that night, and she hated it. Nature had made her somewhat attractive and it had drawn too much unwanted attention from her owner, and any of the male staff. While it wasn't supposed to be the way it was, and because she had no choice in the matter, she had to submit to almost any male who worked for the owner. It had been hell and she couldn't complain to anyone especially the owner. He probably wouldn't have believed her anyway, and besides she was property not a person. So she did not have any rights at all. So with deep resignation she reported to his bed as required. She closed her mind to what she had to perform and fell into a deep exhausted sleep. At least for this night after her duties were performed she wouldn't be bothered.

Coming of the deepest part of the sleep when she was shaken awake she was groggy and could taste metal in her mouth. Looking up through blurry eyes she thought that the master was going to demand more of her, but the shadowy figure above her didn't strike her as her master. *Who is it anyway, and just let me get back to sleep,* were her thoughts. But this one was insistent and finally she awoke sufficiently to know that something was wrong. She glanced over where the master was and saw that the covers were thrown back and he appeared to be quite dead. She did a quick intake of breath. *What's going on?* Then the voice from the one who turned out to be female like she, but one that seemed to be almost a giant, told her that they were escaping and this male would be bothering females no more as well as the two guards, get dressed, head down to the kitchen and help another prepare for their flight and hurry as time was passing much too fast!

She threw the blankets off, at least the little that still covered her, and realized that she was quite naked and grabbed the clothing that was there, dressed, and quickly headed down the stairs in a silent house, with only the sounds of her bare feet and the creaking of the loose floorboards shattering the silence. When she entered the kitchen where the pantry was located she found a young female working hard on putting together a larder for their leaving. There seemed to be no organization, just grab whatever was in sight. Laura knew that this wouldn't necessarily work since whatever they took they'd have to carry. Plus some things wouldn't hold up to travel. She saw this young female turn around and jump. It was obvious she was just about to run, "Don't, I'm here for the same reason you are. I'm to help get food ready for our trip out of here." She saw this other one relax. "Okay let me look at what you have, and we need to think this through."

A quick appraisal of the contents showed that overall the girl had made mostly good choices. She only pulled a few items out, and in the gloom began to prepare a second sack. She told the girl to put together a third so that each of them would have something and while they were in the finishing stages of this the one who had freed them appeared, took one look at what they were wearing, swore a little stating that what they had on wouldn't last a day out in the real world and the wilderness where they would be heading. So go through this house and find something appropriate. Who was this woman anyway? She had to be around two meters tall, but she wasn't fat. In fact she was well proportioned. Yet in the shadows that was all that she could determine. But this one had a voice of authority and she and the young one left to find other clothing.

It was obvious to her now, in the present, after last night's desperate flight that the one that was leading her and the other had been planning this for a very long time – not that any of them weren't. But, they had seen what happened to captured slaves and the examples that had been made of them. And it had a way of keeping the rest of them from doing the same thing. These captured slaves and the deaths that followed were not a pretty sight at all and put fear into all of them. So the thought of escape, while always in the back of their minds, was more fantasy than reality. Yet, here they were far away from that place. Still, she knew that they needed to be much further away than this to avoid capture. She was ecstatic at having escaped, although it wasn't anything she had planned. In fact it was just luck. She wasn't the one who was to warm that bed that night. But the one that was had become ill and her female cycle had reached the point where she was bleeding. So she was sent instead.

Can the three of us really get away? It was a very good question and one that Laura had no answers for. Then this leader stated that none of them were to give each other their names, she could see that again this one had thought long and hard about this. Turning to her she asked, "How long had you been planning this, if I may ask?"

Smiling a sad smile, Madam answered saying, "Since the birth of my last child in my eighteenth year. It would have happened sooner but someone got wind of what I was planning and turned me in. They found my stash. I was beaten, restricted, threatened, and told that if they ever found that I was hording again that I would be sent immediately to the houses."

"The houses? No one ever survives the houses. And yet you went ahead? That I don't understand. It would have been enough for me to consider not taking any further chances."

"Yeah, but you see, because of my size I was beginning to make them fear me. No not purposely, but you see I'm taller than most of the males. Guess I got that from my father, so the rumors were flying that soon I'd be destined for those houses anyway. So I really didn't anything to lose, other than time. It would either be now or later, but the future had been set for me and there was nothing left. So to answer your question, I've been planning this for three years. Although I never planned to take anybody with me, that turned out to be a spur of the moment kind of thing. But there really wasn't anything else I could do about that either. After all if I had just left the two of you, either or both of you would have been accused of those deaths and even though unfair it would have meant your ends. I just couldn't let that happen, and that is why both of you are here with me."

At that moment Laura got a whiff of herself and said, "I stink, smell like sex. Bet the other one does since it is obvious she had to submit from the blood stains."

"Yeah, I found her just after the act and caught the guard naked and still watching her . . . Made it easy to kill him. And now that you mention it you do have an aroma about your person."

"Look, this pile of debris goes all the way to the creek's edge. So I think I'll take the girl with me and we'll go take a dip."

Smiling, Madam said, By all means. Scent can reveal us as well as sight and sound, and that odor is very identifiable."

Laura smiled and headed deeper into the tangle, grabbed Nancse and both of them disappeared towards the creek. Madam shrugged and turned back to watching the wild herd animals. It shouldn't be long until she'd begin to plan the next night's travel.

CHAPTER EIGHT

With the rising of the early morning sun, the air seemed to chill even further. It was something, while invigorating, unexplainable. Why would the air suddenly chill like that with the sun now beginning to heat everything up? It almost seemed like the night saved the coolness to release it at dawn to give one last try at keeping the dawn from arriving. Of course it wasn't true, but he never understood why it always seemed to be that way. Soon Dan knew that they would be looking back on this chill wishing they had it once the heat of the day kicked in – after all this was desert. It would be only a short time until it would be light enough to see and be seen so it was time to leave this location and find a place to remain out of sight for the day. "It's time to move. You said that you had other places to go in case something like this happened, do I have that right?"

With all the discussions that they had over this night Sam had begun to trust this silver haired man who seemed to have an easy way about him, and a confidence that spoke of years of experience. Still, was he ready to reveal any of his personal hiding places? Besides, when he had located them and thought about them most would only hide one individual – himself. This was a new concept the idea of thinking of another. Mentally he shrugged, there was one close by, but it could be exposed, and it was only an emergency one anyway, not that the rest were any different. He realized that this one wouldn't work because it exposed any who left its confines to the ones in the valley allowing them to catch movement.

Dan was becoming impatient; they didn't have time for this delay. If Sam didn't want to reveal any of his secrets he could understand that, but Sam needed to let him know, and he would bid farewell to him and disappear back over the mountainside and find his own hole for the daytime. "If you don't want to reveal anything I can really understand it, but you need to let me know now, time is against us and very soon we will be visible to the ones below, so what will it be?"

"I don't know, part of the problem is the way I planned these hideouts. I mean, I never thought about more than one person, myself. So I don't think that they would work for more than me."

"Okay, that makes sense. I'm heading out over the top and will try to find somewhere that I can remain during the daylight hours. Once it is night I'll come back here and if you want to meet we'll do it here. If I don't show up something has happened to me and it would be good of you to get word back to my family. We have a meeting place that is east of here and on top of one of the hills." Dan went on and described the location precisely so that Sam could locate it. But he didn't figure there would be any need. Yet he felt that this kid was honest. At the same time this location wasn't that close to where they were living and allowed it to remain a secret. He took once last look and left. He hoped that when he returned this night that they would meet. He needed to make a determination as to trust. He knew that while their time in their hidden home was a respite for the family, eventually they would have to find others and try to begin again. Remembering their unknown benefactor, who had provided protection for his family, for the times, when in desperation, they had fled what they had thought was a hidden and safe haven.

He immediately headed up the mountain in the uncertain light. There was no time for caution now. Soon any movement on this side would be visible from below and he needed to be away from any prying eyes. He had plans for only staying out one more night before returning back. He still wasn't sure what these raiders had in mind. And he truly didn't know if one more day would make a difference. He also knew that every day that he remained outside he risked a chance of discovery. He had to know what they were going to do. His hope was that once finished here, taking whatever they found that they would continue west and completely leave the area taking those three shadows with them, and leaving he and his alone once again.

He reached the top just about when the valley shadows began to withdraw. He knew by being up here on top that it would be revealed much earlier and when he slipped over the top and headed down the other side he breathed a sigh of relief – that was much too close. He had learned, with time that the eye had been built to catch movement drawing attention of the one to that movement. And when dealing with the likes as these raiders it would easily be a death sentence. Still, as he had crested the mountain and began his decent down the other side, the light remained uncertain. He needed to slow down and be extra careful. The footing in these desert hills was never certain and the last thing he needed was to have something happen that would cause a fall, and end up with an injury.

Sam watched as Dan disappeared into the gray morning light. Once he was out of sight Sam headed west paralleling the ridgeline. He knew of one of his hideouts in the major ravine that ran down into that valley. Sometime in the past waters had raged down this ravine removing soils that caused a number of buried boulders to be uncovered and they came crashing down forming a number of small caves among and within the piles that were created in that small landslide. A few of those desert trees had grown up around and on the edge of the ravine hiding the numerous entrances into these caves. But if one wanted to be honest they weren't true caves, only gaps that were large enough for someone to climb into when the boulders came to rest. Water, again over time, had enlarged some of the areas, and others had been buried in the silt that had been deposited. He knew that this had to cover a lot of time since it rarely rained here as far as his limited experience had demonstrated.

He thanked whoever was responsible for creating this area since the grounds was hard with many small rocks buried. It would be hard land to farm, but who would want to farm in the desert anyway? The only consistent water source that he knew of was that river in the valley. He never understood why the river existed here in this desert, which meant very little water and less rain. He slipped quietly into one of the many exits and entrances – again important. If one was discovered by an enemy, then he had numerous exits in which to vacate if it came to that. He worked his way back to one of the deepest sections of this particular haven where he had one of his stashes, shivered a bit since it was quite cool – cold really, found the old ragged blanket that he had salvaged laid down and went to sleep. Before passing out an idle thought flashed across his mind – *Here I thought I was the only one hiding out here in this desert, and now I'm finding I've had neighbors all this time.*

Dan, not really familiar with the area, had dropped over the backside and continued down into one of the many shallow canyons that nested close to the peaks of this range of Desert Mountains. It took him a while, actually to the time that the sun began to rise and change the sky from the dawn gray to the familiar blue. What he found wasn't the best solution but within one of the many piles of boulders and trees he found a small burrow that provided shelter and only if someone actually walked up to and climbed the rocks could he be located. It wasn't the most comfortable, but he felt that he'd dealt with worse, and with the bandits, or raiders, or slavers involved with the ruins that they wouldn't be out looking about anyway. He had forgotten about the other three even though he had discussed them with Sam sometime during the period he had been with him at his small hidden fire. Trying to find the most comfortable position he thought. *I'm just not built to do this anymore. Yeah, at one time doing this kind of thing was fun, an*

adventure, and now it's no more than pain . . .
Getting old sucks.

At least he could honestly say that he was getting old, while so many in this world died young. When his mind started in this direction he would always wonder what the world had been like before the ancient fires had struck, but he had no true answer, and really no way to know. Even though they were living in a remnant of that past it was only a small piece, and represented survival for the ones who had originally built it, and of course, he was quite glad they had, since it had meant survival for his family. Slowly the thoughts faded and he fell into a deep exhausted sleep, with his last thoughts being of his mate Marta, and hoping that all was well.

* * *

Abe looked at the other two and shrugged. He really had no answers as to what was happening with the raiders, other than the fact that they were tearing up those ruins trying to get whatever seemed of value. Maybe once they were through they would do as ordered – head west and stay out of the area, but he had no proof. "I wish there was a way we could know what's really going on, but so far we've been able to stay out of sight and I do not want to go down close to their camp and try and overhear something only to give ourselves away. And I have no idea when our army is going to show." He looked over at the one that held their supplies asking, "How are we doing with our travel rations?"

He only shook his head saying, "Not well. We're almost out and being that we are here I don't see an easy way to resupply. My guess is that we have only a couple of days left and we'll have nothing. We don't even have enough to get us back to our people."

Abe looked down at the ground before speaking, "Okay, I guess we don't have much of a choice," he looked over at the third one before continuing, "I guess you'll have to keep tabs on what's happening with the raiders while he and I backtrack down the valley. Once we are away from this area the two of us will hunt down one of those wild cows. It's the only solution I can think of. Then we'll need to haul the meat to a place where we can build a small fire and jerk it, which means a couple of days. Do you think you can keep them under observation that long? I know that there's no way that you could be diligent enough to keep them under constant observation, but hopefully enough to when we return you can pass on enough."

"Yeah, I know it's important, but they don't appear to want to move so it should be a bit easier. Just got to stay out of sight and hope it is enough. Would surely hate to wake up after taking a break, coming back over and find that they had left. That would scare me, since I wouldn't have any idea which way they went."

Again Abe shrugged, after all what choice did they have? As it was they had to sneak down to the river every couple of days to refill their water containers, but those trips had been short and could be completed by one. Now with their food shortage it would leave all of them vulnerable to discovery and the resulting pursuit and possible capture. He looked at both of them and stated, "If either of you have a better solution I'm ready to hear it. If not then we had better head out and get this done. It sucks not knowing what's going on with Madam and the rest, but there's just no way to know and we have to remain with the raiders until someone relieves us." He looked at the other two and neither had a better solution so Abe and the other headed east backtracking through the areas that they had been in earlier before finding a way down off the mountains heading down unseen into the valleys below.

Once they were gone the one that remained sighed. *Why is it that this world, at this time, is as it is? Why must there be so much violence, so much death?* From the short time he had been on this earth he had found only misery. He had been born into slavery and had chaffed at it all of his time as a slave. He never knew his mother since the practice had been to take the newborns from the mothers at birth – no bonding was allowed. As time had passed and he learned his place within this narrow world of abuse, bad food, deception, and of others within this world who would turn on you for little favors from the owners. He saw that females were treated no better by other slaves and at times worse than the owners. It was a hierarchy of the strongest getting what they wanted or needed to the weak losing out almost all of the time. And this placed females right in that area as being the weak. He didn't know where it had come from, but his sense of what was right and what was wrong was very strong. Again since he never knew his mother he didn't know if this came from her.

Then there came that day when there was a brutal attack on the compound by a rival of the owner. In the chaos that followed he, with others escaped. He didn't trust the others knowing that they had betrayed too many others over the years so as darkness fell he slipped away and headed north. He had never been outside the area of the owner's property and only had a vague idea of what lay out there. During his escape he had grabbed a couple of knives, an old bow with a couple of arrows, and some clothing that he hadn't had a chance to look at. He only knew that if he remained in the clothes that he was wearing that he would be identified as an escaped slave and this could only mean death if he was captured. His goals, simply stated, were to get away and head into whatever wilderness he could find. Looking back in the darkness he could see the glow from the fires that had been set in the valley below — so similar to the ones here and now. He hoped that once this battle was over that he would not be missed.

Throughout that first night he stumbled about not sure about anything. Finally when exhaustion overwhelmed him he found a rock and sat down and found that no matter how hard he tried he couldn't move. It took too much effort. His mind kept reminding him that he wasn't far enough away, but his body refused to move. So he slid down the side of the rock leaned back against it, and as his body cooled from the exertion he found that he was chilled, but with the fatigue that lay upon him there was nothing he could do about it. To move required effort and it was something that wasn't within him at the moment. He was mad at himself, since, in his mind, he would be so easy to capture at this moment, but that were the last thoughts he had until the rising sun the morning awakened him.

Looking around through the fog of being deep in sleep he realized that he had to get moving. The place he had chosen – not voluntarily – to spend this first night was quite open, with little to no vegetation and a few small boulders, and nothing else. So he got up quickly, took care of morning's nature call, got a rough bearing and headed out. As far as he could tell, not that he was good at it; there was no one around. Again looking back towards the place he had escaped from he saw thin blue smoke still rising lazily into the morning skies. Well, to be honest he could care less what happened to his previous owners, and at this moment he swore that he would never be a slave again, and he would not become an owner of other human beings. He had experienced it personally and knew that it was a terrible blight on mankind.

In the following days, and moon cycles he continued his trek north. It had not been easy. Throughout this time he had to avoid raiders, and what he suspected were slavers. And because he trusted no one, and had little faith in others he avoided what might have been contacts that would have helped. Slowly his skills were improving, but not fast enough. He was losing weight because he never had enough to eat. At least there had been food back in the compound, not that it was fit to eat. But even the really bad stuff sounded good to him at this time. It was coming onto winter and he still hadn't found what he considered a safe haven, but the nights and mornings had a deadly chill to them, and he hadn't put anything away for this coming time. He knew that the winters on the plains could be rough, but they were far south of him now. He had no idea what they would be like up here.

He decided to change his direction a bit and headed northwest. Then it began to rain, and rain hard. It wasn't some of those warm heavy rains of the plains, it was flat cold, and he was quickly drenched and shivering. He needed to find a place to wait this out and found a small cave, well actually more of a place where soil had collapsed leaving a small indentation that was just about large enough to shelter him. He got some wood together and tried to get a warming fire started but the wood refused to burn. He eventually gave up and sat cross-legged, shivering and miserable waiting for the storm to pass. Only it didn't and the rain began to turn into snow. When it began to do this he knew that he was in serious trouble. He had no clothes that would withstand snow or the cold of winter. But he really didn't have a clue as to what to do. He thought. *At least if I die here it will be as a free person and not a miserable slave. Better to be miserable and cold as someone who is free, than to be the same way and be a slave.* Again somewhere along these thoughts he fell into an uncomfortable light doze.

Somewhere in his subconscious he heard what sounded like the crackling of a fire. But he knew that was impossible. After all he had failed in getting a fire started, so it had to be a dream. Slowly he awakened and found to his surprise a fire and the warmth was one of the greatest things he felt in a long time. It was night, and in the flickering shadows and light being cast by the small fire he found that there were at least four others asleep. He almost panicked, how and when had these showed up? And why hadn't he heard them at all? He almost felt like getting up and leaving, but beyond the fire he could see that it was still snowing and he knew that there would be no way for him to survive. Then he looked across the fire and saw another looking directly at him, which caused him to jump. This other one smiled and whispered, "Don't worry about it. You're safe now."

Somehow the voice rang true and he could feel the fatigue fogging his mind again and he slept. With the dawn he learned that the ones who had found him were a part of Madam's army, and they were out on patrol sweeping the areas to be sure that no one was out and about. They had found him by accident and saw that like them, he was an escaped slave and one that was in very bad shape. With this first storm of winter it had been obvious to them that he wouldn't have made it. They showed him the brands on their right hands that identified them as slaves, but his past experience hadn't been the greatest with his own either. Still there was something about them that he trusted. So he joined them, and before entering the hidden area he had been blindfolded until it would be determined what he truly was and if he would be willing, voluntarily of course, to join them. If not he would have been returned to where they had found him and left there to be on his own.

When he saw what had been accomplished and had spent time to heal and put some meat back on his bones he was eager, very eager to join. That had been at least three years ago and he had never been sorry for that decision back at the first winter when he personally met Madam. He remembered it well. He was in awe of her size. Well over six feet tall, but her proportions were to her height. He was sure that she probably had put fear into her owner once she had grown to what she was now. Then he learned what they would be doing and he was a believer. Being a slave had made him quite aware of the horror of slavery, and to fight against it wherever they could was something he believed strongly in. So here he was part of a scout team watching what they knew to be slavers, and of the worst kind, since it had been recognized that the leader of this raider army had been a slave himself. So it was personal to him that he and they pay.

That led him back to the present and he being left with the assignment of keeping tabs on them. No problem, in his mind. They were not going to escape what they deserved and he wanted to be sure that he was a part of the justice that would be coming in the very near future. So once the other two were out of sight he headed to their lookout point and settled down for a long wait, knowing that he would be on his own for the next couple of days, not unlike when he first escaped back those many years ago. He wondered what Abe's story was. He remained a very private person, yet like the rest of the ones who lived in that hidden northern area Abe had been a slave, and when he had his shirt removed there were scars showing the beatings that he had taken. From what little he knew of Abe he wasn't the type of man who would have deserved that. So his conclusion simply was that the owner was a vicious, violent, hateful person who abused all. At least it hadn't been that bad where he had lived. Still all of this was just conjecture on his part. Yet, what else could account for those scars? He shrugged, it was one of those mysteries that he would probably never have an answer for.

Abe, with the other, continued on the backside of the ridgeline to remain out of sight again passing close to Dan who was asleep and unaware of their passing. Once they were some distance away and far enough in Abe's mind so that they couldn't be overheard. He knew that in the still desert air that voices would travel far, and while they had discussed a number of things back in their hidden camp, they had kept it low almost at a whisper. "How far should we travel back to the east? I was thinking at least a couple of miles, and we can't use the ancient weapons since even at that distance there's too great of chance that they'd be heard. So I guess it will be bow and arrow. Hope you're better at it than I."

The other scout laughed lightly, "Yes, I've seen you with a bow. I really don't understand it because with those ancient weapons you are very good. There's really not much difference between the two, other than the fact that it is easier to kill with what the ancients had."

Smiling Abe said, "That's your opinion. I just cannot keep the bow steady once I pull back the arrow, and if one cannot do that one cannot be accurate. So then, I'll leave it to you, but you didn't answer my first question?"

"First question? Oh right, I think the further we retrace to the east, keeping the river in sight, the better. In fact if we headed back at least four or five miles then there would be no possibility of our discovery, at least by the slavers."

"Makes sense. It will only add a couple of hours to our hike, and I'm all for not being found." Abe looked around and felt the heat of the day beginning. Deserts were funny places, cold at night and very hot during the day, with little of either lasting long as the desert moved from day to night and night to day. "There's a point further east where the canyon narrows considerably and then opens up again. I seem to remember some of those wild cattle being there and it's plenty far so we should be undisturbed. We'll just have to figure out where we can stash much of the meat once we've dried and jerked it. There's no way we can carry that much meat even when it has been smoked."

"Wonder where the rest of them are?"

"Who are you referring to?" Abe asked.

"Oh our people. They've been gone a long time and I really thought that they would have returned to us by now."

"Yeah, it does seem that way. Something about having to wait makes it seem too long. While, when you are traveling the time seems short. I don't understand why, but it just does. As you know they had to travel slower because of the trauma the ones we rescued sustained. And when you think about it, we were at the extreme end of our sweep when we caught up with the slavers and their captives. So even without them it would take a few days to get back and then they would have to organize the better part of our army, resupply, and then return here. I suspect we are looking at another six or seven days before they arrive, and that's if they push it, and I'm sure they will. So we have to make do, and stay out of sight."

"So far we've been able to, but I've been observing their leader and he is a canny one. I know that we've been able to remain hidden, but it's almost like he has another sense or something. It's like he knows that they are being watched."

Smiling Abe said, "Yes I've noticed it also. But he wouldn't be the leader of such as them if he wasn't smart, and had been unsuccessful in the past. Someone would have replaced him by now. In fact I would say that it was we who got lucky when we beat them the last time and he isn't going to . . . what was that?" Both of them could hear a roaring. Looking around and up they caught a fiery streak traveling across the skies leaving a smoky trail behind. Shortly it disappeared from sight and was heard no more. Abe was about to say something when they were hit with a strong blast of air and a crack that set their ears ringing, the force almost knocking them from their feet.

Shaking his head Abe said, "That one had to be somewhat close. I wonder when these ancient fires from the skies will stop. It really must have been hell when the skies were filled with the fires."

"I'm sure it was, after all it destroyed everything, well close to everything that had existed up until that time, and we are simply what are left. I think there are still enough of those things around that they could probably finish the job if we don't do it ourselves."

"Yeah it does look like we are bent on destroying ourselves. Well, enough of this diversion, shall we get this done? I'd like to see an end to this so we can head back home."

"You're not going to get me to argue, I have a mate back there waiting for me."

That ancient fire had been warning enough that destruction could come at anytime from anywhere. They knew, from personal experience and the experience of others they personally knew, that the human race seemed to be bent on destruction. So whatever these objects, these fires from the skies were, they themselves just might bring an end to humankind, and while nature may have been the one who had started them down the road to extinction, it would be only themselves that they could blame if it came about. Only if that did happen there would be no one around to place the blame.

In the distance, and they really had no idea how far, they saw what looked like a small mushroom cloud, and lots of dust. But they might have been mistaken since there seemed to be a haze lying on the land making distances indistinct. So it could just as easily been their imaginations as reality. They continued east away from the encampment, away from their small hidden camp. They needed this additional food so no more time for speculation or sightseeing. What they were dealing with was dead serious, so much so that one minor slip-up could cost them their lives.

* * *

Marta looked out where the grandchildren had been playing, and once that fire in the sky had passed over blasting them with that sound wave they didn't seem too interested in remaining outside. She couldn't blame them. What had been a really nice quiet day, even though she missed Dan desperately, was shattered by another of those ancient fires in the sky and whatever positive mood that the family had was gone. So at this point, other than her second son Joel, who was on watch duty, she was alone. She stared out at nothing and was enjoying the momentary quiet now that the grandchildren had re-entered their hidden home. There was a cool breeze blowing that would have chilled if she had been in a shaded area, but at this time the sun's warmth was almost reassuring. She sighed, the two of them had been together for forty years and with him gone like he was it left her feeling like something was missing. And of course something was – Dan. *Where are you and how are you faring oh mate of mine? Is all well, and have you learned what you wanted?* She knew that she had no way of getting answers to those questions, but she asked them anyway.

She got up from her comfortable chair knowing that once she returned inside that she would have to take it with her. Nothing could be left out to allow someone to discover that there had been people in the area. She quietly approached the point where Joel was watching from knowing that they had picked this location because one could remain hidden right up to the point where they watched from. Here the views of the surrounding areas were complete. She saw Joel turn as she approached. No matter how she tried she couldn't be as quiet as her mate and Joel. Somehow she always gave herself away. When Joel saw her he smiled. She saw that he was relaxed and knew that all was well. She joined him, and felt the breezes blowing a bit harder here. Also she felt the beginnings of the warmth in the breezes up here that had been absent down where she had been sitting. "How's it going?" She asked, even though she knew all was well.

Joel smiled again saying, "All is quiet, except for that thing that passed by a short time ago." He pointed off into the distance saying, "It looks like it might have come down over there, but it's so hazy I can't be sure. Can't see very far today. Suspect that the winds have kicked up the dust and only the areas close by are really visible, but even they seem to have a haze lying on them. Must admit I prefer when it's sharp and clear . . . Makes it so much easier to spot movement. This stuff makes it harder to do that. Fortunately the only movement that I've seen has been the wild cattle down in the valley close to the river – nothing moving up here at all. Suspect that the creatures know that eventually it will get hot and they are finding those cool holes so they can wait out the day and avoid the heat unlike us who seem to be stupid that way."

She climbed up and sat beside him looking out and enjoying the view. If things were not as they were it would be an idyllic scene, or world, with peace abounding. She knew such appearances were deceiving. Since the destruction in the past it had been a struggle to survive and a miracle if you lived as long as she and Dan had. "This is nice, and as I get older I appreciate such moments like this even more. Wonder what it would have been like to have lived before the ancient fires destroyed all they did?" She wasn't looking for answer, after all, she hadn't been born then, and what had been was long gone. She knew that it was wishful thinking to be in what in her mind had to be a better situation than what they were in now. But was it really? After all, someone had built this place that they were living in, and that spoke of issues, of problems that their ancient ancestors faced. Still, after living here as long as they had, they found nothing to explain the wherefores and whys.

"I know", Joel said, "that you're not looking for an answer because there is no way to know. The destruction was just too great, and we've been quite guilty of taking anything that may have survived. Oh don't get me wrong, I think our dead ancestors would have wanted us to. Still by the time that the scavenging is done there will be nothing of value left to even identify to any that there was a people before, or that they were advanced beyond what is known presently. I suspect that the ones who live then will make those that died into tales of the deep past creating a myth, and it will be only a generation or two beyond this time that we who still have access to their technology and know that they are real. And once it is used up – nothing, no proof of existence. Of course, this is contingent on us as a species surviving to be able to look back and wonder. And both of us know that might be our legacy."

Shaking her head she said, "I really hope not. I hate to think that you and the rest of the family only have an empty future to look forward to. Your father and I have lived our lives and have less left to us than what has already passed. But you and the rest have your whole lives yet to live, and being the mother that I am, I would love to see all of you happy and safe for all of what is yours. I'm also enough of a realist, again a mother must be, to know that wishes are empty and bring no promises. We do not control anything out here, or those events that end up influencing outcomes. Look at what is happening right now. We have been here in this desert, a different one I know, left alone, happy in our ignorance, and suddenly it's like the whole world has shown up at our door and is demanding attention. So here we sit wondering if, such a small word, if, we are going to survive this. As you know, it is the reason that your father is away and by himself. I wish he would have taken someone else with him, but understand why he didn't. But he's not getting any younger and while I know that he is very good, like you, at this it still scares me to death that he hasn't come back."

Joel really didn't know how to answer her, but again he knew that mom was just talking to pass on her fears so that they didn't overwhelm her. He could appreciate that. After all he was worried too. He reached out and drew his mother close and they sat like that for a while neither saying anything. Finally Joel said, "I know it's tough. It is for me also, but he's right, and you know he'll be careful. It's so hard when you have nothing to hold on to, and have heard nothing. It's so easy for the imagination to see the worst, and most of the time that worry is just that – worry. I'm sure that he's okay. After all he trained me, and I have confidence in what I've learned from him. So far it has served both of us and the family well. I know that it's impossible not to worry, but I suspect that soon we'll see him again, and all of us will be glad and joyful that he's back. Until then all we can do is trust."

She smiled back at him although he could see that it was somewhat forced. Yes his mother and father had been together a very long time – together longer than they ever were single. So it had to be very tough on her this forced separation. He looked at her, sighed, and looked back out over the distances. She quietly said, "I know that it's all worry and worry only makes the imagination work in ways that none of us like. But every time that he leaves like this, or the two of you go out, I naturally worry and think the worst. I know that it's very important that someone must stay behind and that we must be so careful – especially with all of this going on. I still wonder who those three are and what threat they represent. As far as I know they seem only interested in the raiders, but . . ." She stopped when Joel placed his hand on her shoulder and squeezed slightly. She had been staring out into the distances while she had been talking. Now she looked at Joel and could see him signaling her to remain quiet. He followed this by pointing off to the north. She quickly glanced in that direction and caught some movement.

Together they dropped down out of sight and watched as two people continued to the east remaining north of them. Joel whispered, "I think that's part of the three, the ones scouting the raiders . . . Can't be sure because of the distance. If I hadn't been sweeping that area when they showed it would have been easy to miss them. Still they are far enough out that they are unrecognizable. Looks like we'll have to remain inside once again, at least until we know where these are going. At least it's only them and not the raiders also. So I guess we can be thankful for that."

Marta only nodded in response. She watched as did Joel until they were out of sight heading ever east, and shortly they dropped down into one of the larger ravines and were gone. Both continued to search the area where they had disappeared and beyond in what might be their possible direction. "You said that there were three", Marta commented, "Wonder where the other is? Or are there more that have showed up at this time? I surely hope not!"

Joel hoped not also, but to his mind they looked much like the others that had been scouting out the raiders, and that was a good question, where was the other one if indeed they were the ones. "At least they kept going and didn't look this way at all. Guess it's good that we had that thing burn in the sky today. The children would have been out playing and making lots of noise which would have carried for quite a distance, maybe enough to have alerted them." He took a deep breath looked over the surrounding area once again and came to a decision. "Mom, go get Seth and have him take over my watch. I'm going to trail those two and see where they are heading and see if they will pose any threat to us." He looked into her eyes and said, "Yes, I'll be careful, and yes I'll stay here until Seth replaces me. With all this movement we can't leave this place uncovered for a moment." He smiled, "And yes before you say it, I repeat I'll be careful." He then gently pushed her away and watched as she headed for one hidden entrances.

He turned back and swept the full horizon working his searches closer and then back out again to be sure that he was seeing everything. Eventually Seth arrived saying, "Mom told me to come see you and that I needed to relieve you. What's going on? She was awfully quiet, not that is unusual with dad gone."

"We just had two pass by to the north of us. In a way that ancient fire in the sky was a good thing, but now I need to find out where and what these two are up to and how it will influence what we will do here."

"So you plan on following them?"

"Yes, but not too closely. I just need, we need to be aware of where they are going and what they plan on doing. If they remain close by then we face another period where all of us must stay inside until they move on. I think that we've been extraordinarily lucky so far with all these masses moving through and around the area like they have been. I really don't know how much longer we can count on that and what worries me more is that we have no idea what these represent or why they are following the raiders. Dad and I first thought that they were just outriders from the raiders, but we could see, after observing them that they were staying out of sight and being careful to remain totally hidden form the raiders. So they represent something else, and we haven't a clue."

"Okay, bro, something more to think about. I've got it here. Go find out what they are doing. Be careful and get back as soon as you can. It's bad enough that dad is away, but with you gone our best outdoorsmen are gone. I was always jealous of you when we were growing up. Yeah I had the size, but I never could move like you or dad, and as a kid that was frustrating."

Laughing a little Joel replied, "Yeah, well you sure took advantage of your size often enough. It took all the skill I had to avoid you at times. Okay, I'm out of here – hope to be back by dark."

Seth watched as his brother headed north and then disappeared down the same ravine that the other two had. It was now quiet and he stared at the point where Joel had disappeared, turned around and began his watch time, wishing his brother well.

CHAPTER NINE

Had it really been nine years disappearing into the past since she'd escaped? It didn't seem possible but she knew that she was thirty so it was a fact. She wondered how; well, why the years had moved so quickly. Yet, as she left her shelter, yes she found that she had begun to call it that instead of her home, she could see the growth in the surrounding area. And that couldn't have happened overnight or even in a year or two. Even now with the gray of dawn there was much activity, the shouting of orders, the organizing of equipment. It wouldn't be long until they would be heading back out again with a goal to eliminate another group or army of slavers. As she advanced to the center of the village she shivered since there was a heavy chill in the air. It felt like fall. There was that familiar bite to the air, crisp, clean, and sharp, leaving one feeling a little more alive.

When the sun finally showed she would see the many fields ready for harvest, something to help get all of them through the tough winters that existed up this far north. She was sorry that they were immediately turning around because she had to admit that she loved it here. Loved the mornings where there would be wisps of fog laying low intermingled with the sunshine giving a mystical look to the land. It also gave one a false sense of peace saying that all is right with the world, which was the furthest thing from the truth. Was there ever a time that man didn't fight, didn't steal, didn't try and take advantage of the gullible or the weaker members? She didn't know the answer, and in this present time only hidden islands like this gave one a chance to appreciate how it might be. Yet, even here she knew that there were problems. It seemed that once you brought more than a couple of people together that conflict was the result. Just what was it about them that said it had to be this way?

She spied the large fire in the center was drawn to it for its warmth, with the crackling sound, which seemed to lift her spirits somewhat. As she reached the fire someone, she didn't see who, shoved a cup of coffee in her hand. She knew that eventually this stuff would run out. Nobody alive knew where it had originally come from, but with the destruction by those ancient fires and the subsequent loss of life there had been plenty available even after all this time. But there were signs that it was disappearing –

getting rarer. And because of this every time that they were out she would send forgers out to search for more cans of this stuff. Right now they had a warehouse full of just coffee, but even that would eventually go away. Also, always with an eye to the future, she knew that it would become an important trading tool.

Just like when she found that cache of weapons that her army used, she had found the remains of a warehouse where coffee had been stored and distributed. Most of what was there had been ruined but there had been enough that survived that they had been able to fill their own small warehouse. Since then they added as they found it trying to keep it to overflowing. They had found teas also and while used by many, coffee by far was the favorite. Still anything that could be used for trade was taken and stored. One never knew what would be important in the negotiations, and when trading. After all, they couldn't do or have everything needed to keep this settlement operating. When the army left, they took the ones with them that had a natural affinity for trading with them. That way if they ran into trouble because of someone who was less than honest, they could enforce and protect their own. She thought that maybe before she got together with her army, and after the meal, she would check in with the traders who would be going with them. But right this moment, with the coffee and the fire, she decided that she would simply remain and enjoy both.

She reached up and scratched the back of her neck, twisted her head trying to eliminate the kinks and pains that seemed to happen more often now. Finally, she headed over to one of the communal tables and sat down, where almost immediately a plate of food was set before her. In a way she hated this type of servitude, since in her mind in bordered on slavery. Still she did understand the sentiment. After all, she and her army were the reason that many of the ones living here were here and no longer slaves. Many had been like that last few that they had rescued from the slavers who were on the way to market. So she gritted her teeth, smiled and accepted the food graciously . . . *So much to do, and on such a short notice. I hope our scouts are faring well.* Lost a moment in her thoughts she hadn't seen the beverage set down in front of her, and once she did she turned and saw what she suspected was a girl of about 9 years smiling shyly at her. Madam turned, with her own smile, reached out and hugged her saying, "Thank you very much." The young one clung to her for a moment returning the hug and once released skipped off towards the table where the beverages were being poured. *Was I ever that young or innocent?* Yes, she knew it was so. But her innocent ended at that age, and she buried that day deep inside her, protected by the strongest defenses that she had and only to be visiting her in her nightmares.

She took a deep breath shaking off those few resurfacing memories and turned back to her meal. There was just too much to do and she had better get at it. As she ate the noise and activity increased as others joined at the morning tables for the meal. This would be the last until they returned, either victorious or whatever. She ate quickly, because of the morning chill, food had a tendency to get cold quick, and once finished she took her dirty plates and such to the cleaning area, scraped it of the debris and dumped in the hot rinsing water where it would be taken and placed in the soapy water and cleaned thoroughly. From here she headed immediately to the shack where the traders met before heading out with the army. She needed to know what was needed so that the army could be on the lookout for those needs. After all, the more eyes searching, the better the chance of finding those needed items. Looking over the roof she saw smoke coming out of the chimney and knew that it would be warm inside.

She entered to a blast of heat that was in heavy contrast to the chill outside. In fact it seemed to be a little too warm for her taste, but knew that she'd adjust quickly and once back outside it would seem colder – funny how that worked. There were no windows in the shack and only one oil lantern burning so it was somewhat dark inside and once her eyes adjusted she found the leader of the traders and asked him what was the biggest need this time out. She learned that they needed iron, or metals of some kind, so that they could keep the farming equipment operating. The animals that worked the fields needed shoes, and yes while they reused what they had there was always some loss. So it was always a search for replacement metals and of course the normal things such as seed, and such to keep them supplied. With the continual growth in the population of their village, both naturally, and the new ones brought in, there was an ever increasing demand for shelters, and foodstuffs. And once she had a handle on the needs and what they would be taking as trade goods she headed back out into the cool morning air and headed for the meeting area for her staff. It was getting late and they needed to move. Still she shivered involuntarily, to move from that heated room back outside made one appreciate the heat.

The plan was a simple one, to protect their location the army never moved out together as a single large moving group. Such things were invariably picked up. While the movement of small groups were more the norm, and unless someone was scouting another, ignored. So it would take them all of this day and the many passes out of this "hole in the wall" to vacate the valley. She would be tying in with the traders as would be her second. When, she with the other two women, had discovered that cache so many years ago they had also discovered books on war, and methods of attacking, counter attacking, retreating, and so many other aspects of engagements that she couldn't believe it. Of course they only marked its location that time and made sure that it remained quite hidden. Now they had everything that was there here and protected right here on site.

She reached the tent which was becoming to be known as portable shelters, entered and saw her staff waiting. She smiled saying, "Sorry to keep you waiting, but had to check in on the traders so that I could relate to all of you what they want to collect this time out." She then passed on the information. "Now for the meeting point, once we are all safely out and away from here", She went over to an ancient map, again recovered from that same cache of weapons and equipment, and pointed to an area that was on the border of the Wyoming and Montana territory she continued, "here in this place is where we will meet two days hence. Enter from the south and use your colors so that our guards can identify you. Until we are sure that you are you, we will remain on alert and hidden. Once identified and the password given you can join up. Once we are all together as a complete army, we will force march back into the Oregon territory there close to the border between the Idaho territory and Oregon. There we'll bivouac until we can make contact with our advance scouts that have been following our target.

They will bring us up to date as to what the slavers are doing.

"Of course, once we know that we can begin our planning for how to eliminate them. Remember, I want as little loss on our side as possible. So no one get eager here, this must be another surprise as the first was. Although, their leader is not the type that will be surprised twice, we have to approach it that way. As to why they've remained in the area when they were ordered to head completely out I have no idea, and truthfully don't care. We are trying to bring about a change, and hopefully a change for the better. Unfortunately it requires violence, and that is never a good thing. Still, it is something that some out that only understands. They consider negotiation and talk a weakness. And will take advantage of any which think they can compromise, promising much and delivering nothing. We will not trust the likes of the ones we are going after for I feel that they are that type. The only promise I will make is that we will leave none alive to destroy families and lives. They are like the locus, only destroying what others are trying to build."

She looked around the tent; she always used this before a campaign. It was a symbol of an upcoming operation showing the others that she was quite serious about what was about to transpire. "Do any of you have questions?" Again she looked over her staff and could tell that they had none, "Okay all let's get this operation moving. Time is always an enemy and the longer we take the greater chance of failure." Once she finished her speech, so to speak, she turned around and headed back outside of the tent to allow the rest of her army to view her as their leader. She waved and smiled, and then headed back over to the traders who were now out of their building. They had the animals with them that would be pulling the carts, carts that were hidden outside of the area to prevent someone from tracking them back into this area. She nodded to the head trader for which he returned. He turned to the rest of the traders and signaled move out and with that the operation was now officially on the move. Yet, before they actually got started a signal from one of the outposts stated that a large group was moving just outside of one of the passes. This meant that everything would be put on hold until they received the all-clear signal. *Why now?* She asked herself. *Why now.*

* * *

Joel remained far enough back that there would be no possible way that he would crest a ridge and highlight himself, exposing him to the ones he was following. *Why only two, and where is the third one?* Again the question was unanswerable. He decided that he would try and get close enough, once the two reached their destination, to find out who they were, what they were doing, and why were they following the raiders? He knew that it was a risk since it was also obvious that these were very good at keeping out of sight. It was only because they were unaware that there were others in the area that had exposed them at all. Still they moved with the ease of ones long in the wilderness, so this made his task doubly difficult. They continued for only a short distance and changed their direction heading down towards that river. Joel was always amazed that a river existed like this in the desert. Had it been a different time he might have traced this river back to its source. It was something that he knew would not be happening in his lifetime. It was hard enough to stay out of sight and to stay alive.

In a sense all of this activity angered him. After all, he and the family had found respite in this remote area, had a couple of years of peace, and now in this short period of time all the chaos of those days on the run had returned. True they were not running, but with the running came uncertainty, hiding, hoping to be passed by, undiscovered by a greater force, and so many other little things, like finding enough to eat or water to drink. Yes, this incident had brought all that back to him and had fueled his anger. *Why?* He thought. *Yes, why indeed.* Then a little voice in his head said, *why not?* He shrugged inwardly. *Yeah, why not indeed.* After all there was nothing special about him or his family. They were like the thousands who lost, or were lost to these raiders. There was nothing about them that meant that they should be above anybody else. It had only been luck that day when the village was attacked. The event that had saved them originally had been planned for another day, but circumstances forced the change and because of this they survived and were here, while the rest did not.

He watched, curious as to what these two were up to, and again appreciated the skill that they were showing as they moved silently through the lands. It became obvious as to why the ones that they were shadowing probably hadn't seen them or had a clue that they were being watched. The two were just that good. Eventually they dropped down to the valley floor near a herd of wild cattle. He remained above and continued to watch. He saw them searching out a location for a temporary camp that was a little distance from the animals. Close enough to observe, but far enough to be safely away from them. Also the site that they picked was partially hidden. *Even their ability to hide their camps is well developed.* It came to him suddenly that these two must be here to hunt. It was something he and his family did periodically to supplement their food. Of course with as long as all of these outsiders had been here, food would have become an issue. After all you can only carry so much before you have to replenish.

Now aware of what was transpiring with these two he quietly stood up, turned to leave, with plans on remaining hidden when he stepped on an unseen loose rock which rolled from under his foot, crashing down the hillside where he was hidden making too much noise. Unfortunately it wasn't the worst as it caused him to fall hard and slide on some of the loose pebbles that sat on top of the hard pack making additional noise. Getting back up he quickly headed behind some of the vegetation and crouched down and stared back into the valley, but the two had disappeared. It was obvious that they had heard the rolling stone and the subsequent sound of the rolling pebbles – how could they not? He froze in position not sure what their intent was. He hoped that they would eventually think it was just one of those things that happened now and then and go back to what they were doing. But he suspected that to be as good as they appeared to be that they would search out the area to be sure. Unfortunately, while hidden from any looking from below, if one of them got higher than his location he would be quite visible. What to do? Moving wasn't necessarily smart, but staying here wasn't either.

* * *

With the sound of the stone crashing down the hillside, small as it was, both froze for a moment. After all, in the quiet of the surrounding area any such noise would seem abnormally loud. Abe looked at the other and signaled to hide, and both disappeared into the brush alongside the river bank. Unfortunately being this close to the river wasn't a good thing. With the rapidly flowing water they only heard the river and not what was transpiring away from it. Looking across to where his partner was hidden he signaled that they both needed to move away from the river and to the base of the hillside that they had just left when they entered the valley. It was obvious to him that both of them had heard it so it wasn't his imagination. Now the question was, was it natural, caused by the heat, maybe an animal, or was someone up above them watching them? They needed to know one way or the other before they could continue with their hunt. If they had been followed, and that would surprise him, then they needed to eliminate whoever it was. But with the care that they had taken he couldn't see how that would have happened. Yet, as good as they were he knew, from personal experience that there was always someone better at it.

This got him to thinking, because with all the time that they had been observing the slavers nobody in that camp appeared to have that skill. In fact he was sure of it. They had shadowed their patrols, their searches, and most seemed somewhat sloppy and careless. A few appeared to be better at it, like the one called Bear. He had to admit that he was in awe of that one. For his size and strength he moved with surprising quickness, and seemed to be able to move silently. He appeared to be almost as good in the wilderness as they. It was a grudging admission. Yet, as big as he was Abe was sure that he would have been spotted if he had been following them. Again, as far as he knew, the slavers had no idea that they were around. Could he be wrong? At least if it did turn out to be one of the slavers, with them being this far from their camp he would be easy to eliminate and make disappear. He was sure that he would recognize any from that camp. So with a decision made he signaled the other and they began to work their way back up the hillside to check these possibilities out, and until he was satisfied one way or the other they would remain on alert. It could mean the difference between life and death, the difference of keeping the slavers in ignorance or giving it all away.

Joel watched the empty valley below and knew that he was in trouble. He was sure that the two he had been following would search the area until they were satisfied that what they heard was natural. After all, it was something that he would do. In this present world you had to if you wanted to survive another day. His problem now was his location. His fall had brought him briefly into the open and had exposed him to them, and he wasn't sure that he had been seen or not. But his placement now, because of that fall, left him open in almost every direction except down with no easy way to move that would keep him under cover. *Now what? Everything I've done up until that fall was right. And I was done, finished, thinking of heading back.* Yes he had been satisfied as to what the intent of these two had been and if he hadn't fallen he would be well on his way back feeling that they were still safe. Now, again with that fall, it might all go out the window forever.

Abe worked the right flank while the one with him worked the left. Both had been in this game much too long not to know what the consequences would be if they became careless. So with as much stealth and cover that they could find both worked their way back up the mountain. Because their back had been turned at the moment of the rolling stone, and they had been close to the river neither were sure where the sound had come from other than generally – too much interference from the sound of the flowing water. Careful not to lose their footing and keeping a good distance between them they worked their way approximately one third of the way back up. At this point both worked back towards each other studying carefully the lands around them looking for anything that was out of place. But so far nothing had revealed itself. Abe shrugging thought. *Might have been a small animal or just the heat . . . Still we have to be sure. After all that's why we came this far away from our camp. We wanted to be sure that no one would find us or hear us, or smell our fires as we jerked the meat.*

Eventually the two of them came together with the other scout asking, "Anything, anything at all?"

Abe shook his head saying, "No, nothing. Maybe it was our imagination. After all it's very quiet here other than the cattle and the running water." He smiled before continuing, "Yeah I know we both heard it so it was real. Unfortunately neither of us can say exactly where it came from. Let's work our way back down through the center now and if we find nothing rack it up to nature." To be truthful what else could they do? They had been so very careful when they came this way, changing direction often, heading back and checking their back trail and they had not seen anyone or even tracks. Of course with this hard soil tracks would be few and far between.

What to do? What to do? Joel heard them directly above him. They had been conversing softly and while he couldn't understand them he knew that if they came straight down from where they were he would be seen. And he knew that if he moved it would mean the same thing. There had to be some way to avoid being located. Yet looking desperately around he knew it was next to hopeless. When he had fallen and then slid down the slope he ended up against one of the desert trees, but other than that tree there was nothing. This one wasn't large so he couldn't climb it and hide in its branches, and with no cover behind him other than what was higher up the slope, somewhere close to where the two were, he knew that he would be visible almost immediately once they came through that cover. Finally realizing that there would be no escape from this he decided that maybe it would be just better to quietly stand up, show no weapons, and talk. At least if he died here the family would still be safe and these two might just tie him into the bandits and not look further.

Taking a deep nervous breath he stood up, looking back up the slope, but even though he had heard their voices he didn't immediately see them. Apparently they were further up than he thought. Okay, if that was so, he decided that he would walk on down to the valley floor where if it came to a fight that he would be in a better situation. Luck held with him as he hiked down the remainder of the slope and was now standing in the grass that was growing on the flats. For some reason they hadn't seen him yet, might he still escape? It was a thought but he knew that any movement would be caught immediately and it was probably because neither had been looking his way was the only reason that they hadn't spotted him as of yet. *Might as well get this over with and see what will happen.* "Hey you two come down to the valley floor and join me if you would."

Abe's head snapped around. Where had that voice come from? He looked over at the other scout and saw surprise in his face. Both of them looked down the slope and saw a single individual standing there with no weapons in his hands. Whoever this was had to be good. After all they had been careful coming here, and at no time had they seen whoever this person was. Yet there he stood, which meant that he had followed them at least long enough to know that there were two of them. Of course, as another thought entered his mind, maybe this one had been in the area. After all, how much did they really know about it? Abe signaled the other scout to stand and he followed suit. Abe saw someone who probably was in his mid-twenties if not a little older. Built much as he was and had the look of one who was good moving through the wilderness. There always was a certain air to the ones who had that ability. He had never been able to put his finger exactly what it was that made them different, but he could always spot them. "Are you so sure that there are only two of us? After all we could have more just around the bend in this river."

The one who was below them smiled saying, "That might be true, but I know better, and I could say the very same thing, but it wouldn't necessary be true either."

One thing for sure this one, whoever he was, appeared to have confidence. Maybe what he was saying was absolutely true. Maybe he wasn't alone. Abe was at an impasse. *Now what?* They came to this remote area confident that they wouldn't be discovered and before they were even set up to hunt and prepare the meat they had been discovered. Again, who is this individual? Abe looked over at the other scout with a questioning look and only got a slight shrug in response. It was obvious he didn't have a clue either. "So, if I may ask . . ."

The one down below interrupted and said, "You may ask, but I may decide not to answer. After all it is my choice."

Abe had to concede that. It is his right. And again he had shown no hostile action. Abe suspected that if that rock hadn't rolled under this one's foot and he conjectured that was what had happened, that he would have been long gone and they would have been none the wiser. It was only through such an accident that could have happened to any one of them that had revealed him to them. "Point taken. I was just going to ask how long you had been following us, that's all."

The one below smilcd and asked, "Who's to say that I was following you at all? After all I could have been in this area and spied you once the two of you entered the floor of the valley."

Abe smiled back saying, "I don't think so. First off even though we haven't been here long, a few moments only, there are no signs that anybody has been here or has camped in the area. It's something we always check when we enter an unknown area."

"That might be true, but maybe, like you, I was just passing through and we just happened upon each other. I know with as few of us that exist that such seems unlikely, but that doesn't mean it isn't possible." Joel at least felt a little of the nervousness leave. It was becoming obvious that they were not going to immediately attack and as long as they kept talking there would be a chance to get out of this situation healthy. He thought that he could drop a verbal bomb on them by letting them know that he knew there were three of them, but decided to wait a little longer.

Abe signaled the other scout to join him. So far this one hadn't threatened them in any way and he suspected that he wasn't going to. And in many ways this one also seemed to be a little smarter than the ones that they had been watching. Again he didn't look like any they had observed, so who is he? "Okay, look we'll come down and join you, but keep our distance so that neither of us will provoke something that we don't want." At this point Abe nodded to the other scout and they carefully hiked down the slope until both of them stood on the valley floor a short distance away from the other one. He saw that if they attacked him that he was quite ready to return the favor. But he really didn't want to do that. This one left him curious. There were just too many unanswered questions. "Okay now what? I think that we could stand here all day bristling at each other and get nowhere."

"True," Joel answered, "but I would prefer that it not be that way. If I hadn't fallen up there you would never have known I had been here. And that was the way I wanted it. But it's not the way of it now. Look, my name is Joel; can I have at least yours?"

Over the time that they had been following the slavers this was a name he had never heard. "Yeah, I guess that would be okay. I'm known as Abe. As to my true name I have no idea."

When Joel looked at the right hands of the two he saw the markings of slaves and it made him mad. He hated slavery and what it was doing to families, and communities. In fact he was sure that it had been slavers that had attacked and destroyed the village they had escaped from. The signs had all been there – all adult males killed, and most of the women and children taken – a standard practice. "Ah, I think I understand – escaped slaves, so one has to be very careful. To be taken alive after such a thing means a very slow, painful, and unpleasant death." Now he had to be careful, because it would be so easy to mention his own history, and he had come close to revealing it. So once he realized that he stopped speaking waiting on Abe's response.

"Yes, what you say is true and I can tell that you've been fortunate enough to avoid what we couldn't." Here he stopped also. *What to do, what to do?* Abe was sure it was the same question this Joel was asking himself right now. Again this Joel was right in the fact that if he hadn't fallen the two of them would be none the wiser. And that was very bothersome. To be spied upon as they had been and not have a clue. Then he smiled slightly, after all this was what they had been doing to the slavers, so why should it be different for them? "One of the problems for any of us in this present time is trust. With the slavers, raiders , and who knows how many bad ones are out there one can never be sure that the one they are meeting, the one that they may be willing to trust could be one of the ones that I just mentioned. As you know, trust has to be earned, and especially for us knowing that if someone turned us back in that there would be a reward for our return. So how do we proceed?"

Joel looked down took a deep breath and slowly let it out. "It is something that has been an issue as long as I can remember. In the village that I was from, which was destroyed by we think were slavers by the way, we trusted each other because we knew, worked, and lived with these people. So it was easy to trust — well easier anyway. But out here it's nearly impossible, and I wish I had a simple and direct answer, but I don't. It makes this world a lonely place when you dare not trust another, but at the same time knowing that if you do there is a great chance that you will be betrayed." Again he stopped for a second. "Okay, to change the subject for a moment before we get back to what we are trying to solve here, why have you come here to this remote spot?"

"Oh," Abe replied, "I thought that would be obvious. We came here to this spot to hunt. We are running low on food and wanted to be sure we could find a place where we would be unobserved.

Obviously I was wrong, and while questions are being asked, you said 'we' when you were describing trust."

"Did I? Is that not surprising since, if I remember right, I was talking about the village I'm from. And if it is a village it means more than one. And when I spoke, it wasn't just speaking of now, the present, this moment. Again, obviously if you need food and you were just passing through you would have had prepared for this desert and would have had enough to get one through safely. This speaks of one staying around somewhere."

Abe laughed because both of them were trying to learn much about the other one and each was being very careful in their verbal fencing. "I have to admit that I like you. You're, like me, not willing to give away anything that could reveal to the other something that would show a weakness or a specific location. Yet, both of us sense that we are not getting the total truth." Abe shook his head and smiled once again. "Yeah trust, such a small word, with big meaning and bad consequences when broken. "You're right though, it would seem that the best course since we are escaped slaves would be to kill you to keep it a secret, and you know it. But I have a feeling that if we tried that at least one of us would be dead if not both. And personally I would rather take my violence and put it towards destroying slavers."

The scout that was with Abe stood silent as he listened to the verbal sparring and seeing that most likely this would not end up in a fight finally grew tired of just standing and sat down cross legged on the ground leaning forward to catch the nuances of the conversation. Joel took this as a positive step, since that left this other vulnerable to attack if he so desired, and made it more of a one on one with this Abe if it came down to it. "I don't know if we can work out to trust in the short time that we are together here, and I know that your time, as it is for all of us, is limited. Even in an empty land like this desert one can be discovered and killed for what little they have. I have often wondered if the world that was destroyed by the ancient fires was a safer place then the one we presently occupy. But none of us will ever know. We only have the present violent world and all of us try and find a place of peace and isolation where there might be some respite from the outside world." Joel shrugged, "I have no answers, only questions. I'm sure that somewhere in the distant future things may change for the better but neither you or I was born to such a time. We are here and are continually fighting for survival against nature, against ourselves, against greed and destruction, and of course those ancient fires from the skies. While they do not fall as often, they still do and they still do a lot of damage when they crash into the earth. My father has said that if we, meaning mankind, are not careful that in the end it may not matter. We may just destroy ourselves, leaving only ourselves to blame. We have a chance, a slim one for sure, of surviving as a race and recovering from the destruction that fell. But with the evil that seems to be in control, it is something that could be that final tipping point, the one that ends us forever. I know that most of us are just trying to survive another day to really look to the future, and that really isn't a good thing, but what can one do?"

"Not much really." Abe was surprised with the words that this Joel had just stated. "Profound if I do say. I think that I would have liked to have met your father. But if you are here alone I know that would be impossible. Could it be that he was one of the ones who died in that village?" Abe was fishing for information, and hoped that Joel would slip up and fill in more of the blank pages. "Also I noticed that you spoke of him in the present tense so I might assume that he is alive and close by."

"Yes, you might assume anything you like, but that doesn't necessarily bring forth any truth. No, he did not die at that village. In fact it was his skill that allowed us to escape. But he is not with me now, or very close." Of course Joel knew that both statements were quite true, and while it gave an impression that his father wasn't around, which is what he wanted them to believe, it wasn't quite the truth. "Look, if you allow me to I'll head out and be out of your hair and let you know that your secret is safe. I hate slavers and everything that they represent. Oh, by the way where is the other?" And with that question Joel smiled a knowing smile. He also saw the surprise on Abe's face.

"Other? What other? You see me and the one standing over there. If I count it right that makes two and that is all that is here."

"Yes it is all that is here, but when you came into this area there were three. You see I've been watching you and yours for quite a while. Never had an inkling of what this was all about. Couldn't even decide if you were just outriders for that raider army that is north of here, which is a bothersome thing. It has been difficult to stay out of sight of the army and you three. But until I fell I've been successful."

Abe thought about this most recent statement and it seemed to confirm that there was only this one. Just how long had they been under observation and none the wiser, as they were observing the slavers? It was a good question. Maybe he was the one that they had thought they had seen back where the slavers were presently located. He remembered that one of the other two had thought they had seen someone leaving that place but could never confirm it. At least if he was the same one it would now be confirmed . . . But how to approach it without giving anything away? "I really cannot believe that statement. Here we stand and that's all there are, no more, no less."

Shaking his head inwardly Joel said, "Say what you want, but we were just talking about trust, and here you lie. Maybe it isn't a total one after all if I took what you said literally then you are quite correct. Here you stand with another and it is only you two, but if we were to travel back in time I would see three of you trailing that army staying out of sight and avoiding any of their patrols."

Abe got his answer. Even though it wasn't quite the way he expected it. When they had possibly seen someone leaving it was after the time of the major patrols or searches that the slavers had done. Although, he did have to admit that the slavers still ran some small patrols after discovering the ruins and this could qualify also. Yet, from the descriptions that this Joel had presented it had to be those major patrols and searches that they had to be quick to avoid discovery . . . Which again, meant that the three of them were under observation from the beginning. Just how many people were in this desert, in this area? It seemed ludicrous to him that there should be a lot of people around. They were in a desert. True there was this river, and along its narrow belt of green many could survive. But there was no sign that anybody was living along the river where one would expect people to be. He had to admit that it would be an obvious place making any who did a target for such as the slavers. But in all the time that they had been in the area, not that it was a great amount over all, there had been no sign of anybody living here, and as far as he knew, other than that army, there was nobody around at all. But this one proved him wrong. Yet, one was all he saw. There were enough resources around to support that many. "If I may ask, when did you first spot us, and I'm not admitting at this moment that there's more than what you see here."

"Oh I don't know for sure. After all out here days and such mean little. No real seasons to speak of, although there's a hot season, and one that is a little more bearable. The river never seems to go away, but if I was to venture a guess close to a moon cycle. Might have been less, might have been more." He really did know, and it had been greater than a moon cycle, but he wanted to give the appearance that time wasn't something he was concerned with. He knew that with these three and the army around that it had been hell in their shelter and it made the time that all of these strangers were around seem much too long. He really would like to see all of them gone and then he and the family could get back to some normalcy. What a thought really, to have all of this be gone like a bad dream, a nightmare that fades with the dawn.

"Okay, I will admit", Abe stated quietly, "that we followed that army in and remained out of sight. You see this wasn't the first encounter we had with them and we had to be sure that they were leaving the area. None of us can afford to be discovered, again for obvious reasons. So it behooves us to keep track of them and to keep far enough away not to be caught. As you have stated the consequences are too terrible to contemplate. Although one of the things we have found to be strange is that leader with the raiders. He carries the same mark that you observed, but he seems to be able to move freely and not have to worry about the punishment. So I do not know if he escaped like we did, or whether there is some other arrangement. But he is one of the worst. Just had a thought, how long ago was your village, or maybe I should say the village where you were living, how long ago was it attacked and destroyed?"

"Let's just say that it has been a while. Why would you ask such a thing? After all it has little bearing on what we are discussing here."

"Yes, and no. You see we are part of more . . ." Glancing over at the other scout he could see him signaling him to be careful. He nodded slightly showing him that he had confidence in what he was doing. He saw the other shrug slightly and could understand his concern. ". . . and we saved some women and children from this army. I'll not go into the details since they, ah, the details are not important. Let's just say that the rescued had been sorely abused, and I was hoping, in a way that maybe they might be related, but the destruction and capture of these had to have been in the recent past, while what you are saying happened to the village where you lived was much further back in time. Do I have it about right?"

"Yes, you do. I have been here a while, and the incident happened far to the west of here. It took me a long time to get here and then to set up a hidden camp. I didn't want to have to face any of them again, and figured that this desert was a great place to avoid any more confrontations."

"Normally I would agree with you, but it seems that this desert has become quite the busy place."

CHAPTER TEN

Madam was restless and eager to be going, but with whoever it was outside of their hidden place they could not afford to move. So far no one had thought to look here, and with the number of years that they had lived here, nine if she wanted to count from the time she had first arrived, there had never been a threat to or a discovery of their hideout. The village had grown over time as she led escaped slaves into this oasis. Now the problem that she and the rest faced was that all adults and some of the younger ones all had the mark of slavery. The children that had arrived since the establishment had no such marks but were much too young to make contact with whoever this large group that was moving through the area truly was. There was no way to establish facts about them, and with the size of her army, if they left even going out the number of passes that led into and out of the area it would set off alarms.

It would be so nice if we had someone here as a part of our growing community that had never been a slave. Then it would be easy for them, with support of course, to go out and determine who these people are, and what their intentions are. But no, we don't and so here we sit. I don't know how much longer our opportunity to remove that blight will be, but the window is always small. All she could at this point was pace to burn off some of the pent up energy and continue to wait. She knew that the ones that were out there were under constant surveillance, and that the runners would keep her and the rest informed as to what was transpiring. *Why now?* Then she laughed after all why *not* now? No one was guaranteed any favors in this world, or was special. Even though she knew that many thought they were just that. And in most cases they were not necessarily ones that she wanted to be around. Many of them were the slave owners, or the market owners where slaves were bought and sold.

She saw her second and saw that he was just as eager to get out and move on the slavers, but again there was no way that he or the rest would compromise their home. Finally as the day had moved towards the zenith she decided that she would go out to one of the lookout points and see for herself. After all the information that she was receiving was third hand and she preferred to make the observations herself. It was between the zenith and dusk when she finally arrived at the point where she'd make her own observations. She signaled the one watching that she was approaching and quietly joined him. While she had believed the information that had been passed to her she was surprised at the very size of the group that was out there in the distance. She turned to the lookout and asked, "Really?"

Quietly and in a subdued voice he replied, "Yeah, really."

She saw a good sized camp. And considering the distance from where they were to the location of the camp, well, the sheer size would have been a small village. She saw wagons that were built to last, and it appeared that there had to be at least fifty fires going with a large one in the center of the group. With the distance glasses she peered into the campsite and saw family groups, children running around playing their games, and much movement within that all spoke of some purpose. "Gypsies, or nomads, and we cannot trust them at all", she said softly. From what little knowledge she had of them she guessed that they didn't deal in slavery directly. But they were always looking for ways to improve their lot, so capturing and selling escaped slaves back to the owners could easily fall into that category. She had known that these people existed, but had never run into them. In a way it did not surprise her that such as they existed.

Again from the very size of their camp very few would attack them and with their continual movement it was difficult to surprise and then attack them.

The winds began to blow up canyon a little harder and she thought she heard the sounds of bleating coming from whatever herd animals that they had with them. She knew that the animals provided most of the needs for the gypsies, and they protected them to their own death. She also knew, from rumor that they were fierce fighters, and if one attacked them they could expect the gypsies to fight to their personal death, and that included the women and children. It was one of the reasons that raiders and slavers avoided them. It wasn't worth the effort or loss even though from a distance the gypsies appeared to be a temping and easy target. Very clannish, the rules and laws were theirs alone, and everyone who was outside of these clans was unimportant, and as such, could easily fall victim. Turning to the one who had duty she signaled that she would be leaving. She asked, even though no one had an answer, "How long before they move on?"

He just shrugged showing he had no idea. In truth no one did. The ones that they were observing was a secret society and very little was truly known. To her it was obvious that they were camped for tonight. Since this was the first time she had ever seen them in the area, she hoped that it would only be tonight. She and her army needed to move. But now they were delayed. Add to it the fact that the gypsies were here, and even if they moved on the morrow, they would have to avoid them, which could delay her even more. They couldn't afford to be seen by anybody. To be locked into someone's memory that they were seen in this area, this might give her enemies a clue to their location.

It was dusk when she got back down to the area where her army was bivouacked. She called a quick meeting and told the ones in charge of the different elements to send all home for this night. She would evaluate the situation in the morning with the ones who would be watching the gypsies and determine then what they would do. With a deep drawn breath, followed by slowly letting it out she dismissed the lieutenants and stood in an empty portable shelter staring out at nothing. *Why does it have to go this way?* She wanted to be far away from here, but here was where she and the army were – stuck. So with a somewhat black mood, she vacated the tent and headed back to her shelter and hoped that in the morning the news from the ones guarding the entrances would be good and they'd move out – with stealth of course. After all it still would be bad if the nomads left and then shortly after her army was on their way they ended up making contact. It would leave too many unanswered questions in the minds of the gypsies, and she knew that they were a curious lot with long memories.

On her way back to her shelter she had a thought and stopped for a moment. She thought that maybe it would be a good idea to check in on the ones that they had rescued to see how they were recovering now that they were no longer on the move and there would be time to heal – at least physically. She knew personally that it would take much longer to heal the mind and spirit from the abuse that these had faced. In a way she laughed inwardly because she almost feared, yes feared was the correct word, actually talking with these people. It had nothing to do with them personally, but what they had lived through. It seemed that every time that they had been successful in saving ones like these from the slavers that it brought back the nightmares of her past, and for her it was a place hidden deep in the recesses of her mind that she wanted to avoid. In her sleep she could not control what her mind presented in living color.

While her beginning as a slave had happened twenty-one years in the past in her dreams she relived that time too many times to count, and it seemed that these visits to the ones who had just faced was she had those so many years in the past always brought the nightmares back – not that they weren't constant companions because the nightmares were. She wondered if she would ever get over them, come to terms with her personal demons. She wondered if the nightmares were slowly bringing her to accept what had happened, something for which she had no control over, and eventually move on with her life. She had to admit that it would be great to finally be rid of this horror from her past. Yet, again, she had to admit that for all the hell that she lived through those many years, she now was a stronger person. She didn't know what her life would have been if they had been missed by the slavers that faithful day, but she was sure that she would have traded almost anything to find out.

She didn't know who was stressed more, the ones they had rescued or herself when she talked with them. Even though they were unaware of her past, they knew from the markings on her right hand that she had been a slave, and that wouldn't have been a good thing at all. And they knew that if it hadn't been for her and her army that they would have been carrying the same mark and she and the rest around here had, so they were quite grateful for their rescue. Most would put on a brave face when she'd join them, but it was easy to see through their attempts. The wounds were too new, the abuse too fresh and it showed. It was these signs that pushed her stress levels because she saw herself in each and every one of these victims. And every time – she still had no defense against her own mind – those bad memories from that time in her life always arose and she tried to avoid those memories like she tried to avoid death.

At least this meeting was over and with it being night she realized that she hadn't eaten since earlier today but instead of heading for the kitchens that were always going, she decided that a cold meal at her home would have to do. After being keyed up to begin the return run and have it stall had burned her out. She felt her energy flagging, and even though she dreaded the idea of sleep, she knew that she would need to be sharp on the morrow. She hoped that the nomads had moved on and this was just a camp for the night before they continued to wherever they were headed. She also hated this waiting game. After all she wanted to get this distasteful chore over with and return to continue her life, what was left of it.

With the visit to the ones they had rescued it always brought back memories of her own children, the ones taken from her at birth, the ones she had never been allowed to see, to hold, or touch. Not that the pregnancies were anything she had wanted, or the children produced were from a loving relationship, but to have them taken as they had been had left her, in each case, wanting to die. She would always ask herself if this was what her life was to be, and if there would be no one to mourn her when she passed from the living to the dead. As a slave she knew the answer, and it wasn't encouraging. Once they were finished with her she would be sold to the houses and there she would die. No one escaped or lived long once sent there. So her legacy would have been no different than the many who had preceded her into those houses, or the ones who were still being sold to them. She would have died a slave, and would have died with no one caring at all – just something to throw out with the garbage, and to be replaced with another.

She stumbled into her shelter or home or whatever they were calling these things now days, and cursed a little. Because it was dark she had, once again, forgotten to lift her foot high enough to clear the ledge that went across the doorway at foot level. It had been placed there to help keep dirt, mud, and yes snow out as much as possible. It had always been there and she had tripped on it too many times. One would have thought that she would have remembered, but she had been lost in thought and hadn't really been paying attention. No one to blame but herself that was for sure. The place felt stuffy, and again that was obvious. After all she had closed it up with plans on being away for however long it would take. She lit a candle that sat on a small table next to the door and carrying it with her went around and opened up the windows to let in fresh air. *It surely doesn't take long for this place to smell like it has been closed up for a long time,* she thought.

Standing close to one of those open windows she took a deep breath of that sweet cool mountain air. She knew that they were a few moon cycles from winter, and even if they hadn't tracked the time, the crispness of the morning and night air would have informed them that fall was on its way. She continued her circuit lighting lamps, and when satisfied headed back out with a lantern to go use the outhouse. She'd make one more trip before sleeping. When she approached the outhouse it always made her think about the very cold treks to here in the winter. She really wished that there was some way to have such a thing inside the living space where there was a chance that it would be warm. She knew, from her reading, and actually observing that at one time it was common, but that was before the ancient fires had destroyed everything. Now very few had the ability, let alone the understanding of how it had been accomplished.

Back inside the house felt cooler now and now longer smelled stale. She went to her pantry and found some smoked meat and canned fruit, putting together a quick cold meal, going to her comfortable chair where she picked up one of her favorite books. She smiled, because she had read this one so many times that she had almost memorized it. Yet it was precious to her. She knew that as time continued on that most of these books would disappear, either through use, or loss due to fires, floods and such. At least there were still a few around. This one had been responsible for her knowing about where they were now, and when she had escaped she had taken it with her. The memories came flooding back. Had it really been that long ago? The three of them had spent the day by that small river hidden, learning how to do just the basic things. After all, even though they had been slaves and had to do as ordered or pay a severe penalty at least the conveniences were available. But here in the wilds there were none. So taking care of those nature calls and figuring out what would work the best was a new experience.

If their situation hadn't been so desperate she would have laughed. Because any of the books she had read as a slave never mentioned these difficulties, just glossing over them as if they were unimportant. *Might be if a male had written these stories. After all such things seemed to be so much easier for a man. Just whip that thing out and take a leak.* But she and the others weren't built that way so had to find other solutions. When darkness arrived the three headed out again in a general northwesterly direction. They still needed to put distance between them and she had hated the idea of remaining in that spot all day, but knew that they would stick out and be out of place to any who would see them during the day, so they waited. She hoped that she had marked their direction well in her mind using the night sky, and some landmarks that she had pointed them towards at dusk. Yet, she knew that she was anything but an expert at this.

That first seven days, well nights, that was how they traveled – in the darkness only – in that time they had only seen wild game, and the two dogs had alerted them more than once to possible situations that might have put them in jeopardy. So what she first thought could have been a real hindrance became an asset. She had really worried that the pursuit would be instant. She felt that the slave owners, many times, considered their dogs, their animals, more important than the slaves that they owned, and because she had taken the two dogs with her they would double in their effort to recover their property. Of course with her killing the owner, it may have thrown a lot of chaos and delays in the situation. Or, because of the death of the owner there was no pursuit at all as the others fought over the suddenly available properties. She never learned, and she really never cared.

It was early in that second week that they finally ran out of the supplies that they had stolen from the house. The food had served them well, but now they had to slow down and learn to hunt. Again, although this time it was frustration, those books made it seem so easy, so simple to hunt, to set traps and catch food. But time and time again they failed as the wild animals outsmarted them. For the animals it was an old game. To reach the age they were meant that they had been outsmarting the predators for all of their lives and it did not matter whether they had four legs or two. Again, early on, it was the dogs that had come to the rescue bringing down some rabbits. And with none of them working with the butchers or the kitchen they had made a complete mess of skinning and gutting their future food. In fact, she had to admit that all of them became ill over the process. Yet, she knew, as the other two that if they were to survive they had no choice. Any of the three of them could become a meal for other predators out here.

It was finally through trial and error that they finally became successful with their deadfalls and snares. They were still afraid of using their guns for two reasons – first their ammo was very finite, and second they were loud. Sound carried a very long way out where they were, and they knew that such things, while available, were rare and becoming rarer as time continued to pass them by. It was obvious that there would be a time when any of this ancient technology would not function or be unavailable. And because they were eating small game, and whatever wild grains they found all three were losing weight. She didn't know why since there had been plenty of rabbits and birds like quail to keep them fed. Then she remembered reading that one's body required a certain amount of fat in the diet to remain healthy and most of what they were eating would be considered lean with little or no fat. It became obvious that they would need to bring down a larger grazer if they wanted to supplement their meat.

One day just beyond where they were camping sat a large herd of wild cattle. It seemed that they had taken over the prairies once the ancient fires had done their damage, releasing the cattle to fend for themselves, and it appeared that they had done this quite well. Luck was with them this day as one of the younger cows had gotten stuck in mud besides a place where the herd came to water. They saw that others of the same herd had gotten caught and died here and the one that they were eyeing had been struggling for a long time and appeared to be weak. A couple of problems faced them. First off they weren't the only ones eyeing this animal for a possible meal. There were coyotes, or wolves, or maybe wild dogs, she didn't know enough to separate them. Secondly, that mud that the animal was buried in might be a trap for them just as much as it was for the cow. With the help of the dogs they were able to run off the pack, but they only withdrew a short distance and lay down to watch seeking out any opportunity that might come to light. Then with long sticks they probed the mud trying to find the best way in eventually reaching the struggling animal and with a quick strike with their knives finished off the cow. It was probably more merciful anyway since the animal would have had a slow death stuck as it was.

Again, this was the first time they had slaughtered a large animal and had difficulty cutting out the meat they thought would do them the most good. They made three or four trips cutting only what they could carry and retreated back to their camp where they smoked and dried the meat over their fires, roasting a large chunk which they consumed rapidly. It was one of the best tasting meals that any of them remembered. Watching the dogs eating their share it seemed to be the same for them. They found that they had to remain for a couple of days to get the meat prepared, but when they were able to move on their supplies and packs had been replenished.

It had been late spring when they had made their escape from the compound where they had spent their lives as slaves and it now felt that time was moving them towards summer. Their muscles had hardened from the constant travel and their senses sharpened. They were three hardened women apparently born to the wilderness who avoided everybody. Madam had a destination in mind but truly did not know how long it would take them to reach it. The small map that she had was from that old paperback book and did not give distances or a scale. Its small size made it difficult to even determine the lay of the land. Yet, she was determined that they push through until they reach her Shangri-La, a term that she had picked up from another one of those old books. Again, it was one of her favorite fictional worlds, although she had no idea where the Himalayas were, or whether they really existed at all. Her world was the slave compound and the areas around it, being limited to where the owner allowed her to go. Well, she wouldn't be worrying about that anymore. Her owner was now dead and she would not be taken back to that world – period. Since their escape their world had been expanding daily and all were surprised at the size of the prairies that they were traveling through.

The weeks were passing rapidly and the days were becoming warmer. Again from trial and error, they learned how to carry water with them. It was one of those things that none of them had considered when they escaped. Food yes, and they had originally brought quite a bit of that, but water wasn't even considered. It didn't take them long to realize the importance once they were away from the streams and rivers heading deep into the badlands of what they had learned was the Kansas territory. They had come across a sign somewhere in the past welcoming them to Kansas along one of the old roads. Here Madam knew that they were not traveling far enough to the west and needed to move that way. So using the sun as a guide they went directly that way picking up a major road that was marked seventy. Even though the road showed major damage in a number of areas, where the fires from the sky had destroyed it, and at times making it impassable, they stuck to it.

It was along this road that they found a partially destroyed building somewhat hidden, a place where they spent the night. It was here that they found some items to replenish the meager supplies. It seemed that this had been one of the stopping points along this route. It had been a small store selling all sorts of odds and ends. And it appeared that at one time that this was a jumping off point for hikers and campers. Here they found fishing gear, knives, bows, arrows, and small caches of ammo that would work with what they had stolen, tents, lanterns, and so many other important items. They were surprised that most of it was still here. It appeared that they were the first to have found it and so most of what was here was still here. Now outfitted with packs and bottles for carrying water, and something marked as canteens, fire starting materials, books on survival, and of all things maps. Maps – so many maps! Ones that showed routes, others were topographic, showing the lay of the land, most being local to the area where they presently were, but a few covered surrounding areas far to the west and far to the north., and next to the discovery of the armory that was still ahead and in the future this had been their greatest find.

She smiled as she thought back on all of this because the next find in that partially destroyed building was clothing. None of them had ever owned anything new, or had anything that wasn't made by them or patched from what was passed on from the owners. Here were racks upon racks of outdoor clothing for both male and female. Pants, shirts, jackets, socks, shoes, boots, and those all-important, although most of the time lacking, underwear. She had to admit that this place was like discovering a great treasure. And along with those most important items they found old medicines, and feminine hygiene items from the past. All of them had wondered how women had taken care of that problem, and now they knew. But now what? They could only carry so much, and they knew that if they had found this place, others would. And once others had discovered it would all be gone. Since they were taking their share so it was obvious others would also. Still they spent a few of their precious days here gathering what they considered would be the best for them, packing a few extra packs that they would take with them, and cache somewhere. They'd mark the locations on their maps so they could return some time in the future to recover these precious items.

All three of them were heavily laden with the goods that they had removed from the building and headed back down the I-70 corridor once again, generally following the road but at the same time trying to remain off of it as much as possible. It was along this route that they made three caches of the extra equipment that they were carrying with plans of returning and recovering these supplies. It was soon after the placing of the last cache that they came across their first major city – at least that is what they were called on the maps. There was very little left standing, and all that they heard were the winds whistling down the broken streets and rubble that marked a building. They had approached the area towards dusk and decided to remain outside of this city until they knew more. There was a possibility that people might be living here, scrounging and stripping the carcass of what this place once was and they could not afford to be seen, let alone be captured. So they pulled back into a hidden copse of trees that sat away from the road, and was completely hidden from all directions. That night with no fire to alert anyone, and once it was full dark, they'd come out to the top of the hill that they were behind and see if any fires could be seen alerting them to ones who would still be here in those ruins.

She broke from her thoughts briefly, smiling as she looked at the wall in the darkening room. It was here that once this place had been built that she had framed and then hung the one map that had led them here those many years ago. Looking at it brought her back to those thoughts of that first run to find this hidden place. Yes when they had left that partially buried building they had made sure to remove all the maps and take them with them. They didn't want someone in the future time to locate their planned destination. It had to remain a secret place, and so far it had, but eventually she knew that it would change as all things did. She hoped that when that time came that this place would be too large to become a target of the bad that existed out there. She took a deep breath as the emotions of looking down on that dead city so many years in the past surfaced and it was like they were standing in the darkness searching for anything that signaled that there were still people there, but the area was blacker than the surrounding land. If there were any there at all they were doing a great job of hiding. So with no real sign of occupation the three of them returned to their camp wondering what tomorrow would bring let alone their future.

In the morning they went back up that same hill to watch the sun rise behind them and see what it would reveal in the shadows created in the early morning light. The first thing that they noticed that had been missed in the failing light of the previous day was a river. Somehow if they were to enter this place they would have to find a way across. From what little they knew of their past, it had been said that their ancestors had created bridges to go over such places. Few remained standing, and many still spanned the rivers but were traps for the any who tried to cross – damage had been too great and many had fallen to their deaths. Silently and in awe they began to discern the size of this dead city. It was well beyond anything they had ever imagined. The largest of towns would easily disappear in just one small section of this place. Were there really that many people in the past before the fires from the skies? She felt that if they took all the population that she imagined that still existed that it might, and in her mind it was a slight possibility, might fill this place and still leave empty buildings.

With care, keeping hidden they headed down to that river and behind some of the growth sat and stared at the flowing waters and the great bridge that at one time had spanned over this river, now a rusting hulk with a large gap in the center. It sagged and showed signs that soon it would disappear into the flowing river – a sad reminder of all that had been lost. She wondered what that world had been like, and how her ancestors had ever created such marvels as this dead and dying bridge, let alone the dead city. It appeared that the city followed the edge of the river on the west side as this one seemed to flow generally north to south. One of the most precious items that they had recovered from that store was a compass, well many of them. With the maps and with the compasses it made it easier to plan and then go where they needed. Looking at the map they were presently using they saw that eventually the river changed and flowed easterly further south. So there was a possibility of crossing it further to the north where they suspected it changed direction once again.

As the day progressed and they followed the river their curiosity was growing, that dead city so close and at the same time so far away. That river continued to be a barrier that kept them away from exploring these ruins. Maybe it was one of the reasons for no obvious signs of anybody being here. Eventually they found a place where the river widened tremendously and seemed to flow much slower and seemed to be somewhat shallow at the same time. There were rocks that were above the surface of the flowing water and with care they tried crossing at this point only to find that the rocks were extremely slick and all of them took an unexpected bath when they slipped and fell into the cold water. For whatever reason once they hit the water and found that they could stand, first when they looked at each other soaked as they were, all of them began to laugh, and the youngest Nance who was now getting her adult shape and features started a water fight that helped all of them release much of the stress and tension that had been building over their travels.

Once across they found a copse of trees built a small smokeless fire stripped and hung their wet clothes close to the fire to dry. To their surprise, the packs they were using seemed to be mostly waterproof and their extra clothing was only damp. They gratefully got into their fresh clean clothing with Laura stating, "I guess that river figured that we needed a bath, and our clothes needed washing." All of them had to admit that it had been a while since they had dipped in a stream or river to clean up. After all, their main goal was to reach the" hole-in-the-wall" well before winter and prepare for a tough first winter there. They still did not know what they would find if anything. All three hoped that all they would find was empty land and wild animals, nothing more. It would be such a disappointment to find that others had the same idea and had acted upon that idea and beat them to this hoped for sanctuary.

While their flight had been hard she had to admit that she still had pleasant memories of that flight from slavery. And later in time they had gone back to pick up their hidden caches and to check on that building that had supplied them. With the caches they found were untouched, and as she expected the somewhat buried building had been found by others and had been stripped of anything of value. She smiled as she glanced once again at the wall in the gloom for that framed map that they used to find this place. And that dead city, so large, and nothing more than a corpse that probably had been picked clean by the few survivors long ago in the past still beckoned them to explore. This was something that none of them had ever seen in their short lives.

It was just after the zenith when the clothes finally dried and they were able to repack everything. During this idle time they had reconnoitered the area close to their temporary camp looking for any sign that others had been in the area but the only sign they found were the scat and tracks of small animals, rodents most likely. While their wilderness skills had improved tremendously over the time they had been on the run, there were still many tracks that they couldn't identify. And in their minds it wasn't critical to know all, only the ones that they hunted and the ones that could and would hunt them. Madam looking at the other two asked, "Are you ready for this?" After all it was a worrisome thing. With it being as large as it appeared to be there still could be others living there deep within the ruins and with them only being three women they would be easy targets. It probably would have been a better plan to skip their exploring; still to possibly see how their ancestors had lived their lives was too great a draw to the three of them.

Laura shook her head saying, "I know that it's probably stupid that we do this, but like a bug drawn to the fire at night, something about this place is pulling me in demanding that I look around, to visit. I just hope that it doesn't become a place that we cannot leave."

"I know that we can go around this place," Nancse commented, "but it just seems like such a waste of a chance to see something that won't be around much longer. Look, it's falling in on itself. I think if we are careful we should be okay. Besides we have to go in that direction anyway and if we went around we might run into something that would force us back this way anyway."

Madam knew that it was just the three of them trying to convince each other that they needed to go this way, but in reality it was more they wanted to then needed to. So with some trepidation for what lay before them they headed into the outskirts of this city. The first thing that struck them was the silence. From personal experience, in the villages and towns that they had been in, and even the compound where they had lived as slaves, there seemed to always be background noises that spoke of activity and of life. Here just the gusts of wind as it whistled, the movement of the grasses in that same wind giving illusions of movement, and very little else. As they entered into the ruins they saw that this place had been struck at least twice of not more times which had led to the mass destruction they were seeing. Very little remained standing and much more showed heavy fire damage, and with time nature was slowly taking over. Everywhere they looked were these strange metal hulks that sat by many of the ruins. For lack of a better word they thought that people moved about this place in them so they simply thought of them as people carts.

They came upon an area that was flat with some what appeared to be white lines painted on the surface, and there were many of these people carts here. The gray-black surface was cracked and broken with grasses growing up through those cracks. Here the building that had been here was huge. So large in fact that the whole compound that they had lived in probably would have fit inside of it. What was it that required something this size? From their brief explorations on the edges of some of these individual ruins they felt that it would be completely unsafe to try to enter them. And from the size of some of the rubble piles these building had to been tall, much taller than the tallest in their time which was no more than two to three stories high. How did their ancestors ever build these things? In that rubble they found what looked to be stone and metal, but how it all went together they hadn't a clue. Laura looked at the other two saying, "I don't know about you, but this place depresses me and I'm more than ready to leave."

Madam had to admit that there seemed to be something that lay over the area that was depressing all of them, and if Laura hadn't put it into words she probably wouldn't have figured it out. It then came to her that they were basically in a massive grave yard. The ones who had lived here had no warning of the impending disaster that was about to fall upon them, and within a moment's time they were no more. Looking at Nancse she could see that it was affecting her heavily. "Yeah, I agree. Let's just get out of here. We need to be back into the wilderness by dark anyway." It was obvious that the others agreed totally with her statement. So they picked up their pace and wound their way through this dead place trying to shake the feeling of dread that was now upon all of them. Still it took until darkness for them to transverse this place and they knew that they had only crossed a small section. It left them wondering how much area this place actually covered, but it was an idle question, and one answer that weren't important anyway. And once clear and back into the trees that were slowly encroaching on this place they felt a lifting of their spirits. They went a little further in the darkness to put additional distance between themselves and this city of death before setting up for the night.

Eventually with the tasks of the day, and the frustrations of not being able to leave, taking their toll she felt the fatigue rolling over her, but she dreaded going to bed, afraid that the nightmares would return. Still with her trip down memory lane maybe it wouldn't happen. Yet, she knew that sleep was needed, especially for the tasks that lay before all of them. So with some reluctance she took her final trip outside, and went to bed, thinking. *Has so much time passed since we made that mad dash for our freedom?* She looked at herself, and the shelter she was in, *yes it really has. Where did the time go? It seems like yesterday, really just a short time ago when we came into this place, yet it was years ago – what happened?* These were the last thoughts as she drifted off into a deep sleep.

CHAPTER ELEVEN

Unaware of what was transpiring further east Dan slept through the day undisturbed. It was a nature call that awakened him at dusk. From the fog in his mind and the taste of metal in his mouth he knew that he had slept hard – so hard in fact that it would have been easy for someone to have found him and he would never had heard them. Lying there he stared up into the dimming sky trying to bring everything into focus. Taking deep breaths and letting them out slowly he realized that as uncomfortable as this place was he didn't feel like moving. Yet his bladder was telling him that he'd have no choice. Shaking his head he slowly sat up and carefully peered around to be sure that there was no one in the area quite unaware that two of the scouts had passed by this location much earlier in the day. He was finding new aches and pains thinking. *I'm really getting much too old to be out and doing this kind of thing, and my body is really letting me know.* He grunted slightly as he had a sharp pain in his back. Carefully he worked it out and finally with care left his small hidden shelter and went over to one of those many desert trees and relieved himself. It felt like he could just head back to where he had just left and go right back to sleep. It was difficult to shake off the fog in his mind, and his mind kept drifting – very dangerous.

Moving back to the rocks he sat down trying to come fully awake. He couldn't remember when this was so hard to do – another sign of age that was attacking him full on. It would be so easy just to say "forget it", and simply head back to their hidden shelter, but that still wouldn't answer the questions that needed answers. *Oh yeah, and there's that kid, hmmm, what was his name anyway?* He was finding that this was another aspect of age, the loss of memory, and it sucked. To survive out here memory was critical and any delay in an action or reaction could mean death. *Sam, that's right. Got to go back once it's full dark and meet up with him once again . . . still haven't decided about him yet.* Making a wrong decision might mean the loss of his family and that was the very reason he was reluctant to trust this Sam fully. Yet it was obvious that Sam had lost his family and was now on his own. And it was further obvious that he had been doing well on his own. Still it was a big risk to bring him fully on board.

Yet, their circumstances, and the pressures of the times could force it anyway. And having another to help was a nice idea. But that led to another mouth to feed, and his daughters possibly looking at him as a prospective mate, and he understood that. After all for the last at least a year they were it – just family. And while you could bring more lives into the world with just family it wasn't healthy. *Maybe it won't come up and he won't be there, or if he is then he may want to remain on his own. And who can blame him? After all if there is only you, then you have no one to fall back on, or to worry about.* All of this was conjecture anyway. He found that he was still having problems shaking off those cobwebs in his mind and knew better to remain here until his mind cleared. If he didn't move there was a better chance of not being seen.

He reached into his pack pulling out some jerked meat and began gnawing on it allowing his saliva to soak into the meat. At the same time he grabbed his water bottle and took a slight swig. It would have to be refilled soon. Besides the water was tepid and was beginning to taste bad. *Time to rinse it well and refill it with fresh water,* he thought. Unfortunately he wouldn't be getting close to that river any time soon. Finally with some food in his belly he felt awake enough to head back to the meeting place. While not fully dark it was close and probably safe to move. With a sigh and a deep cleansing breath he headed out. Soon he would know one way or the other, and from that he would have to make a decision, one that had a possibility, in the end, to destroy all that they had.

* * *

With dusk fully upon her Marta worried. Both her mate and one of her sons had yet to return. She really had no idea what she would do if they didn't return. And she didn't know which would be worse, the loss or not knowing that they were dead or alive and have no way of ever finding out. She had stayed outside of the shelter for as long as she dared and it was time to go back inside and put on a brave face for the rest of the family. With all that had been happening, in the last cycle or two, it had been almost as stressful and downright scary as their escape from the destruction of the village. The last couple of years had been so peaceful, so much like it had been before their world had been torn apart, so much so that she had almost hoped, almost felt like they would be safe and not face these difficulties again. And now here they were in the midst of the chaos, the danger, and somehow, and so far while it had been happening all around them, they had been able to remain unseen. For how much longer she had no real idea. And with the number of those raiders they had no chance if discovered. And just who were the three, well for a better word, scouts who kept this army in their sight? What and who did they represent? Was it a rival, or maybe worse part of the same that remained out of sight, hidden, to uncover their next victims?

And Joel had followed two of them, which left the third one. She was sure that both of them stated that there were three. So where was the other one? Was he watching them, ready to report to whomever that he had found others? This thought scared her, because, if she remembered right, both her son and her mate stated that whoever these three were, they were good. This caused her to nervously look around, but then she smiled and inwardly shook her head. To be truthful if he was watching them she would never see him anyway. She knew that shortly Jake would be out to relieve his brother, and then later it would be no one. Dan had insisted that none of the women ever do this since they were one of the specific targets of the bad element that roamed this world. And if one of them had been captured by one from the bad side, there would be little chance of ever finding them – not that they wouldn't try.

She heard the outer door open; still unless one was attuned to the sound it would appear to be just one of the many random sounds that existed in this world. Shortly Jake stood beside her saying, "Mom, you really need to get inside. The others are really beginning to worry and I know that it's tough on you with dad and Joel out, but you know as well as I do that they are good at what they do, and we have to trust them."

She smiled at her son, even though it was forced, and she knew that most likely he couldn't see it anyway. "I know, but I've never been good at waiting and being a woman, a female, it seems to be our lot. I know that it's more dangerous for us to do what they are doing because we become the victims and targets for the others. Especially since they know that they can get away with whatever they want to do, but it's still not easy for me. I think it's the 'not knowing' that's the worst part of all of this. It makes time drag, and until they come back to us I suspect it will always be that way."

Jake couldn't think of anything to say, and simply nodded his head in reply. What she said was true and for this time in their history, and in their lifetime nothing would change. It seemed that in most of the areas the lawless ruled. He knew it wasn't true, but all of them were refugees because of the likes of the ones further east. There had been a girl he had seriously been interested in back when the village still existed, but now she was forever gone. Either dead, or a slave to who knew who, and there was no way to know. Why did it have to be this way? "Guess I better relieve Seth, he's been there most of the day since Joel left. Be sure to go back inside with him when he comes this way. And I'll be telling him that you're out here."

Laughing a little she asked, "So you're going to tattle on your mother are you?" She looked at her youngest son and thought. *He's grown up to be a really nice looking man, and very responsible. I know that he was sweet on that girl back in our past, and we, Dan and I, thought that there was something between them. But fate intervened, and here we are.* "Okay, when your brother comes I'll go with him."

"Thanks mom. Remember that all of us love you, and want only the best for you and dad – at least for what this time allows us." He turned and headed out into the darkness disappearing from sight, and the silence of the night closed in around her once again. Shortly Seth arrived, put his arm around her shoulder and gently guided her toward the entrance.

* * *

Joel had not planned on being out this long, but at this moment in time had no choice in the matter. He suspected that he would be spending the night with the two of them. While it might not be called trust as of yet, at least there was an uneasy truce between the three of them. After all, even more than he and his family, these two and the one who wasn't with them had to be aware of the many dangers that an escaped slave faced. There was no way to remove the mark that was branded on the right hands so they would always be identified as what they were. It made absolutely everyone a potential enemy. At least he was beginning to understand why they kept the raiders under surveillance, and why they might consider him part of the same raider army, but it seemed that they had been observing them long enough to know that he wasn't. Now they were trying to figure out, like he about them, what he was doing here, and why he was shadowing them. He could tell that he had surprised them completely when he asked about the other, but they had hid their reaction relatively well.

The small fire that the three were around and back far enough to sit only in the shadows, snapped and crackled quietly, giving a false sense of peace to the night. The silence at the campsite gave the same impression until one would approach and then it was possible to sense the tension in the air. "So", Joel asked, "where do we go from here? You know that I've been observing you long enough to know your true numbers and that you've been following those raiders. Plus you've pretty much admitted that I'm not a part of them, and that's quite true. But it's left you with the mystery of where I came from and how I know what I know. But these doubts and questions go both ways. There has to be a reason why you've been shadowing those raiders and have remained completely out of sight." He leaned forward briefly into the light to emphasize what he was saying. "When you passed me earlier today and again didn't see me I was curious as to why and what happened to your other member so I followed, slipped and fell, and here we are."

Abe shrugged. He didn't know if this Joel could see him do this in the uncertain light of their small fire. He was still worried that there was more here than met the eye. This one was young in years but not experience. It had proved out when he remained unseen and unknown to them – they who considered themselves very good at this. Yet, like a spirit he suddenly appeared. Even though he knew that it was only through one of those accidents that happen to everybody. If that hadn't happened then the two of them would have no clue that they were being watched like they were doing to those slavers. What to say, what to say, he had to admit he was at a loss. In truth scouting, trailing, and watching was what he was good at not solving problems or speaking. His first reaction when this one became known was to just kill him to protect who they were, but he quickly squashed that notion. There was fluidity to his motion that spoke of one who was familiar with the wild lands and how to defend himself. Taking a deep breath and letting it out slowly he asked, "So where do we go from here? Because of this world and the fact that no one can allow too much trust since it can lead to one's downfall, and as you have seen, our situation, again how do we proceed?"

"Honestly, I don't know." It was a big problem. Too many out there would sell information for whatever advantage it would give them. Joel knew he wasn't one of them, although to protect his family, which was something he was doing right now, he really didn't know how far he would go. And, he had to admit, that giving up something was never any guarantee that the other side would live up to their promises. It seemed that one's word in today's world was worth nothing. He suspected that sometime in the future that it might, or had better change; otherwise they were doomed to eventual extinction. "How does one gain trust in this place when it is something that is broken more often than kept? Yet, I suspect that if we are to get beyond this time in our climb back from the destruction that fell here, those ancient fires that wiped out our pasts, then somewhere a person's word, the idea of extending trust must come to fruition otherwise we are doomed. I don't know any other way of speaking it.

"Being a slave has shown you the bad, and while I've never been one I've had my own taste of the bad when that village was attacked and destroyed. Our, my home was there and it was only luck that kept me from death. I suspect that it was slavers who were responsible. All the signs said so, but I have no proof or any way to get it. Besides, what would it matter anyway? There's no one out here who could bring justice to the ones who suffer at their hands, or are captured and then sold. So it just leads one to survive and avoid others, and not to believe what is said when one meets others, like now. It is a real dilemma, because one wants to trust, to believe that there are others who believe like you do, but one cannot take the chance, so what do you do? Somewhere along the line we have to, otherwise we are dead."

"Yes, trust is a very hard thing. And you're quite right, as a slave you cannot even trust other slaves. Because the conditions are so bad, they will give up anything to have it a little better. And 'accidents' happen to some who go too far. For some a reminder is never enough and they just disappear. And with the marks that all of us have we are forever reminded of what our position is and that we are just property and not people. We're something to be used, and once used up thrown away like trash. It is a life that I wish upon no one." Abe was silent for a moment thinking trying to find a way out but still not coming up with any solutions – *What to do, what to do?*

"This is a very troublesome thing here you meeting us. We had enough complications trying to remain hidden to the ones you are calling raiders. Obviously our concentration was too much on them and trying to avoid them to realize that others were around." Here he stopped once again, not sure how to continue, "Look I would love to trust. In fact I ache to trust beyond what I know, but you've stated it well, this world at the present doesn't allow it. Promises are no better. We've all witnessed the results of this when raiders attack a village or group, and if not immediately successful make all sorts of promises that if accepted the ones who then learn quickly that the promises were no more than the smoke rising in the air and disappearing. Then when they state, 'you promised', all they get is laughter and whatever the ones from the position of strength have planned for them."

"Yeah, but you know what, here neither side is bargaining from a position of strength. The situation is close to equal. Yes I know that there's two of you and only one of me, but its night and I could easily disappear into the darkness before either of you could react and then come back and take you out one at a time, but I have no plans on doing that. I have yet to find out the reason for what you are doing here, and because I'm in the area I need to be aware so that I can avoid any unforeseen problems because of your actions and the actions of those raiders. Does this make sense?" Joel hoped so, because he needed to find a way out of this. Silence followed as no one seemed to be inclined to carry on the conversation. So they remained with their own thoughts and neither side wanting to make the first move that could be a mistake.

* * *

The night was becoming a restless one for Madam. She really hoped that they would be well on their way to whatever destiny lay ahead. But it was not going to happen for a while. The openness of the land made it easy to spot anyone or anything moving, and the size of her army would be impossible to miss. She was beat but her mind wouldn't stop. Angry with herself, she got up and began pacing trying to will her active mind to stop and just allow her to sleep. Eventually she gave up, put on something warm and headed outside to sit in a chair that was on her covered porch. The fresh cool – cold actually – air felt refreshing. She sat in the chair with her head up against the wall of her shelter staring out at nothing in particular. Every once in a while her eyes would catch something moving in the shadows, or see a streak crossing the night sky. Other than the breeze it was quiet. The whole area slept, so why couldn't she? Finally shaking her head and sighing she headed back inside and back to bed hoping that sleep would finally come. And she fervently hoped that the nomads would be gone on the morrow. They really needed to get on the trail. There would be only so long that the window of opportunity would exist where she could remove another scourge from this earth.

* * *

Scar walked through the camp with his second Bear. Their camps were never quiet. With drinking whenever alcohol was found, arguments, fights and disagreements among members of this army, loud snoring, and when they had females even screaming. But one got used to what became the normal sounds. It was a rough group of misfits, murderers, thieves, and whatever else bad that one would think up. He knew that these gatherings of such corrupt souls would break up and go their own way at any time, and there were the beginning signs that this was in the near future for this army. With the failure of the delivery and sale of the ones that they had captured and taken their pleasure upon, the imagined rewards had not materialized, and most had already spent their loot in their own minds. He knew that this loss had been his first major failure with them, and with this attempt to salvage whatever they could from this bad situation it wasn't looking any better. He saw that Bear understood and was patient. Nobody was successful all the time.

Whoever it was that had been living in these ruins had been cleaning them out and caching what they found. They had yet to see or find whoever it was. But from what caches that they had located the feeling was male. This brought further disappointment to the riffraff as they had lost their entertainment to that slave army. Although none of them felt like demanding that their prizes be returned to them. Skar had hoped that there would be enough here to at least allow some recovery of their losses, and that there would be enough buried booze to allow the army to let off some steam – *So far, very little has been located.* Whoever this was had hidden his caches well and this added to the frustration. Turning to Bear he asked, "What's your feeling on all of this? Should we just chalk these whole episodes up to one of those things that happen to everyone and move on, or should we continue to look for those caches? I know that we've added a couple of those ancient weapons, and a bit of ammo for them, but not much else. Whoever it is that was living here had time to go through most of the ruins and get whatever is of value. I feel that we are running out of time."

"I don't know boss. These caches leave a tantalizing sense that there's more and that they would be of more value than the ones that we've located. I know that we are up against time here. Although we've seen nothing that has said that she will reinforce what she ordered us to do." Bear shrugged, "But like you I sense that we are being watched. I even ran up that ridge on the other side of this small lake and up the mountain at night to see if I could catch the light of a distance campfire, but there was nothing. And all the patrols and searching we've done have come up empty. This would normally say that there's nothing here to worry about."

"Yeah, but I know that we are being watched. I don't know how I know, but I do. The problem I face is to who is doing the watching. The one thing we know is that there was someone living here and escaped just before we arrived. I can almost eliminate this one since I've had this feeling of being watched long before we arrived here. And I know that this is desert, although I've never experienced one like it. With that river running through the area there's a good possibility that there are others living out here.

Again we've found no sign. But because we've not found anything doesn't mean that somebody isn't here. In fact there might be hundreds out here and we never the wiser." Skar looked up from their campsite by the lake towards the ridgelines that rose above their location on both sides to see the stars shining and not a sign of life, or of movement. It truly appeared to be a dead world once one left the river.

"I don't know Bear. I have a feeling, a pressure building that says we need to move. But I also sense that this army is just about ready to come apart at the seams. I think that we've had too many successes. Now it is expected and life just doesn't work that way. I suspect that we are in for a period of bad and with what I'm sensing here it will be enough to scatter us to the four winds. I really hope that I'm wrong, but I don't think so.

"So you feel that it is wise to continue to search for these caches. That maybe there's a chance of finding one of the bigger ones and maybe risk the time necessary to locate them. Okay I agree, but we can only remain about one more moon cycle then what we find or don't find will not matter. We will move."

"Works for me boss. There seemed to be a small store here in this place and it has been stripped clean, but from the destruction I would guess that nobody came back to clean it out other than maybe the one who passed the info on to you. But, again from what you said he only took what he could carry and said that he would never go back into these ruins let alone this desert. So I can only conclude that the one who lived here is responsible and has cached it somewhere, and this is the cache I would love to find. Okay then, we have one more moon cycle and at the end we move." At this point both were standing in the middle of the camp not really hearing the activity happening around them. Breaking up they went their separate ways, Bear thinking. *He's sure is on edge. Don't remember him ever being this way. I really believe that he was ready to leave in the morning, to just abandon it. What is it he is sensing anyway?* Bear had to admit that Skar always seemed to have a sixth sense about such things and it was beginning to worry at him. It was time to send out the patrols again.

He found that somehow he was now in front of his tent. *Funny*, he thought, *how names for common things change, and just where had that thought come from?* There were too many other problems so why the stray thought? So names change, after all he personally had changed his too many years in the past to become just Bear. It had been his nickname for a long time anyway, and he felt that it was better to leave his family and heritage and become what he was presently. He knew that if his family, a large clan really, ever knew of the direction that he had taken in his life that they would turn their backs on him anyway. So he did it first and never looked back.

Taking a deep breath he pulled the flap back and entered into his, and he smiled saying the new name, portable shelter.

Skar watched him go and shrugged. The foreboding was becoming stronger and he felt that it was time to leave. Not in a cycle but now. Yet when he looked around the camp, listened to the sounds, walked the perimeter everything appeared to be normal. The camp was never quiet even after a really hard day's work, which was a rare thing. But there had been a number of force marches over time that had consumed great amount of distances running from before dawn to well after dark leaving them all exhausted. Yet, even here this camp never completely slept, or was totally quiet. Somehow as the two of them had walked through the camp they had stopped by the center fire which was close to their personal tents. He watched Bear enter his and with the sense of something terribly wrong still hanging over him he turned and entered his. He needed sleep and if he was to be as sharp as he should he had better get it. But his mind wouldn't let him and all sorts of "what ifs" continued to run through his mind. Disgusted he said out loud, "Stop it!" As if doing this would cause his mind to cease. Finally resigned to it he stared at the flickering shadows on the wall created by the fire outside and somewhere during the time of being mesmerized by the shifting shadows and with his mind finally slowing down he drifted off into a troubled sleep.

* * *

Marta allowed her son Seth to lead her back to their hidden shelter, but her mind was still out with her two men. *Why hasn't Joel returned?* Not knowing what he had run into she had no way to answer, but she hoped that nothing bad had fallen upon him. He might be out there hurt and helpless, but there was absolutely nothing that could be done if this was so. So all she could do was put her faith in his skills and know that there had to be a valid reason for his delay. And her mate, where was he? Again she knew that there was no time limit on him being away. And she realized that what both of them were doing was critical to their personal safety and survival, but that didn't make it any easier.

Once back inside Seth smiled at his mother and saw the worry on her face, but it was always there when any of them had to be away. He guessed it was part of being a woman. Although he knew that men worried also, it wasn't as obvious. He suspected that part of the problem lie in the fact that they had to remain behind while the men went out, so it had a chance to build since there was no way to know what was truly happening or whether the ones away were safe. He had to admit that he had to see his mate and their two daughters and to reassure them that all was right for now. But he really wasn't sure if he should do that because he honestly didn't know. So all he could do was reassure them, and hope for the best.

When he entered the rooms where his family slept he found the two girls asleep in their bed and Tasha sitting in a rocking chair under a soft light pretending to be reading. The only problem was the book that she was holding was upside down. Smiling inwardly he saw that she was worrying also, and it was understandable. While time had passed since that fateful day a few years ago, it was still fresh enough that when they had situations like the one that was around them presently that it brought back those horrible memories of that time. "Tasha", he said quietly, "I didn't know that you read upside down."

She glanced down at the book saying, "So it is. But dear mate of mine, you learn once you have children that you can read from about any angle. If you think about it when they present something to you that they've created and are proud of it, it's not necessarily in a direction that makes it easy for you to see."

"True, but we haven't been together the time that we have not to know each other better than that."

"I can't deny that and truthfully I could use a little encouragement tonight. These last few cycles have been rough on all of us. Your dad is doing the best he can to keep us safe, but there's a good chance all his work can fail in the end. Not his fault, but that's the way life goes. So tonight while our children sleep I need to get very close and feel your body next to mine to allow me to escape even if it is only for a very short time from all of what is happening around us at this time. I know that after we've enjoyed each other the real world and its problems will still be here and nothing will have changed . . ."

"Yeah, I understand. For at least a couple of minutes we will be in our own private little world where only you and I matter and the rest will have to wait. I'll go clean up and join you in our bed shortly. Then he smiled a wicked smile, "And for our sake may our daughters stay asleep. I think that we need our time together uninterrupted so that we can concentrate on each other." He quietly left the room heading for the shower area.

She watched him go, looked over lovingly at their daughters who were dead to the world, sprawled in awkward positions, partially uncovered and all she could do was shake her head, *To be able to sleep that way what a gift.* She got up and headed for their area within the same room, the same space with only a curtain dividing the area. *We are going to have to be quiet*, she thought. *Too bad really, because there are times that I could scream in joy. Oh well, such is the life of parents.*

* * *

The night was cold and he found that he hadn't dressed warm enough. Jake decided that he would just suffer. At least by being somewhat chilled he would remain awake. Even with all that had been happening around them and the few times someone had passed close to their hidden home they remained somewhat untouched. Even though it had been this way up to now it might change in a moment's time and their family could be destroyed. He surely didn't want to be the instrument of that destruction. So for now it was only he and Seth that would watch, to guard, to warn if some danger was near which meant that it would be after the mid-point in the night before Seth returned to relieve him. Fortunately he became most chilled when the soft breezes would reach him, and because of their location for watching he remained mostly out of them. He was shivering when Seth came to relieve him. Looking up at his brother who was smiling and shaking his head he heard him whisper, "Now you know what mom has always said, bring something warm and even if you don't need it at least you would have had it if you did. And I can tell you didn't do that and you have suffered because of it."

What could he say, since every word of it was true, "Yeah, I know, at least it kept me awake and that's more important than my comfort. It's been quiet, not even a night bird flew by. Guess overall it's a good thing. I think I'd rather be bored than face that fear, tension, and flight once again. And if we did have to leave I know that the odds of finding anything like this would be so high that our success would be zero."

Looking around in the dim light Seth knew that what his brother just stated was fact. He didn't know why they were allowed to find this one, but to have it happen once again seemed impossible. "Before you freeze, better head inside, get something hot to drink and maybe a hot shower to remove the chill. We, you and I, are all the stands between until dad and Joel return. I really hope it's soon. This not knowing is tearing mom apart on the inside. I know that she puts on a good front, but we know better. Still we cannot let on that we know, although I suspect she knows anyway.

"We have our women to protect. I know my mate Tasha is the only one who is not directly related, but with our children she might as well be blood. I think I understand so much more now as a mate, as a father to my daughters. I know that I would fight to my death trying to protect them. But we are too few and it would be futile, and in the end they would suffer a fate worse than death. We saw the results or at least part of the results when slavers wiped out that village killing all the adult males and removing all the women and children. It isn't a pleasant future, and one I definitely do not want for our family. Okay bro, I got this. Be back just after the sun rises after you eat. It's going to be long shifts until the others return and it's just you and me between them and us."

Jake left gratefully heading back to their shelter. It wasn't real close since they did not want to tie the location of the shelter with their lookout post. *It's so fortunate,* Jake thought, *that whoever built this place really thought about how the lay of the land would help conceal a shelter.* It was located in such a place that anybody, even standing right on top of it wouldn't give it a second thought. It just didn't appear to be a place where anybody would build such a hideout. With a slow careful hike he found that after about ten minutes he was approaching their home when he heard the flapping wings of one of those night birds, stopped a moment and continued to listen until he heard it no more. It was then that he realized that the hike had warmed him and he was no longer chilled. With one more careful look around he entered into the shelter deciding to skip all the suggestions his brother had given him and go straight to bed. He needed to be sharp when he relieved him in the morn, and in the light of day to be ever so much more careful.

* * *

Madam awoke in the grayness of the dawn shaking and soaked with sweat. *Damn, that nightmare came back again.* She honestly wished that there was some way beyond it. Her real problem lay in the fact that it was based on what had happened to her so many years in her past. It was one of the reasons that she hated raiders and slavers in particular. And every time that she and her army rescued any from the grips of them inevitably she would have to relive, in her dreams that time in her life that had been the beginning of her personal misery and slavery.

It had been a beautiful late spring day and she had just turned nine. She had two younger brothers who had remained with other family members. They were hidden deep in a forest where they had seen no others for a very long time. She remembered begging her parents to go out where those wild berry bushes had to be ripening and it would make a great dessert for their evening meal. She knew nothing of what transpired in the adult world and was innocent of such things. And for a day that started out as one of happiness and being carefree it ended with just the opposite. Fortunately for the rest of the ones who were living in this area the place where the berries grew wasn't close. She suspected that it was the only thing that had saved them. She remembered the sweet smell of the flowers, and of the colors that surrounded her. The breeze was cool in the warming temperatures – temperatures that spoke of summer just over the horizon. Maybe they had gotten careless, or maybe not, but for whatever reason once they had reached the bushes deep in the forest all three of them relaxed and were enjoying the peace that surrounded them at that moment. Unfortunately it wasn't going to last.

The three of them had a quiet mid-day meal when her mother asked, "Well daughter, do you think we have enough of these berries?" Her mother had always seemed short when standing next to her father. She now realized that this was because her father was so tall, and that because of his frame it made it appear that he wasn't. She realized that her height and her build had to have come from his side of the family. Although in retrospect she knew that her mother wasn't short for a woman either. Together their influences insured her size.

She remembered laughing, and realized that this would be the last time she'd laugh for many years. She remembered begging them to just get a few more so that they would have a few days' worth. Had they left at that point and returned back to their hidden shelters then she wouldn't be here at this point in time. Who knew that such a decision would change all of their lives and after this day was over that she would lose both her parents and the world became dark and ominous. She remembered her father smiling and teasing her saying that they had enough to feed everybody back there for at least seven days. But in the end he relented and they stayed. By the middle of the after zenith they were quite loaded and began their return. It was shortly after this that the hell in her life began and she learned the harsh lessons of life and slavers. In a way she was grateful that they hadn't gotten further. At least it meant that they were the only three to suffer the cruelty of these animals. She had no better word for them. Although even animals treated others better and remained within their nature.

It was then they heard a voice ask, "Well, what do we have here?" It wasn't a nice question the way it had been asked and she knew that they were in deep trouble – although how deep she wouldn't know until later. Her father only said one word – "Run!" They tried but there were too many. Where they had come from and the reason that they happened to be in this area she never learned, but in short order they were captured. She fought hard trying to get away, but a nine year old girl, no matter how strong, wouldn't be able to break away from the likes of these. And they were none to gentle, again with what would be happening later this was just a taste. It was the beginning of her learning fear and hate that remained with her all of her life.

They were brought back to a large camp. She guessed that there had to be at least twenty to thirty dirty unkempt men here and there was a strong unpleasant odor speaking of a lack of concern for any who were here. She heard one speak that she suspected was the leader. "So I see we have some entertainment for tonight, and the beginnings of our next supply of slaves to sell in the markets to the east. Who'd have expected to find such as these out here? After all we were just cutting across to save some time before we went after others to add to our collection." This brought out a laugh from many, and she had to admit at this moment she really hadn't a clue to what he was talking about. They were all thrown into separate cages and she found that she was scared to death. She didn't know what would be happening shortly but whatever it was it wouldn't be good.

Her thoughts were interrupted when there was a knock on the door. With difficulty she tried to shake off the remnants of the nightmare, took a deep breath, pushed herself off the bed looking down at her nightclothes and seeing that they were soaked with sweat. She stumbled across to the door and opened it seeing her second standing there.

"You look like hell," the second said. "Must have been one hell of a night . . . That nightmare again?" It wasn't the first time he had seen her like this and it had always been that one particular nightmare that did this to her.

"Yeah," was all that she said. Taking slow deep breaths she tried to wake up fully, but the cotton that seemed to be in her mind wouldn't leave. "What's happening?"

"At first I figured this would be good news, but looking at you right now I'm not sure. Anyway, words from our guards – the gypsies are moving . . . Looks like we will be able to head out later today, once they clear the area."

CHAPTER TWELVE

With the gray of dawn Joel felt the need for additional sleep. It had been a horrible night and he was sure for the two in this small hidden camp it wasn't any better. Since that trust they had been speaking of the night before didn't come about in one day or one night. This world, as it now existed, didn't allow it. Too few left and no one that would hold another accountable, and with these conditions it seemed to bring out the worst. Taking a deep breath he stared at nothing trying to make his mind work, he needed to figure out something that would allow this tense situation to end, but how? He saw that the two at the small fire that had burned to coals and mostly white ash were looking as bad as he probably did. At least he thought so considering how he felt. "I need to leave, and since, as I've said, I know that there are three of you and I haven't informed that army of raiders of you being in the area it should be enough to know that I won't."

Abe felt that he had been run over by one of those wild cows who were unhappy with him being here. It had been a horrible night – stranger in the camp, and one that seemed to know more than he should. Just how did he know about the other one, the one that was still watching the slavers? It had been a shock that out of nowhere he asked that question. He was worried that the three of them had been careless but no matter how he searched his mind or went over their past coming into this area he didn't find anything to suggest it. He could have denied it but it was obvious that this Joel knew. And again he understood it. For one to survive out here it was necessary to know as much as one could about who was around you, and what the countryside consisted of. If you did not, then, most likely, your chances of seeing the next sunset or sunrise diminished tremendously. Fools did not last long in this present world. Even the best were surprised or caught off guard and the best of plans would easily go astray – that was the way of life, and death.

He also had to face another issue and because of this it complicated this already convoluted situation. It seemed to be simple at the beginning. After defeating the slavers in that one battle, even though they were unable to complete the job at that time, to scout them out, to follow, to remain out of sight until the full army could be brought to bear seemed straight forward. Yet, as Madam had suspected the slavers hadn't left, and with the brief contact made he had expected them, their army to already be here, and they weren't. He knew that with the ones that they had rescued that there were many injuries and that it would be a slow trek back. But knowing Madam he knew that once the word was given then she would be eager to return and wrap this nasty business up.

It wasn't that he looked forward to the battle that lay in their future; he just wanted this to be done so that they could return to what he considered his home. So many twists and turns on this journey already, including this one sitting across the dying fire from him. His hard statements ringing of truth, but he had no proof that anything he had said was in fact truth. Yes it was obvious that he knew about the ones that they watched, and that there were three of them, but that might have been a recent discovery. The rest could easily be a guess with him trying to get information from him about their plans. *What to do? What to do?* In a way he wished that the one that they had left to watch was here. This was more to his abilities while he and the one with him were better at hunting and taking care of the meats afterwards. That meant that that one's skills were better served on keeping them under surveillance than being here helping them get food. "Look, I know we keep going over the same ground time and time again. I think that you can understand why. With these marks we are forever a target, and it would be easier to kill whoever discovers this. Of course that leads to other problems. Problems that can make it worse than just being an escaped slave, such as being tagged a murderer or killer. And as always seems to be the way, the word does get around. I'd love to let you go and pretend that this never happened, and yes I know that it would be easy for you to leave and that there is a great possibility that you would escape, yet there is just as great of a chance that you would get hurt or killed as much as it is for us." Abe stretched his tired muscles; he was getting too old for this. *In fact,* he thought, *once this assignment is over I think I'll bow out and let some of the younger ones take over and maybe stay back home and just pull guard duty now and then.*

He came to a decision at that moment. He saw that the other with him was leaving it all to him. But first he needed some additional reassurances and get a couple of other questions answered. "I believe you when you say that you were following us since we have confirmation of that. I know not by choice but by accident that you sit here. We've all faced such disasters and sometimes we live and sometimes we don't. I just have a problem with other parts of your story. You say you are just passing through but your knowledge is too great for one who is doing that. I suspect that you are protecting others, and that is one point that I understand completely. Truthfully if I had family around, or loved ones or others that require protecting then I would be doing exactly what you are. So I suspect that is what we are facing here. Again it comes down to the little word – trust. I can almost see that this is probably closer to fact just by your reaction. No you haven't really given yourself away, but your attention grew sharper when I mentioned this. And you know that we are not or cannot say too much either again because of that little word. Until yesterday we didn't know each other, and from the looks of all of us we still don't and we have no trust at all.

"From your need to get away, it is another sign to me that you have someone waiting for you. After all, if you didn't, spending a day or two with us wouldn't change a thing and it would give each side a chance to learn more about the other. So it seems to me that we are both protecting something. I'm sure that if you do have a family or others close by that when all of the chaos arrived it has left everybody worried. Especially if what you described earlier is fact, and I don't doubt it. After all, this desert would be a great place to escape to. Very few would come through it and if they did they would stay to the known trails. We all know to leave them in the desert is one way to commit suicide. So to have all of this descend on one would make any of us nervous. Since you know who we are you must come to the conclusion that we have a place similar that we would never reveal. And if something like this came down upon us there we would want to know why, and attempt to come up with any way to protect our assets."

Joel listened carefully. This Abe was making sense, but again should he trust him enough to reveal what he was guessing? He, even if it meant his life, had to keep his family safe. So what could he reveal? This Abe wasn't stupid and his conclusions were dead on, and even though he had tried to hide it, somehow he had given himself away. So what would he feel comfortable with giving up as far as information was concerned? "Go on", was all he said, trying to see where this was going.

* * *

The shifts he and his brother were dealing with at this time were very difficult. But what can one do, after all with both dad and Joel away and with no idea when either would return or, heaven forbid, not return, they had no choice. Soon his brother Jake would be relieving him, and he had to admit that it had become difficult to remain awake. Night was the time to be sleeping, to recharge, but with the situation still completely unknown there was no choice. He felt his eyes burning from the lack of sleep and he was sure that if he could look at them they'd be red. At least he hadn't inherited the dark circles that his mother had when she didn't get enough sleep. He smiled inwardly as he could almost hear his mother complaining about them.

Slowly his subconscious mind began to pick up a sound that wasn't natural and he realized that there was someone out there. This brought him wide awake and he hunkered down straining to hear and to determine where the sound was coming from. At this point it was too subtle to be able to determine the direction let alone the source. Eventually the sound became louder and he determined that it had to be someone carefully hiking in his direction. Suddenly the sounds quit and this panicked him for a moment. Had he given himself away? Other than his brother and father there was no one out here that could be considered a friend. He strained harder to try and pinpoint the location, but with no movement it was impossible. He was almost afraid to breathe thinking that the very act would give him away. So he took slow shallow breaths while looking around. *Still nothing!* Whoever it was that was out there had to be good. He felt that he was decent at doing this and better than most. Yet, he knew that he would never be as good as his father or brother Joel.

He didn't want to fail here, and with the change in guard coming soon, he didn't need his brother Jake walking into something. It was easy to be too relaxed as you came in to take your shift never thinking that something might be going on. They all had spent too much time doing this assignment with nothing happening, and even a chance of something happening. Now if he came in here unawares it might undo everything that they had done, revealing their hidden oasis to all. As cool as it was he could almost feel himself sweat. *Why now, why just at this time?* Suddenly standing right before him was someone hidden in the shadows, and his first reaction was he had been discovered, but just as quickly he realized that the one standing there was his father. He didn't know how he knew but he did. His father crouched and whispered, "Go get your mother and return here. Do this quickly if you please." He heard the fatigue in his voice, and had too many questions, but immediately left as he had been requested.

Dan watched him as he left until he disappeared into the darkness. Dawn wasn't far off and he needed this to be over before the light of day exposed everything. He couldn't remember when he felt this tired. In his mind there was still too much that was unknown. He really needed to be updated to what had been happening since he had been away, and was frustrated that he had returned with so little to help them.

She was really deep in sleep. The first half of the night she had tossed and turned unable to get comfortable. She still worried heavily about her mate and all the unknowns tied to that situation. Every little sound seemed to be magnified and she stared up at the ceiling in the darkness wide awake. She didn't know when it happened but somewhere through this restlessness she had drifted off to sleep and now there seemed to be a voice that was urging her to wake up. It had to be a dream and she wanted to simply sleep now. But the voice was insistent and finally something was gently shaking her. As she slowly dug out from the depths of her sleep she realized that the voice was from her oldest son and as consciousness came to her she asked through a raw throat, "Yes?" She realized to have a sore throat she must have been snoring – something she always denied, but knew that everybody did. Then a thought crossed her mind. *This is highly unusual, is there a danger or did someone get hurt?* This brought her wide awake and she sat up and immediately regretted it. For a moment she was dizzy as the blood caught up with her. "Something wrong?" She asked.

Seth shook his head, although he realized that she couldn't see it in the darkness of the room. "Not that I know of, but dad is out at the outlook and wants you there immediately. He didn't say why . . ."

"He's back?" She asked incredulously.

"Yeah, but I don't know much more than that."

Taking a deep cleansing breath and trying to shake the cobwebs out of her head she said, "Okay, give me a few moments to come to life and I'll meet you out in the hall and you can take me to him." She watched as the shadow that was her son left, swung her legs over the edge of the bed and headed for the necessary room to take care of nature and get dressed with none of this taking very long. Shortly she met Seth in the hallway and he led the way back outside and when the cool night air struck her she shivered because of the difference. She saw that Seth had noticed so she smiled and whispered it was just the change in temperature from inside to outside and that she would be fine. "Why did your dad not come in? I mean I would have expected him to come to bed and not do this. Is he hurt or something?"

Shaking his head Seth shrugged. "I can't answer any of those questions mom. He came quietly out of the darkness and once I recognized who it was, he asked me to get you and bring back. As to why I don't know. He looks tired, which is no surprise, but said no more."

* * *

He didn't know where it came from, this sixth sense of his, but for whatever the reason it was one of the reasons for their success over time and it was screaming at him right now warning him to get out. In fact it had snapped him right out of a deep sleep and left him wide awake staring wildly around trying to locate the danger. Yet, all was quiet, nothing more than the normal night camp sounds. *Not going to get any more sleep now*, he thought. Skar got up from his sleep sack and because he was fully dressed headed out in the cool darkness of the night. He really had no idea what time of the night it was. It wasn't like the daytime where one could follow the progress of the sun and feel the heat, which helped one to know. The night, other than when the moon was full had no such clues. Yet, from the silence of the camp he suspected that it probably was getting towards dawn. Another sign that it was this late lay in the fires themselves. Most were down to coals. With no one up to maintain them they had burned down to almost nothing.

He went to the closest one and threw a few sticks on it causing sparks to rise into the sky. Even though he knew better he stared into the coals watching the few sticks he had added begin to burn. It had always fascinated him how fire consumed its victims. One of the guards, seeing the flaring of one of the fires, curious headed over and saw Skar sitting by it and staring into the fire. He approached cautiously and asked, "Why are you up boss? It's still a while before the sun rises above the ridges."

Skar looked up and glared at him and saw the guard pull back a little. "Sorry, didn't mean to look at you that way. Was awakened from a deep sleep and couldn't go back to sleep so that's why I'm here. Something awakened me and I can't figure it out – didn't expect anybody to notice."

Concerned since he and the rest knew of his premonitions and the subsequent successes that they had because of them he asked, "Is all okay?"

"As far as I know, but I've been getting a feeling that's been building and I don't know why or what it means yet. Believe me when I know, all of you will. So let's just chalk it up to nerves right now. We've hung around this place longer than almost any other place that we've been. So maybe it's just because of that. When one is in the business that we are in it's never wise to stay in one place too long. Although out here in this desert there's no one around to let anybody know that we are here. As you know we've made a lot of enemies over time and one I don't want to face again anytime soon is that Madam and her army."

"I know that they surprised us and that's why they won, but why would she and what runs with her scare you?"

"You weren't there when we faced her. There's a passion and fanaticism for what she does. You can read it in her and it was obvious that the others who were with her have it also. Bear, who was with me, both of us saw and felt it. They will follow her into the depths of hell itself if she felt it's necessary. And you must realize that they have nothing to lose."

"Nothing to Lose? That doesn't make sense. All of us have something to lose . . . Our lives if nothing else."

"You've never been a slave so it's something that you'll not understand. Since they are all escaped slaves they know that if they are caught that only death awaits them. So whether it is from being recaptured or from fighting the result is the same. Thusly, nothing to lose, and nobody that they can trust – not even each other. Once you've been living that life you learn that anybody and especially another slave will sell what he or she knows for whatever small advantage it might bring. Of course, that isn't a safe thing to do since one cannot be protected all the time and retaliation from others will always come in its time."

"Guess I never thought about it that way." The guard waited a few moments to see if Skar had anything further to add, but he remained quiet and staring into the fire. When it was obvious that nothing else would be said he headed back out somewhat disturbed, but the night had been quiet and his shift would be over soon, then some sack time before joining one of the parties that was searching for the caches that whoever had been living here had hidden. He knew that soon they would be moving on to the west and maybe south looking for another village to ravage and captives to sell into slavery. What they gathered here would be just a small respite, something to allow them to resupply at one of the many places where their kind were welcome. With a little left over to at least get some alcohol, even though it could barely be called that and blow off a little steam. Not enough for a female in one of the houses so if they had interest in that direction it would have to be with the next village that they attacked and ravaged.

Skar watched him go back to his assigned duties. He should have remembered to ask him what time of night it was, but had forgotten. He knew that he would be on edge this day whenever day arrived, and his patience would be nonexistent. No matter what he did there was no way to remove that dark cloud that had been building for days. Trouble was brewing in their future and he suspected that it was the same trouble that had struck them in the recent past. But he could be completely wrong. But there had yet to be any proof other than his feelings that they were being trailed, being followed, yet his was sure of it. He looked back into the fire and realized that the few sticks that he had added were consumed and he was bathed in shadows once more.

He found that he was restless and couldn't sit here any longer. Looking around he decided that the camp wasn't a place he needed to be at the moment so he headed out of the camp letting the guards know that he was out. With no real destination in mind he found himself by the small lake. If the mythology was right this had been created by one of those ancient fires falling from the sky. He wondered how it must have been to realize that one of them was just about to strike close to where you were living. Then he laughed at himself. The few that he had seen streaking across the sky spoke of a speed that wouldn't give one time to realize such a thing was going to happen. The only warning would be the glow of the impact followed by the sound and heat, and then the blast would destroy everything close by. No time to even realize that your death was at hand. Kind of like when that slave army hit them although much quicker. He heard the water lapping the shore as the river pushed through it to continue to wherever it went. At times he was curious and thought it would be something he'd like to do, follow one to its source, but it was something that would never happen.

He pulled back a little from the water's edge and heard something moving in the distance. The light was too dim to be able to see what it was, and curious he slowly advanced towards the sound keeping his hand poised over his knife should he need it. Soon he began to discern some indistinct shapes and realized that it was a small herd of wild cattle grazing close to the river. He suspected that by dawn, whenever that would be, that they would be gone. All that meat and with time they'd jerk much of it. He turned and looked up the ridgeline that he only identified because it blocked out the stars and presented a darker area. Something up there held his interest. Might it be that the ones following them, scouting them were up there? He thought that he could see a slight flickering glow of a fire, but realized that it was close to the top and could just as easily be a star . . . So no answer there. He remembered that Bear had stated that he had climbed the ridge the opposite of the lake, close to their camp and had seen nothing.

So, was all of this uneasiness just him, or was something about to happen? He really wished he knew. He had learned long ago to trust his instincts, as they had saved him a number of times. But there were other times when nothing happened even though he had a strong feeling that something would. Maybe in those times of failure he had changed his direction, his destination, and because of these changes had avoided whatever it was that his sixth sense had warned him about. He just didn't know. It would be nice if the feelings would be more exact instead of the heavy vague uneasiness that lay upon him. He needed to talk with Bear again. He needed to have something happen to ease this foreboding, but all was quiet and seemed to be quite normal. Withdrawing from the wild herd he walked around the other side of the lake until he reached the edge of the fast flowing river. Here he could only hear the moving water, and like the fire watching the water flow catching starlight now and then and the splashing of the moving water he briefly became mesmerized and stared out at nothing.

He was in deep thought when he heard someone approaching and turned back looking in the direction of camp. There silhouetted against the camp he saw a shadow approaching and from the size he knew it was Bear. For a man of his size he moved silently and many learned of this skill just before they died. He waited as Bear approached. What brought him out? Was he feeling something also? He didn't have long to wait. He saw that Bear was aware that he was being watched. "So", Skar asked, "what brings you out here on a lovely night like this?"

"You", he simply said. Bear continued his approach until he was standing next to Skar. He turned and faced the camp as Skar was presently doing. He gestured back towards the camp saying, "The guard you talked to felt that you were uneasy about something and eventually it worried him enough that he came and woke me. He passed on some of what the two of you were talking about, and that he sensed that something was wrong. So he decided to get me and here I am. So what's happening boss?"

* * *

As Marta continued her walk with her son she really wondered why Dan hadn't just come back in. *Was he hurt, had he discovered something that might be a problem, was there an immediate danger to them? Oh stop it Marta! You know better than this, the answers will be given shortly. Just go and I'll have my answers.* Even with the walking she found that she wasn't warming yet. That night desert air really chilled one unless you were out in it for a while. Eventually they reached the perch where they kept watch and she saw the silhouette of Dan and she knew it immediately. She tried to restrain herself, but to see him standing there safe caused her to choke up with emotion. But she held back from running to him although it took all of her will. Finally after what seemed an eternity she was next to him, reached out and hugged him desperately. She had really missed her mate and to have him back in one piece and to actually be here was all she wanted at this moment. In a way she wished that they were the only two because she would really tell him and show him what she thought, but that wasn't possible. Finally she asked, "Why didn't you just come in?"

"Because lady of my life, I needed you here."

She laughed lightly and quietly saying, "I thought that was what the bedroom was for."

He cocked his head to the side as he smiled, "True, but this time it isn't quite that need. Although the offer is something I can't refuse." Taking a slow breath and letting it out he continued, "No that's definitely hard to refuse." He paused a moment. "Sorry but you distracted me from what I need of you. I found something when I went to keep track of that army, and before we invite this something in I need your advice and opinion."

"Can I assume that this something is a person?"

"Yes you can. I have him waiting a short distance from here. I wasn't willing to compromise our oasis until someone else checked him out and I've always found that you're a pretty good judge of character."

Smiling teasingly she said, "Oh I don't know about that. After all I picked you the rogue that you are."

"Me? Rogue? I don't think so. I mean I think we've done pretty well over the years."

"I can't complain about our time together and the care that you've always shown me and our family, but my parents didn't consider you good enough for me, but I knew better and we proved it, in the end. So who is this person by the way?"

Oh someone around eighteen who has lost his whole family to raiders and had barely escaped. He found a place to hide and make his own only to have these raiders invade his home. He almost didn't escape and he suspected that they figured out that he was male so didn't pursue to hard. I suspect, as well as he that if he had been female that they would have torn these hills apart to find her. But with them ripping into everything and going through the ruins there is no place for him to go at this time. From what I've learned he and his family were herders, and had been with a larger group of the same. They had taken their animals out and away from the others looking for some better grazing when they were attacked and killed. He happened to be away, kind of like us, when it came down so he was able to escape. Although he watched as they killed everybody. He never learned if they backtracked and found the rest or not. But he couldn't take a chance and headed out his own eventually finding those ruins and living there for a couple of years – Just a little shorter period of time than us.

"We've spent a few nights talking, and trying to see if we could trust each other. It's quite obvious that he hasn't been around people in a long time. It seems that he wondered around for quite a while avoiding anyone that he saw before entering this desert and stumbling across the ruins close to that river. So after careful thought I asked him to accompany me and haven't told him too much more than that. With him now over in one of the side canyons he isn't aware of us or how many of us are here. So, are you willing to check him out? If you accept him then I'll feel comfortable in bringing him in."

"Well, why are standing here? Lead on oh mighty mate. You've made me curious now, and you know women, if we are curious we want answers."

"Yes ma'am", Dan answered. He turned and with his mate headed off into the darkness as Seth watched them disappear. *Another one out here in the desert, who'd have thought? I really thought that we were it at least until these raiders showed up.* Once they were out of sight he went back to watching. He really had no idea how long they would be gone or what the outcome of the encounter would be. Yet, one way or the other eventually there would be an answer.

* * *

Joel stared at the two who still remained a safe distance across the fire from him. There had to be an answer to this impasse, there just had to be. "Look, I know you're here to add to your dwindling food supply and that once that is accomplished you will move on. So why not leave it at that, and I'll leave, going where I was going before finding you two, how does that sound?"

Looking across that fire Abe knew that dawn wasn't far off and they were definitely at an impasse, so what to do – really, what to do? He wished that the second was here or maybe Madam herself, but he really didn't know how far away they were or if they were close enough that it wouldn't matter how this played out. At this moment everything was up in the air, and he really didn't know enough to feel safe around this Joel. Yet, why not? Why not just let him leave. Had he not fallen they wouldn't have been the wiser anyway. Maybe there was another way out of this, but dare he even think it? It was a dangerous idea. If this one was actually part of the slavers he would be giving himself to them freely, and he knew what his future would be then. Still this one didn't have that taint that seemed to be part of the raiders and slavers. He almost trusted him just by who he was, and that was very dangerous. He knew that there were many who would lie through their teeth and give the appearance of being totally truthful. Madam had pointed that out to him, in the past before the fall, before the ancient fires, there were people known as politicians, whoever they were, who made their living by this method. He really didn't believe her, it had to be a tale, a myth, after all what would such benefit anyone?

He saw that Joel was waiting for his answer but he really wasn't sure what answer to give him. So pushing for additional time to continue his thinking he said, "I don't know. I just don't know, after all neither you nor I have any proof that we are who we are saying we are. I suspect that had you not fallen then we would not have been aware of you, and you would have returned to wherever you came from and we would have been hunting both of us going about our business, but that's not what happened. We haven't been hunting, which, as you have so aptly pointed out by showing me that you knew that there were three of us instead of the two that sits before you, so he would be expecting us back soon. But by delaying what we are doing then it could lead to his worry when we don't show up when he expects.

"Then we, and I include you in this we, are faced with the fact that I suspect you have someone waiting also. I know I have no proof other than the way you reacted when I stated it. So I suspect that soon you will have the same problem. If this is the way of things then, as usual, what happens with the ones that are not here are beyond yours or my control and they might come looking, get the wrong impression, and what might have worked out for the benefit to both of us could go south even further."

Joel listened and cursed himself for reacting like he did, but there was nothing he could do about it. He knew from scouting that one learns to see and interpret subtle movements and reactions, much more than the average person out there. He suspected that if they hadn't been as he they wouldn't have caught his reaction. So now he was stuck. "I feel that you're heading towards something here, but I'm not sure what that might be, so please continue."

Laughing a nervous laugh Abe said, "To tell the truth, I'm not quite sure where I'm going with this either, but somehow we've got to solve this and soon otherwise we can sit by this fire staring at each other until we are dead and still not solve anything. So one side has to give in a little and maybe . . . maybe put forth a small seed of trust but not so much that it leaves one vulnerable to the other side."

Still suspicious, as he suspected that they were of him Joel said, "Go on."

Abe really wasn't sure where he was going with this either. He found that he was making this up as he went, but did he dare go where this was leading, and that was the real question. He turned to the other scout signaling him to remain sitting, carefully rose, stretched since he was beginning to cramp a little, and paced a bit as he worked through this in his mind. "Okay, here's what I propose, and I hope that neither of us pays for this, how can I say it – stupidity? And I really cannot believe that I'm even suggesting this, but here goes. With what both sides are facing we will solve nothing. So I propose that the two of us head back to where you came from and leave my companion here to do what the two of us were originally going to do. That once we have determined the truthfulness of each other, then once satisfied, we can continue whatever it is that we had originally planned on doing."

Alarmed at what was being suggested, Joel realized that what he was offering, while a concession on his part, meant that he would be exposing his whole family to an unknown danger. He still had no idea what or who these scouts worked for or represented? Did he dare, was it worth the chance? After all, all of them knew that eventually they would have to leave their hidden shelter and seek out others. By staying where they were, yes they were safe, it was a dead end and eventually if they remained long enough the desert would take them one by one until they were no more. *What would dad do in this situation? He has so much more experience in such things.* But, as he was well aware, dad wasn't here and the decision would have to be his and his alone. He leaned forward putting his elbows on his crossed legs. He knew that it gave the appearance, sitting cross legged like this, that he was sitting in such a way that prevented his leaving with any speed, but he knew better. It was something that his father had made him practice, rising from this position and disappearing before others could react.

He raised his right hand and put his chin on his thumb thinking. He always did this and inwardly he shook his head, why did he? It was a dead giveaway and he noticed that he wasn't the only one who did it. Maybe it was something he had learned from his family, he wasn't sure, but he noticed that this Abe did it also. So maybe it was just a common thing. "You're asking me to risk everything here. So while on the surface it seems a simple thing, it is anything but." At this point Joel also stood up, doing it with a slow careful motion so as not to alarm either of them. He then put his arms behind his back and looked down. "Since you and the other two came in this area from the outside you risk very little, while I risk almost too much. Yes you are right, there are more here than just me and I will die before I would betray them, and that's the truth."

"Yes, you're right, we came from the outside. But did you not see that it would be the same for us? As you are quite aware we are escaped slaves and as such our lives and all the lives of our friends and families would be also. So while we may not be close that does not mean that what we protect is any less."

Joel shook his head. "I'm not saying that especially since it is a fact. But that doesn't mean that you couldn't be a part of an army – slave army for the lack of a better term, who would have it in for anybody who isn't or hasn't been a slave. And by me revealing this information for which I haven't confirmed by the way, it would be the death of all that I love."

"No, not by your words, but you did give it away. I just don't know how many may be there, wherever there is." Anger began to rise as this fencing with words was something that he left to others. He preferred action or trailing or scouting to this. He left this to others who were good at it. He fought down the urge to lash out at Joel who was only protecting his own. How could he fault that? And if what had transpired in Joel's past was accurate he had a right not to trust. And knowing the world as he did he suspected that it was the truth. So he forced the irritation down with an iron will took a deep breath and letting it out slowly. "Again from what you saying I think you're wrong, by me coming with you and making sure that he stays here and does what we are supposed to be doing it is just you and me, and no one else and that evens the odds to very equal. We have to solve this one way or the other, and I would prefer for it to be other than violence." Abe shrugged, "Although if it must be that way I can be very violent."

Smiling Joel said, "I'm sure you can – to have survived captivity and now to be free means that there had to have been violence in your past, and in a way a past not much different than mine, except that we escaped. And there is one other difference, being that I'm a grown male I wouldn't be alive. It is well known what slavers do to us. They only want the women and children."

CHAPTER THIRTEEN

Even though they had planned to be on the way a day or two in the past it still took a while to get everything organized once again. Madam was impatient and hated the time lost waiting for the gypsies, or the nomads to leave. In a way she felt lucky that they had only remained at this camp for a very short time. They could have stayed quite a while. Yet she wondered why they had been here at all. This was the first time, in the nine years that they had been here; the nomads had shown up and decided to use this area. Maybe they were beginning to extend their range. She truly hoped not because that would eventually mean a confrontation with them and she did not want to make enemies of these gypsies at all. While not a large group as of yet, still they appeared to be almost everywhere that she and her army had been. And so far there had remained an uneasy truce between the two sides, and she wanted it to remain that way. There were enough issues dealing with thieves, murderers, raiders, and slavers.

So as the sun was climbing into the sky, instead of dawn, they were finally on the trail once again. This time with her full army, and it was understood by any who lived within her protection that they were required to be part of this army – except, of course, the women and children. Bringing them along left them weak and vulnerable to counter attacks and exposed them to possible capture and slavery at the very least. Like they had originally planned the traders were with them to try and purchase and trade for items that they lacked, things that they could not make or provide for themselves. She knew that it wouldn't be violence that ended the way life that existed now, but the needs and trade between communities that would eventually force the bad elements out into the wastelands breaking their hold and their destruction. But until then it would be people like she that would try to keep the chaos under control.

With the late start her plan was simple. They were to push through into the Montana territory, spend the night, then push west and then south to come out of the north to surprise the slavers. Yet to be successful they would have to push from dawn to dark to cover as much as possible and at the same time to avoid any outpost that existed along the way. There had to be no warning to allow their target to be prepared. She wanted this to be quick and dirty and done with complete surprise and as little casualties as possible on her side. Yet, she was realistic enough to know that what she wanted and what happened were two different things altogether. Very rarely did plans work when you finally made contact with your target, your enemy. The goal that first night was to bivouac in that destroyed city where they had found their cache of ancient weapons. It was an armory that had been buried under a collapsed building within one of the many destroyed cities and towns. One of the damaged signs had stated the city's name which was Missoula. Like the other that they had gone through many years in the past it had been completely destroyed. This Missoula sat in a valley surrounded by mountains and the lands were very similar to the high plains of Wyoming. Yet in many ways it was more rugged with lakes jagged peaks and heavy forested areas. There were places where the snow never melted – a land in transition. But she knew that it would now be the second night instead.

The Montana territory was different when comparing it to the Wyoming territory since most of Wyoming was high plains, rolling hills, and quite open, making it easy to spot anything moving – one of the very reasons that they had to wait until the gypsies moved. With the size of her army even with them divided and taking the different passes out of the area they would have been easily spotted and however the nomads did it, all of the different clans would have been aware of their movement. She wished she had the same ability as they seemed to have. Then it would be easy to remain in contact with her scouts. Montana had some of the same high plains areas, but also was part of the mountain range that blocked one from the coast, leaving many areas within the territory heavily timbered and easy to move and remain hidden. And it was very dark when they reached their first planned stop – a day away from Missoula.

The camp was quiet, but again, no surprise there since it had been a hard exhausting push to reach this point. It was decided since they had pushed so hard that they would set guards, as they always did, eat travel rations, and then turn in. No tents or portable shelters tonight, just the stars overhead. She wanted to be back on the trail before the morning sun rose over the hills. In fact she wanted to be well on their way by the time sunlight kissed the earth with its warmth. She heard the groaning and little else. It had been a while since the full army had been on the move. And with simple patrols many hadn't been out in a season, since all rotated to give them as much time at home as possible. But this wasn't one of those times. She picked a spot somewhat away from the rest but not so far as to leave her a target. In truth she was the only female in this army and that was fine with her. She laid out her sleep sack made a final trip outside of camp for nature, slid gratefully into her sack and was almost instantly asleep. Before drifting off she hoped that she was too tired to dream. It was a place where she was helpless and weak and it was a place she tried to avoid. But the nightmare returned.

She stood in her cage scared to death. She was alone and her mother was in another where they could barely see each other. They watched as these bad men tortured him, her father, her mother's mate. He had looked at both of them with despair and pain in his eyes whispering that he loved them, and he was so sorry for what was happening. She could say that she honestly did not know what was happening or what her future was and why they did this. Eventually her father died and these evil men laughed about it. There was a deep anger within her now even though the fear that she felt was overwhelming. What was to become of them, and what of her brothers who happened not to be with them on this day? Would these bad men have killed them too? She watched as they took the body of her father and dragged it out of their camp and dumped it somewhere. He meant nothing to them and it was obvious that they cared less. For them it had been entertainment nothing more and lives were forfeit and were cheap.

Then a number of the men went over the cage where her mother was held, opened it up, grabbed her, and with her screaming and fighting, dragged her off somewhere. It was the last time she ever saw her. Now she was completely alone. There were five who kept glancing her way and she didn't have to pretend to not know why. They had a way of looking at her that she didn't understand until much later in life. But what was about to happen would haunt her the rest of her life. It seemed that they were what her father had called gambling, but for what she again had no idea. She didn't know that it was for and about her. Finally they came over and one smiled an ugly smile at her saying, "My friends here say that I won't be the first but I think they're wrong. They believe that you must be ten or eleven, is that true?"

She didn't know what to say or how to react. She shook from her fear with tears staining her face. Why did her age mean anything? "I'm nine", she croaked out through her raw throat.

Turning to the other four her said, "Ha, I'm right. There's no way that she's been touched before." This brought out ugly laughter from the others. He turned and looked right at her in a way that made her fear even more, even though she didn't think that was possible. She was scared to death right now and could barely control any of her bodily functions. "Then missy, I will be your first, but by no means your last. In fact we share don't we?" This brought out more laughter and it was of the type that caused her to pull back. Again she had no idea what was coming but she knew it was something that she wanted no part, but knew that there was no escape. She remained silent; it was obvious that begging wasn't going to change a thing.

She noticed that one of them had a ragged blanket as they opened her cage and grabbed her. She fought as hard as she could, but what can a nine year old girl do against five grown men? Nothing really, nothing at all. She was at the age of wanting privacy and rarely showed her body to anyone but herself, but they quickly ripped her clothing off leaving her to stand naked before them. She felt something warm running down one of her legs and realized that she was leaking a little bit. If she hadn't been as scared as she was she might have been embarrassed. One of her age didn't do such things. She heard one of them state, "Nine huh, big for her age. Guess that makes sense if that one was her father." With them holding her arms there was no way to hide what was showing and she began to hyperventilate. They dragged her a short distance to a somewhat flat area threw the blanket down and proceeded to pin her there with four holding her arms and legs – legs spread. *What are they going to do?* She still didn't know but had an awful feeling. She struggled but they held her firm and there was absolutely nothing that she could do. She was completely at their mercy and that was one thing that she knew for sure – they had no mercy.

The one who had been talking got down between her legs and wet his finger. He then pushed it up inside of her, which was a shock. Nobody or anything like this had been done to her before. She struggled with new energy but failed to dislodge that finger. He pulled it out and stated, "Got to get something to help here otherwise we won't have our fun." Again this brought out laughter. He got up and disappeared for a moment returning and going once more between her legs. He smeared something and once again slid that finger inside of her which went easier but she didn't want it there at all. He was on his knees and dropped his pants and she saw that thing and screamed. She had an awful feeling what he was going to do and she definitely wanted no part of it. She had seen her younger brothers' things but they were nothing like this.

He got over the top of her, further pinning her, and she could feel that thing come up against her and then he pushed and it began to go inside and she screamed again as it hurt. He wasn't gentle and pushed hard until it seemed that she was going to be torn in two. She fought but found that no matter what she did that it seemed to help him and not her. It was like she was on fire, it hurt so much. Her panic was rising even higher and he began to push that thing in and out of her with each stroke bringing heavy raw pain. She felt herself becoming light headed from her rapid breathing and the sheer pain and fear. Yet he was relentless continuing his pushing and pulling with it increasing in tempo. She didn't know what to do, or how to fight this. It was all new and all unwanted but there was no way out. Finally in what seemed to be an eternity his breathing got ragged and he pushed very deep inside of her, which brought on even more pain, shuddered and was moving no more. It was somewhere along this time that she mercifully passed out and remembered nothing. Later she awoke because she heard someone crying and finding herself back in her cage, still naked, thrown on that dirty ragged blanket, with tears still running down her face, feeling totally torn and broken up inside. It was like she was on fire, like she had been burned. She suspected that it was her crying that had awakened her. She further suspected that once she had passed out that all of them had taken their turn at her. She felt dirty, and there was an odor that clung to her now. She had heard the word rape before but until now it had only been that – a word. Now she fully understood and wished what had just happened to her on no one.

She snapped wide awake trying to orient where she was and finally realized that once again that nightmare had returned and she was in her camp and she was no longer nine but thirty. Twenty one years in the past and it still haunted her like it was yesterday. She remembered the horrible days and nights that followed, with much of the same happening to her often. She knew that this had happened to her mother also. She learned that the females were not the only ones to face this. Young boys were also the target and it sickened her to think that it would be this way. Maybe the reason this dream, this nightmare stayed with her for all of this time, allowed her to keep her passion on the destroying the very thing that had destroyed her family, and her innocence. To eliminate just one of these slavers meant that some other young girl or boy would not suffer from their abuses and then be sold into slavery where the abuses would continue until death.

She found that she was once again soaked in sweat and so was her sleep sack. She glanced to one side and saw her second crouched next to her and even in the uncertain light saw the concern on his face. "Bad dream?" He asked.

With remnants still hanging on as sleep slowly left her she replied in a somewhat hoarse voice, "Yeah, the one I wish would just go away and never return."

"I was sleeping close by and could hear you struggling in your sleep and thought that I had better come over and make sure that that was all it was, and not someone sneaking in camp to do damage."

Sighing and slowly letting out her breath she replied, "Yeah, that's all it was, and at times I would prefer to stay awake then to relive that. Guess it was just too much of a shock so that it's always with me no matter how I try and bury it."

He shrugged, even though he knew she couldn't see it. "What do you expect? You've told me of that incident that happened when you were still a child, still innocent, not understanding anything about that kind of thing. It was still a few years in your future. It was still time for you to be a child and enjoy those things. To be brought into the adult world and that way wasn't and isn't right at all. But we both know that we live in a violent dangerous world." Here he smiled knowing that while not visible it would be heard in his voice. "But, we are changing that one death at a time.

"You know, I wonder what any of our lives would have been if we had gone on with our lives before we were captured. To not have those scars that we hide because of what was done to us. Would our lives be such that we'd have our own families, have that loving touch, to know what it is to be loved even during intimacy? Instead of what we had to do or face punishment, or face the threats of being sold to the houses, always holding onto the fears which were always a part of us. I'd almost give anything to know. But that wasn't our destiny and here we are on another march to right another wrong. You know that I can see your passion and compassion every time we rescue another group of captives from the slavers. I can see the hurt and pain that it brings every time you see the abuse and rape that has taken place among the rescued. It's one of the reasons I'm still here with you, here as your second. I know that we live in a time where the bad seem to rule, but I can only hope that eventually this will change and the good will finally rule putting this scum in its place.

"I don't know how long such will rule, and how long people who only want to live their lives, raise their families, to live in peace, will have to fear such, but I can only hope that there will be an end to this. I know that I won't live to see it, but I hope that we are part of the beginnings that lead to that change. I see what it has done to you, and of course, others and it makes me curse our species. Maybe it would be better if we did just die off and let something else take our place. Yet, I know that by looking at what we were before the ancient fires destroyed we were so much more. So if it was that way before there is no reason it can't be again."

She sat up leaning back on her arms, "Yes, very well said. Look I don't have any idea what time it is but I've got to move." She laughed a little, "And actually I've got to hang this sleep sack as it's soaked as I . . . Which means that I'll have to change out of these wet clothes, go hang them by our small fire that marks our camp center, so they'll dry. After that I'll check on our guards. Maybe, if it's close to dawn, I'll rouse the camp and we'll head out. Long way to go and time never stops moving."

"Yeah, except in our dreams." The second got up and headed back to his area and disappeared into the darkness. She slid out of her wet sleep sack, grabbed her pack, sliding deeper into the wilderness where she quickly changed feeling a chill every time her wet hair touched her bare skin. *Better now than then,* she thought. Yet the remnants of the nightmare hung with her and took her back to those first few moon cycles before she was sold into slavery. When she had awakened after that rape she found that she was still crying and she was shaking from both reaction and cold. Her clothes had been torn off of her and the only thing she now found in her enclosure was a large dirty and worn shirt. She eagerly put it on to hide her nakedness and found that it at least covered her below her rear end, but not much more. The only other item she had was her sandals. In a very short time she had gone from a happy carefree life with her family to an orphan and shortly one to be sold into slavery.

The slavers who had captured her and her parents which she was sure were dead pushed east attacking other outposts of humanity and capturing others – women and children, all falling to the same fate that she had. No one was immune to the rapes and abuse. Even feeling torn up inside as she felt this didn't keep it from becoming something that she faced every day. The first few times she fought as hard as she could but she always lost and still was raped in the end. It seemed that these slavers were very familiar with the surrounding area and had stops and camps just about a day apart where there were cages that they placed their captives into, only bringing them out for their own pleasure. And that ragged shirt that she wore made it easy for them. She hated them and what they had done and were still doing. She didn't know how she would do it but she vowed that somehow she would get even for what they were doing to her and all the others that had become their captives.

Eventually one night, after being on the plains for a few days, in the distance, they saw many fires. She overheard it said that this was the marketplace where they would sell their merchandise. Even at this point it hadn't clicked that she and the others were that merchandise. At least until all of them were forced down into a large stream under threats of more of the same and of physical harm. Here they were forced to wash off the caked dirt and grime of the abuse and travels. The water was cold and when she finally was allowed to leave the waters she had turned blue and was covered in goose bumps. The breeze didn't help either as it chilled her further. It was obvious that they weren't going to be given anything to dry off with so most of them huddled as close together as they could trying to share each other's body heat – what little there was. Then when the slavers were satisfied they moved towards where those fires were and then all of them were herded into a large fenced enclosure. It was a pole-fence something that one could climb over, but there were campfires all around it lighting the area making it impossible to escape. Even though the other fires were still in the distance they were now much closer. It was obvious that they were old hands at this.

In the morning the slavers took all the ragged clothing leaving their captives naked and herded them once again towards that area in the distance where those fires had been. As they got closer it turned out to be a town of some sort, and now to her and the rest they knew what was about to happen. For the first time since their capture none of them had been touched the night before, and with the removal of clothing there was nothing to hide. As they were pushed through this town there were many hoots and hollers, with many looking at them with the look that said that they would love to take her right then and there. Her fear returned in full force and what little hope she had held on to was now gone. Despair was her companion and that wouldn't change for many years.

Eventually they were pushed to the middle of this place and found once again the pole fences all around a platform. Many were filled with ones just like her and others were being placed on the platform and then there would be bidding and what was used as currency would change hands and the one or ones would be led away. All were presented without clothes so that anything that might raise or lower the price would be seen. She had never seen so many people in all her life, and it seemed that all of them were bad. Were there that many bad people in this world? The buying and selling went on all day and with nothing being brought to them she was quite thirsty when she was grabbed and pushed up onto the platform. She tried to hide her private parts but this wasn't allowed. From here it was all a blur and finally someone had won. At that point a stranger grabbed her and herded her off to another area where there were others such as she all without clothes, all without hope, and now all were slaves.

Again none of them were offered food or water and as the sun set they were led over to a fire where they received the brand on the right hand marking them forever as property – as a slave. It hurt like hell, and continued that way for many days afterwards. Again she cried from the branding and actually cried herself to sleep for a very long time. It was here that she had her children and had at twenty one escaped. In a way it was an anniversary year since it had been twenty one years in the past that she had been raped, followed by becoming a slave and she had escaped slavery at twenty one. And now for nine years after her escape she was doing exactly what she had promised herself that she would do.

Now changed she took her wet clothes to the small fire and draped them close to receive what little heat the fire was putting out. She didn't know what to do about that sleep sack since there wasn't time to dry it out. All she could do was hang it open across one of the pack animals and hope that it would both air out, and dry. She was sure that it had to stink somewhat because of her sweating. She saw what appeared to be a coffee pot sitting on the coals, smiled, looked around and found a battered metal cup hanging from a cross bar that they put over the fires. With a cloth that was there for handling the hot pot she poured herself a cup of that liquid. Someone close by commented, "I wouldn't if I were you . . . That's been on the fire all night and is quite old. Suspect that if you turned your back that it would attack you."

She smiled replying, "Right now I'll take that chance. And if it wants to attack me I look forward to the fight."

The voice was unfamiliar and with the shadows she really couldn't see who it was, but he shrugged saying, "Your funeral." He withdrew and became part of the night. She carefully brought the hot liquid up to her lips and smelled the strength of the dark brown liquid. She seemed to remember a comment that one of her favorite authors had used through his characters, "Strong enough to float a horseshoe." It seemed appropriate for this brew.

* * *

It had taken until dark to reach Missoula, or probably better stated, the ruins of Missoula. From here the plan was to move more southerly dropping down to catch the southeastern edge of the Idaho territory. Why all the territories, and why the names she had no idea, but felt that eventually even these names would fade away or be changed. Time seemed to do that. As the old ones moved on or died, and the new moved in or were born they took it as their own and named the regions as their own. Many times they mistakenly believing that they are the first to be here, and with no proof otherwise felt confident in their appraisal of the facts. She knew that eventually the ruins would be buried or return to the earth to be no more. In fact she could see much of that happening and it had only been a short time – two hundred years, give or take a couple. She really didn't have much time to contemplate such things with the effort to remain alive in this present violent world. This would be left to future generations – if there were to be any.

As they had approached the area of where this city had lived memories began to flood her mind. She knew that at this time she would allow herself the luxury to go down that trail once again. Since it had been here that had changed her fortune – her and the other two that was with her during their escape. As she remembered it, those nine years in the past, she learned that she wasn't read a map as well as she thought she could. So far after the discovery of that buried building and the cache of clothing and such that they had recovered they were feeling pretty good about themselves. They now had recovered topography maps – at least that was what they had written on top of them. She didn't fully understand what that meant or what all those lines, numbers, color, scale, and such really were. The only map that she had seen prior to this was in that book, and it didn't look anything like this. The map in that book was small and the detail poor because of its size. So she had mistakenly figured distances weren't great, but had learned otherwise. She really had no idea what miles or kilometers were or what they represented. So reading these maps were more trial and error than skill.

So the three of them Laura, Nancse and herself as the unspoken leader, ended up traveling too far to the west. She, for whatever the reasons, couldn't make the orientation of the maps work no matter how she tried. It was when they had stumbled upon Missoula that they realized their mistake. Time was beginning to be against them as it was now fall and the morning air was crisp with a bite in the air. It began to rain a lot and many of the trees showed unbelievable colors in their leaves as they began to turn, flashing reds, yellows, and golden colors. She turned to the other two and said, "I'm sorry. I really thought that I understood these things, but we are too far west." She stopped unrolled one of the maps pointing so that the others could see saying, "Look here. This is that place that is just below us, and we are trying to go here which is east of us."

Laura shook her head before commenting. "Look there's no reason to apologize about this. You've got us this far and let's be honest here, none of us is good at this kind of thing. With all the distance that we've traveled we could easily be dead, or worse captured and returned for the reward that I'm sure is out there on us. Come on, we did the worst thing a slave can do, and that is kill our master and others who were in charge of us. I know we've talked about this before, but it's true. And Nancse or I would never have made it this far if it wasn't for your tenacity, or willingness to push us. So we made a mistake and came too far west. It just means we have a little further to travel." At this point she had her hands on her hips as she made her point. It seemed that all of them did that when pushing some point that they were passionate about. Was it particular to them personally, or did everybody do it?

Nancse looking down at those ruins shivered a bit. "Look, I don't know 'bout you two but I really don't want to go walking among those ruins. That other place where we did that scared me to death, and I don't need a repeat thank you." All three of them looked down on the ruins when she had stated her position. There was a silence between them as they looked over the area. Again there appeared to be no movement, nothing to signify that there was anybody alive down in those ruins. In a way all of them had to agree that the previous experience was overwhelming. The feeling of constantly being watched, of expecting to have someone or something jump out at them, the feeling that they would be attacked, had left them leery of repeating.

What to do, what to do? She thought. She saw the reluctance in both Nancse and Laura, but there might be something down there that would help them. They had burned through most of their food, and with the feel of the air she felt that winter had to be closing in on them. And not knowing anything about the winters here in the place she could only equate to what she knew. Winters on the plains sucked. So why should it be any different up here further north – other than worse? They would have to figure out something soon, and by coming too far west they had lengthened their time on the trails, and shortened their time to prepare – not good, not good at all. "Look, we are just about out of everything, and there's a good possibility that we may be able to find something down there among those ruins that will let us resupply. I know that the last place that we went through gave all of us the willies. Yet, other than the feeling of being constantly watched, feeling like we were being followed, nothing happened. And that is the only one we've ever gone through. Who's to say that it will be that way in all of the ruins? We've skirted around a number of them avoiding ones that we saw that was still occupied, and even the ones that had no sign that anybody was around.

"Yes, I know, we are three women alone, and that marks us as targets for any out here. Another reason that we've avoided any contact, with the big one being our marks identifying us for what we are, escaped slaves. Being women alone is bad enough, but not so bad that if we were pursued that we couldn't escape. Add in the discovery that we are escaped slaves and there are many out there that would not stop until we are captured. Still, is it fear that is stopping us from searching these ruins, especially when they appear to be abandoned, I wish I knew. Because, you see, I'm just as scared about it as you. We need to determine which it is, and if it's just fear, then fight it and do our own scavenging. We need supplies, and we need them badly."

It was late in the day when they overlooked the ruins and decided that they would camp back away from them and make their decision in the morning. So over a small fire they ate a hot meal and pulled back into the shadows, each withdrawing individually into the darkness to take care of nature. While this was something that wasn't easy for a woman they had become expert at it over time. Not that they didn't end up with wet feet now and then. After all they weren't built like a man who could redirect the stream away from them. Laura came back in from the shadows anger showing in every move heading for her pack. Curious as to why she was mad Nancse asked, "What's going on?"

Laura looked up with fire in her eyes saying rather loudly, "I've started! Damn I hate this."

She smiled back at her even though it was a sad one. "Look I know that it isn't something that any of us like and that means that in a couple Nancse will start followed by me. We seem to run close together on this, but it is so much better than the alternative."

"Alternative?" Laura asked, "What alternative? This is messy, has its own particular smell, makes me feel uncomfortable, and coming up with enough fur, since we ran out of the old stuff, to keep it from going everywhere it a pain."

"Yes, everything you've just said is true, and I know that none of us look forward to that time in our female cycles, but we, as in the past could be carrying for some male that we had no desire to lay with but by who we are were required, or forced, or whatever. And then we wouldn't be facing these things once a moon cycle. Instead we would eventually be bringing into this world a new life . . . . One that we wouldn't get a chance to mother, to love, to become part of our own family, by the way. You know how it is. Once you've birthed that child they take it immediately and all you're left with is the pain, and not only the pain of birthing, but the pain of an empty womb and nothing to show for it . . . And – as you well know – to repeat the process down the trail with no way to prevent it from happening again. I'll take this, thank you, over the loss of another child, over another carrying of one that I had no desire to be carrying in the first place.

"It makes me wonder what the women who were alive before the ancient fires did. And I guess all the way back in time. I mean it's not like we are the first ever to face this problem. Back where we were living we used rags, and while it wasn't the best it worked. Since we've been on the trails we've all tried many things, grass, leaves," which brought laughter from all of them since that failed miserably, "and so far the best has been rabbit fur. Or whatever other pelt that we can come up with at the time. Yeah the other stuff was nice, but we've only found that little bit and its long gone. I guess it's just another part of being a woman, being a female – just part of the suffering that we live with. Again, I know we had a limited supply for these times that had to be from before the fires, but we have no more, and are back to what we are using. At times I think that it would have been great to have been born a male. Then I wouldn't have to face this or being the smaller and more vulnerable of the two, and so many other things that makes it harder for us, but we cannot change who we are or our sex." Looking at the two of them she smiled saying, "Sorry about that. Didn't mean to climb on a rock and say all of that."

Nancse who had been quiet during the exchange spoke up quietly. She was still the youngest by six years and had only been facing her cycle for a year or so. "Madam, you are so right! Look, I've not had the, well I can't say pleasure, because these things aren't pleasant at all. I fight headaches and I get cramps, and I feel miserable and wish that it would go away and just leave me alone. And I guess, fortunately, I've not carried yet, although as often as I had to submit to them it probably would have happened soon. So I've never carried. Yet from the women I've seen carry there seems to be a magic to it. No I'm not talking about the sickness that one faces when they realize that they are carrying, but the wonder at each stage. I always wondered what it would be like to feel a life inside of me. Feel something moving, and be in awe that such a thing could and can happen. I guess it's part of being a woman, a female. It's what we do."

Laura laughed, "Yes, all of that is true, but when you birth that child you feel like you're being torn in half. You can't believe that your skin can stretch that much, and that something that big is going to come out of you down there between your legs. I mean, if you think about it the first time you saw that thing between a male's legs standing up and coming to you, you wondered how something that big was going to fit inside of you. And that first time with these idiots hurt. They don't care about you at all; all they are interested in is their own needs, not yours. We are just something to be used, and boy did they use us. Then you deliver that child – something so many times larger and it just seems impossible.

"I guess that's why there are deaths for us during that time. So much can go wrong. I've witnessed too many of us dying at that time. And what makes it worse is two things, first many times both die, and second, at least in our situation, if the mother dies and the child lives the ones who are there taking the baby anyway couldn't care less. After all there's always another female to replace the one they just lost."

She thought about this, and for the first time in a very long time she thought about her mother and father. It seemed that they had a very good relationship and it was obvious that they had been physical because she and her brothers were here. And she knew that it was the only way that happened. Was there a difference between what they had and what she and the other women faced as slaves? She had to admit that there must have been something. It was obvious that her father had cared. She found that she had been staring into the fire – a mistake – looked up saying, "Laura, you better take care of it before you stain your clothing. We don't have a lot, and if we can't get anything in those ruins, or decide to pass them by then we are stuck with what we have." She knew that all of them and all of their clothing had minor stains from travel and from that time in their cycles. Yet, it had been important to find something to absorb this fluid because they had to keep moving. To have gone without and left a trail would have been bad. Many predators were attracted by the smell of blood, and there was always blood in that fluid. "Oh one last thing and I really don't understand this at all."

"What", Laura asked, "is there to understand? It seems that we are cursed by this and the males have a free ride."

"Yeah, I can see that, but have you noticed that when we started our escape from the compound that our cycles were all over the place, and now we are only a few days apart – that's what I don't understand. I thought they were locked in but now I just don't know."

"I hadn't thought about that", Laura said, "but you're right. Still does it really mean anything?"

She shrugged, "No, I guess it doesn't. It was just a surprise when I thought about it." They spent over seven days in the area, and all three were bleeding. For a couple of days in that time it was almost war. As emotions, feeling bad, and the normal problems of that time arose.

They had decided the next morning to search the ruins. Again that previous night they watched the area of the ruins and saw nothing that reflected life. No sounds, no fires, nothing but the normal night sounds. It appeared the night time was a great time to listen. Sound carried so much further, and with the silence of night anything spoken in a normal voice would carry. In a sense, even though it was unspoken they decided to use this time when they were indisposed, so to speak, and stay here to see what they could find, to salvage, to add to what little they had. With the morning light as they looked over the ruins they saw that this one was smaller than the other ruins that they had passed through. They waited until the full rise of the morning sun and searched with their eyes the surrounding areas to see if they could spot any movement. Only seeing what they thought were deer grazing quietly. That previous night somewhere towards the middle of it one of those ancient fires streaked across the sky lighting the area to almost daylight. A short time later they heard and felt an explosion – the shockwave being somewhat strong, but not so strong to signal that it had struck close by.

Once they reached the ruins they didn't feel the same uneasiness, the feeling that someone was watching them. Other than the destruction that lay all around them it might have been any chilly fall day. As with the others that they had observed, it appeared that the ones who had lived here had their homes on the outskirts. They found row after row of homes completely leveled. It was also obvious that many of these had been searched over time. As they penetrated deeper they found less and less sign of salvage. It was like the ones who had, became discouraged. It could be that the pickings had been slim and whoever it had been had simply given up. No way to know since it appeared the area had been undisturbed for a long time. Yet, at this time, they had to agree, there appeared to have been little that survived the devastation that had struck this area. They kept at it since there were only three of them figuring that they should find enough to resupply.

But after the first day within the ruins they had found little and were discouraged. She remembered that all of them argued that first night. Smiling a little at that memory she wondered now if it was because all of them were either there or approaching that time of their cycles. She remembered that after the arguments that they remained apart and with an uncomfortable silence for the rest of that night. But with the light of day they made up and headed back to the ruins confident that they were here alone and undisturbed. It was on that third day, while searching an unpromising area of rubble that they found their greatest discovery. Although once found they worried that others would find it before they would recover what was here. There definitely was more here than the three of them could handle many times over. Somehow once they had located where they had planned to stay then there would have to be many trips back and forth until they had it all.

She looked around in the darkness, had really been nine years ago that this had happened? She shook her head, it seemed impossible. Now here she was, once again, but this time she had her army, not three women alone. The other two had found males and had become mates. Both had children now from those unions – so different from the years as slaves. In a way she envied them, but she never had found one that would fulfill that empty spot in her life. Her passion had been, and she felt probably would always be, wiping out slavers and raiders, the ones who destroyed what was good in this world. She felt that she had no room for anything else, let alone a male. At least she knew where she was going and probably how her life would end. It would be of her choosing, not some slave owner or the houses where no one lived long. She figured that it would take them another three days to reach the desert where the slavers were, and she hoped that they were still there.

Her thoughts briefly returned to that search through these ruins. After all it was here that as far as she was concerned, it was fate that led her to this far off destination. Because they found their hidden weapons cache here in a buried armory that had belonged to a, what was called, National Guard. With the weapons were cases upon cases of food. It had been an unbelievable discovery and she felt that if they found it so would others. But fortune had been with them and it took them over a year to move all of what they had discovered, and during that time there had been no sign of any others around. It gave them their start, and provided food for that first winter in the hole-in-the-wall. It really had been a cold miserable first winter. But now nine years later, one would never have known how really difficult it had been.

CHAPTER FOURTEEN

As the family gathered for the morning meal Cassie, the middle daughter, turned to Katelyn and whispered something that the rest couldn't hear. Katelyn turned and began looking around and then shrugged. Cassie asked, "Where's mom?"

Seth, who was now in from his shift while Jake had taken over the watch duties said quietly, "She's outside. Dad came home last night – well closer to this morning and asked that she meet him. Other than that I don't know much more."

Suddenly there was an excitement at the table and Cassie asked in an excited voice, "Dad's back? Really? Why didn't you say anything?"

Seth's mate Tasha looked at him with a questioning look, "Yes, Seth, why didn't you tell us? We were all wondering where your mother was, but wasn't expecting this. So if your father is back, could it be that Joel has returned also and you didn't mention that either?"

Shaking his head and feeling like he was under attack. Then again, it seemed that the females had a tendency to gang up on hapless males anyway, and today he was the target. "Look, first off I just came in off my time out there guarding all of you. And when dad came in he stated that for now no one was to know." He put his hands out in front of him palms up, saying, "I don't know why. For all I know he would be heading back out and didn't want to get anybody's hope up that he was back. I've already said too much anyway. But he asked for mom to meet him and that's why she isn't here."

They all jumped when Dan stated, "No Seth, that wasn't the reason that I didn't want anybody aware of my return." They all turned and saw Dan and Marta and with a young stranger. Before he could say anything further their daughters jumped up and came over joining them all talking at once. He saw the joy on their faces when they knew that he was back safe. Then it penetrated that there was another with them and suddenly shy they pulled back and looked down at their feet. Inwardly Dan laughed. Well, it had been a very long time since there had been anybody around other than family. Putting his arm around the shoulders of the stranger he said, "I'd like to introduce you to one who has been living out here in the desert just as we. Only in his case it was a bit harder. His full name is Samuel E Kaytrova, but prefers Sam." He turned to Sam saying, "Be careful you're the only male these females have seen other than family for a while so I suspect that you will be a favorite target of them for a while."

Both of the younger girls said in unison, "Dad!" Then both looked at this Sam and smiled a shy smile. All Dan could do was smile. It was obvious that things would become a bit more interesting now that Marta had agreed to allow him in. Of course this was only after much grilling from her. After all she had to have her questions answered, and then her discussion with him, and with some time to think, this was followed by more questions and answers. Of course, this included him. Eventually satisfied that he was "safe", so to speak, and considering the world as it is presently, and with this a very important word, she allowed this Sam to join them. When it came right down to it his home had been destroyed by the same raiders that were giving them problems. Not the same way of course, since theirs hadn't been discovered yet, by the raiders, and they wanted it to remain that way.

Taken back by seeing so many people after all the time he had remained isolated he didn't have much to say. In fact Sam felt too enclosed and almost claustrophobic. After all, other than his escape routes and places to hide, he had been living in the open for the last few years. And before that with his family – before they were killed – they had been living in the open. Simply stated part of what they were, were herders. And while not a part of the gypsies or nomads, which many times seemed to be one and the same since their lifestyle had been similar. He thought back to the grilling he had gotten, first from Dan back where he had been living, and then from Marta. Although of the two Marta's was worse by far, and he finally understood why now that he finally met the rest of the family. And even though it had been a while since he had seen any females he had to admit that those two daughters of Dan and Marta were easy on the eyes. Who'd have guessed that there were others here and such a place as this existed – not he.

Quiet, as he listened to the excited conversation around him, it was almost too much. After all as far as conversation went there had only been he talking to himself. One thing for sure, this would take some getting used to. Definitely would take some time to feel comfortable. But at this moment he almost felt like he wanted to run and return to what he had known. But, this couldn't and wouldn't happen. Dan seeing what was going on with him understood the impact that this must be. "Look all. He's been alone for quite a while. I'm sure this is somewhat overwhelming to go from only one to this clan. So give him some air and time to get used to this many people and", here Dan paused and smiled, "all you females."

Sam looked over at Dan and silently thanked him. It was obvious that this man understood how he was feeling. When he could he walked over to him and whispered, "Look, I need to get outside for a while. This is making me really uncomfortable." He saw in Dan's eyes mixed emotions, but when he spoke it was clear.

"Sam, it's only understandable. This chaos takes time for one to get used to." Here he smiled, "But I wouldn't trade it for anything. Okay, follow me and we can go back out for a while. Give you time to think and get familiar with all of this." He led him out through a different exit, a place that was shadowed and cool. Even though the heat of the day hadn't begun yet he could tell that this was a place to escape the heat. Dan basically said the same thing. Then he was left alone. Of course, he realized that to really leave this place that most likely he would have to go back through where all of them lived. He couldn't help but smile on that point. While they might trust him, it wasn't to the point of stupidity. *Wow, this is going to take time to become comfortable around this many. Now, am I going to stay, or will I just say thank you and leave?* It was a very good question. Since he had been living on his own he found that he really hadn't needed anyone. Still, once back among people he began to sense a need to be around others.

Another thought came to him and it caused him to pause a moment. He realized that this family was taking the bigger chance by allowing him into their lives. With those raiders just a short distance away he could betray them and come away with whatever wealth he demanded. But at the same time, knowing what he did about these raiders they would just as easily promise everything and betray him. Well, one thing he knew for sure, he wouldn't do that. He had seen his own die and had been fortunate to escape. Even though he barely knew these people yet he didn't want to see a repeat, or be the one to cause it to happen. So for now, he would stay and learn of these strangers that had put out a welcoming hand to him. Who knew where this would lead – surely not him? But this future would be infinitely better than his, had he remained where he had been. So with a decision made he reveled in the quiet peace that he had for this moment knowing that shortly he would be rejoining that chaos that existed inside those hidden walls.

* * *

It was late afternoon of the same day that Dan with Sam had returned when Joel arrived. Like his father he had the one that was with him waiting with his brother Jake at their watch point. That way Abe could get acquainted with one of his brothers. It had been a difficult decision to allow a stranger this close to their hideaway but what could he do? Yes, he might have attempted to sneak away, but these scouts were now aware and would be looking. So he felt that it would be better to make them into friends and associates instead of enemies. He had to admit that in verbal battles his brother Seth was much better, like he was better at moving through the wilderness. Each of them had their own gifts. Yet, as far as he could see, Abe and the other two had just as much to lose as he did and they had to be infinitely aware of who they were dealing with simply because of those marks that would forever mark them as escaped slaves and a possible target to any that they met.

He learned, from his brother that dad had brought someone home also. *What is this, introduction day or something?* Why, after all of this time alone as a family by ourselves that on the same day strangers come calling? It was so weird how such things worked. It was as if this was all planned, but that's ridiculous, isn't it? He had to seek out his father, bring him up to date, and then the two of them go back and have him talk with Abe. After all, if dad refused to allow this one any further, then their actual location would not be compromised. The first two he ran into were his sisters Cassie and Katelyn who seemed very excited. He had to admit that this was the first time someone who was close to their age and wasn't family had been around in a very long time. He saw their curiosity was piqued, and he had to smile knowing that this meant that whoever this new one was he would be in trouble. The one lesson he'd learned was that you never made a female curious unless you really wanted attention.

They pointed him in the direction of the sleep space for their parents and he was reluctant to go that way not wanting interrupt the reunion of mom and dad. But this was something that couldn't wait so he headed down the short hallway that had storage built into the walls, he knew that whoever had built this place wasted no space, and found his mother sitting at the entrance in a chair. Curious, but before he could ask, his mother looked up from the book she was reading and saw the joy in her eyes saying that both of her men had returned and were safe. "Joel", she exclaimed, "you're back!" She smiled before continuing. "It has been quite a day. First your dad returns with a guest, and now you're back. Most of my worry is lifted and I feel so much better."

"Yes, but mom why are you out here instead of inside with dad?"

She smiled a knowing smile, "Let's just say that your father is exhausted. He's been sleeping the days and working his scouting during the night. And with the passing time he's not as good as he once was as far as sleeping on the hard ground – age does that to you, and that's something you'll learn later in your own life."

Feeling a little guilty he hesitated for a few moments not sure how to continue. But he needed dad for this. "Yeah, as far as this guest, I'm now aware that my sisters seem to be very interested in whoever this is. So I would say that this new person is male, otherwise they wouldn't be this kind of excited."

Again his mother smiled, "Yeah, funny how that works . . . Although I can understand it. As you know there haven't been any eligible males around for them to think about. Not that you don't know but we are kind of isolated here – At least we were."

"Mom, I need to talk to dad. You see I've ended up meeting the ones I was following." He shook his head and smiled. "Not on purpose that's for sure, but I slipped and fell giving myself away. It was crazy for a short time but eventually I spent time in their camp, at least their temporary camp, and we've done a lot of talking. They are escaped slaves so have to be even more careful that we do and I have the leader of the ones who have been trailing the raiders. He's confirmed that the ones we've been watching are slavers. It seems that the three of them are part of a larger group, all escaped slaves by the way, and they had an encounter with the slavers.

"Enough on this, I can tell the whole story later. I need dad to come and meet the one with me." He saw alarm in her eyes. Shaking his head he said, "No, I didn't bring him to our hidden oasis, but left him with Jake at our lookout."

Marta laughed, which surprised Joel. "You and your father are so much alike. I think that the two of you must even think alike. That's exactly what he did before bringing in the one he had with him. He wanted a second opinion – mine. Okay, I'll go wake your father and send him out. You can meet him there. I'm sure your brother who is on watch can use some support. After all you left him in a somewhat of an awkward situation. He knows nothing of the one you left, and I'm sure the silence is getting pretty loud by now. I don't know how long it will take your father to come to life, but I know that he will be there." She got up and went into the room and disappeared from sight. Joel, once she was gone headed back out and returned to the waiting Abe and his brother.

Marta entered their room and looked down upon her sleeping mate. She could see that he was exhausted. He hadn't moved since he had lain down. She suspected that the whole place could come apart around him at this moment and he'd never hear it. She really hated to do this but much was happening and he needed to be involved. Taking a deep breath and letting it out slowly she said in a loving voice and softly, "Dan . . . Dan, you are needed."

In his mind he heard rushing water. He wondered where that was coming from. As far as he recalled he was back in their shelter and such a thing wasn't close. In fact it was a few miles downhill to the river where such sounds would be. But it was just before dark – dusk, so he wasn't able to visually locate the sound. He realized suddenly that there was another sound somewhere in the distance calling his name very softly. But that didn't make sense since the rushing sounds were loud and should have drowned out that other voice. He turned towards that sound and as he did it became stronger actually overriding the sounds of rushing water. In fact the rushing sounds were fading and this other was becoming the dominant sound. Then slowly he awakened and as he opened his eyes he looked up into the smiling loving face of his life mate. Taking a few slow breaths he smiled. "I guess I was tired – must admit still feel that way. What's going on?" His body felt heavy and numb and there still was a rushing sound in his ears. He definitely had been very deep when she had awakened him.

Quietly as she leaned on the bed said, "It seems that your expert advice is needed. I would have preferred to let you sleep, but too much is happening. Funny, but we've been able to remain hidden and more or less out of all that have been happening around us. Now on the very same day it's all changing. You brought that one with you, and as you know Joel was following those others that you and he had spotted earlier. Well, he has one of them out at the overlook and needs you to go and talk with this one. It looks like our secret hideaway won't be a secret much longer."

He had to admit that just lying here on the bed felt like the best thing to do. He had to admit that it would be much too easy to fall back into a deep sleep. He started pushing himself up and off the bed and then thought better of it. Instead he reached up and grabbed his mate and pulled her down to him. Laughing she resisted a little which got him to laughing also. With her on top of him he lightly kissed her saying, "I love you, but of course you knew that."

"Yes, I do know that. But it's always nice to hear it from the one I love."

Sighing, he said, "I guess I have to do the adult thing and be responsible. Honestly it would be more fun to be here with you and do whatever comes to our minds."

Knowing him well she replied, "Yes, wouldn't it. At least I know that I wouldn't have to worry about carrying and we starting over with another child. But I know what you mean. Responsibility always goes ahead of our pleasure and intimacy." She gently pushed him back down getting off the bed and with a lingering look left the room and headed out where the other family members were.

He watched her as she left with a nostalgic smile on his face as his thoughts turned inward briefly. *So much time has passed us by – so much. Just what has happened to all those years that are no more?* He had no answers but knew that he needed to get moving. Because of the fog that was still with him and because he had been down so deep it still took a moment to gather his thoughts into something coherent and head out the door. He found that he was still in his clothes. *Must have been tired to still be in these,* he thought.

Joel headed back out into the bright sunlight momentarily blinded from the difference between the gloom from inside to this brightness. He stopped a moment to allow his eyes to adjust and using a different path headed back to the overlook. He didn't want to make it obvious as to the location of their shelter, but knew that most likely, this would be a futile attempt since Abe and the other two were scouts and knew how to trail and read sign. Given time they'd easily follow any back to where the tracks originated. And as often as they had made this trek to their lookout it would be impossible to cover all the tracks and routes to prevent someone who was good at tracking from backtracking right to their door. So far it had been the utter lack of people and the fact that the location of their shelter was so unlikely. After all no one would put such a thing where it was located – it didn't make sense.

Eventually coming from above the overlook he saw that his brother Jake had spotted him and that Abe was sitting on one of the rocks. From the interest that Jake presented Abe turned around and spied him as he got close. Abe commenting, "Heard you coming, but since your brother didn't react in such a way that said danger, figured it had to be you returning." Abe looked back over the valley before continuing, "Quite a view from up here. I can see why this was chosen as a place to watch from. From what I can remember when we came through this area we were further up, but can't be sure. So what are we waiting for now?"

Looking out over the view it seemed so peaceful, but it was a lie and he knew it. It was wishful and dangerous thinking in this present world that it should be so. Reality spoke of a vast difference from the appearances and the truth. "We will have another joining us shortly."

"Another? So how many are there of you anyway and however did we miss you? We are in the desert and there's really not many out here and because of that it should be easy to spot others."

"I'll let this other one determine what can be revealed. In reality it will come down to his word as to how far we can trust. It's still a small word but has so much power. I know that you are in the very same boat about this – actually more so because of your status."

"Yes, that's so very true. So how long will it be before we have this other join us?"

"Shouldn't be too long but he has been out working the nights to be sure that those, what did you call them, right, slavers, not raiders, weren't going to come back and give us trouble."

"Yeah they're slavers. We rescued a number of captives from them. They were on the way to the markets to the east."

Jake remained silent as the two talked. He had felt quite uncomfortable when this Abe had been left in his care. He knew nothing about him, and Joel really hadn't said anything. So with split attention he watched the valley below and watched Abe. Although he never made a threatening move, just remained sitting on the rock and a safe distance away so as to be non-threating. Turning and looking back towards the hidden shelter Jake finally was able to see his father approaching, although it would be a few moments before he would arrive. *Why is it that we always refer to him when we want something solved?* He wondered. He noticed that the other two – his brother and this Abe were now watching him approach. It was obvious to Jake that he was still tired. It showed in the way he walked which was slow and careful.

Standing Abe watched and remained silent. He wondered how many were really here. But these people were very careful. He had to admit that with the way things are that if one wasn't then one would be dead or worse. Dan seeing three standing up the hill ahead of him recognized two of them as his sons and the third someone who seemed to be deeply tanned, with shoulder length dark hair, and built similarly to him. So this was the one he needed to meet. In a way he looked familiar but couldn't remember where he may have seen him before. Well, he'd have an answer to that problem shortly.

Joel went over and met his father as he approached saying, "I needed someone else to talk to the one I brought back. Mom said that you did the same thing. If we were crowded before we surely will be with all the additions that we are taking in. It was obvious that you were trying to place this one so let me help you. He's one of the others that we barely avoided back when we were dealing with the raiders. Oh I've learned since then that they aren't raiders but much worse. They're slavers. From the conversation that I've had with Abe, oh right, that's his name, they've been following them for a while. But I'll let him tell it." They reached the overlook and Joel turned to Abe saying, "Abe, this is my father Dan, and of course dad, he is Abe."

Both reached out and grabbed each other's forearms as was tradition with Dan taking a deep breath before speaking. "Abe is it. I don't know what Joel has told you, or what your true status is but this desert has been getting quite crowded lately."

Abe smiled saying, "Yes hasn't it. When we came into the area we thought that we would only be dealing with the slavers, but have since learned that there were others like you here. And probably are better at scouting and remaining hidden than we. And the three of us consider ourselves very good at it. In fact I'm pretty sure that the slavers have never spotted us. But their leader is very good and suspects."

"So why are you following them? Oh I can see one of the reasons since you carry the mark of a slave, but that means you're putting yourself in jeopardy of capture and subsequent death by the owners of slaves. Something that I, or we cannot and will not abide by at all."

"What slavery or putting a captured escaped slave to death?" Abe smiled taking the sting out of the question.

"Both to be honest. I don't know how much information you've gotten from Joel, so I'm sort of flying blind here. So let's sit and talk a while and then both of us can be brought up to date. And not to be too distracting to Jake here let's head away from here where we can be safe and talk without worrying that someone who shouldn't overhear will." He turned back to Joel saying, "Okay, we'll talk it out and come to an agreement one way or the other. So either stay with your brother or head back. I know if it's been anything like what I faced since I was away, some down time about now is important."

Joel had to admit that he was tired. The time in the scout camp had been very trying and nerve-racking. He could feel the fatigue rolling over him and it was beginning to cloud his mind somewhat. "Are you sure?"

"As sure as any of us can be during these times son. If you trusted him to bring him this far I'll trust him enough to be off and alone with him. So head back." Dan purposely didn't mention anything about the others. It might easily be a mistake. At this point all Abe could account for was the three of them, and at this point until he knew better it would remain that way.

* * *

Evening was descending upon the family plus one and Dan had called a meeting. After his talk with Abe he returned and had discussed what he had learned with Marta and had followed this by some much needed sleep. He had a much better understanding now of what had transpired before the slavers had entered the area and now knew that things could get much worse before they got better. Seth was now on watch duty and after this meeting he would go out and bring him up to date. He saw the nervousness in the family as they tried to get comfortable. Even the grandchildren were here although with the fidgeting they were doing he was sure that it would distract their mother. He looked over at his mate who gave him an encouraging smile, looked back and began to speak. "After all the quiet and all the time that we've been alone here it lately has become quite crowded around here." This brought a bit of nervous laughter from the ones who were listening. "As you now know we have added another to our already crowded space, and Joel made contact with the others we had seen scouting around the area. What this family meeting is all about is to relay what I have learned from Abe, who is the leader of the three that we've seen following the ones that we had considered raiders. Now I've learned that it's much worse than that. They are slavers, and slavers of the worst kind. So if any of us were captured by them we can expect no mercy at all, and the maximum abuse before the women and children here would be sold into slavery." It was obvious that it was affecting all of them like it did when he learned the truth.

"Now, with what I know, it is going to get more difficult, if that's even possible. You see Abe and the other two with him who are following the slavers are escaped slaves. We all know what that means for them if they are ever captured and returned to the markets. None of us here wants anything to do with the slave trade, but unfortunately it is a part of this world that we presently live. But while this was unknown to us, the knowledge that he passed on told me that soon we will have another army coming down upon us. It seems that this new army that we haven't been introduced to yet has already fought the slavers once, fighting them to a standstill. I asked why they didn't just wipe them out; after all it's a logical question. I was told that when this other army had found the slavers that it was only a patrol and as such really they didn't have as many to fight them as they should. It was only through surprise and bluff that they succeeded. But word was left with the leader of the slavers to clear out or face the consequences, and thusly why the slavers were followed by Abe and his group.

"I've learned that he's sent word back and because these slavers hadn't done as demanded this new army, which will be full strength, will arrive very soon and finish what they started. That means that we must hold up and stay out of this. We don't have the numbers or firepower to get involved anyway. Abe said as much, even though he knows nothing about this place or how many are here. This one is smart. I never stated or identified more than the three of us when I talked with him, but somehow I sensed that he knew. Yet he was kind enough not to say anything or pry. Oh yes, before I forget, this army that will be coming into the area are all escaped slaves and as such has a very good reason to want the destruction of those slavers."

* * *

Skar was becoming more agitated. His inner sense was screaming at him, but there had been nothing. Even with the additional patrols that he had sent out, and the dividing of his camp, with a third now down canyon from the main camp. He felt that it wasn't enough. But with nothing to point to or at he was completely at a loss. He found that he couldn't even sit at the fire but had to be up and pacing. Moving in and out of the flickering light with his arms behind his back – stopping now and then appearing to want to say something, but found he didn't have anything to say.

Bear had seen him this way before and was worried. When the boss got this way something always happened. This inner sense had never been wrong when it reached this point. And because of this he had reinforced the guards, had made it clear to the ones on patrol to look closer at anything, anything at all. They had questioned him on what to look for and he had no real answer, only that something was on the horizon that would affect all of them. So with some grumbling they did as ordered. All of them knew that they would still be here for a least another fourteen days before continuing to the west. It was all because they recently had discovered one of the larger caches that the unknown one who had been living here had created. And while disappointing in comparison to what they would have earned from the sales of their captives in the markets it was enough to keep them looking. Bear, watching Skar as he paced said, "Boss if you don't stop this you'll have me doing it."

"Sorry, but this has just got me. Most of the time by now I know, but there's just nothing. We've not even found a track. And even the one who was living here has eluded us, not that he was important. But this is a desert, different I know with all the trees that are here, but desert anyway. There are just not that many places one can hide. Well, let me restate that. There's a lot of ground out here and it's huge, but as far as ground cover goes, other than around the river there really isn't any. I know this ground is hard and leaves few tracks but we have some pretty good trackers with us and they've found nothing. With this inner thing screaming at me that something is about to happen, and still the silence, still no change, still the sun rising and setting, it's driving me crazy."

"Maybe boss, this time it's wrong."

"Tell me Bear, has it ever been wrong when it's this strong?"

"No. But there's always a first time for anything."

"True, but I don't think it will be this time, the feeling's just too strong – stronger than I ever remember."

"So what do you need me to do?"

"Now that's the question. If I knew then I would let you know, but I don't. And that's the crux of the problem. I always appreciate the ability to know that something is about to happen, something will be coming down, but I've never liked the part that is unknown. I mean it's just a feeling. It doesn't tell me what it will be or where it will come from, and it's this part that drives me crazy."

"I guess we could send another third up canyon making three camps, so that the patrols can go to any of the three when they come in. Plus it spreads us out in such a way that if we are attacked it will be much or difficult."

"True, but Bear there is a downside to this and it could make it tougher for us. If we keep dividing ourselves, then we become weaker, more vulnerable, so I really don't know. Look I'll think about it tonight and let you know in the morn. Just keep the guards awake." With that he was unable to remain by the fire and headed inside his portable shelter. He really hoped that he could sleep, but the way this was screaming at him he doubted it. Instead of being able to lie down and sleep he found that he was pacing inside the small shelter. There really wasn't much room to do this and eventually with the restlessness headed back out walking through the camp approaching one of the guards letting him know that he would be beyond the camp and would come back through this same area so be aware.

Once beyond the camp he had no real destination in mind and hiked past the small lake and headed along the river bank listening to the flow of the water as it moved rapidly to wherever it went. He never had been that curious about such things. Such things were either barriers or something that could be used and nothing more. Finding a place where he could sit he stared out at nothing idly grabbing a pebble or two and throwing it into the moving water. The inner screaming to do something would not abate, but he was no closer to a solution at all. Eventually he heard someone approaching and knew by the sounds that it had to be Bear. Besides he would be the only one to follow him. The others left him alone, let him lead, and left it at that.

He stood up and saw Bear as a lighter shadow against the darker shadows of the trees and vegetation that grew close to the river. He knew that Bear had located him and was making noise in such a way to announce that he was approaching. He always marveled at Bear's abilities. For one so big he moved with surprising grace and silence. And he was quick and deadly showing no mercy. Yet when one who did not know him looked at him from a distance none of this showed. He projected an image of slowness and peacefulness – so the opposite of what this man truly was. So why didn't he want to lead his own? For whatever the reason Bear was content to be the second and never pushed to be the leader. Letting out his breath slowly Skar quietly said, "Okay Bear I know that you've located me and that you've made enough noise so that I would know that you're here, so what's up?"

"Nothing boss. But I know that you're agitated and after our earlier conversation I felt that you wouldn't be able to stay in camp – been with you too long. So after making sure the guards were doubly aware that something was coming down I watched your portable shelter and as I expected you left and headed out of our camp. It was easy for me to follow as I kept you highlighted against the night sky. I know that when these feelings hit you that you get ornery and difficult to be around – like a bear with a sore tooth if I may. Felt that it was necessary to at least come out here and if nothing else *watch*. I know that it is easy for you to become distracted and not really be aware of your surroundings. So I figured to let you know I was here and then withdraw and cover your back and not bother you until you were ready to return to camp."

"I guess we've been together much too long as everything you've said is absolutely true. Why do you stay with me Bear? I've known for a very long time that you could lead your own if you so desired. And yes, I know that I've asked this before, and heard your sundry of answers before, but I really don't understand why you stay with me?"

Bear shrugged. "I do just because I do, that's all. We've made a pretty good team over the years and while there have been a few lean ones, which is the way of life, overall we've been successful. I think that it's because that we simply work well together, or maybe it's just because we've been together doing this business for so long that I cannot imagine any other way. I've never really thought about it, and don't really plan on thinking about it. We'll be together doing this kind of thing until we are not, and that's really how I look at it. I really have no ambitions towards anything other than being somewhat comfortable, having a woman now and then, finding some of that old alcohol that still remains hidden out here, and traveling around seeing something new. We do all of that, and our skills complement each other. In this present time it just works."

"I guess I'll have to accept what you just said, but it is something that's hard for me to understand. I love the aspects of the planning and the ability to lead others and be successful, allowing us, at times, a good reward. To see you as big and as smart as you are not want anything but what you've stated just doesn't seem right, but if there's one thing that has shown over time it has been that what you've stated has been borne out. And I appreciate your willingness to be here tonight to just be my guard so to speak. But there are others who could do that."

"Yes, there are others who could do this, but they would become bored, become careless, and become distracted themselves. After all, out here there would be no one to hold them to the task, and as quiet as it is, it makes one's mind start to drift in too many directions and away from the task at hand. We cannot afford that."

"Okay, I take your point and again you are very right. And to be honest I appreciate it. And no, I still haven't a clue – although, I suspect that because we haven't left the area as demanded that this has something to do with that. I know that we've found no sign that we were followed, but this Madam is too good – too good to leave such a thing to chance. I'm sure that we were followed and just because we've found no proof of it doesn't mean it isn't a reality. Still, there's been nothing to pin this feeling too, nothing at all. I don't want to jump to conclusions and assume that it's her and her army and find out later that it was something totally different, and unexpected.

"Look, on the way to here I thought about what you said and I think that it's a good idea. So in the morn let's split another part of us off and head them up river, just far enough away that they can cover or we can cover them if necessary. That way it will make it more difficult for whoever might come along. And I think that we will move out of here, this area, earlier than planned. We haven't recovered much, but at least it's something and what we've found we can use, with some of it being trading materials. Much better than what we had before we found this place. With the river and the wild cattle we've had no lack of meat or a place to stay. So before this becomes the trap it can easily be I want us to be out of here by the next full moon, which I believe is only a few days away."

* * *

He had pulled far back from the rim and was now camping with an almost invisible fire too far back to watch what was happening with the slaver camp. He had no choice. Too many times he had almost been caught when the patrols suddenly started once again. And they were combing the hills with ferocity and thoroughness that they hadn't the last time the three of them were avoiding patrols. It had been luck that had prevented his discovery so far and the fact that Abe made sure that their fires was small and that they never camped in the same place twice. Once they prepared to move to a different location then all traces of their previous camp was eliminated. It had been the only thing that had saved him so far. Had he done something to trigger this? He surely hoped not. With Abe gone with the other it made it easier to stay out of sight, but easier did not mean that it hadn't been difficult. With so many bodies out and about he might have easily been spotted.

It was full on dark and now he had to be at least a mile from the rim where they watched the camp below. And for now that was how it would be. Maybe later he would chance it and venture back from a different direction and try to update his information, but if he was caught then everything they had accomplished up to this moment would be lost. So was it better to remain hidden and have old information, or was it better to take that chance and at least come closer and see what was transpiring? He honestly didn't know. At least, for the moment, it seemed that the patrols had returned to the main camp. The last thing he saw, or suspected was that it appeared that they were splitting the camp and preparing to create a second one. The only issue for him was that he hadn't been able to stay long enough to know what direction the split, if it did happen, and he had no direct proof, went. So thinking this over, and he wished that there was one of the others to discuss this; he decided that it would be better to see if the slavers had made a second camp.

So with a decision made he extinguished his small fire and headed overland in the direction that would put him upriver of the present camp. Even with his eyes adjusted to the night he had to be careful in the uncertain light as everything was indistinct and shadowed. Much was hidden in the deeper shadows that hid who knew what. As a result his movement was slow and it had taken him until late in the night to finally reach an area where, once again, he could overlook the river and still be high enough above that he would be able to pinpoint the slaver camp by the fires and determine if another had been established further up the river. Yet where he surveyed the area there was nothing. This was not to say that there wasn't a camp down there as it was much too dark to determine what existed in that valley floor. There might be a camp there with many, and without fires to establish a location like their main camp, it would have been missed.

It meant that if he wanted to be sure he would have to work his way to the floor of the narrow valley, but decided that slavers without their fires would be out of character and while he wasn't a hundred percent sure, for now it would have to do. He needed to work his way back and then down river to find out if maybe they had gone that way. In a sense, now that he thought about it, that direction probably made more sense. The river and the corresponding valley or canyon took a sharp turn hiding anything that would be established from the main camp rendering it invisible for any who wouldn't be searching for it. It would leave an attacking force vulnerable to a counter attack to the rear and flank by an unexpected enemy. With those thoughts in mind he didn't know if he had the time to work his way around before daylight, but knew that it was critical that he do so. He withdrew not knowing that right below him sitting by that river were the two leaders of the slavers, and just as ignorant were the two of him.

He was exhausted. Between the dodging of the patrols and this all night scout he was finding it difficult to concentrate but at least he felt better now. He had located the second camp and indeed it was downriver from the main camp and it appeared to consist of at least one third of the army. Why had the leader done this, and would it be that the leader would do it again? This worried him. Had they given themselves away? He had no answers, but knew that he needed to pull back and find a hiding place where he'd be able to sleep. The patrols would be on the move again. Fortunately he had everything with him in his pack and the last camp had been well hidden. Now in this new area he simply had to find a place to hide during the daylight hours.

CHAPTER FIFTEEN

Even though nothing had been going on and everything appeared to be normal – well as normal as possible considering the slavers were close – that anybody could either see or sense, well there seemed to be electricity in the air that charged the atmosphere and put everyone in the region on edge. It was like the very soils were holding their collective breath waiting for something. In the shelter the tension made everybody short, with tempers coming to the surface much too quick over nothing, followed by the need to get away and be alone. But the problem was where could they go? So, all of them were stuck. At any time that other army would be arriving and then the fireworks would begin with no guarantees of who the victor would be. In any battle the outcome was never known until it was done. At least with their location they would be somewhat on the outside of the area, but there were no guarantees in this as in life. No one is promised an easy time, or that they will live to old age. In a sense war was coming to their quiet world, and while it would only be for a short time, it reflected the world that they lived.

With the help of Joel Abe and the one other scout successfully brought down one of the wild cows, and had rapidly prepared the meat, and with enough to last them for half a moon cycle were returning to their meeting place to tie in with the one they had left to watch. Abe knew that Madam would be here any time now and he needed to be able to update her with the most recent information. So with heavy packs they took off with Joel watching them leave. He had grown to like this Abe, with his quiet strength and his wisdom. They had discussed much over the night fires and he had learned more of a slave's life and even with his dislike for the ones who did this, his dislike had almost grown into hatred for the destruction caused by slavers and slave owners. He found that he now felt strongly that this blight had to disappear. How, he hadn't a clue, only that it had to. So once they were out of sight he headed, in a roundabout way, back to the shelter where the family was waiting.

When they came to the meeting point that the three of them had set up the other wasn't there and there was no sign that he had been in the recent past. Just what happened? They had been away for a few days to get additional food which they now had, but it was apparent that things had changed drastically in that time. Not sure what to do the two of them pulled further back to a point where they had marked as an emergency camp if it became necessary. It was here that they found Joseph. He was severely injured and was barely hanging on. It was obvious that he was staying alive by sheer will, and at this moment was unconscious. Turning to the one that had hunted with him he said, "Look, we don't have the supplies or the knowledge necessary to help him, but I know of others who might. Take care of him, and do what you can. I know where to go and unfortunately you don't, so I have no choice but to leave to you here with him. Apparently something went terribly wrong." Taking a deep breath and shaking his head he finished by saying, "Be back as quickly as I can."

He immediately headed back in the direction that they had just come. He needed to get to that point where he had met the three men. It was obvious that there was something close by that was sheltering them. He only hoped that he would make it in time and that they had something to help. Now he wondered if they had finally been compromised. But there was no way of knowing. If Joseph regained consciousness then he might be able to tell them, but if he didn't then it would be an unknown and a dangerous time.

* * *

When Joel returned Dan was on duty. Joel stopped briefly and brought him up to date on what had transpired and that the two were on their way back to continue their surveillance of the slavers. After that he headed back to their shelter. Dan thought it over and knew that the danger was far from over for them. Yes they were now a few miles to east of where the slavers were camping and scavenging, but there was that other army now approaching and who knew what would come out of that? In the end this new army could decide that he and his family were liabilities and as such destroy them too. All of it was just an unknown and with this came fear that it might end for them here and in the near future. So far nothing was happening and if he didn't know better it easily could have been any of the too many days of the past where the most excitement was the watching of the predator birds riding the thermals looking for food. After all that had already happened, it was the past, and it would be nice to return to those boring days. *Yes, and if wishes came true we would be living in peace.* He thought.

He wondered how the world was before the ancient fires arrived. He imagined much but with the destruction there were only slight hints of what the past had been. And here it was only a couple of hundred years after it had happened. He knew that in the future, if there was to be one for them, that most if not all of what had been before would completely disappear, leaving them as they lived through their time, ghosts of a past that might be considered fiction. How did one leave something that could be found further down the trails of time to say to the world that, "Hey world, I was here, and I am real. I lived, hoped, dreamed for better things, and tried my best to make it happen." He hadn't a clue. From what little was left there was little proof that others had lived before them.

As these thoughts went through his mind his subconscious picked up movement that took a few moments to reach his consciousness. He realized that someone was approaching his post and seemed to be jogging, but not coming from the direction expected. There was something familiar about him, but not so much that he could identify the individual. Being on the ready he waited partially hidden. As the individual came closer he began to recognize some of the features, but as of yet was unable to identify him. Then in the next few moments he realized that it had to be Abe. He stood up wondering what brought him back so soon. And as he came into voice range Dan asked, "What's going on? Has your army arrived already?" A valid question since that had been one of the subjects that had been discussed.

Arriving and leaning on a rock Abe said, "Give me a second here as I catch my breath. I'm finding that I'm not as good at this as I once was." It took a short while before he had his wind back. "Okay, look we need your help, and we need it now. When we got back to our meeting place the one that we had left didn't show. We became alarmed and moved back to an emergency camp that we had established and it was there that we found him. He's in bad shape and needs some medical help. Can't say that he'll survive until I get back, but he has a family back where we are living and I really don't want to bring them any bad news."

"Thinking a moment before commenting Dan said, "Okay, look you stay here and watch for us. I have no idea if anybody may have followed you, but can't take that chance. I'll be gone as short of time as I can and then we'll head back and see what can be done if anything." Abe agreed and Dan took off jogging in a different direction so as to hide the true location of their shelter. He hadn't been around this one long enough to put his full trust in him and felt that this could be a ruse to learn the location and who might be there.

In what seemed much too long Dan returned with Joel who replaced him as watcher. Abe noticed the unusual pack that Dan was carrying and asked him about it. "This? It was a discovery that I made a few back. It is from the time before the ancient fires that have ravaged this earth. Carry the important things in it. Okay I'm ready, lead on."

Smiling and shaking his head Abe said, "Okay we'll have to jog for a few miles. And it would be nice if I could make a similar discovery. That thing's so much better than anything I've either used or seen on others." His tone changed before continuing, "I hope we are in time. He's in really bad shape when I left."

"Yes," Dan replied, "I've seen much too much death as it is and would love to see it end. At least deaths from the violence, I know that we all face death in the end, it's just a part of living." He watched as Abe led off and began to jog; retracing the steps he had taken to bring him here. Dan was barely recovered from his time out scouting himself so taking a deep breath he began his own distance eating jog and because he needed to be a little faster to begin with he realized that he would need to move it up to a run and catch up with Abe. Once even he paced him and as his muscles warmed to the task began to fall into an old rhythm and his breathing eased. For a period of time all he heard was the sound of their feet hitting the hard ground and their breathing.

Time meant nothing as the gait that Abe had set ate up the miles in quick time. And as they entered the area where the ruins existed he veered to the backside of one of the hills away from the overlook to the ruins, down into one of the smaller valleys and to their hidden camp. When they entered into it Abe saw the one that he had left with Joseph standing. Giving himself a moment to catch his breath Abe asked, "How's our patient?"

The other stared at him not saying anything for what seemed like a very long time. Finally saying, "He passed while you were gone. He had been lying here with no help for too long and there was just nothing we could have done – nothing at all."

Abe's shoulder slumped, I'd really hoped . . ." He was silent for a moment looking down at the ground. It was obvious to the other two that he was trying to control his emotions. Abe turned to Dan saying, "Sorry to have brought you here, and for nothing."

Dan not quite sure how to answer asked, "Would you like me to stay for a bit?"

Shaking his head Abe said, "No, it won't be necessary. We'll take care of our friend. Damn! He has family back where we live and now he will never get the chance to see his children grow. I'm not looking forward to informing his mate. They have been close for many years. Although we all knew the price we could pay. Why is it that it seems to be the good ones that get killed like this?"

Dan shrugged, "There are no answers to questions like that, but I suspect you weren't expecting one anyway." Taking a deep breath he said his good byes and headed back leaving the two standing there. There had been hope that they might have saved this one, but it had been dashed.

Abe watched him go and inwardly had wished that the outcome had been different. Yet the fates had said it would be as it was presently. Turning to the other scout he asked, "Did he say anything before he passed?"

"Yeah, a couple of things. Obviously he wanted to be sure his family would be okay. I think he knew that he wasn't going to survive. He left me with a couple of private messages for his mate and his children. Then, as it became obvious to me that he wasn't going to make it, he passed on the information that the slavers have begun their patrols once again and they have divided their camp into three camps. His evaluation was that they were spreading their forces out with the idea of support from any of the camps and they are placed in such a way that support would be easy, but at the same time hidden from someone attacking them. It's obvious that either they know we are here or they suspect something.

". . . Oh yeah, one more thing. He overheard them say, when one of the patrols spotted him that they thought he was the one who had been living in the ruins, so at least from that information we can assume that they don't know that we are here. It was soon after that his breathing became ragged, and then it seemed, as this went away, his breathing eased. At this point I thought there was a chance, especially if you got back with help. Then it just stopped and I knew that he had held on as long as he could and whatever strength he had was gone and there was nothing left. It was just before you returned."

Quiet for a while Abe finally said, "So near, yet so far. I guess we had better find a place to bury him. At least we know that we haven't been compromised, but how does that leader of the slavers know?" They reverently wrapped their friend and comrade in his sleep sack, carrying him further down the hill on the opposite side of the mountain from the ruins and into a ravine, where the soils were easier to work, buried him saying a few words of comfort over the grave before returning to the camp, both silent within their own thoughts. They'd surely miss him.

* * *

Dan was almost back when he began to discern a light dust that seemed to be hanging in the air to the east. Either the winds were beginning to blow from that direction or there was someone or something approaching from that direction. It would be a while before the answer would be known. In a way he hoped that it was just the hot winds, but suspected with what he knew that it was the approaching army that would be here to eradicate the slavers. *Will all this fighting and death ever end?* He really wished he knew. Maybe this species that he was a part was such that violence is just the way of it until all of them were dead. He had no answers, just questions, and knew that these were ones that probably would never be answered.

* * *

From the advance scouts Madam knew that it would be soon and they would meet up with the ones who had been trailing the slavers. She needed to know what had transpired since the last time there had been contact. There had to be a way to keep on top of something like this. Without the knowledge of the movement of her enemy how could she and her second ever plan a successful campaign? She thought that this must have been the bane of every leader whoever led their people into battle. It's never is smart to just go in blindly. It was a great way to be destroyed. Soon, one way or the other, this would be over. It was midday and would be late before they reached their projected camp. On the morrow they would attack. She wouldn't waste time to allow her enemy to discover her and their location giving them the upper hand. So that meeting with her scouts was critical.

After the burial of their friend Abe sent the other that was with him out to the meeting point where forward scouts of the army would be informed. He still had no idea how long it would be, but now it was critical that one of them remain at that meeting point until someone showed. With Joseph dead it made their job that much more difficult. Still, to eliminate such as the ones that they were watching was foremost on his mind. And now with a very personal reason because of the death of his friend at their hands, he wanted to see it even more. He needed to scout out the changes so that the information that they were gathering was the best it could be. If they missed anything it could make the difference between success and failure. But how did one do that now that for whatever the reason, the slavers were sending out patrols and making it that much more difficult to watch? And, he wondered, what had alerted them? He knew from the information that Joseph had passed on before he died, that the slavers had considered him as the one living in the ruins. So it appeared that they were still unknown and unaccounted. Yet something had ratcheted up the alertness of the slavers, and he didn't have a clue.

He thought of those three males that he had made an acquaintance and knew how careful they were. So careful in fact that it had only been an accident that had finally revealed them to him. So he knew that they weren't the reason for this heightened alert from the slavers. Finally running out of ideas he worked his way down the backside of the hills proceeded down a ravine coming out to the west of the furthest encampment. His position was still above and he saw there was much activity in the camp as well as people coming and going. Whoever was the leader of these slavers pushed them into some semblance of order and demanded respect. Otherwise what he witnessed here wouldn't be happening. *Who is he anyway?* He knew that from the grapevine, after the meeting on that hillside, the impression was one of strength, personal strength. It had been rumored that this leader had the mark of a slave which made him even worse in their minds. But what had alerted him? Was it something that he and the others had done?

Seeing all the activity he pulled back and worked his way deeper into desert away from this camp and headed east. He needed to see the locations for himself. This one wasn't that far from the original camp and both could easily support each other if attacked. Staying hidden he continued past the original camp and worked his way deeper in the direction where the third camp should be located. Eventually he found it and it was around a bend in the river with a full ridgeline separating it from the center camp. It would be a little more difficult to defend this one, and with that ridgeline between them and the center camp it would be a bit harder to defend the original camp. All of this was good to know. Pulling back to the north he carefully skirted the patrols that now seemed to be everywhere. Someone surely must have stirred up a hornet's nest. He found that he had to travel further north than he wanted before working his way back to their emergency camp, which had become their new base.

As he came into the camp he found that there were others there now. At first he was alarmed that one of the patrols had located their camp and was presently waiting for the ones who were using it to return. But he, once he was closer, recognized a couple of the people and realized that they were normally, as he, advance scouts for Madam's army. He joined them and they exchanged greetings. The army was finally here and this would be over soon. Finally the waiting and wondering would be at an end, but he felt that somewhere along this line that those three males might want to talk with their leader. He knew that she was looking for others to join her that was not escaped slaves. Ones that would help in purchasing items that they couldn't create themselves. Maybe they'd be interested in such a proposition? Of course, he knew that he would have to clear it with her first, but opportunities like this didn't just drop in on you that often.

It was time to abandon their camp and join with the army. He wouldn't be sorry. This duty had grown old long before they lost Joseph. Now he wanted it to end and return to their home deep in the wilderness where they lived untouched and unknown.

* * *

Madam's camp had been set up far enough away from the location of the slavers to keep them unknown to them, yet she was disturbed. What was it that made this leader, ah Skar if she remembered correctly, prepare for an attack? From the information that Abe had passed on to her he and the other scouts had never been seen or located. And other than the loss of Joseph to the slavers and the report from him before he died that they had mistaken him for the one who had been living in the ruins and had escaped before the slavers arrived there was nothing. Then there were these others that Abe had met living in this wasteland. She didn't have any other word for it. Sure where they were living back in the-hole-in-the-wall it was high plains with few trees whereas this place had the illusion because of the trees of being a good area to live but in fact was desert.

She was awaiting updated intelligence on the three camps and was pacing the camp. Now that the time was at hand she just wanted to get it over with. Yet she knew if she simply charged recklessly into the fray that they would be the ones who would lose, so she forced herself to be patient. Even with the advantages she had she knew that it would be too easy to become enamored with what they had recovered in that armory and become careless. She also saw that with all her pacing and restlessness that she was beginning to have an effect on the others so she forced herself to relax. It was going to be tough enough once they went into battle and she didn't need to make it worse.

Abe approached knowing that Madam became this way when she prepared for a battle. After all she's female, a woman, and as such had compassion for her people. Yes, like any leader, she'd use someone to accomplish what needed to be done, and at times sacrifice an individual or small force if it meant that they would survive. And she could be cold and hard as necessary, but underneath it all was that part of her that wanted to mother them, to protect them like a mother hen with her chicks. If one didn't know her, this part of her would be hidden, unknown, but for the ones, who did, it revealed the true strength and caring that was all a part of her. "Madam, if you would like, we are not very far from where the three males are living. I could make contact and bring the oldest male here and the two of you can talk. I know that part of our needs is to find ones who will live with us that can barter for items we cannot make ourselves and who do not have the mark of slaves."

"They've impressed you that much. You who have been so careful to avoid contact with others, and the one who refuses to become involved in negotiations of any kind. What makes you want to trust these others? After all we've found little sympathy from ones who are not slaves. In fact they would prefer to stay away from any contact with escaped slaves. Not that I can blame them because the penalty from the slavers and slave owners is just as bad for any who harbor us as it is for us."

"Let's just say that I've had a chance to get to know at least one of them. Yes, I know it was only for a short time, but it's obvious what he felt about slavers and when I met his father, I felt the same from him, only it's much stronger. As I said earlier, even though I have no way to confirm what they've said, their stories have been consistent." He then related everything that had transpired with the accidental meeting between Joel and him, followed by his meeting with Dan. She sat quietly and listened, only interrupting when she wanted something explained.

"Yes", Madam said after a pause, "they do sound like ones who could help us. But there is a problem here and it's a worrisome thing. We haven't been around them as much as they haven't been around us. How much should we reveal, and how would others see them? If you think about it there's a good chance that there will be resentment. Even though it's obvious that they have been through tough times with the loss of the village, and who knows who, since they haven't mentioned anything about that. Remember if the two younger ones that you saw were his offspring, then somewhere there had to be a mother – possibly a sister or two. And that means that they were lost, or maybe not."

"Or maybe not? What do you mean by that?"

"Only this and there's no proof one way or the other. First off you were never allowed to get close to where they are actually living – not that I can blame them for that. What if they have females who are with them? Wouldn't you want to protect them and keep them hidden? And if they do, who are they? What I mean by this question is this; are they relatives or are these females ones who have been captured by these males and are forced to live with them? Either question could be correct, or they could be exactly what and who they say they are. We don't know, so it means that we must be as careful, as they apparently are being."

Silent for a moment Abe looked down on the ground as he thought about the questions and the possible conclusions. "Yes, I have to admit that some of what you said came to mind, but I've seen nothing to show it to be one way or the other. Either these three are very good actors or the reactions I saw were genuine. It's exactly why I thought about bringing this up with you. And no, I did not mention anything at all to them about what my thoughts were or are on this subject. You are our leader and as such would make the decision, not me. So before I presented anything at all it would only be after your approval. I know you've kept most of us safe since our escapes from wherever we came from, and that deserves respect."

"Look, I think it is something worth pursuing later. Maybe once this fight is over and done with, but until then we will keep any of this between us and then once there is time it will be better considered."

Abe had to admit that what she had brought to his attention left so many other answers to what he encountered. It was why he left such things to others. He was good at what he did, but the complicated direction of this world was beyond him. Just give him a trail to work out or an area that needed to be scouted. Here it was something that he understood. "Okay, I'll not say another word until you are ready to meet them, or not."

* * *

The final meeting had been called and with the updated information about the three camps which was now in their hands it was time for a council of war. Madam looked over the few that were in this council of war and inwardly smiled even though it was tempered with the knowledge that there was a good chance that once this was over there would be fewer of them to return home. Yet, in such things, loss of life, no matter how one tried to avoid it, was a part of this. "The original main camp", she said as she turned to a roughly drawn map of the areas, "has been split into three. The one furthest to the east is around a projection of the mountain that comes down to the river's edge. This makes it invisible to the other two camps, and probably the most vulnerable of the three. Still it is, as is the one furthest to the west, easily defended by support from the middle camp.

"From the information that has been passed on these three camps were only one a short time ago. It appears that something has alerted them. Whatever has caused this change in tactics I honestly don't know. As you know we did lose one of our scouts to the slavers, but what he passed on before he died said that they, the slavers, thought he was the one who had been living in the ruins that they are presently scavenging. I suspect it is the reason that they disobeyed the order we gave them, but we are not here to determine what their reasons may have been. Only that they did not clear out. So we will remind them." This brought a bit of laughter from the ones present. She paused long enough to allow it to quiet once more.

"Okay, I'm going to keep it simple – Complicated gives us too many chances for things to go wrong. First off we must avoid the patrols that are now working the areas close to the ruins. We are going to divide into two forces with the majority staying with me, and the smaller going with the Second. Timing, other than when we will attack, is not critical. We will attack just as the sun is rising, coming out of the east putting the sun at our backs; making it harder for the ones we are attacking to see us. I'm going to have our sharpshooters on the ridges both to the north and south. We must keep this high ground. Once we start, the ones with me will attack the camp furthest east. Once the sound of battle starts it will alert the other two camps. It is here that it is very important that the second remain hidden and prepared."

She pointed to the camp that was furthest to the west, looking back to the Second, she said, "Here is where you and your smaller force comes into play. You must wait until they are beginning to head east putting their backs to you making them unaware that anything is behind them. Again, like from the initial attack, I want a number of your people on the ridgelines to be able to shoot into the enemy. Once you engage it must be from a position of strength since you will have less to work with. If you can surprise this third camp then before they can join the middle camp and then head towards us and engage you need to do as much damage as you can.

"Now comes the hard part for you. I expect to take the brunt of this and once you have made your attack I expect you to withdraw, swing up along the ridges and begin to work the ridgelines targeting any you see in that middle camp. You shouldn't have to worry about any friendlies there as we will remain around that outcropping and with all of yours on the ridges that leaves only enemy targets. You will need to leave a small force back where the western camp is located to cover any of the slavers who may decide to retreat in that direction, or counter your attack and try and flank you. Your people must be in such a location that they have a clear field of fire and at the same time not easily targeted or seen.

"In a sense while the heaviest fighting will be with me, it will be you and your smaller group that will hold the more important position or role in this. There is a good chance that once the surprise is over that there will be an attempt to head your way, work their way up the mountains then sweep back around to try and catch us on the lower ground. This one who runs this army of slavers is not stupid and the division into three camps at this time is ample proof of that. He seems to have some inborn sense that alerts him to danger. It's the only answer I have since from everything we know, he has no proof that we've been following him. And for the ones who were with us when we met him and his second, he has the mark of a slave. So somehow he has been smart enough to convince the slave owners that he more use to them alive and doing what he is doing then dead and an example of what will happen to any escaped slave.

"If you think about it, this makes him even more dangerous – more dangerous to us and our kind because of that mark. It would be easy for him to infiltrate camps where others like us exist and then bring in his army, capture the unsuspecting escaped slaves, return them for whatever reward and continue. So we must end his reign so to speak. We have enough problems without one of our own being a traitor. And again if you think this one is stupid consider how well they reacted to our first attack. Even though we surprised them, there was no panic and they worked as a team trying to find a way out of their situation. Of course there was none for them since we had them covered with them in the open and we hidden."

She looked over the group before continuing. "When we are finished here we will divide the forces up." Again she stopped giving them time to absorb all that had been said. "Are there any questions at this point?" There was a silence in the portable shelter with none coming forth. "Okay then, we move out at dusk and with the rising sun on the morrow this will begin with the rising sun and be done, one way or the other, by the setting sun. Good luck to all. Let's get this over with and return home where we can rejoin our families."

Abe wasn't a part of the gathering of leaders, but had a rough idea of what was just about to go down. He wished there was a way to warn the ones he had recently met, but knew that there was nothing he could do about it now. They were on their own until this was done. He knew that if this battle went the way he hoped it would that by being successful then many of the slavers, who survived, would be running and spreading out. This would leave the ones he talked with vulnerable to a small group of the survivors coming upon them and surprising them. Well, wherever they were living it had to be well hidden, since they hadn't been located by the slavers when they came into the area, and from the conversations that he had with both Joel and Dan it was obvious that the slaver patrols had been everywhere. All he could do was wish them luck from a distance and hoped they survived.

The word had come down that they would be moving out at dusk moving all of them close to the point of attack, bed down for a few hours then in the grayness of dawn move into position. This would have been the largest slaver army that they had ever attacked, and even though they were evenly matched as far as manpower went, they, with their ancient weapons, had the superiority. But no battle has a guaranteed outcome and they could lose just as easily as the slavers. After all Abe had heard that battle plans only work until the first contact with the enemy, after that it becomes chaos.

* * *

It was cold as dawn approached. It always seemed to be that way. Just before the sun rose the surrounding earth seemed to drop in temperatures. It would have been nice if they could have moved a bit to get the circulation going and warm a bit, but silence was critical. Abe, because of his position as lead scout, was back with Madam. He had just returned from a brief overlook of the camp of the slavers, the one furthest east. In a short time they would begin their attack and he needed to be sure that they were unaware. When he had looked it over, from the high point, it seemed that everything appeared to be normal. The campfires were down to coals, and the four guards were in their positions. So now it was just a waiting game until the time of attack.

Yet, when he had watched the camp something didn't feel right and he couldn't figure it out. So at this moment he kept his feelings to himself. *Everything is normal, right? Guards out, fires down, little movement, all normal . . . yet, yet what?* In his mind's eye he went over it once again and could find nothing to support this feeling.

The next few hours went by slowly and he asked and received permission to do one last reconnoiters of the camp. He just couldn't shake it that something wasn't right, but kept these thoughts to himself. He headed out and as he approached the camp area from above he took one last look. It was lighter now and soon the sun would rise so this was the last chance to place everything within this first camp, but still nothing seemed out of place. He double checked everything and still his feeling lingered. *What is it that I'm missing?* He was sure that he was missing something. Eventually putting it up to nerves before the upcoming battle, he finally withdrew and rejoined Madam at her high point. It was now light enough for the land to be visible and the attack was almost here.

Madam asked, "So is all okay? Is all like we expect?"

Not sure how to answer Abe said, "Everything seems just as we expect it." There must have been something in his voice that expressed his doubts since she looked at him in a way that said she knew that something was up.

"Okay Abe, that's how the camp appears, but from the tone of your voice I would say that something isn't right."

"Yeah, it's just a feeling I have. There's nothing in that camp that seems out of place, everything appears to be what you would expect, what we would expect."

"And that bothers you, is that what it is?"

Shaking his head Abe said, "No, that isn't what bothers me, and I wish I knew, but while it all appears right something is telling me that it isn't, and I don't know if it's just nerves of the upcoming battle or I've seen something that's alerting me."

"I've found that with you Abe, if you get those feelings there's something to it." She stopped and was silent as she thought. *This one that we're going up against is smart and seems to have anticipated our arrival. Until recently there was only the one camp, with no patrols. Suddenly there were two and now three camps, with heavy patrols. It's obvious he's expecting something and I've really got to take that into consideration. Okay we need to change this. Fortunately our other force will not begin to attack until they hear the beginnings of the battle.* She turned back to Abe saying, "Assemble the scouts. I'm going to signal in my other leaders and we are changing this a little. Meet me back here with the other scouts and do it quickly. We are running out of time."

Abe took off and in short order had the full scout compliment with him returning to Madam. In his absence she had her lieutenants with her now and all she was waiting for was him. "Abe take your scouts quickly up the river and sneak into that camp, or as close as you dare and see what we are really facing. Right behind you we will send a small force to give the illusion that we are attacking. If you find out that there is no ruse then you will pull back downriver towards the smaller force informing them of what you've discovered. If it is a camp that is unsuspecting then we will, through hand signals bring down the full force. If it turns out to be different, then we'll see if we cannot make them react to our smaller force. The one advantage we have is that they have no idea the size of this army while we do know theirs. Let's get to it people time once again is against us.

* * *

With care Abe and his scouts worked their way up to the edge of the camp, and it immediately became clear that there was definitely something wrong with the camp. He quickly withdrew his people heading back down river. Now it made sense that little voice saying something wasn't right. The four guards that he was watching from the heights were dummies. It was their lack of movement that his subconscious had picked up. Real people always moved a little bit while dummies were static. Now he was glad that she had asked. They would have come into a trap. He smiled because they were going to turn that trap around on the enemy. He didn't know where the ones from the camp were hiding but knew as soon as the smaller force entered into the camp to attack that they would come out of hiding and counter attack supposedly surprising the attackers.

Shortly they tied in with the smaller force and he relayed what they had learned. The one responsible for signals sent the message, and the altered attack plans went into effect. It was still a little time before the sun touched the top of the ridge so Abe used this to search some of the surrounding area to see if he could find the hidden forces, but there really wasn't enough time to be able to find them. He only hoped that they would. He knew that he wasn't a part of this first initial attack, and now these first were only going to draw the hidden attackers out and then immediately withdraw back down the canyon giving the appearance of a rout, looking like they had panicked – all a part of drawing them out into the open and into their own trap that they would close from both ends surrounding the enemy.

The signalman received the acknowledgement from the main force and it was time since the sun now touched the ridgeline. With a roar and yells the smaller force charged into the camp maintaining the illusion that they expected someone to be there. As they entered the camp the yells and roars ceased leading to what had to appear to be confusion. It was at that moment that the slavers attacked coming from the river side. Immediately the small attacking force fired towards the attacking slavers halfheartedly and began a quick disorganized retreat back down the river. It looked real enough to Abe as he watched. This was the critical point where their trap would be sprung catching the slavers with a trap of their own.

The small force led the slavers down the river, and quite a distance from the camp, before closing the door, so to speak, on them. The ones, who had retreated, retreated in a haphazard way, running past the ones from their army, who were hidden behind boulders and other such objects, turned, crouched, and fired into the approaching slavers signaling the rest that the trap had been closed. The slavers, realizing too late, that the tables had been turned on them put up a desperate fight. While they did not have as many of the ancient weapons as they did, there was enough to make a fight of it. But they were outnumbered by a factor of three and were caught in the open. Abe knew that with all of the sounds of fighting that soon the other camps would be diving into the fray so they needed to finish this quickly.

They all heard it, which caused the battle to pause for a second or two. At this point in the fight it was almost finished with the slavers down to only a couple who had found cover making it difficult to take them out. Then came the flash followed by an explosion that seemed to originate somewhere just past that ridge that projected towards the river forcing the river to bend around it. After the explosion they felt heat and a heavy blast of air, following by a crack that almost deafened them. All of them were knocked down and it began to rain rock and debris in large amounts injuring some from being hit by some of the larger rocks that seemed to rain from the sky for what seemed forever. Eventually everything became silent, but they weren't sure if the silence was real. Their ears were ringing heavily from that sound wave that had struck them.

Shaken, and with the last of the slavers dead from this most eastern of the three camps they got up shakily and out of their defensive positions standing as they tried to assess what had just happened.

One of the lieutenants yelled, "Get back under cover. We might be under attack from the other two camps." Immediately the rest reacted and returned to their defensive positions. Whatever had just happened placed them in a dazed condition and they had let down their guard for those few moments. Fortunately no one from the slavers had shown up. But they were expecting to hear the battle as their rear guard attacked the camp that should have been moving east towards them, but there was nothing, nothing at all. After waiting what seemed to be too long they began their move west up the river and as they came around that outcropping they stopped with weapons at their side. Where there once had been a camp there now was a smoking crater. And the third camp, which was visible to this one, had been destroyed from the shock wave. Nothing remained standing in that third camp, and anything that could burn was now burning. "What happened here?" One of them asked.

Abe, with Madam, came forth to the head of her army and stood as shocked as the others. She looked desperately to the west looking for the other part of her army, but at this moment because of the haze that hung over the river could see nothing clearly. Quietly she said, "Abe, take your scouts, with some of the army, and see if any of our survived this. And kill any of the slavers you find that are still alive."

With the others Abe found that they had to skirt the area where the crater was located. The ground was hot and still smoking. It was then that he realized that there had been a shaking of the earth when this happened and it was one of the things responsible for knocking them off their feet. In a way it was good that it had happened as it preceded the hot blast of air. By them being on the ground already the heated blast had swept over the top of them. As they had looked at the trees and other greenery they found a lot of damage with most of the trees snapped right off. The area where the crater now existed was wiped clean of all vegetation taking the whole area down to the soils. With care they worked their way past this devastation which seemed to go far to the west right up the valley where the river flowed. It seemed that with the narrowness of the valley at this point it had funneled the blast right down it and to the west. Anyone or anything that was there at the time of the blast would have or should have been killed.

It was still raining debris from the sky, although it was more the fine particles than the larger rocks. Still it kept the area in a haze that made it difficult to see. Eventually they reached the sight of the third camp and there was no one alive, let alone a camp. Many of the bodies that were there were smoking. So far he hadn't seen anybody that he recognized. But with what he was seeing he couldn't see how anyone would have survived. Standing in the middle of the devastated site his shoulder drooped. He had many friends in that smaller force. Eventually as the skies began to clear a little he caught movement on the hill sides above the canyon or valley. He realized, at that moment that at least some had survived – how many was an unknown. He shook his head. How lucky these few were. And to be honest, all of them, since they were still on the ridge at the time it happened. It would have only been a short time until all of them would have been close to that center camp. Whatever this was would have destroyed them all.

* * *

Dan was on shift watching from their overlook when he spied another of those ancient fires streaking across the sky. Dawn had just arrived and it rivaled the sun for brightness. This was followed immediately by a brighter flash as it struck close. He saw, heard, and felt the impact a short time later watching a mushroom cloud rise high into the sky. This one had been really close. In fact this was the closest any of them had been to one of these fires crashing into the earth. It gave him a sense of how it must have been when these things were raining from the skies with no place for anybody to escape. As he continued to watch he saw a fine dark cloud forming from the falling debris, with what looked to be steam rising from the valley below. He suspected that this one had hit close to that river, but from here he really didn't know where other than towards the east and possibly close to those ruins. But honestly there was no way to know for sure other than going there. Something, with two armies in the ficld meant that none of them would be doing such a thing. It was much too dangerous.

Shortly the whole family had joined him with them asking what had happened. Marta had stated that most were up for whatever reason and had gathered in the family space was simply discussing breakfast when there came a deep rumble and a quick shaking that set the dust to flying filling the lit areas with dust mites that floated in the air creating patterns as they settled back to the surfaces that they had been on. He pointed to the east, not that it wasn't obvious to all as the cloud had continued to rise into the sky, and even from this distance there began a slight shading of the sun as the morning winds brought the dust east with some starting to fall even here. It was awe inspiring to see the power of these ancient fires when they collided with the ground – such power, such destruction, no wonder so much had been lost.

* * *

As the morning progressed Madam established a temporary camp up from the river and the valley where that ancient fire had met the ground. Slowly the losses were totaled and she hated this part of being the leader. This loss of life, which could be directly brought back and laid upon her, she was a woman, and as such, was full of compassion. Fully half of the smaller force, including her second, had been killed in the blast. There would be families back at home that would be without their mates, making a tough situation even harder. Her army was searching the area for any survivors, and so far it had only been the ones who had been on the ridgelines above the valley that had been spared. It appeared that all of the slavers had been wiped out. Absolutely anything that had been in the area had been killed – animals, vegetation, you name it, it was gone. It was time to bury their dead and wish them well. She really hoped that there was an afterlife and that their spirits would continue on watching them. The old religions spoke of such, but once dead nobody could come back and tell the living, so it had to be taken on faith.

She called Abe over and she waited until he arrived. It had taken some time as he was still working the devastated camp furthest to the west. When he arrived she said, "Look, you've been with me close to the longest. Yes there were others before you and I know that they found you on one of their patrols so many years in the past. But you've always been strong, always willing to be the leader of our scouts, and have done it quite well. I'd like you to replace the Second and become my second. Your insight and understanding has been invaluable over time." saw that he was about to protest and put up her hand to keep him from saying anything. "I don't want an answer now. In fact I just want you to think about it and once we are home then you can tell me. Whatever answer you give me I'll accept. I just hope that it will be yes. Now that this is finished, you spoke of others in the area. The army will be tied up for quite a while finding and burying the bodies – ours and theirs. So go and talk with them, come back and let me know if they will meet with me. If they will then I can make my own call. If it is positive then I can ask if they would be interested."

* * *

Seth was on duty when Abe approached and presented him with the information and that Madam wished to meet. He told Abe to wait and he left heading for the shelter. And once there related to all of them that what they had witnessed had landed in the camp of the slavers destroying them completely, and that the leader of the escaped slaves wanted to talk. This was too important for only one of them to make a decision, so the family discussed it and with some reservations said that they would. The meeting would have to take place at the overlook to keep their shelter hidden and safe. Although Dan knew that with the size of that army, and the knowledge of their overlook location, that it wouldn't take them very long to find this place. It was better to learn what this leader was interested in and keep her on the good side. With as small amount of bodies that they had here there would be no chance of survival.

It was late after zenith when Madam and Abe arrived at the overlook. She saw the three males standing there and waiting. For some reason the one with the silver hair even from a distance seemed familiar, but that was impossible. As far as she knew she had never met any of them. And from what Abe had said he knew none of them either and from what he could gather they had been in this desert for a number of years after the raid and destruction of the village where they were living at the time.

Dan watched as the two approached their location. He was surprised that it was only the two of them. That was being trustful in a time where trust had to be earned. Yet he had to admit that the woman coming towards him was tall. He suspected that she had to be well over six feet tall, and was well proportioned for her size. He saw her strength and a flow to her walk that spoke of confidence and like he good in the natural world. As she approached there seemed to be something vaguely familiar about her, but just shook it off as coincidence. If this went well then he'd bring out his mate and the two of them could talk. He knew that Marta would nail a personality almost instantly, but until he'd be able to guarantee her safety, she, as the other females, would remain in their shelter.

When she reached the overlook she held out her arms in the normal greeting saying, "I'm Madam and you already know Abe."

Dan replied saying, "I know that Abe knows the three of us but you do not. I'm Dan, and these are my two sons Seth, and Joel. I understand you want to discuss something with us."

"Yes, but let us get acquainted first. *This is strange. Even his voice is familiar. How can it be? I'm sure I've never met this one . . . yet.* She inwardly shivered. It was as if she was seeing this through two sets of eyes and didn't know who that second set belonged. They talked a bit of recent personal history, small talk as she learned of the three. There was nothing inconsistent and it was obvious that they hated slavers. Everything that Abe had said seemed to be true.

Dan found that he was comfortable around this woman who would tower over him if they stood. Finally he said, once he felt safe, "I'll be right back. There's someone I would like both of you to meet." He saw the concern and caution in his sons' eyes. Saying simply, "It's important that this happens."

This left Madam curious since there only seemed to be the three, but obviously there was another. She could see the reaction of the other two and knew that this was a surprise to them also. She watched as Dan left, even his walk seemed familiar. *Damn, what is it about him?* In the time that he was away she turned and was looking at the valley below from the overlook. What a view and it did give one a good idea as to what was happening down in that river valley. She saw that cloud of silt still hung in the air. It appeared that it would remain this way for a number of days.

Marta reluctantly followed Dan back to the overlook where she saw the back of this woman. She stopped shocked. *No it can't be. Not after all of this time.* Marta with a quiet trembling voice asked, "Anna?"

Madam froze. She hadn't heard that name since that day over twenty one years ago. *Just who are these people anyway?* She slowly turned around and even though this woman was quite a bit older, she recognized her immediately. That was why this man looked familiar. With a small voice she said, "It has been much too long."

Abe, completely out of his element and at a loss for what was happening remained silent. *Just who is this Anna anyway?* It was a name he was unfamiliar with. *And who are these people?*

It suddenly came to Dan who this was and the resulting knowledge left his speechless. He watched as Marta went to the woman and hugged her desperately. She was that niece that had disappeared with Marta's brother and mate so many years in the past. Nothing had ever been found of any of them and it had been a mystery in the family one that they felt would never have an answer. He heard his mate sobbing and he understood completely. It was obvious also that the one that went by the name of Madam was also.

Marta in this woman's arm kept whispering, "Anna, oh Anna, I'm so sorry."

Madam with her real name revealed said nothing as she clung to Marta. Who would have thought that something like this could happen, especially to her?

It finally dawned on Abe that this woman that he had always known as Madam was a part of these people that he had met a part of their family. How it happened or what the odds were he didn't know, but for the first time he now knew her real name, one that she refused to tell any. With shock he sat down and simply watched unbelieving.

Dan turned to his sons and said, "Get the rest of the family out here it is time for all of us to meet your cousin who has been lost and now is back among us."

E P I L O G U E

It had been a complete and total surprise when Anna, known as Madam had been found after all the intervening years. And as everybody caught up on her past history, Madam felt herself drawn to these people – *her* people. It brought many smiles to her. And yes, the family would join her back at her hidden settlement, and of course they would be willing to help. Even the one known as Sam agreed to join them. In the short time that he had been with them he and Cassie had become close, and who knew where this would go? Besides he had much knowledge on the care of herd animals the beasts of the field. After all it was what his family had done for a few generations before they had been killed by those marauders. Eventually he wanted to work back down south where he had heard that the weather was better and it would be easier for the herd animals to survive. But for now this would work.

* * *

He didn't know how long he had been unconscious or how he had ended up in this, well for lack of a better word, hole. But it had been fortuitous as it had saved his life. When he crawled out he found that he hurt just about everywhere. He noticed that his right side had some light burns and whatever hair was on that side was gone. Just what had happened? As he stood up, even though this took effort, what he surveyed below was total devastation. There didn't appear to be anything alive. Yet, there hung a haze over the area obscuring the valley floor. He had hiked up this ridgeline to survey the surrounding area just as the sun rose and heard the beginnings of an attack on the camp set up to the east. He remembered starting back down when something like a heavy fist hit him with heat and flying rock and then he remembered nothing, until just now.

Stumbling down to the valley floor, skirting the lake, although it didn't look quite like he remembered, and finally crossing the stream he found himself back at the center camp. Only there was nothing to mark that such had ever existed. Taking a deep ragged breath he smelled smoke. *Smells like a campfire* – it had to be coming somewhere to the west since that was the way of the winds. With care, he stumbled up the silent river valley towards what would have been the west camp. Again like the other one it was completely gone. How long had he been out? Looking around there was nobody and nothing. Yet, where the camp would have been was a small campfire – *how can that be?* Then he recognized the figure that was huddled around this small fire. He seemed as shaken as he was. He asked quietly, "Bear?"

With the one answering saying, "Yes boss."

ABOUT THE AUTHOR

Storytelling and writing has always been F.D. Brant's passion, but responsibilities took preference. And because of those responsibilities it took retiring to allow those passions to come to fruition. Since retiring he has written 9 books, and maintains a weekly eclectic blog, Words in the Wind.

Growing up in the backcountry he learned the appreciation of "doing things for yourself". Because it was impossible to call in someone to repair anything one either did it themselves or went without. This led to the appreciation of the natural world, and the daily struggles that one faced as nature threw problems at the family that had to be overcome, leading to confidence and self-sufficiency. This led to the strong characters that populate his stories and books. And his female protagonists are strong willed and confident – something that he saw in both in his mother and sister.